Thrilling r...

RHYANNO

Primal Instinct series

Edge of Hunger

Byrd successfully combines a haunting
...ve story with complex world-building."
—Publishers Weekly

Edge of Danger

...Ms Byrd had me first intrigued and then
...ellbound from the first page to the last."
—Joyfully Reviewed

Edge of Desire

...rd] serves up plenty of action and passion
...hat won't be denied… Great stuff!"
—RT Book Reviews

New instalments are coming soon:

Touch of Seduction
(July 2010)

Touch of Surrender
(September 2010)

Touch of Temptation
(December 2010)

...nly from Mills & Boon® Nocturne™

Available in July 2010
from Mills & Boon® Nocturne™

RHYANNON BYRD

TOUCH OF
SEDUCTION

®™MILLS & BOON®

All the characters in this book have no existence outside the imagination of the author, and have no relation whatsoever to anyone bearing the same name or names. They are not even distantly inspired by any individual known or unknown to the author, and all the incidents are pure invention.

First published in Great Britain in 2010
Harlequin Mills & Boon Limited, Eton House,
18-24 Paradise Road,
Richmond, Surrey TW9 1SR

© Tabitha Bird 2010

ISBN: 978 0 263 88292 6

89-0710

Harlequin Mills & Boon policy is to use papers that are natural, renewable and recyclable products and made from wood grown in sustainable forests. The logging and manufacturing processes conform to the legal environmental regulations of the country of origin.

Printed in Great Britain
by Clays Ltd, St Ives plc

Rhyannon Byrd fell in love with a Brit whose accent was just too sexy to resist. Luckily for her, he turned out to be a keeper, so she married him and they now have two adorable children who constantly keep her on her toes. Living in the Southwest, she spends her days creating provocative romances with her favourite kind of heroes – intense alpha males who cherish their women. When not writing, Rhyannon loves to travel, lose herself in books and watch as much football as humanly possible with her loud, fun-loving family.

For information on Rhyannon's books and the latest news, you can visit her website at www.rhyannonbyrd.com

This book is dedicated with much appreciation to
the incomparable, awesome and ever-supportive
Charles Griemsman.
Oceans of thanks for all that you do, Charles!
You are and will forever be an absolute lifesaver.

CHAPTER ONE

Lennox, Kentucky
Friday night

SOMEONE SMELLED GOOD. No, better than good. Someone smelled downright sinful. And as the warm, womanly, mouthwatering scent filled his head, Aiden Shrader began thinking that his current assignment was an even bigger mistake than he'd thought it would be. After all, he was standing on a human female's doorstep at nine o'clock at night, ready to tell her that she was now under his protection, for God only knew how long, whether she liked it or not. And he was probably going to have to toss in the fact that he wasn't just an armed, badass-looking bodyguard set on keeping her and her three-year-old niece alive, but a shape-shifter, as well. One who could take the form of a massive, deadly predator. An actual tiger-shifter, to be precise.

Oh, yeah, he thought, pushing his windblown hair back

with one tattooed hand while the bitter December night twined itself around his long body like a cold, clinging lover. *There isn't a chance in hell that little tidbit is going to go down well.*

Aiden and his colleagues didn't know how much Olivia Harcourt's stepsisters had told her about the world of preternatural creatures who lived hidden among humanity, the various races collectively referred to as "the ancient clans." And since they also didn't know how much she might have been told about the Watchmen—the organization of shapeshifters that Aiden belonged to, whose job it was to watch over the remaining clansmen—there was a good chance the chick was probably going to run screaming, hell-bent for leather, the instant he laid things out for her. She might even run the second she set eyes on him. Not that he'd blame her, if she was the skittish type. At nearly six and a half feet, packed with long, solid muscle and sporting a multitude of tattoos and shaggy hair that he hadn't bothered to cut in months, Aiden was used to sending some women running for cover. They either loved what they saw or didn't stick around long enough to discover if the "bad boy" was really as wicked as he looked.

The simple fact was that some women had a taste for danger…and some didn't. Aiden had never cared much, one way or another, seeing as how his interest in the female gender remained purely physical—his inner animal far easier to control when he kept it sated. The only rules he lived by were that he never messed around with a woman unless she understood exactly how much he was willing to offer, that she was built to handle a hard ride and that she didn't touch the darker, more primal aspects of his nature.

Of the three, that last rule was by far the most important, and now he had to face the unsavory realization that someone in that goddamn house smelled good enough to arouse the dangerous, possessive hungers of his beast… and he was going to be so screwed because of it.

Aiden half prayed the mouthwatering scent didn't belong to the Harcourt woman, but doubted he would be that lucky. Pulling his hand down his face, he stifled a frustrated snarl and figured he might as well stop stalling and get on with it. As the wind stretched a dark, ominous string of clouds across the hazy glow of the moon, he lifted his right hand and banged his fist against the front door of the brick two-story. While he waited impatiently for someone to answer, he silently cursed the fact that he needed to get laid, in a bad way, while doing his best to convince himself that he was reacting to *that* scent only because he'd been forced to live like a monk for too many weeks. He wasn't the type of man to go without, his primal instincts constantly driving his sexual hungers to an urgent, aggressive level, but it was bloody hard to pick up women in the middle of a war. He'd been so busy in the past month, most nights he just collapsed into bed and didn't move until it was time to get up and start all over again the next day.

Not that the Merrick and the Watchmen were making a lot of progress. Though the Merrick were one of the most powerful of the ancient clans, their bloodline had been dormant for centuries, until the recent return of the Casus and the beginnings of the war. A vile race of immortal creatures who'd been imprisoned over a thousand years ago for their crimes against humanity and the other clans, the Casus had somehow begun escaping from Meridian— the metaphysical holding ground that served as their prison—and returning to this world. The first had returned at the end of the summer, with more and more following in recent months. They were now hunting down the Merrick, one by one, exacting a bloodthirsty revenge against their ancient enemy.

As a result of the Casus's return, the Merrick blood within the original clan's descendants was awakening, and some Merrick, like the Buchanans, were now waging a fight against the monsters, along with the help of the Watchmen. Ian Buchanan had actually been the first Merrick to be awakened, and thanks to Ian's sister, Saige, it was the Buchanans' and Shrader's Watchmen unit who were conducting the search for the Dark Markers. As the only known weapons that could destroy a Casus's soul and send it to hell, the Markers were invaluable in their fight against the Casus. The mysterious crosses had been hidden across Europe and the Americas in order to keep them from falling into the wrong hands, and Aiden and his friends were doing everything they could to track them down. But it wasn't enough. Despite the fact that they'd now managed to find five of the hidden Markers, giving up only one to the enemy, their side was losing the war—and Aiden wasn't a man who liked to lose. He'd spent too many years under the thumb of his enemies when he was younger. Now, at the age of thirty-four, he was a man who liked to fight hard and come out on top, no matter what it took to get there. He'd been working his ass off to make sure that he and his friends were going to end this conflict as the victors, and he wanted to be out in the field, continuing the fight. Not acting as a goddamn baby-sitter.

Around him, the night was strangely silent but for the rustling of the leaves in the trees, the other four houses in the cul-de-sac already dark, though strands of Christmas lights continued to flicker around two of them. Just as he raised his hand to knock for a second time, he heard the back door open and close. It barely made a sound—just a soft brushing of the mechanism clicking into place—but it was enough for his sensitive hearing to pick up. Cocking his head to the side, he listened as someone quickly made their way down a set of steps, their gait uneven, as if they were carrying something heavy on one side of their body.

With his left hand braced on the porch's wooden railing,

Aiden vaulted over the top, landing with a soft thud in the damp grass at the side of the house. His mouth watered when he drew in a deeper take of that warm, rich scent as it rode the wintry breeze, stroking his senses like a physical touch. The predatory beast within him stretched into a fuller awareness, its gravelly voice rumbling from deep within, vibrating through his body like a shock wave.

Stalk. Cover. Take.

Cursing under his breath with a bitter surge of frustration, Aiden wondered why things just kept getting crappier for him, rather than better, since this was the last damn thing that he needed. One would think that fighting on the "good" side against a sadistic, merciless evil would earn him some karma points from at least one freaking entity in the universe, but his luck just kept slipping deeper into shit.

Then again, he mused, scraping his rough palm against the bristled surface of his jaw as he moved silently through the shadows, maybe he shouldn't be so surprised. Aiden knew firsthand that the good didn't always come out on top. And if they did, it usually took a hell of a lot of time and pain to get there.

Coming around the corner of the house, he stepped into the backyard…and instantly caught sight of the woman, his exceptional night vision enabling him to clearly make out her form in the darkness. He could see that she wasn't overly tall for a female, probably no more than five-five, her shoulders narrow, graceful hands struggling to control a bulky piece of luggage. She looked as though she was in a hurry as she hefted the suitcase into the trunk of a compact Honda, then slammed it closed. She also looked nervous as hell, her hands visibly shaking as she seemed to take a moment to listen to the night. Did she know that trouble was on its way, then? Know that the ones who'd killed Monica Harcourt, her eldest stepsister, and kidnapped the youngest one were now after the little girl she was protecting? Is that why she'd left her home to stay here, at the house of a friend who'd gone out of town?

If so, it had been a foolish move on her part, because the house couldn't have been in a worse location. It sat at the far end of a quiet country neighborhood in a sprawling cul-de-sac, surrounded by woods, the only access road providing the perfect place for an ambush. Aiden had spent the past week about a hundred miles south of Lennox, searching for the fifth Dark Marker along with fellow Watchman Kellan Scott and their human colleague, Noah Winston. They'd found the Marker that morning, and would have already been on their way back to Colorado with it, where the compound they called home was located in the Rocky Mountains, if it weren't for the unexpected phone call that had brought them to Lennox instead. Aiden now carried the ornate cross in his back pocket, and Kellan and Noah were patrolling the woods, on the lookout for the Casus. Monica Harcourt's ghost had been in contact with them, warning that the bastards were coming for her daughter, and Aiden knew better than to underestimate them. If he'd managed to find Olivia Harcourt and her niece at this remote location, the Casus would, as well.

As if she suddenly sensed his presence, the woman turned, caught sight of him at the corner of the house, then immediately started to run. Without thinking about which direction she was headed, simply reacting to the fact that she was running *from* him, Aiden found himself sprinting across the grassy backyard and taking her down. She started to cry out, but the sharp sound was cut off as they landed heavily on the cold ground, momentarily knocking the wind out of them both.

Soft. That was the first word that came to mind as he lay heavily against her, his chest to her back. *Sweet* was the second. He usually went for his women a little sturdier than this one, so that he didn't have to worry about hurting them when he let go, but he couldn't deny that he liked the feeling of her lush, feminine little body trapped beneath him.

Without thinking it through, acting purely on animal instinct, Aiden lowered his head and nuzzled the warm, tender patch of skin just behind her right ear. The heavy silk of her red hair tickled his nose, the sleek strands smelling of flowers and spring and things that were too damn tender for his world. His long frame began to shake, something thick and hot rushing through his body, as if a biting, visceral craving unlike anything he'd ever experienced had been injected directly into his veins, poisoning his reason.

A rough noise vibrated in the back of his throat, and he jerked from shock when he realized he was actually purring.

Bad, he silently snarled, and he stilled, not even breathing, while a deeper, more guttural voice chanted *"Keep her"* within the darkness of his mind.

No, he growled, shaking his head so hard that his long hair flew around his shoulders. *No way. Not possible,* the rational, human part of his mind argued, while the rest of him went into total meltdown, coming undone, something dark and possessive clawing against his insides, demanding its freedom.

Need her. Naked. Now.

He was, to put it bluntly, completely screwed, and as his body crushed hers against the ground, two thoughts fired simultaneously through Aiden's brain, obliterating everything else. The first was that she felt better than any other woman he'd ever had beneath him, even if she was a human. The second was that he needed to get the hell away from her, before he ended up making the biggest mistake of his life.

This second idea was completely born from the first, and the first had so many tangled layers to it, it was difficult to find his way through them all. He'd known she smelled good, but now that he was so close to her, the effect was staggering, like some tantalizing cross between the dangerously forbidden and the comforting warmth of home. Illicit, and yet strangely familiar, as if it was a part of him. Despite the difference in their heights, she fit against him in a way that just seemed *right,* and there was something painfully erotic about the soft, gasping sound of her breathing…the way she squirmed to get free.

Just calm down, he thought, struggling to hold himself together. *And while you're at it, get a friggin' grip.*

All right. Okay. He could do this, damn it. He just had to think it through. Wrap his mind around it. There had to be a reasonable explanation for his reaction, because human females did *not* call to his beast this way. That was why he slept with them—for the sheer fact that they did *not* affect him…that they were safe. If someone had asked him to explain why he liked to bed down with the things he most hated, that would have been the answer right there—the fact that he remained completely untouched by the humans he had sex with. For the most part, he still considered humanity to be nothing more than a cesspool of greed, filth and perversion, aside from the select few he now considered his friends. And yet, even though he loathed their species, he never hurt the human females he slept with. Never allowed that darker side of his nature its freedom.

You're just in a bad way. It's been too long for you. That's all it is, he silently argued, forcing his locked muscles to move, and he managed to lift himself away just enough that the woman could roll over beneath him. Then everything went to hell, because the instant Olivia Harcourt was on her back, she stared directly up into his narrowed, no doubt "changing" eyes, and the only thing Aiden could manage to say was "Shit." A red, steamy haze instantly filled his vision, and his cock went so hard he was half afraid he would go off right there, inside his friggin' jeans. She might have been on the delicate side, but her breasts were incredible, cushioned against his chest, her nipples hard beneath the fabric of her sweater. Her soft, glossy lips were moving, no doubt cursing him to hell and back, but he couldn't hear her words over the roar in his ears. Through the dizzying, deafening storm of hunger, Aiden watched helplessly as he stretched her arms above her head and pinned her wrists against the cold ground with his left hand, the aggressive action so at odds with the way his right thumb tenderly stroked the fragile edge of her jaw.

It didn't matter how hard he tried, he simply couldn't stop staring down at the strange little human, completely mesmerized by the things he could see…and even more so by the things he could *sense*.

The heat blooming beneath the pale, pearl-like luster of her skin.

The provocative rush of blood pounding through her veins.

The heady rise of desire as it softened her body.

Then she exhaled a sharp, shivery breath, the scent of her mouth filling his head, and Aiden realized he'd made a fatal error. A serious miscalculation. He'd thought she smelled good on the outside, but it was nothing compared to her scent on the *inside,* the sweetness of her inner secrets breaking him down. He could only imagine how perfect it would smell when her warm juices were slipping from her sex like honey, pooling like melted sunshine between her thighs. They would be mouthwatering—hot and slick and exquisite—and in that instant the man faded to the background of his mind...and the animal took over.

One second he was poised above her, and the next thing Aiden knew, he'd taken her mouth, thrusting his tongue deep, tasting her completely, the kiss just shy of violent as he sought out that rich burn of flavor. A devastating burst of pleasure poured through his muscles and his limbs, scorching every inch of his body, inside and out—the painful, gnawing need so much worse than it'd been before.

She smelled deliciously ripe...and somehow tasted even better. Though he knew it was madness, the feral part of his soul was roaring that he needed to mount her, penetrate her and fill her up with a hot, thick surge of come before she could get away. He growled low in his throat, wondering where that strange urge was coming from, compelling him to do the unthinkable as he pushed himself between her thighs in a hard, aggressive movement. He'd never willingly spilled himself inside *any* woman, and he sure as hell wasn't going to start now.

A chilling shadow from his past crept through him, but he mentally shoved it away, fighting against that slick, nauseating pull. *Never.* He would never go down that path again. Which meant that he needed to get away from Olivia Harcourt…and stay away. Now. The sooner the better, for both their sakes.

If he could just get her and the kid out of there, he could take them to a motel. Then he could switch up—to hell with the promise he'd made his friends back in Colorado—and hand her over to Kellan. Let the wolf deal with her, while he protected them from a distance.

Struggling to find the presence of mind to break away from her, Aiden became painfully aware of the fact that he was grinding against her now, thrusting his hardened cock against the warm, tender notch between her thighs. Even as he fought to hold back the release of his claws and fangs, his fingers and gums burning with the need to change, he was eating his way into her mouth, unable to stop. His beast had hijacked his body and he was helpless in the face of its primitive demands. Once he'd started kissing her, he was lost. And God help him, it felt as if she was actually kissing him back, her small tongue rubbing against his, her sweet breaths filling his mouth as he shifted his head from one side to the other, searching for a deeper angle…a way to get even more of those pansy-soft lips and the sleek, lush warmth that lay within.

It completely unnerved him, how lost he was to the act, considering he'd never been all that interested in losing himself in the taste of a woman's mouth before. After all, there were always more interesting things a female could be doing with her lips and her tongue. And for some strange reason, Aiden had always viewed a kiss as something a little too intimate for the kind of affairs he had with women.

But he was kissing the hell out of the little human trapped beneath his body and the cold, hard ground, and he never wanted to stop. He was also dangerously close to taking her right there, and he could *not* let that happen, for too many reasons to count.

She's one of them, you idiot. A friggin' human. Do you even know what you're doing?

With a deep, bitter snarl, Aiden finally managed to pull away from the drugging depths of pleasure, breaking the contact of his mouth against hers. But it wasn't easy. Breathing hard, his heavy chest rising and falling beneath his black T-shirt, he forced himself to change the position of their bodies, pinning her hips between his rigid thighs. With that done, he wiped the back of his wrist over his damp mouth as he struggled to calm his thundering heart rate.

"Who are y-you?" she stammered. "G-get off me!"

For some reason he couldn't understand, Aiden found that stutter of hers completely charming. It probably made him nine different kinds of insane, but watching the way her mouth trembled when she got stuck on a word just made him want to kiss her again.

"Are you deaf?" she cried out in a shrill voice. "I said to g-get off!"

He kept her wrists pinned against the weak blades of winter grass and did his best to ignore the devastating effect of her struggling body beneath him. "Just take a deep breath and calm down," he choked out. "I'm a good guy, okay? I'm not going to hurt you."

Her eyes went wide with disbelief. "Yeah, r-right. What kind of moron do you think I am?"

Even in the frosty, moon-drenched darkness, Aiden could see her clearly, though he knew he remained mostly in shadow to her human vision. Her unusual violet eyes were bright with shock, her mouth swollen from the hard aggression of his kiss—the pink, full lips glossy and smooth, tempting him to take them again. The rational part of his brain knew that her individual features weren't the most beautiful he'd ever seen—that they were more cute and feylike than exotically sculpted—and yet he was completely mesmerized by them. She was undoubtedly pretty, but he couldn't stop staring with rapt absorption, as if he were gazing down at the most exquisite, provocative female ever created.

Clearing his throat, he somehow managed to say, "Seriously. I mean you no harm," then immediately winced, thinking he sounded like some geeked-out alien trying to reassure the panicked earthlings that he came in peace. What in God's name was wrong with him?

"How do I know that?"

"Because if I wanted to hurt you," he countered in a gravelly tone he was determined to keep even and calm, "I'd have already done it."

A bitter laugh spilled from her lips. "And that's supposed to make me t-trust you?"

"I don't give a damn if you trust me or not. But you'd better do what I tell you if you want to make it through this alive, because the bad guys probably aren't far behind me."

"What do you want from me?" She forced each word through her gritted teeth. "Why are you here?"

She continued to pull at her trapped hands, but Aiden wasn't ready to let them go, knowing she would only try to strike out at him and end up hurting herself. "I'm someone who was sent here to keep you alive."

"That's not p-possible." Her stammering words suddenly trailed off, the look of rising horror on her pale face tearing at him like claws. "Oh, my God," she whispered. "You're one of *them,* aren't you? You son of a bitch. Monica said they could look human. You're one of the bastards who killed my sisters!"

"I'm not a bloody Casus," he growled, scowling down at her.

"Right! And I'm just meant to b-believe you?"

"Well, if I was, you could bet your sweet little ass that I wouldn't have been knocking on your front door. And I wouldn't be taking the time to talk to you, either," he finished in a guttural snarl, his own temper beginning to get the better of him.

She calmed a little at his words, sinking her teeth into that full lower lip that Aiden knew was going to play front and center in his dreams, obviously thinking over what he'd said. Then she took a deep breath, slowly exhaled… and finally stopped fighting his hold. "If you're not one of the monsters," she questioned in a soft, hesitant voice, "then just who in God's name are you?"

CHAPTER TWO

KNOWING THIS WAS GOING to be the tricky part, Aiden stalled, using the time to simply appreciate the way her curly hair spread out against the ground beneath her, the vibrant color shimmering like bloodred jewels in the silvery glow of moonlight. It contrasted sharply with the paleness of her skin, the violet smoke of her eyes. When he found himself fighting the urge to lean down and nuzzle his nose against the crimson strands, he coughed to clear his throat again. "I've come here to help you," he told her. "Your sister's the one who sent me."

"Now I know you're lying." She bit out the words, resuming her struggles. "My sisters are dead!"

"One of them is." His tone turned gruff as he noticed the liquid rush of tears glistening in her eyes. "The other's been taken."

"What?" She visibly swallowed, trembling beneath him. "What are you talking about?"

"The youngest witch. The Casus have taken her prisoner." Rough, husky words that, if he didn't know better, almost sounded as if they had an undercurrent of emotion to them. "We're not sure where they're keeping her, but we're working on it."

"You mean Chloe isn't dead?" Her voice cracked as the tears spilled from those violet eyes, and the tip of her nose turned an adorable shade of pink. Though Aiden figured she had to be at least in her mid-twenties, there was an innocence about her that made her seem younger…and made him feel like a lecherous old geezer. "Answer me, damn it. Are you saying that Chloe wasn't m-murdered?"

"As far as we know, she's still alive."

Her shock was obvious, as was her hope that he was telling her the truth. "We never found a body," she whispered, "but…she's been missing for over a month. When Monica's body was found three weeks ago, I…I just assumed that they'd gotten Chloe, too."

"Yeah, well, they *do* have her," he said in a low voice. "But for some reason they haven't killed her yet."

His gut twisted at the realization that he would eventually have to reveal the specifics of her eldest stepsister's death, and how it had led to the hunt for her niece. "It's Monica, though, who is communicating with Molly."

She shook her head, her confusion obvious. "I don't understand. Who is Molly? How can she communicate with my sister?"

Biting back a groan of frustration, Aiden finally levered himself off her body and stood, then offered her his hand, pulling her to her feet. He'd have been lying if he'd said he didn't ache to pull her against him, molding her curves against his hardness, but she quickly released his hand, taking a shaky step back, her fingers swiping nervously at the tears glistening on her cheeks. As he ran his gaze down her body, he realized he'd been wrong to think of her as a "chick." Though she was dressed in faded jeans and a simple, long gray sweater, she had class written all over her. A fact that set her even further out of his reach, seeing as how he avoided classy females like the plague, since they tended to turn their noses up at what he was willing to offer. Which wasn't a hell of a lot.

"I'm w-waiting for an explanation," she stammered, though her voice was beginning to even out.

"Aw, hell." He lifted one hand, rubbing at the back of his neck. "This is the part I'm no good at."

"Well, give it a try," she snapped, crossing her arms under her breasts. "Because I'm completely freaking out here."

Aiden did his best to keep his eyes focused on her face, and not on those hefted breasts, knowing without a doubt that she wouldn't be holding her arms that way if she realized what it was doing to her chest. "First, where's the kid?"

She tried to give him an innocent blink. "What kid?"

"You can't lie worth a damn," he said in a low voice, "so don't even try it. It's just going to waste our time, and we don't have any time to lose. You're taking care of Monica's daughter. I think Molly said her name was Jamie."

Her eyes tightened, her expression filling with hard determination. "She's my niece, and I'm not just taking care of her. I'm going to adopt her and raise her as my own. And God help anyone who tries to stand in my way."

Aiden arched his right eyebrow. "If you're so protective of her, why did you start running off without her the second you laid eyes on me?"

Her fear momentarily forgotten, she vibrated with anger as she pointed one feminine little finger in the direction of the house. "I was running *toward* the back door, you ass! I was running to get back to Jamie, not away from her!"

He grunted, feeling every bit like the ass she'd just accused him of being. "Where is she?" he asked, hoping the kid wasn't watching them from one of the windows.

For a moment all she did was glare up at him, her gaze piercing and sharp, making him feel as if she was sizing him up, doing her best to figure him out. Just when his patience was about to snap, she said, "Jamie's watching *Hercules* upstairs."

Nodding his head toward her car, he asked, "And where exactly were you headed?"

"I was going to search for help," she replied with a slight shrug.

He didn't like hearing that, though he couldn't explain why. Any explanations he could have come up with didn't make any sense—and he wasn't about to own up to any of them, anyway. Determined to ignore the strange, possessive edge of his reaction, he simply said, "Help from who?"

"I was going to try to find the Watchmen."

He couldn't help it; he laughed. When she frowned at him, he gave her a mock salute with two fingers against his temple and drawled, "Watchman Aiden Shrader, at your service."

She narrowed her eyes. "That's not funny."

Another dark rumble of laughter vibrated in his chest and he shook his head. "Christ, you're telling me."

"Then do you care to explain why you're laughing?" she asked tightly.

The gusting wind pulled the long sun-bronzed strands of his hair across his face, and he lifted his hands, pushing it back. "Because I'm telling you the truth."

"You're really one of the shifters?" she whispered, her violet gaze moving with slow precision over his body, from his scuffed boots, up his jeans-clad legs, over his ridged stomach and broad chest, until she was once again staring into his eyes.

Feeling as if there were a fire burning inside him, Aiden

nodded in response to her question, waiting for her to ask what kind of shape-shifter he was. But she didn't. Instead, she pulled that lower lip through her teeth again and said, "You know, m-maybe this isn't necessary." Soft, quiet words that betrayed her uneasiness. "I'm sure that I can get Jamie somewhere safe, and you can just get back to…whatever it is that you do."

"It's too late for you to run and hide," he muttered, absurdly irritated by her reaction. "I've said I'm going to protect you, and I will. Which means you're stuck with me."

She frowned again, her arms tightening across her chest. "I wasn't planning on running, but I b-bet I could hide if I wanted to."

The slow smile spreading over his mouth had her blinking, and he could literally hear her heart rate speeding up as her face went hot. There was a healthy dose of worry and fear in her tense expression, but there was also desire. Olivia Harcourt might not like him, but Aiden would have been willing to bet his favorite body part that she was fully aware of the connection sizzling between them.

And the woman thought she could hide from him. Hah. He'd like to see her try.

"Not from me you couldn't," he finally rasped.

"Do you have any idea how arrogant that sounds?"

He shrugged his shoulders, liking the way her gaze kept

slipping to the bulge of his biceps, across the broad expanse of his T-shirt-covered chest, before whipping back to his face. "Not arrogant. It's just fact. One that you'd be smart to accept. Now that I know your scent, I could find you no matter where you tried to hide from me."

The words practically reeked of possession, and Aiden inwardly groaned. Oh yeah, touching her had been a bad idea, all right. Because now that he knew how she felt beneath him, he just wanted to keep on touching. Hell, who was he trying to fool? He wanted to do a heck of a lot more than *touch* Olivia Harcourt. What he wanted was to lay her down, spread her open and bury his face between her soft little thighs until she was wet enough to take every inch that he had to give her.

Then he wanted to do it again…and again, until they were both completely destroyed, their bodies wrecked, bruised and limp with exhaustion.

As one of the most primal breeds of shifter, Aiden often felt the need for hard, aggressive sex. But this was different, as if "need" were just some paltry emotion that didn't come close to describing how badly he wanted this woman. He didn't like it. Didn't like being drawn to a human this way, and his instincts were screaming that he should be wary…cautious. That she could spell trouble for him in so many ways.

He'd known it could happen. There were always certain females who were more attractive to his kind. Ones who could draw him in. Mesmerize the beast. He didn't know why it happened. Was the phenomenon based purely on scent? Bloodline? Random chance or the fickle hand of fate? Whatever the reason, these women were the ones to be avoided, and not just because of that "mate for life" crap. That wasn't possible unless his emotions were to become involved and he was driven to bite her, but they were still dangerous. If anyone had the ability to become his true mate, it *would* be one of them. One of the ones who personally awakened his beast…who managed to touch the hungers of the animal that prowled within him, as well as those of the man. Aiden had heard it referred to as "the Eve effect"—named for that first feminine temptation— but it was exceptionally rare for it to happen to a Prime predator. And to experience it with a human wasn't just odd, it was downright wrong. Not to mention potentially disastrous, considering humans were fickle, untrustworthy creatures at best, and his kind mated for life.

For all the catting around the males of his species liked to do, when they stuck, they stuck hard, like friggin' super-glue. It was like that with all the Prime predatory breeds. Sure, Raptors were renowned for their possessiveness and their insatiable sex drives, but then so were the furry ones, from the tigers to the wolf breeds, like Kellan and his brother Kierland. But the Prime predators took their hungers a step further than the Raptors, needing their fangs buried in the neck of the woman they chose to mate for all eternity. They needed the hot, metallic taste of her blood on their lips. Needed to mark her flesh with the provocative power of their bite. Needed her in every possible position that had ever been used between two consenting adults…and a few more thrown in for good measure.

The mere fact that Olivia Harcourt was human should have soured him to her taste and her scent, but it hadn't. No, there was obviously something about the woman that did it for him, but Aiden wasn't going to let it screw with his mind. Not if he could help it. If he'd learned anything in his life, it was that humans weren't to be trusted, no matter how damn appealing they were.

Scrubbing his hand over his jaw, he suddenly asked, "So what is it you do, anyway?" He knew the question was out of left field, but his growing curiosity was too much to ignore.

"I'm a teacher," she replied. "But I've taken a leave of absence."

"Teacher, huh? What exactly do you teach?"

"Not that it's any of your business," she said defensively, as if anticipating his reaction, "but I teach kindergarten."

For a moment all he could do was stare, the word running itself around and around in his head while his brain tried to make it compute. He had it bad for a freaking kindergarten teacher? So bad he could hardly see straight? When the others heard about this, they were going to be relentless with their ribbing.

Her eyes narrowed as she studied his expression. "I said *kindergarten,* Mr. Shrader."

"Yeah, I heard you. And for the love of God, call me Aiden."

"Then why are you staring at me like I have two heads and just told you that I'm a professional snake charmer?" she asked, her tone as dry as a desert wind.

Aiden rubbed his hand over his mouth. "No offense," he muttered, "but I think I'd have been less surprised by the snake-charming gig."

"You are such a strange man," she murmured, shaking her head, her windblown hair just reaching the tops of her shoulders.

"Lady, you have no idea." He sent her a crooked smile, then took a quick glance at the sturdy watch on his wrist. "Go ahead and call down the kid. We gotta get going."

She stared, unmoving, and he made a thick sound of impatience. "Honest to God, Olivia, we don't have the time for you to turn difficult. Not if you want to get out of here alive."

When she still didn't move, he ground his teeth together and shoved his hands into his pockets, trying to appear as nonthreatening as possible. "Look, I'm…sorry for what happened," he offered in a rough voice. "I don't force myself on women. Ever." No, he knew too well what it was like to have something taken from you against your will, and he'd vowed at a young age to never make anyone feel that same sense of helplessness, which was why he never even got close to a woman unless she made it clear that that's what she wanted. Tonight had been a first, and he was still pissed off at himself for losing control, which was why he was forcing out this awkward-assed apology. He also figured it would probably be a good idea to throw in *I won't ever kiss you again* for good measure, but couldn't quite get the words out, so he simply tacked on "It, uh, wasn't my intention to scare you."

She nodded, still looking a little wary. A second later she opened her mouth, then closed it again, and he wondered what she'd stopped herself from saying. Whatever it was, she'd obviously decided against it. After a moment she simply asked, "How did you manage to find us here, anyway?"

"I talked to your elderly neighbor back in town."

"Georgia told you we were here?" she groaned, her expression an adorable mix of worry, anger and frustration as she pressed one palm to her forehead. "What was she thinking? I made her promise not to tell anyone!"

Aiden shrugged one shoulder and grinned. "Don't be pissed at Georgia. She tried to hold firm, but I can be pretty charming when the occasion calls for it."

"What'd you do to her?" she gasped, eyeing him with a heavy dose of suspicion.

He snorted and rolled his eyes. "She's seventy if a day, Liv. It wasn't like I put any moves on her. All I did was eat some of her lemon cookies and tell her I was a cousin who'd decided to come into town to surprise you. After that she was only too happy to tell me where I could find you. I warned her not to talk to anyone else, but who knows if she'll do it. So the sooner we can get out of here, the better."

"I'll go get Jamie," she told him, heading for the house. After she climbed the porch steps and disappeared inside, Aiden paced back and forth across the lawn, sweating despite the chill in the air, his head still dazed from her strange effect on him. It was a good five minutes before she came back out, holding a small child bundled against her chest, the little girl's face buried in her shoulder.

"Jamie, honey, this is the man I just told you about." She spoke the gentle words into the child's dark curls, her hold one of tender affection that made him strangely envious. "He's going to help take care of us on our trip."

The child lifted her head, flashing him a shy grin. She had big, heavily lashed eyes, delicate features and round, rosy cheeks that made her look like a little cherub. Aiden could see the strain on her small face, and could only imagine the hell she'd been through since her world had started falling apart. It made him furious that her family had been left on their own, with no one to look out for them. Cutting a sharp look toward Olivia, he said, "If your stepsisters are descended from a Merrick bloodline, then why haven't you ever been given Watchmen supervision?" He knew that only the dormant Merrick/human bloodlines had been under strict surveillance, but it seemed criminal that an exception wouldn't have been made for a family of females, even if they were witches.

"According to Monica, there was never any supervision because we're not human," she said, telling him what he already knew. Before he could point out the obvious flaw in her statement, she added, "Now that my father's gone, I'm the only human Harcourt. But my stepsisters were... *are* Mallory witches."

"So it's true," he murmured. "The child is part Merrick and part Mallory?"

She nodded again, then quietly said, "But only half. Her father was human."

"Doesn't matter," he said in a low voice. "The Casus are still going to be champing at the bit to get their hands on her."

"But it doesn't make any sense!" she protested softly, tightening her grip on the three-year-old. Pressing Jamie's head to her shoulder, she covered the little girl's ear with her hand. "She's only a child. She can't be awakened! And her Mallory powers aren't even manifested yet."

"They'll want her anyway. Monica said her Mallory-Merrick blood mix is too strong a lure for them. They're going to value her power and her bloodline, even if she hasn't awakened."

Her rage was obvious, the furious blaze in her violet

eyes so intense he could have sworn he felt its heat. "Well, they're not going to get her."

"That's where I come in," he told her, taking a step closer.

She tilted her head back to stare up at him, and Aiden could sense just how badly she wanted to believe him. "You're really here to help us?"

"I really am." He reached out and ran his thumb over her lower lip, mesmerized by the sight of his dark skin against that smooth, glossy surface. Her breath caught, and he pulled his hand away as he lifted his gaze. "You know, you're not stuttering anymore. What gives?"

The look she sent him was suddenly pure teacher, thick with disappointment and reproach, and the corner of his mouth kicked up with another crooked grin. "What? Too rude of me to mention? You gonna smack my hand with a ruler?"

Jamie wiggled down from her aunt's arms, then tugged on the leg of his jeans, demanding his attention. When he glanced down, she lifted her chubby arms into the air and said, "Up."

Praying that he didn't accidentally hurt her, doing his best to be gentle, Aiden lifted the little runt off the ground, perching her small body on his right arm. "Yeah?" he asked, quietly noting the latent power he could feel humming within her. The keen intelligence burning in her big eyes seemed almost too sharp for a mere toddler, and he made a mental note to question Olivia about it when they were alone.

Acting as though she was about to tell him a secret, Jamie leaned her face close to his and whispered, "Livie only talks like that when she's weally nervous. Or when she's scared."

He arched both brows. "Is that so?" he asked, ignoring the almost silent curse that Olivia muttered under her breath, her embarrassment obvious.

The child nodded, her dark curls tumbling over her smooth forehead. Looking into her small face made something in Aiden's chest hurt, as if he'd been dealt a physical pain. It was unthinkable that anyone would want to harm something so precious and innocent, but then that was what the Casus specialized in, things too gruesome and wrong for any normal person to comprehend.

He slanted a curious look toward Olivia. "And the idea of the Casus hunting you down doesn't make you nervous?"

She crossed her arms, her voice hard with anger as she said, "It ticks me off even more."

Well, hell, he couldn't help but admire her spunk. For a kindergarten teacher, she was pretty feisty.

"You take care of us now?" Jamie asked, pulling his face back to her with the slightly sticky touch of her small hand against his cheek, the scent of chocolate and peanut butter reaching his nose. Her big eyes were so dark, he could see the stars reflected in their depths—and yet there were too many shadows lingering in her solemn gaze, and the pain in his chest got sharper. Aiden swallowed against the tight knot of emotion in his throat, but before he could say anything to reassure her, his phone started buzzing on his hip. Olivia moved forward, taking Jamie from him, and he pulled the phone from its case, thumbing the keypad as he lifted it to his ear.

"S'up?" he grunted, knowing Kellan wouldn't have been calling unless there was trouble.

"Get the hell out of there!" the Lycan shouted, breathing hard as if he was running. "They're closing in on you!"

"How many?" he asked as he dug his truck keys from his pocket, wondering if they had enough time to get out without having to fight.

Before Kellan could respond, a series of stark, guttural howls cut through the silent night…and Aiden had his answer.

CHAPTER THREE

IT SHOULD HAVE BEEN a criminal offense for a man to look…well, like this one did.

As she watched him talking on the phone, Olivia couldn't stop staring, soaking up the physical details as if they were something that would prove vital to her existence. Something she might someday need in order to breathe…to live, which probably meant that she was completely losing it. The Watchman was outrageously tall, towering well over six foot, his mouthwatering body clearly made for fighting, as well as a multitude of sins. All ones she was seriously wishing she had the courage to commit, no matter how dangerous he looked.

And he *did* look dangerous. With his long, wavy, caramel-colored hair falling around his wide shoulders, golden skin and long, corded muscles, he was her ultimate Celtic-warrior fantasy come to life, complete with mesmerizing tattoos. The dark designs covered the backs of his knuckles and his strong, sinewy forearms from wrist to elbow in a beautiful blend of what looked like pagan symbols. She wanted to lean close and study the intricate patterns. Trace them with the tip of her finger. Feel the strength of his thick, ropy muscles and the heat of his skin beneath the touch of her hand.

But unlike her fantasy lovers, Aiden Shrader was so much more than a gorgeous, compelling hunk. Though she still didn't know what specific kind of shape-shifter he was, Olivia had seen the way his eyes had changed as they'd argued, shifting from a gray-green hazel to a hot, glowing amber. There was a primal, predatory edge to the way he moved, and her breath caught as she recalled what it had felt like when he'd been pressing that powerful body against hers, thrusting heavily between her thighs. The erotic friction had been so overpowering…so achingly delicious, she'd nearly gone screaming over the edge, and her face burned with the thought, even as her conscience argued that she must be out of her ever-loving mind.

Stranger danger, you pleasure-starved idiot. Ring any bells?

Not that he was acting like a stranger. No, he was taking charge as if he'd been born to it, and God help her, Olivia was scared and tired enough to let him, the past few weeks of horror and heartbreak leaving her shaken and raw and needing a badass warrior she could rely on. He looked the type that could handle anything, his muscles coiled hard and tight beneath his golden skin, stretching the seams of his black T-shirt as he paced before her, muttering into the phone about the howls being some sort of warning to others that the Watchmen were there. His glowing amber eyes constantly surveyed their surroundings, looking for danger, and she began to wonder about things she simply didn't have time to wonder about. She wanted to know if he had a girlfriend, though she doubted it, the idea of monogamy probably repugnant to a guy who threw off his kind of sexual vibe. Wanted to know why he'd become a Watchman. What kind of life he'd led to become so hard and lethal-looking.

But most of all, Olivia wanted to know why he'd kissed her. Not that she could actually ask him at the moment, considering something was out in the woods, making the most god-awful sounds she'd ever imagined.

"Don't be scared, honey," she whispered against Jamie's silky curls, covering her little ear once again as she pressed the other against her shoulder. She hated that her niece was about to go through what would surely be another horrific situation. Thankfully, Jamie hadn't been with Monica when she was killed, but the traumatic loss of her mother had come just weeks after the disappearance of her beloved aunt Chloe. Olivia honestly didn't know how much more the little girl could take, when she'd already been through more than any child should ever have to endure.

Olivia was still lost in thought, worrying about Jamie, when Aiden disconnected his call and reached out, taking hold of her arm. "Come on," he muttered. "We've gotta go."

"What's g-going on?" she stammered, though she had a good idea of what was making those terrifying howls.

"I have some friends with me who're patrolling the woods. The Casus are on their way."

As he spoke, he started guiding her around the side of the house, toward a massive black truck she could see parked out on the curb. At first she was too shell-shocked to react, but then panic took hold and Olivia dug in her heels, pulling against his grasp as much as she could with Jamie in her arms. "Wait!" she panted, her breaths coming hard and fast. "I have to think f-for a minute. I need to—"

"Look, you might not be happy about being stuck with me," he snapped, cutting her off as he spun toward her, "but I'm your best shot at getting out of here alive. And I'll take apart anyone who tries to hurt the kid," he added, jerking his chin toward Jamie, who had her small arms wrapped tight around Olivia's neck.

"How do I know you're not lying?" she whispered, rubbing her hand against Jamie's small back. "How do I know this hasn't all been some sort of elaborate setup?"

"You don't." Grim lines creased his expression as he held her stare. "You're just going to have to trust me."

Taking a deep breath, she prayed she was making the right choice. "Okay, all right. What do we do?"

"We're going to take my truck and get out of here. Then the guys I'm with will come back for your car."

"No," she argued, already shaking her head. "We can't go in your truck."

He pulled his hand down his face, his gravelly voice thick with frustration. "Christ, Liv. This is no time to argue."

She spoke quickly, knowing they were running out of time. "We have to take my car. It's already packed with Jamie's things and I can't risk losing them. They're all she has from home. From her mother."

He muttered something foul under his breath, but stopped arguing and barked out a gritty command for her to wait there for him. Olivia watched as he ran to his truck, grabbed a duffel bag from the extended cab, then came back, latching on to her arm again as he headed straight for her car. She ran to keep up with his long strides, then buckled Jamie into the car seat belted into the middle of the backseat, while Aiden held the door open for her. After pressing a quick kiss to Jamie's forehead, she promised her niece that everything was going to be okay and climbed back out.

Olivia was about to hand her car keys over to Aiden, thinking he'd want to drive, when he dropped his bag on the ground, leaned into the car and slipped something over Jamie's tousled curls. Before she could ask what it was, he looked back, snagging her gaze over his broad shoulder. "You've heard of the Dark Markers, right?"

Her gaze swung to the ornate Maltese cross now hanging around Jamie's neck from a black velvet cord, resting against the fuzzy pink heart on the front of her pajamas. It was incredibly beautiful, etched with tiny intricate symbols that covered every inch of its dark, metallic surface. "Are you serious? That's one of the ancient Markers?"

He nodded, saying, "We just found this one earlier today," before turning back toward Jamie. He lifted her tiny chin with one tattooed finger. "Whatever you do, honey, do not take that off, okay? It's magic and it's going to keep you safe. You can even feel its magic when you touch it because it'll be warm against your skin. Why don't you try it?"

Jamie looked down at the Marker and grabbed hold of it, then stared back up at Aiden. "It's pwetty."

"Yeah, but not as pretty as you," he told her, ruffling her curls. "Now, promise me you won't take it off. No matter what happens."

"Pwomise," she whispered, gripping the cross tight with both hands, as if she understood just how serious the danger was.

"Good girl." He grabbed his bag and shoved it onto the floorboard, closed the door, then turned toward Olivia just as another series of screeching howls echoed through the quiet night. "Shit," he growled, glaring toward the thick line of trees at the edge of the yard. "They're too close."

"Too close for what?" she asked, worrying about the neighbors waking up and coming out to investigate the strange noise.

"There's no way we're going to make it out before they get here. So we go with plan B," he explained in a low voice, quickly moving around the back of the car and ripping open the driver's door.

Following him, she stammered, "What on earth is p-plan B?"

"You drive, I'll shoot." He motioned for her to get into the car, then shut her door and reached behind him. Olivia's eyes went wide as he pulled a heavy black handgun from behind his back, where it must have been tucked into the waistband of his jeans, hidden beneath the hem of his shirt.

Silently chanting a mixture of curses and prayers, Olivia quickly belted herself in while Aiden moved around to the passenger's side. He folded his long body inside the compact interior, then sent her a strange look that would have been funny if she hadn't been so terrified. "Christ," he muttered, "I feel like a friggin' pretzel in this thing."

"Fwiggin' pwetzel." Jamie giggled from the backseat.

Olivia glared at him and he winced, grumbling something about small-ass cars quietly enough that Jamie couldn't overhear him as he moved the seat back as far as it would go.

"So what happens if we m-make it out of here?" she asked, her hands shaking even harder than her voice as she looked over her shoulder and began reversing out of the driveway. At any moment Olivia expected the monsters to come leaping out of the dark, and she fought to brace herself, worried she was going to panic and steer the car straight into a tree, or one of the neighboring houses.

The gun clicked as he checked the clip, his voice somehow confident and calm as he said, "I need to get you and Jamie to the Watchmen compound in Colorado as soon as possible. It's called Ravenswing and it's where I live. It's also one of the safest places there is."

"We can't fly there," she told him, wondering how long she and Jamie would need to stay at the compound. It seemed so bizarre, the idea of living under the same roof with a group of strangers. Not to mention with Aiden Shrader. "Jamie has an inner-ear condition that causes extreme pain at the kind of high altitudes a plane flies. I've heard that there's a new medication for children her age that can help, but the prescriptions are just about impossible to come by."

"That's okay. Probably safer right now to stay on the ground anyway, where we're in control," he murmured, making her wonder if he didn't care much for flying himself.

Turning the wheel so that they were facing the road out

of the cul-de-sac, she put the car into Drive. "Aiden, I, um, I have n-no idea what to do."

"Just make it fast." His voice was rough, his expression focused as he started to roll down his window.

Taking a deep breath, Olivia gripped the wheel with both hands and floored the gas pedal. The back wheels made a god-awful noise, searching for traction, and then the car finally lurched forward, tearing down the moonlit road. A scraping, sinister howl sounded from somewhere in the darkness up ahead, and she shivered, praying she wasn't going to throw up from the churning rush of adrenaline and fear.

"What are you doing?" she asked when Aiden turned around, reaching into the backseat.

"Putting Jamie's blanket and pillow over her head. The Marker will protect her from the Casus's claws and fangs, but she could be cut by the glass if any of the windows get shattered. That's why I'm covering her up."

"Oh, God," she groaned, feeling as if she'd slipped into some kind of horrific action movie that had been horribly miscast, terrified she would make a mistake that could cost Jamie her life. "Please keep her safe," she whispered under her breath. "Please, please, please keep her safe."

Continuing to send up the quiet prayer, Olivia flicked on the high beams and glanced over to see Aiden watching her with a kind of confused expression on his rugged face, as if he couldn't quite understand what she was doing.

"What?" she asked, sinking her teeth into her trembling lower lip.

"You really care about her, don't you?" It was obvious from his tone that the idea surprised him.

"Of course I do," she snapped. Then, in a calmer voice, she said, "Why do you find that so hard to believe?"

He shrugged his broad shoulders, looking as if he was almost embarrassed as he turned his attention back to the road. "I just don't think a lot of humans feel that way about our kind."

"You mean I shouldn't love her because she isn't human? That's ridiculous. I couldn't care less if she's human or Merrick, a mermaid or a fluffy little bunny rabbit."

"You'd be surprised by some people, then," he muttered. "Not everyone feels the same way."

Anger made her voice hard. "Then they're jerks. And brainless ones at that."

"Can't argue with you there," he drawled in a husky slide of words, and from the corner of her eye she could see his mouth curve with a wicked, endearingly lopsided grin.

The howls suddenly came again, sounding considerably closer, and Olivia gripped the wheel tighter, silently cursing the damn road for being so long. Funny how it had never seemed that way before, and now it felt as if it stretched out forever, like an endless pathway leading straight into hell.

"You see anything big and ugly and gray, hit it," Aiden instructed her in a low voice. "Just try to avoid a tall guy with auburn hair, and one whose hair is short and black, if you see them. They're with me."

"Both Watchmen?" she asked, wincing as she took the next curve too fast and the wheels screeched in protest.

"The redhead is. His name's Kellan. The other's a human, but Noah's fighting with us against the Casus."

Looking over his shoulder, he reached back and patted Jamie's leg, his voice raised so that he could be heard over the roaring engine and the guttural howls. "Jamie, baby, I need you to cover your ears, okay?"

Olivia steered them around the next bend in the road, and without any warning, the first monster came out of the woods, charging the car head-on. The impact as it slammed onto the hood reminded her of the time she'd been rear-ended on the interstate by a drunk driver, the jolt slamming through Olivia's body hard enough to make her bones rattle. Claws screeched against the metal hood as the beast struggled to hold on, the nightmarish sound making her want to scream with terror, though she refused to give in to her panic. Not yet. Not until she'd gotten Jamie out of there alive and away from the monsters.

As Aiden braced himself in the open window and fired the gun, she knew why he'd instructed Jamie to cover her ears. The blast was painfully loud, making her flinch. The car swerved, and Aiden slammed into the window frame, a coarse four-letter word jerking from his throat.

"Sorry!" she shouted.

"Don't worry about it," he grunted, resettling himself in the open window. "You're doing great."

It all happened so fast after that, the details were like a blur. Olivia fought to keep the car steady while the other Casus attacked, jumping onto the roof...the hood. Each time she thought they were going to die, Aiden would unload a round of bullets, and even with her untrained eye she knew his aim was lethally accurate. Only one of the vile creatures managed to get too close, its razorlike claws just missing his chest as it fought for purchase on the roof of the car. Before it could swipe at him a second time, Aiden reached out with his left hand, caught its arm and cracked the bone in half while bringing his gun arm around and nailing the bastard right between its pale, ice-blue eyes. Olivia struggled not to gag as its heavy body rolled down the windshield, leaving a bloody streak across the glass as another Casus launched itself toward the car, only to be jerked off its feet as Aiden drilled it with a bullet that tore right through the center of its leathery forehead.

"Don't freak out," she whispered to herself, her hands curled in a death grip around the wheel. "Just focus...and keep breathing, and whatever you do, don't pass out."

One minute the car seemed to be buried in the bowels

of hell, and in the next, it was over and they were speeding down the winding road all alone, with nothing but the moonlight and the surrounding forest for company. "Is Jamie okay?" she shouted the second Aiden had slipped back into his seat and rolled up the window.

Sensing her panic, he quickly turned and leaned into the backseat, pulling the blanket and pillow off Jamie's little body. "She's fine. A little pale, but she isn't even crying." To Jamie, he said, "You were so brave, sweetheart. It's all over now, but I want you to keep the cross for me. Can you do that?"

In the rearview mirror Olivia could see Jamie nod her head, but it was difficult to make out her expression in the shadowed interior. She took a deep breath, trying to sound as normal as possible as she said, "I love you, Jamie."

"Love you, too, Livie," Jamie called back. From the sound of her voice, you'd never have guessed the child had just gone through a living nightmare, and it made Olivia's insides clench with worry, the fear taking hold of the back of her neck with a cold, clammy clasp. It had a different flavor than the terror that had been riding her during the attack—this one slower, digging down deeper, rooting its way into her heart.

Settling back into his seat, Aiden quietly asked, "Is, uh, that normal?"

Olivia knew he meant Jamie's reaction—or lack of one—and she shook her head. "I don't know. She's been really closed down lately." She swallowed, trying hard to keep it together. Softly she said, "I'd be lying if I said I wasn't worried about her."

She flinched as he reached out and settled his large hand on her forearm, its startling heat sinking into her flesh. "You can slow down now, Liv. Just pull over here on the shoulder for a minute and get your breath back."

She hadn't realized she was still driving at top speed until he pointed it out, and she immediately did as he said. The night seemed unusually silent without the engine roaring, and as the car came to a slow stop, she pressed her forehead to the steering wheel, her chest hurting from the ragged force of her breathing. "They're going to keep coming for her, aren't they?" she whispered, wondering if she would finally throw up now.

"Yeah." Olivia turned her head to look at him, her expression obviously stricken, and she felt the powerful intensity of his stare as he studied her face all the way down to her bones. Felt it in her blood and her stomach and the tightness of her chest. "I know that's not what you wanted to hear, but I'm not going to lie to you, Liv."

"Well, that's something, then," she murmured, unable to ignore the strange sensation that he was actually telling her the truth. Honest men, in her experience, were few and far between. She'd have pegged Aiden Shrader as the kind of guy who could smooth talk his way right out of any uncomfortable situation, sugarcoating the truth if it made things easier for him, but maybe she'd been wrong. "Have you had to do that a lot?"

"Do what?" he rumbled as he undid his seat belt again. Leaning forward, he reached behind him and slipped the handgun back into the waistband of his jeans.

"The gun thing," she explained. "You were deadly accurate with it."

Pushing back the thick strands of his hair, he slid her a wary glance, as if worried about how she was going to take his answer. "I've had to make kills, when the circumstances called for it."

Olivia nodded, squeezing her cold fingers around the padded wheel. "That's not surprising, I guess, except that I thought the Watchmen were meant to be neutral or something like that."

"For the most part, yeah, we are," he rasped. "When it comes to the clans, our directive is to simply monitor and report our findings. But there are times when we're called on to take down something that needs to be taken down."

A shiver traveled up her spine. "Well, I think the Casus certainly fit into that category."

"You'd think, wouldn't you?" he muttered, his tone bitter. Before she could ask what he meant, he changed the subject, saying, "Why hadn't you left town, anyway? After what happened to your stepsisters, I would have thought you understood how dangerous it was for the two of you here."

"Well, we haven't been alone," she explained, noticing that his eyes had bled back to hazel, though they still smoldered with an unearthly glow of light. "Up until this morning, Jamie and I had a houseful of aunts and uncles from my father's side of the family staying with us. Two of them are actually retired law enforcement, so I felt we were safe with them there. They came in for Monica's funeral, but after being here for several weeks, they needed to get back to their lives, especially with the holidays coming up. The house finally cleared out this morning."

"So they just abandoned the two of you?" Rough words that practically vibrated with outrage.

"It wasn't like that," she told him, turning to stare through the front windshield. "Remember, they're human, like me. They don't know anything about the clans or how Monica really died or what's happened to Chloe. As far as they know, a wild animal attacked Monica, and most of them believe Chloe's flighty enough to take off on her own without telling anybody. Several of my aunts invited me and Jamie to stay with them, but how could I say yes, knowing the danger we would have brought with us? I can only assume that the sheer number of people we've had at the house forced the Casus to bide their time, but they wouldn't be daunted by a few humans once our numbers were smaller."

"So you decided to leave?"

Olivia nodded. "I packed up the car early this morning

and we left the house. I figured it would be safer to drive out of town at night, and I actually had an important meeting in town late this afternoon with Monica's lawyer that I couldn't miss. So we went to my friend Connie's house for the day. I thought we'd be safe there, but I guess my mistake was in telling Georgia where we were going."

Slanting him a worried look, she said, "You don't think the Casus have hurt her, do you? She must have told them about Connie's house, the same way she told you."

"Maybe not. Depending on how good a lead they had on your scent, they might have simply tracked you there."

"They can do that?" she whispered, feeling as if every ounce of blood had just drained from her face.

"Yeah, and you didn't travel that far from home." He took a deep breath, and his voice seemed even deeper as he said, "Your scent is…unique, Liv. Different. I'm not sure if they can track Jamie's Merrick blood, like they do with the other Merrick, since she's so young, but there's a good chance they could have followed you."

"Great," she groaned, wondering why she would have to be the freak with the "unique" scent, whatever *that* meant. "Will they be able to track us out of town?"

"Not as easily, and we can keep ahead of them if we're careful. But it's still going to be a dangerous trip. They're going to guess we're headed for Colorado, which means we're going to need to avoid the direct routes as much as possible."

"This all seems so unreal." She shook her head again, her voice thick with emotion. "I don't even know what I'm doing."

"Naw, you're doing fine. Hell, just look at how you handled yourself tonight. You drove like a demon, and not everyone could have done that." Her pulse rate climbed as he gave her another one of those sexy, lopsided smiles that just seemed to intensify his outrageous appeal. "I never thought I would say these words, but you are one badass kindergarten teacher."

Though she felt oddly torn between laughter and tears, his husky words filled Olivia with a strange bubble of warmth that managed to ease some of her fear, which was probably what he'd been after. "You know," she said shakily, looking away as she felt her face go warm, "this is probably going to sound crazy, but I think that's the nicest compliment anyone has ever given me, Aiden. Thank you."

As the heat from his gaze lingered on her profile, she wondered what he was gearing up to say, but then his phone rang, interrupting the moment. He quickly took the call, asking if everyone was okay, while Olivia twisted around in her seat to check on Jamie, who seemed to be quite happy as she studied the beautiful cross that Aiden had hung around her neck.

"When you're done taking care of the bodies," he said into the phone a moment later, "meet us over at the gas station we stopped at earlier. Had to leave my truck back at the house, so we're in a red Honda."

"Are they all right?" she asked when he ended the call.

"Yeah." He slipped the phone back into its case, then raked his hair away from his face again. "A little banged up, it sounds like, but then they're used to that. Kellan thinks they took down around seven of the bastards in the woods, which means there were about twelve of them altogether, if you count the ones that attacked the car."

"That seems like a lot," she murmured, pulling back out onto the road. The only gas station remotely close to their location was a mile away, so Olivia headed in that direction, assuming that's where his friends would be meeting them.

"They're coming through faster and faster," Aiden grunted, his right arm braced against the door, his hand resting against his mouth as he sprawled against the back of the seat in one of those casual poses that had always struck her as beautifully male. "But to send that many tells us that your sister was right. They're eager to get their hands—" He cut himself off, obviously not wanting Jamie to hear, but Olivia knew what he'd been about to say. The monsters wanted to get their hands on her niece. On a precious, innocent little girl.

"I don't understand," she whispered. "It just…it doesn't make any sense."

"Yeah, well, you can't apply logic to these things, Liv."

The words were straightforward enough, but she could tell from his tone that there was something more. Something he either didn't want her to know or that he couldn't say in front of Jamie. Her body ached as the worry settled deeper into her bones, the past few weeks making her feel as though she'd aged ten years.

They pulled into the gas station a few moments later, and she parked in the back of the lot. While they waited for his friends to arrive on foot, Olivia made a quick call to Georgia, who thankfully was fine. The elderly woman claimed that Aiden had been the only person to come asking about her and Jamie, which meant that the Casus had likely followed her scent to Connie's house, just as Aiden had suggested. Unnerved by the chilling thought, Olivia fought to put a smile on her face as she twisted back around in her seat and chatted with Jamie some more. The little girl still seemed remarkably calm, considering what they'd just been through, and she couldn't help but wonder what was going on in her clever little mind.

Though Jamie was like a human child in so many ways, Olivia knew that her niece was far from what the world would consider normal. Her Merrick blood might have been dormant, but she was still a Mallory. Once a powerful, diverse clan of witches, the clan's magical powers had been bound by a curse—and it was because of this centuries-old curse that the Mallory now magnified the emotions of all those around them. All of which meant that Jamie would carry a tremendous amount of power trapped inside her body as she grew older. She would also eventually suffer from the curse, the same as her mother and her aunt Chloe. But Olivia didn't care that Jamie wasn't normal. The fact that she wasn't human certainly didn't make her love the little girl any less, as Aiden had suspected.

And yet she couldn't help but worry, not only about the dangers that lay ahead but whether she understood enough about the world of the clans to be a good protector for Jamie.

You'll learn what you need to know, because you love her. Because you love her enough to do whatever it takes.

Silently praying that she wouldn't fail, Olivia tucked a fuzzy pink blanket around Jamie's small body as the child cuddled up with her teddy bear to watch a Disney movie on Olivia's iPod. She'd just turned around and settled back into her seat when Aiden said, "That's Kellan and Noah over there." He nodded toward two dark, muscular men who were making their way across the empty parking lot, and she shook her head, wondering what it was about these guys. Did all the Watchmen look like this? The one named Kellan was tall, and nearly as gorgeous as Aiden, though he looked as if he'd just taken part in a vicious fight, his face scraped down one side, his black T-shirt ripped at the shoulder. He had auburn hair a few shades darker than her own, so that it appeared almost black in the moonlight, and piercing blue-green eyes that were still glowing unusually bright, attesting to the fact that he was something more than a mere man.

While Kellan's heavily muscled physique reminded her of a professional football player, the guy walking beside him could have stepped right out of a rock video. He was attractive in a dark, sinister kind of way, his long body wrapped entirely in black, the corner of his sensual mouth bloodied from their run-in with the Casus. His thick black hair was spiky from the wind, and despite being human, his eyes burned a pale, unusual shade of blue, almost like that of the creatures that had just attacked them. Trying not to stare, Olivia wondered if Aiden had been completely honest with her about Noah's species, but couldn't imagine why he would have lied.

"I need a few minutes to talk to them," Aiden said in a low voice, the gruff edge to his words making Olivia wonder if he didn't care for the way she'd been looking over the other two men. Not that *that* made any sense either, but then, it truly seemed a night for the bizarre. To be honest, at this point she didn't think anything could surprise her.

She didn't realize how lost she was in her own little world until he barked her name so sharply it made her jump. "You in there?"

"Sorry," she murmured, gesturing her hand toward his door. "You go on and talk to your friends. We'll wait for you here."

SO THIS IS IT, he thought, shutting the car door and heading across the tarmac. *Crunch time.*

If he was going to pass her off to Kellan, Aiden knew it was now or never.

Glancing back at the car, he felt the idiotic urge to go and toss Jamie's blanket over Olivia's head. He didn't want the guys ogling her, knowing damn well that they would. Noah's reputation with women was nearly as sordid as his and Kell's. And Olivia wasn't the type of woman that a man could miss. Everything about her was designed to draw a male's attention, from her smoky gaze to her full mouth, and that red hair of hers was something else. Even with the fiery strands tangled around her face from their earlier scuffle on the lawn, she looked delicious. Touchable. Earthy and soft and warm.

She'd actually put her trust in him to get her and Jamie out of there alive, and he couldn't stop thinking about it, even though he knew it was dangerous to make too much of it. To allow it to mean anything to him. Who knew what she was really like? What she was really after? Women were tricky creatures at the best of times. After a lifetime of experience, Aiden knew this as a given fact, just as he knew that he'd do well to stay as far away as possible from the very female, *very human* Olivia Harcourt. And yet he couldn't do it.

Alarm bells were going off left, right and center in his head, but he ground his teeth and ignored them. It just wasn't going to happen. He couldn't simply walk away, knowing her life was in danger, and leave her under another man's protection.

Hell, even if he passed her off to Kellan and tried to protect her from afar, he knew the Lycan would charm his way into her pants the second he got the chance. Then Aiden would end up having to kill Kierland's little brother, and he'd have the bloody wolf at his throat night and day.

Thanks, but no thanks.

"So is that the little lady?" Kellan asked when they drew closer, the Watchman's curious gaze trained on the car…and the captivating woman sitting in the front seat. Kell drew in a deep breath, pulling in her scent, then gave a low, rumbling groan. "Oh, man. This just isn't fair, Ade. How come I get stuck with Winston and you get the yummy redhead?"

"Don't start," he warned, taking note of the Watchman's bloodied knuckles and battered face. Kellan looked as if he'd single-handedly taken on the entire force of Casus himself, and Aiden sent a questioning look toward Noah, who responded with a slight roll of his shoulders. Ever since the crap that had gone down in Washington the month before, when Kellan had unknowingly hooked up with a female Casus who'd been plotting against them, the Lycan had been playing an increasingly dangerous, risky game with his safety—one that was worrying everyone who cared about him.

"Where's the kid?" Noah asked as he turned his attention toward the car, his ice-blue gaze searching the windows. Though they'd gotten off to a rocky start when they'd first met, Noah had quickly proven invaluable to their unit, and Aiden liked the guy's dry sense of humor. He also admired the human's wicked fighting skills.

Answering Noah's question, he said, "She's cuddled up in the backseat watching a movie."

"She isn't freaking out?" Kellan asked, his concern obvious as he eyed the gouges the Casus's claws had made in the Honda's doors. "Looks like the bastards hit you guys pretty hard."

Aiden shoved his hands into his pockets and frowned. "She's holding together a lot better than I would have expected. But I imagine her nightmares are going to be bad."

Kellan all but vibrated with leftover adrenaline as he finally looked Aiden in the eye. Rolling back on his heels, he said, "Well, knowing how you feel about humans and kids, I guess I'll go introduce myself and let 'em know that Noah and I will be taking over from here."

Without any conscious direction from his brain, Aiden's hand shot out and caught hold of the Watchman as he started to move past, his fingers digging deep into Kell's powerful biceps. "Not. So. Fast." He ground out the words, his throat feeling as if he'd swallowed a mouthful of gravel.

Kellan cocked his head a little to the side as he studied

his face, and Aiden fought to keep his expression neutral. "What's going on, Ade? I mean, I know Molly had some weird bug up her ass about you taking the job, but everyone knows you'd rather die than be stuck with a human for longer than it takes to screw her."

Aiden pulled in a deep breath, counted to five, then slowly exhaled. With his ears roaring, he barely heard himself as he said, "This is different," and let go of Kellan's arm.

The Watchman's eyes went wide with surprise, then narrowed with concern. "You sure you're okay?"

"Just dandy," he forced out through his gritted teeth, while Kellan looked between him and Olivia, the Lycan's expression confused…until a slow, jackass kind of smile began to curl his mouth. "If you value your life," Aiden growled, knowing Kell was going to say something that would just piss him off, "you'll keep your mouth shut."

Kellan raised his hands in a teasing sign of surrender, his blue-green eyes glittering with silent laughter.

Ignoring the younger Watchman, Aiden tossed his keys to Noah. "The kid's got an ear condition that makes flying impossible right now, so we'll be driving back. I'm going to get them out of town, but I need you guys to go back to the house and grab my truck for me. We'll head north, and when I've found a motel, I'll call and let you know where we are. We can meet up again tomorrow morning."

"Whatever's going on with you," Noah drawled, one dark brow lifted in a cynical arch as he pocketed the keys, "just remember to stay sharp. I've heard you tiger breeds can go a little light-headed when you get a whiff of something tasty."

"Go to hell," Aiden muttered, curling his lip.

"Winston's right." Kellan snickered. "Don't let the female catnip go to your head, Ade."

After shooting the grinning bastard the finger, Aiden forced himself to turn and walk away before his temper got the better of him…and he got himself into trouble. As he drew nearer to the car, Olivia lifted her face, sending him a shy smile that shot straight to his head, damn near making him dizzy, and he cursed something ugly under his breath, wondering just who in God's name he was trying to fool.

He was *already* neck-deep in trouble. And he was sinking fast.

CHAPTER FOUR

Prague, Czech Republic

THE AIR TASTED LIKE DEATH. Cold and thick…and lonely.

Walking headlong into the piercing wind blowing in off the Vltava River, Kierland Scott scowled as the bitter flavor filled his lungs, while his head continued to pound from the mother of all headaches. But then, arguing with the Consortium tended to have that effect on him. Comprised of representatives from each of the remaining ancient clans, the Consortium was a sort of preternatural United Nations whose job it was to govern the clans. The only problem was that the pompous bastards wasted so much time bickering amongst themselves, it wasn't any wonder that it often took years for them to come to any sort of a decision, much less take aggressive action.

And time was something that Kierland and his friends didn't have.

After the Merrick awakenings of Ian, Saige and Riley

Buchanan, the Watchmen knew more than they had last summer, when the first Casus—Malcolm DeKreznick— had escaped back to this realm. And thanks to Noah Winston, a human who'd stepped in to help during Riley's awakening, they now knew a lot more, such as the fact that the Casus were working with a race known as the Kraven. According to Noah, the Kraven—offspring of female De- schanel vampires who had been raped by Casus males before their imprisonment—were a closely guarded secret outside the Deschanel clan, their existence hidden not only from the majority of the Consortium, but from the Watchmen, as well.

Until now.

Slowly but surely, the pieces of this macabre puzzle were finally clicking into place, but there were still too many unanswered questions. Why did Ross Westmore, the Kraven who had somehow instigated the Casus's return, want the Dark Markers? What use did he have for the ancient weapons if he didn't intend to use them to kill the Casus? And what, if any, credence was there to Westmore's warnings that a time of anarchy was coming to the clans? Yeah, they had some answers. But it was the truths that still lingered in the shadows that worried them most. That had the Watchmen and the Merrick driving themselves into the ground to uncover as many of the Markers as they could before Westmore and the Casus got their hands on them.

Hunching his shoulders against the wintry midnight chill, Kierland ran over the arguments he'd made to the leaders throughout the long night, explaining why it was so important that the Consortium give its full support to the Merrick in their fight against the Casus, before it was too late. Arguments that had fallen on deaf ears, until his temper had finally gotten the better of him. He'd been told to leave the ancient mansion that was now serving as the Consortium's temporary headquarters in Prague, the stern directive capped off by a warning to cool down before he returned.

"Miserable old bastards," he muttered under his breath, scraping his fingers through his hair. "They'll be begging for our help when the Casus have worked their way through the Merrick and start gunning for them instead."

The road curved to the right, the street silent and dark ahead of him, but as Kierland neared the famous Charles Bridge, the unsettling sensation that he was no longer alone began to slither across the back of his neck, bringing a soft curse to his lips. Looking over his shoulder, he stared into the shadowed depths of the moonlit street, wondering if the Consortium leaders had sent someone to track him, but no one was there. The curling, serpentine tendrils of fog appeared to be his only companion…until he caught sight of the Deschanel, or what the human world would have simply called a vampire, moving stealthily through the shadows.

Shoving his hands deep into the pockets of his jeans, Kierland turned and stood his ground, an old, familiar hatred coiling through his insides as he waited for Gideon Granger to reach him. Though he had no direct reason to dislike the vampire, his lip still curled with disgust. After all, he despised the man's older brother, Ashe, enough that the wrathful emotion had eventually spread like a disease, until he'd come to loathe the entire bloody race. The prejudice was as unjust as it was juvenile, but Kierland had learned long ago that matters involving headstrong, impetuous females were seldom reasonable…much less logical.

Especially when the female ripped your heart out by shacking up with another man.

As Gideon stepped into a milky stream of moonlight breaking through the clouds, he sent Kierland a crooked, cautious grin, as if he knew his reception was going to be less than civil. Thinking it must have been years now since he and Gideon had exchanged so much as a passing greeting, Kierland couldn't help but wonder just what in God's name the vampire wanted with him.

"Tei," Gideon murmured in one of his many fluent languages, only a trace of his Scandinavian accent shaping the husky greeting. Seeing as how Kierland didn't speak a word of Finnish, Norwegian *or* Swedish, he had no way of knowing if the vamp had just said hello or called him a jackass…and he didn't particularly care.

"Granger," he grunted in reply. Pulling in a deep breath,

he searched for a trace of any other nearby Deschanel, but could find no others. Not that it meant anything. If they chose, a Deschanel could mask their unusually distinctive scent, making them impossible to track, even for a Lycanthrope.

"How does that saying go?" Gideon murmured from the corner of his mouth as he came closer, his pocketed hands mirroring Kierland's, though his trousers were black silk, rather than well-worn denim. Despite his size, he moved with the smooth, effortless ease of his race, as if he were merely gliding over the street like a phantom, the moonlight glinting blue off the rich sable strands of his hair. "You know, that one about how if looks could kill?"

Kierland arched his right brow. "Aren't you already dead?" he offered in a bored drawl.

Gideon's sharp smile flashed with his low rumble of laughter, his fangs just visible beneath the curve of his upper lip. "Aw, you know very well that I'm not dead, Lycan. But then, Hollywood rarely gets those types of things right, do they? I mean, look what they did with that movie about the Watchmen."

Hardly in the mood for jokes, Kierland cut to the chase. "What the hell do you want from me, Gideon?"

The Deschanel moved closer, leaning against one of the historic street signs that lined the sweeping road. Though his pose remained casual, the rigid set of his muscled shoulders hinted at an inner fury, as did the tightness around his eyes. While a Kraven's irises bled to crimson when they released their fangs, a pure-blooded vampire's were actually a pale, pure gray that would glow silver for several hours after they'd fed.

Instead of answering the question, the vamp simply said, "It wasn't one of ours who made the kill."

Granger didn't elaborate, but Kierland knew exactly what the man was referring to. Two days ago a Watchman had been found murdered in Russia, his mutilated corpse left in the center of a small town seventy miles south of Moscow. The fact that his body had been drained of every last drop of blood had started rumors flying among the clans that the kill had been made by a rogue Deschanel, but Kierland wasn't entirely convinced. Something about the killing made him...uneasy. The Watchman hadn't been hunting a rogue vamp, and yet for some reason Kierland had the oddest feeling that the kill had been deliberate, as if the Watchman had been targeted on purpose.

Then again, maybe he was just being paranoid, allowing his imagination to get the better of him, and the guy had simply been in the wrong place at the wrong time. God only knew he was maxed out to his stress limit these days, which was why he'd kept his suspicions to himself for the time being, instead of sharing them with the others back at home. Between the Casus and the search for the Markers, they had enough to deal with right now, without adding this to the rest of it. Plus, with the Casus on the loose, every Watchmen unit around the world knew to be guarding their backs.

And yet, despite the fact that Kierland obviously had doubts about the kill being a rogue vamp, it didn't mean he had to admit as much to the cocky-assed vampire standing before him.

"Come on, Granger. How can you be certain it wasn't a Deschanel kill? You know how easy it is for those of your kind to lose their…perspective."

The vampire snorted. "That's pretty rich coming from you, Scott. Considering rogue wolves gnaw their victims to the bone."

"And your kind drains them dry," he countered, his voice going softer as his temper sparked like kindling. "In either case, a life is lost."

"And we could keep going round and round with this bullshit, but I'm not looking to waste what little's left of my night on arguments. My first purpose in approaching you was to make it clear to the Watchmen that we're not responsible for the killing."

Wishing like hell that he hadn't quit smoking— seeing as how he was jonesing for a cigarette so badly he could taste it—Kierland tilted his head a little to the side, his eyes narrowed on the vamp's handsome face as he tried to get a read on him. Though he hated the Deschanel with a passion, he had to admit that he'd never actually met a vampire who wasn't beautiful in a cold, deadly way. "Why do you even care what we believe?" he rasped.

"War is coming," Gideon replied in a low rumble. "We intend to play a part in it."

"Do you, now?" Kierland murmured, lifting his brows. "I find that hard to buy, considering how the Deschanel have never given a crap about anyone but themselves. What's your interest in the Merrick's war?"

"Have you forgotten that four nesting grounds have been massacred by the Collective? Have you ever seen a murdered vampire, Watchman?" A low, humorless laugh fell softly from Gideon's lips. "But of course you have. After all, when the clans refuse to take care of their own business, the Consortium often calls on their *pets* to take care of the monsters. I'm sure the killing of a Deschanel isn't a memory that would fade, seeing as how it's such a colorful sight. Now, imagine what it's like looking out over a blood-covered field that's littered with the decapitated bodies of innocent women and children."

Raking one hand back through his hair, Kierland swore softly as the macabre scene took shape within his mind, making his stomach turn. The Collective was an army of human mercenaries who sought to purge the world of every nonhuman species that walked the earth, their tactics as brutal as they were merciless. In an ironic twist, the army had partnered up with the Kraven and the Casus in exchange for information that would further their ends. As a result, dozens of Deschanel families had been slaughtered in their ancestral nesting grounds. Located throughout Scandinavia and other parts of Europe, the grounds were ancient, sprawling castlelike communities where families lived for security, the lands protected by powerful magic that kept them hidden from the world—until their trust was betrayed.

Clearing his throat, Kierland slid the vamp a grim look of regret. "The nesting grounds had slipped my mind."

"Yeah, well, the locations of those nesting grounds were given to the Collective by Ross Westmore." The man's hatred and rage were unmistakable in the huskily spoken words, though his deep voice remained eerily quiet. "You know that as well as I."

And the Deschanel obviously wanted revenge, he thought, reflecting that this could easily get ugly. Not to mention complicated as hell. "So because of the nesting grounds, you want to join forces with us?"

"We're not asking to become a part of the party." The vampire's dry tone suggested that he knew damn well Kierland would never agree to work with the Deschanel. "But we're willing to help you learn more about the things you don't know," he offered suggestively. "Willing to get you information that you're going to need."

Certain there had to be a catch, he asked, "And just what would you want in return?"

"That brings me to my second purpose." With his hands

still buried in his pockets, Gideon straightened away from the street sign and stepped forward, narrowing the space between them to no more than a few feet. "If you find Westmore before we do, we want him."

"We?" Kierland asked, acutely aware of his beast's repulsion at having the vamp so near. "You mean the Deschanel?"

Gideon shook his head. "This is a personal matter for my family, considering our positions and the fact that we had cousins who died in the massacre. My brother and I intend to deal with Westmore alone."

Fury scraped down Kierland's nerve endings like a blade, and it was a physical effort to keep his fangs from descending. Taking an aggressive step forward, he ignored the wolf's vicious snarls vibrating inside his skull and got right in Gideon's face, going nose to nose with him. "You've got a lot of balls," he growled, longing to throw the first punch, "thinking I'd agree to anything that involves Ashe."

Granger's lips twitched with bitter humor. "You're not the first man who's accused me of that, but I'm sure as hell not going to show them to you, Lycan. And yeah, I think you'll cooperate. You need this information too badly."

"I don't need anything *that* badly," Kierland drawled with a mean smile. "And your brother can go screw himself for all I care."

The vampire's eyes narrowed, until nothing but a thin

slice of gray burned through the dark veil of his lashes. "Regardless of how you feel about Ashe, you know the code. It's our right to destroy the ones who have turned against us. We intend to keep searching for Westmore, doing everything we can to find him. But we want this deal, in the event that you get to him first."

For a moment Kierland thought his hatred would actually get the better of him, the wolf punching against his insides, eager to act on the rage that continued to seethe beneath his surface. The only thing that held him back was the vampire's eyes. The gray was darkening, proof that Gideon hadn't fed before approaching him. In the world of the Deschanel, that was a sign that he'd come in peace, and not aggression. The vamp would still be capable of giving Kierland a hell of a fight, but he'd purposely constrained his strength as a show of good faith—one that Kierland couldn't ignore, no matter how badly he wanted to.

Taking a deep breath, he retreated back a step, needing to put a little breathing room between them as he struggled for control. "You know, word on the street has it that the Deschanel treat the Kraven like slaves," he pointed out with thick sarcasm. "When you look at it like that, you can hardly blame them for revolting."

"I didn't say that their lot in life was fair," Gideon muttered, his rough tone cut with shades of anger and frustration. "But as *Förmyndares,* my brother and I have a duty to protect the interests of the Northern clans."

Though he wanted to argue the point, Kierland knew the bastard was right. It *was* the duty of the Deschanel *Förmyndares,* or Protectors, to destroy any threats to the vampire clans. And considering how much he knew about the Deschanel, Westmore was definitely a threat. "You still haven't told me what you have to offer," he muttered before easing back another step, needing to put a little more distance between them if he wanted to keep the wolf from taking over and going for the vamp's throat. "This information you think I need so badly. What is it?"

"The Markers," Gideon replied, his pale eyes holding Kierland's hostile stare. "There are things you don't know about them. In truth, they're not all that they seem."

"Meaning?"

A low, bitter laugh rumbled up from the vampire's chest, his expression shadowed by something ugly and dark. "Meaning that no good deed in this world goes unpunished, Lycan. Or haven't you learned that by now?"

A scowl pulled Kierland's features tight. "And just what the hell's that supposed to mean?"

"It means that your precious Dark Markers are far from perfect. The Deschanel Elders believe that in order to pour the necessary power into those little bits of metal, the Consortium had to travel into places that you righteous bastards would never think of going. They had to meddle with things that were better left alone." Taking his right hand from his pocket, Gideon rubbed his fingers against the shadow of bristle that roughened his jaw. "In short," he rasped, "they had to go begging to the darkness."

"The darkness," Kierland echoed, noticing that from where he stood, only half of Gideon's face was actually illuminated by the moonlight, while the other half remained shrouded in the shadows. Darkness and light. Although duality was a common feature among many of the clans, the trait was especially strong within the Deschanel, whose very natures were a dichotomy. A trait that made them complex friends…and dangerous enemies. "Are you actually going to stand there and tell me that they used dark magic to make the Markers?"

Gideon shrugged, the casual gesture pulling the black silk of his shirt tight across his muscular chest. "It's all about compromise," he murmured. "Sometimes if you want something badly enough, you have to lower your morals to get it."

"They wouldn't have," Kierland argued in a low voice, the horrific idea burning its way through his brain like acid.

"Oh, but they would." Gideon's mouth twisted into a wry shape that didn't quite make its way into a smile. "And they did."

"If you expect me to believe that, then you're going to have to show me proof, Granger."

"I have a feeling you're going to have your proof soon enough," the Deschanel told him as he stepped back, retreating once more into the thick shadows that blanketed the far side of the street. "Something is coming, Lycan. Something that has the Deschanel Elders worried, and the whispers are beginning to spread like wildfire. It won't be pleasant, but I'm willing to get you the answers you need, in exchange for Westmore."

"What do you mean something's coming?" he snarled. "The Casus are already here."

"Remember the murdered Watchman, Scott. The Casus aren't the only evil that wants a piece of this world. Not by a long shot. And if you want to survive," Gideon drawled from the murky shadows, the darkness swallowing his form like an eager, hungry mouth, "you just might have to sell a bit of your lily-white soul to make it happen."

CHAPTER FIVE

Kentucky, near the Ohio state line

THERE WERE TIMES when "hell on earth" wasn't simply an expression. Times when a man created his own misery in this world, simply because of the decisions he made. Decisions that led to circumstances that were not only torture, but a painful, living extension of his nightmares.

Kierland had given Aiden a book about it once, but then that was Kierland Scott for you. The unofficial leader of their Watchmen unit was always trying to help the others through the nasty minefields of their emotional issues, without ever tackling his own. Personally, Aiden thought it was an "avoid and deflect" instinct, but Kierland had just told him off when he'd offered the advice.

The Lycanthrope liked to dish it out. He just didn't like to take it. Still, Aiden had read the book and found a certain element of truth to it. For the moment, his own personal hell was being stuck inside a car with a human female who sorely tested his control and an adorable child the monsters wanted to get their claws into. He could have passed her off to Kellan and Noah, removing himself from the situation, but he hadn't. No, he'd chosen this version of hell, and now he was just going to have to deal with the consequences.

Of course, Molly was to blame, as well. He'd bloody well known that having a woman for a friend was going to be trouble, and now look at him.

Friendship was something he never offered to women, for the sole reason that friendship gave them ideas. The kind that could seriously screw with a bachelor's peace of mind—and ones that a man like Aiden had neither the desire nor the intent to ever fulfill. That alone was reason enough to keep his relationships simple and to the point. The point being that he needed women for physical release, but had little use for them beyond sex. While he might leave them humming with pleasure, it was a God-given fact that he *always* left them.

But it wasn't just the ones that Aiden got hot and sweaty with who could turn into trouble. He was fast discovering that having a simple, platonic relationship with a woman created its own set of issues. And when you made that woman a human female like Molly, who happened to possess the ability to talk to ghosts, the problems coalesced into one huge, irritating pain in the ass.

Case in point: his current situation. Aiden had never so

much as even lip-locked with the pretty little blonde who was set to marry Ian Buchanan, a man Aiden now considered a friend as well as a colleague, and yet here he was, simply because Molly had called and asked him to find Olivia Harcourt. Of course, she'd been backed up by Hope Summers, her soon-to-be sister-in-law. The bloody women had finagled their way into Shrader's heart and he'd somehow found himself becoming "friends" with them. It was enough to make a hardcore son of a bitch's stomach turn.

And Molly had had no qualms about sending "her buddy Shrader" on her quest.

Frustration rode him hard, and he could feel the same sizzling emotion vibrating off Olivia as her car ate up miles of highway. Now that he was driving and she'd had time to sit and think about everything that had happened, he was sure she'd put together a long list of questions for him about her stepsisters, but they could hardly have that conversation now, while Jamie was in the backseat, not quite asleep yet. Needing something to drown out the buzz of lust and restlessness in his brain, he finally reached down and turned on her radio. The latest Kings of Leon began playing from the CD player, and he smiled. "At least you have better taste in music than you do in cars," he drawled.

As she looked toward him in the shadowed interior, Aiden could feel the heat from her gaze touching quietly upon the sharp angles of his profile. It swept across the high slash of his right cheekbone, skimming down the surprisingly straight line of his nose—considering how many times it'd been broken—until it settled warmly against the corner of his mouth. His beast reacted to the visual caress with an impatient stretch, as if to remind him of its hungers. Not that he was in any danger of forgetting them.

"There's nothing wrong with my car," she finally replied, the slight huskiness of her words settling like a ball of fire in the pit of his stomach, the heat spreading out to his extremities, burning beneath his skin. Even his goddamn fingers and toes were prickling.

Forcing himself to focus on her words, and not the million and one other things he wanted to be doing to her at that moment, Aiden bit down hard on the inside of his cheek until the pain helped him calm down a little. "Yeah?" he managed to snort after a moment. "Doesn't seem to be much right with it, either."

"Did I momentarily space out and miss something? Because I don't recall asking for your opinion on the subject."

He whistled softly under his breath before flashing her a cocky smile. "You're quite the puzzle, aren't you?"

She appeared baffled by the question. "Is that supposed to make sense to me?"

He shrugged, flicking the windshield wipers on low as an easy rain began beading against the glass. "Just that you're not easy to peg. To figure out. I mean, you've gone from being scared to death of me tonight to mouthing off like a little hellion. I'd be lying if I said I wasn't enjoying it. It's somehow oddly refreshing."

"Glad to be so entertaining." Her tone was dry, her posture tense as she crossed her arms over the heavy swell of her chest.

"Well, you'll fit in great back at Ravenswing. Molly and Hope are gonna love you. Hell, they'll probably even ask you to join their little human sisterhood."

"And who are Molly and Hope?" The sudden, unmistakable edge to her words had him smiling again. "Your girlfriends?"

Aiden gave another low whistle, strangely enjoying their easy banter. "You think I've got two women living under the same roof? Impressive."

"I can't say that it would surprise me," she murmured, shaking her head.

"Ya know, I think that's the nicest compliment anyone's ever given me," he drawled, parroting her earlier words when he'd complimented her driving. "But they're not *my* women. They're engaged to the Buchanan brothers."

"The Buchanan brothers?"

"Ian Buchanan was the first Merrick to awaken, followed by his sister, Saige, and then his brother, Riley. Molly is set to marry Ian any day now. They were supposed to get married last month, but had to postpone when things started getting crazy. Hope is engaged to Riley, but I don't know that they've settled on a date yet. And the last I heard, Saige is marrying Quinn, one of the other Watchmen in my unit, on New Year's Day, though he keeps claiming that he's gonna drag her off to Vegas before then because he doesn't want to wait that long."

"Wow. It, um, sounds like there's going to be quite a few weddings taking place around there." Hooking her hair behind her ear, she looked away and stared silently out the passenger's side window, making him wonder where she'd wandered off to in her head. The Kings of Leon's lead singer had just finished belting out another husky chorus about lust and loneliness when she turned back toward him and spoke in a soft rush, as if she was in a hurry to get the words out. "So how did you end up getting stuck with the job?"

"The job?"

"Protecting me and Jamie."

Well, hell. Aiden ran his tongue over his teeth, fighting the urge to fidget like a guilty kid. "What makes you think I didn't volunteer for it?"

She didn't answer right away, as if she was giving some careful thought to her response. The next song had already wound to a soulful conclusion, the tires eating up another long stretch of country road, before she finally said, "You just seem like the last man someone would send to look after a schoolteacher and a child."

Scowling, he lifted one tattooed hand to his long hair. "Well, I can't do anything about the tats," he muttered. "But I'll be sure to get a haircut so you think I look respectable enough to be seen with you."

"I don't—I mean, what's wrong with your hair?" she asked, sounding confused.

Shaking his head, Aiden wondered when he'd become such a woman, allowing his freaking feelings to be hurt by her comment. "Look, you're the one who just suggested I didn't look the par—"

"I meant your attitude," she interrupted, cutting him off as she gestured toward him with a fluttering of her fingers. It was one of those wholly feminine gestures that a guy couldn't have pulled off to save his life. "It hasn't really seemed as if you wanted the assignment or job or whatever we are. In fact, I think your friends expected you to pass us over to them. Is it that you don't like kids, women or humans? Or a combination of all three?"

Huh, so she'd picked up on that while watching his exchange with Kellan. The woman was obviously observant for a human, which meant he was going to have to be damn careful around her. He didn't want her getting inside his head. He just wanted to get her to Colorado, where she and Jamie would be safe, while somehow managing to keep the animal half of his nature from completely screwing up his life.

"Well?" she asked, prompting him for a response.

Aiden kept his attention focused on the long, moonlit stretch of highway. "I like women and kids just fine."

"But...not human ones? Is that it?"

"Yeah," he muttered, knowing damn well that he sounded like a prick. "That's pretty much it."

A soft, wry sound that didn't quite make its way into a laugh fell from her lips. "Um, ouch."

His face felt tight, his mouth dry. "It's nothing personal, Liv."

"Oh, no. Not at all." Flexing his hands around the wheel, Aiden figured he'd have to be deaf to miss the sarcasm behind those simple words. "Will you at least tell me why?"

He worked his jaw, managing to scrape out a gruff refusal. "The why isn't important, so just drop it."

She nodded, as if that was the response she'd been expecting. "So, uh, whose brilliant idea was it to send you after us, then?"

"Kellan and I have been in Kentucky searching for the Marker that Jamie's wearing. Noah joined up with us two days ago. Since we were closest, it made sense that we come after you." Aiden kept to himself the part about Molly insisting that *he* be the one to personally watch over them, unsure why the little psychic had done it.

"And Molly was the one who told you about us?" she asked, rubbing her palms along the tops of her thighs.

"That's right."

"You mentioned that Molly was...contacted." She cast

a quick look into the backseat, then shifted her gaze back to his face. "Since Jamie's asleep now, I'd like you to explain what that means."

Lifting his left hand, Aiden rubbed at the tight knots in the back of his neck that seemed to be growing more painful by the minute. "Molly's human, but she has certain...powers," he explained. "I'm not real clear on all the details, but when she sleeps, ghosts are sometimes able to communicate with her."

Her breath sucked in on a sharp, shaky gasp, and she turned her face to the side, staring out the window again. Softly she said, "So Monica made contact with her? Did she tell her where Chloe is?"

"Yeah, Monica contacted her," he rasped, uncomfortable with the topic, wishing he knew how to handle this kind of crap. A certain level of compassion would probably have helped, but that just wasn't him. He'd spent so many years honing his cynical, smart-ass attitude, he'd forgotten how to be...easy. If he'd ever even known in the first place. "But she, uh, wasn't able to tell her where Chloe is. All we know is that she's been taken."

"And Monica told Molly that the Casus were coming for me and Jamie?"

Aiden nodded, saying, "After seeing how ruthless those bastards can be when they go after a target, we knew we didn't have any time to lose. So we headed to Lennox and tracked you down as quickly as we could."

She took a deep breath, obviously working to take it all in. "You make it sound as if there have been a lot of Merrick losses already. Is it really that bad out there?"

"It's gone from bad to worse," he admitted in a hard voice, "and things are moving faster every day. Saige Buchanan, who's an anthropologist, managed to get possession of some encrypted maps that give the locations of the Markers, and has been able to decode a few of them. We've already got four of the crosses in our possession, but there are still too many that need to be found before the Casus, along with their Kraven buddies, get hold of them."

She turned toward him, her gaze settling back on his profile, making him burn. "What's a Kraven?"

"The Kraven are a species that's half Casus, half vampire, but who can pass damn easily for a human. There's one named Westmore who seems to be orchestrating this whole thing, pulling the strings from this side of Meridian, which is what they call the Casus holding ground where the shades are imprisoned."

"Shades?"

"Because of their immortality," he explained, "the Casus can't die in Meridian. They've simply wasted away to 'shades' of the creatures they once were, which is why they're forced to take human hosts when they return to this world. We think Westmore has partnered up with a Casus shade named Calder, but we don't know much about him.

What we do know is that the Kraven are a nasty piece of work, and seeing as how they have the backing of the Collective, as well—"

"They what?" she gasped, cutting him off. "The Collective? But I thought the Collective was some kind of army of humans who tracked down clan members and executed them."

"It is," he told her, flicking the wipers onto high as the rain began to come down in a hard, steady pour. "But the human soldiers are working with Westmore, which means they're working with the Casus, as well."

Twisting toward him in her seat, she pulled her left leg beneath her and shook her head. "Okay, you're going to have to explain that one."

Aiden could understand her disbelief. Hell, he hadn't believed it himself when he'd first been told. "From what I understand, it all started because the Collective found the ancient archives—documents that apparently hold endless amounts of information about the clans. They were lost not long after the Casus were imprisoned and the Collective Army began hunting down the clans."

"How did they find them?" she asked. "And where?"

Frustration coiled through his body, cranking his tension. "We have no idea, but from what we've been told, Westmore found out that the Collective had discovered the archives, so he went to the Army Generals, offering them a trade. In exchange for allowing him access to the archives, their bank accounts and even their men, he offered them the one thing they apparently couldn't resist—the location of every ancient clan that remains in existence."

"Oh, m-my God," she whispered, her stammer returning. "C-could he actually do that?"

Aiden blew out a rough breath, hating that she was afraid. And hating that he hated it, because it meant that he gave a crap, when he knew he shouldn't. "I hope to hell not," he muttered. "But he already gave the bastards four vampire nesting grounds. The Collective caught the Deschanel completely off guard, and from what I understand, it was a complete slaughter."

She shuddered, wrapping her arms around her middle. "Have you ever f-fought against the Collective?"

Nodding again, he decided not to tell her exactly how many of the human soldiers he had taken down over the years. Instead, he simply said, "We may need orders to take down a clansman, as far as the Consortium is concerned, but the Collective are free game."

"Sounds d-dangerous."

"It can be. But they haven't given us much trouble since Riley's awakening last month. Idiots are probably wondering what they've gotten themselves into, teaming up with those psychopaths."

Quietly she said, "And so their greed will be their downfall."

"Who said that?" he asked, thinking the words sounded vaguely familiar.

She gave a soft laugh. "To be honest, I have no idea. The words just came to me."

"Well, whoever it was, it about sums things up. By making the deal with Westmore, the Collective Generals have created a hell of a mess for themselves. Now it's the Merrick and Watchmen against the Casus, Collective and Kraven, with all of us in a race to get our hands on the Markers before the other side."

"Why do they want them?" she asked, resting the side of her face against the back of the seat.

"We wish like hell that we knew. But some of us have started to suspect it has something to do with bringing the flood. We just don't know how."

"The flood?"

"When all the Casus escape at once."

"God. That would be…" Her voice trailed off, and he knew she was trying to think of a word that would do the horrific idea justice.

"Yeah." Lifting his hand, Aiden scraped his palm against the hard edge of his jaw. "That's why we're doing everything we can to keep it from happening. Kierland Scott, Kellan's older brother, is in Prague right now, addressing the Consortium. You know who they are?"

"I know a little. Monica and Chloe told me about them."

Aiden was about to explain the purpose of Kierland's

visit when he caught the flickering glow of a neon sign through the driving sheets of rain. After being in the car with her for so long, he was covered in Olivia's scent, the drugging perfume seeping into his pores, filling his head—and driving his goddamn beast to the edge. If he didn't get out and give himself some breathing room, the thing was going to shatter his control. And then there'd be hell to pay.

Reaching down, he turned off the music, then jerked his chin toward the sign. "That looks like a good-size motel up there. We should probably go ahead and stop."

"Will it be safe?" she asked, leaning forward to peer through the windshield, as if to see if any monsters were lurking out there in the dark.

"As safe as anything else we'll come across."

After heading around to the back of the building, Aiden parked and turned off the engine, his tension cranking even higher now that they'd stopped for the night. If he hadn't been such a bastard, he knew he would have told her that he'd wait outside until Kellan and Noah arrived, then do the right thing for everyone involved and step aside. Every second he spent in her presence was tempting fate. Tempting him to make a costly mistake. It didn't matter that he should keep his distance. Didn't matter that she was human and he didn't trust her.

No, the only thing that mattered, other than keeping her and the kid alive, was getting her under him—which meant that he was just going to have to suck it up and throw together a game plan. He was good at working through shitty situations. He'd had to be, or he wouldn't still be around.

And it could be worse, he thought. *She could be freaking out. Screaming and crying and blaming you for the mess that her life is in.*

Yeah, when he looked at it that way, he'd gotten off lucky, all things considered. Thanks to her stepsisters, she understood enough about the clans to save them all a lot of arguing and headaches.

And who knew? Maybe he was getting worked up over nothing. After all, what were the chances that she was going to be anywhere near as tempting as his imagination believed she would be?

So stop getting so jacked up. After you bed her, you can forget about her. Just like you've done with all the others.

As far as game plans went, it wasn't much, but Aiden was willing to give it a go. He'd screw her a few times, making sure the itch was scratched to the point that it bled clean, and God willing, once he did, he'd find out that Olivia Harcourt was the same as every other woman he'd ever had, even with that goddamn "Eve effect" going on. Then he'd be able to leave her behind, and get on with his life, searching for the next Marker...and then the next.

The plan should have brought him a measure of peace, but it didn't. Instead, Aiden's gut twisted tighter, and he swore something foul under his breath. Christ, when had he become such a bloody head case?

"You okay?"

Jarred out of his thoughts by her question, Aiden caught himself staring at her mouth. He could feel her embarrassment, thick and hot in the air, but he couldn't seem to look away, fascinated by the sensual shape, the impossible softness. Not for the first time that night, he found himself wondering if she'd actually kissed him back when he'd taken her to the ground back at the house. Or if he'd just imagined it. And if she had, why?

Frustrated at himself for mulling over it like an old woman, he forced out a gritty admission. "I don't want to leave you out here unprotected."

She glanced around the quiet parking lot. "Do you really think it's dangerous?"

Shrugging his shoulders, he said, "The odds are unlikely that they could track us this quickly, especially with all the rain that was coming down, but I also don't see the point in taking unnecessary risks."

She nodded, already undoing her seat belt. "Then we'll go in with you."

"That was the plan," he murmured, already unfolding his long body from behind the wheel. Aiden opened the back door and reached inside for Jamie, who was slowly waking up. When he unbuckled her from her car seat and lifted her into his arms, she cuddled against his chest as if it was the safest place in the world for her to be. Looking half-asleep, she gave him a shy smile and ran her pudgy fingers along his arm.

"Pwetty," she whispered, touching her little fingers to his tattooed forearm.

Blinking, Aiden choked back a gruff burst of laughter. God only knew he'd been called a lot of things in life, but pretty wasn't one of them. He slid a laughing look toward Olivia, and found her watching them with a strange smile on her face. "You're going to have your hands full with this one when she hits sixteen. She's already a charmer."

"Don't I know it," she groaned, giving a soft shake of her head that sent the fiery strands brushing against her cheeks.

Thinking of Olivia raising Jamie alone and without help, he suddenly found an uneasy frown working its way into his expression. "She's gonna need some big, mean-looking daddy to beat off all the boys."

"I'll beat them off. With a shovel, if I have to."

Aiden lifted his brows at the forcefulness of her tone. "It's a huge responsibility you've taken on, raising her by yourself."

She reached up and ran her hand down Jamie's back, her own expression one of fierce determination. "We'll manage."

"Well," he rasped, "the good thing is that you don't have to manage on your own anymore."

She sent him a startled, questioning look that made something in his chest go tight. "What do you mean?"

"You've got friends now, Liv."

For a moment all she did was stare back at him, her eyes wide...wary. She looked somehow afraid to believe him, and equally afraid not to. "Do I really?" she asked, the soft, whispered words nearly silent beneath the gentle rasp of the wind.

"Yeah," he muttered, knowing there was no way out of this. He was just going to keep sinking deeper, but man, there had to be worse ways to go. Right?

"You've got friends who can be ruthless as hell when they need to be," he told her, holding her misty gaze. "So stop worrying so much, because we're not about to let anything happen to either one of you."

CHAPTER SIX

OLIVIA HAD MEANT TO TELL Aiden she wouldn't need all their luggage, but by the time she'd recovered from hearing those low words on the Watchman's lips, he'd already paid for a suite, tucked Jamie up in the room's king-size bed and headed back out the door. Jamie was snuggled into her pillow, half-asleep, so Olivia found the bathroom and quickly splashed some water on her face, while silently lecturing herself for being such an emotional sap. God, the guy told her she wasn't alone anymore and she almost bawled like a baby.

But there was no denying how good it had felt to hear those words. Even from a man who'd already admitted he didn't like her…kind. It probably made her fifty different kinds of pathetic, but she was honestly too tired to care.

When he came back a few minutes later, she walked into the small blue-and-cream living room…and could only blink at the fact that he was carrying *all* of Jamie's and her luggage at once. The bags must have weighed four hundred pounds combined, and the muscles in his arms were bulging against the seams of his T-shirt, yet he hadn't even broken a sweat.

"What the hell do you have in here?" he grunted as he tossed the heaviest bag onto the striped sofa.

"Um, my books are in that one."

Surprise shone in his eyes. "Christ, woman, how many books do you need?"

"Don't you like to read?" she asked defensively.

"Well, yeah." He arched one tawny brow, adding, "But I don't usually feel the need to travel with an entire library."

Aware of the warmth burning in her cheeks, Olivia knew she should have shown a little more restraint when packing, but damn it, she *loved* her books. It no doubt seemed crazy to someone like Aiden, but she'd been leaving everything else behind. Her furniture. Her job. Her life. At least her books had been something she could take with her. "You don't have to make a big deal out of it, Aiden. All I did was put in a few favorites."

"A few favorites?" he repeated with a low bark of laughter. "Okay, this I gotta see."

Realizing he was going to look inside, Olivia screeched, lunging for the suitcase. Aiden was too fast, though, and as he lifted the top section, his low whistle blended with her groan. "Liv," he said with a wicked, lopsided grin curling the edges of his mouth, "I'm shocked."

"Yeah, right," she muttered.

He clucked his tongue against the roof of his mouth, clearly enjoying himself, his hazel gaze teasing and bright. "What would the other teachers say?"

Olivia rolled her eyes. "Oh, honestly. There's no crime in reading erotica, Aiden. So stop making such a big deal out of it. I wouldn't have expected you to be such a prude."

"But books like these?" he teased, waving one of the trade paperbacks in the air.

She shrugged, smoothing her hands down the front of her sweater, doing her best to school her features into an expression of cool, womanly confidence. Rolling one shoulder, she said, "What can I say? Women have needs, too, you know."

He gave her one of those fallen-angel kind of smiles. One that was slow and smooth and dangerously suggestive. Then he winked at her. "Just for the record, if you ever need help with those needs, you just give me the word."

"That wasn't a come-on," she said primly, the heat in her face flaming hotter. "And I don't happen to need a man's help."

From one instant to the next, his eyes shot from playful hazel to deep, golden amber, the glow burning brighter… hotter, as if someone had cranked up the gas. "You like to go it alone, then? Wow. Kinky."

Olivia gritted her teeth. "No…I just…what I mean is, I don't need—" She broke off with a sharp sound of frustration, knowing that anything she might say was only going to make it worse.

His voice turned deeper…huskier. "Not that the idea of you getting yourself off doesn't do it for me. Because it does. But you know, Liv, there are some things that are just better when you let someone else lend a hand."

It took a moment before she could think of a suitable response, the provocative words dazing her, as if she'd just been dealt a sensual jolt of pleasure. They hit her low in the abdomen, where she felt hot and empty, a heaviness there that felt like a gnawing, aching need. Finally she wet her lips and managed to say, "I realize this might come as a painful shock to you, Aiden, but I disagree. Actually, to be perfectly honest, I think the whole sex thing is a little overrated."

He winced, pulling his hand down his face. "Now, that's just not fair," he muttered, his rough voice sounding somehow pained.

"Fair?"

"Comments like that are the equivalent of waving a red flag in front of a bull. Just makes a guy want to charge in and prove how good the ol' sex thing can really be, when it's done right."

Ignoring the loaded remark, Olivia opted to steer the conversation back into safer territory. "So do you like to read?" she asked, following him as he picked up two of the suitcases and carried them into the bedroom.

He sent her a look over his shoulder that said he would let her get away with avoiding the sex topic for now—but not forever—and said, "Yeah. I'm a big Rowling fan, as well as Koontz and King." Setting the bags on the upholstered bench at the foot of the bed, he turned to face her, his thumbs hooked in the front pockets of his jeans. "But I like to play, as well."

She arched a brow in perfect imitation of his own. "Play what?"

"Piano."

"Are you serious?" she said with a quiet laugh.

He smiled a little, as if to say he knew how hard it was for her to reconcile the idea of a guy like him being cultured enough to play the piano, and guilt had her lowering her gaze, her face prickling with shame. She took a deep breath, knowing she should apologize, but when she lifted her gaze again, her mind stuttered to a jarring stop. Aiden was pulling off his T-shirt, his muscular arms raised in the air, his biceps bulging as he shamelessly revealed his enticing abs, followed by the smooth, sculpted planes of his chest. Olivia's jaw dropped, while drool collected in the corners of her mouth. She might have even whimpered a little, but hoped the hungry sound had been only in her head. Working for her voice, she somehow managed to ask, "Wh-what are you doing?"

"Getting ready for bed." He tossed the T-shirt over the back of a chair, then reached for the top button on his jeans.

"Whoa," she breathed out, holding up her hands. "Stop right there, buddy. You are n-not sleeping in here."

His eyes smoldered under the heavy weight of his lashes. "Why not? You got a snoring problem you don't want me to know about?"

"No," she practically growled. "I do not have a snoring p-problem. I j-just—"

Before she could finish, Jamie rolled over in the bed. Sounding half-asleep, her niece said, "Livie never snores, but she talks in her sleep. Weal loud."

"Is that right?" Aiden asked with a husky, impossibly sexy burst of laughter, his long fingers scratching lazily at his chest.

Olivia sighed, then pushed her hair back from her face. "Jamie, baby, you need to go back to sleep. Okay?"

"Okay," Jamie said around a wide yawn, while Olivia walked to the far side of the bed, leaned down and kissed her cheek, making sure the blankets were tucked in around her body. "Can I have a story?" Jamie asked. "The one you tell about the princess and the dragons?"

"Of course you can, sweetheart." With her back to Aiden, she sat on the edge of the mattress, her tension easing as she smoothed Jamie's soft curls back from her forehead. "Once upon a time," she said, "there was a…"

WHILE OLIVIA WOVE a magical tale of fire-breathing dragons and a princess named Jamie, Aiden went into the living room and called Noah over his unit's secure line, letting him know where they'd stopped for the night. He wanted to grill the guy about Kellan, wondering just how reckless the Lycan had been during their earlier fight with the Casus, but knew Kell would be in the truck with Noah…and able to hear anything he said over the phone. Better to wait until he could get the human alone.

When he was finished with the call, Aiden walked back into the bedroom just as Liv was moving to her feet. He leaned his shoulder against the wall and watched her, taking a moment to simply enjoy the way she gazed down at the little girl with such love. When she shifted her gaze toward him, he was careful to keep his voice soft as he said, "I'll pull the sofa in here and sleep on that, so you and Jamie can have the bed. But I'm not sleeping in the other room. We need to bunk down together for safety. It's stupid to take unnecessary chances, especially when I don't have any of Kellan's gadgets on me."

"Gadgets?"

"His custom-made security alarms," he explained. "Guy's some kind of techno genius when it comes to that stuff." She nodded, busying herself with one of the bags he'd brought in earlier. Aiden could scent her tension in the air, the subtle vibration melting into his body, almost as if he was a predator on the hunt…and it felt *good*. "So I was wondering if there was a reason you didn't want to sleep in the same room as me. I mean, other than the fact that I obviously make you uncomfortable."

Instead of denying it, she pulled her lower lip through her teeth and slanted him a curious look. "Like what?" she asked.

"Some guy who's gonna take exception to you being here with me?"

Her gaze slid away and she gave a quiet, nervous kind of laugh. "Uh, that would be no."

"What about Jamie's dad? Won't he be looking for her?"

She shook her head. "He left Monica before Jamie was born and has never even met his daughter."

"And you're serious about no boyfriend?"

"Yes."

Staring at her delicate profile, Aiden searched for any signs of deceit. When she glanced at him again and caught the way he was looking at her, a warm blush covered her cheeks. "What is it?"

He blew out a rough breath. "I just find that really hard to believe, Liv."

"What?" She ran her hands up and down her biceps, as if she was cold. "That I don't have a boyfriend?"

"Yeah."

She shrugged, turning back to the suitcase. "Sorry to disappoint you, but it's the truth. I ended my last relationship over a year ago."

Without meaning to, Aiden heard himself ask, "What happened?"

Another soft laugh fell from her lips, but this one had a brittle edge to it. "Let's just say that he wasn't the man I thought he was."

Aiden wanted to press her for details, but held back, not knowing what to make of the unfamiliar burn in his chest. It had flared at the thought of her with this unnamed male, as if the idea of her being with another man actually mattered to him. Shaking his head at the bizarre, completely unfamiliar concept, he watched as she sent a longing glance toward the bottles of shampoo and conditioner she'd set on the dresser. "Go on and take your shower," he murmured. "I'll watch over Jamie."

She stared down at her niece, clearly undecided.

"Liv, look at me." He waited until she'd shifted that smoky gaze back to his face, then said, "I'd rather die than hurt a kid. And I'm sure as hell not going to let anything happen to this one. If you're going to make it through this, you've got to start trusting me."

"I know that," she whispered.

"So go on, then. I promise I won't let anything happen to her."

She pulled out some clothes, then grabbed her toiletries. When she reached the doorway she braced one hand against the doorjamb and glanced over her shoulder. "Thank you, Aiden. For everything. I promise I'll figure out a way to repay you for all of this someday."

"Not necessary. And if you need any help in there

scrubbing your back," he drawled, giving her another wink, "just let me know."

SHAKING HER HEAD at his outrageousness, Olivia shut the bathroom door behind her. She showered quickly, and within ten minutes she was dressed in her favorite ratty pair of navy sweats and a gray tank top, her towel-dried hair hanging loose around her freshly scrubbed face. She was ready to race for the covers, but the instant she opened the door, she found Aiden sitting on the sofa that he'd pulled into the room, thumbing through a dog-eared copy of one of her favorite erotic romances.

"What are you doing?" she gasped, while Jamie snored softly from the bed, obviously out for the count.

Without taking his eyes off the page, he said, "I was curious about what you like."

"What I l-like?" she stammered.

The low rasp of his voice stroked her skin like a sensuous touch as he quietly said, "You know. Sexually."

Something isn't right here, she thought, only too aware of the differences between them. Men like Aiden Shrader never even looked twice at women like her, and they certainly didn't admit to being "curious" about their sexual fantasies. Olivia had always been too plain for that. Her older stepsister, Monica, had been the jaw-dropper in the family. Tall and perfectly proportioned. Then there'd been her younger stepsister, Chloe, who was so tiny and slim and ethereal. From the time of her father's marriage to Monica and Chloe's mother, Olivia had always just… been there. Stuck in the middle. Average, except for the overly top-heavy part. She supposed her hair and eyes could be considered assets, but had always felt as if they were kind of wasted on the rest of her.

And the rest didn't add up to much. Especially when you threw in the shyness and the stammer.

Still, she had her pride, and she wasn't going to just stand there and let a man like Aiden poke fun at her, pretending he was actually interested in what got her off. Tears pricked her eyes, her throat burning with a sudden rush of anger. "I get that you don't care for humans, Aiden, but that's no reason to be mean."

When he slid his gaze up from the pages of the book, the smoldering look in his glowing amber eyes made her shiver. "Mean?"

"You're making fun of me," she accused, fisting her hands at her sides.

"And you're making assumptions, Liv. I was serious about what I said." He shrugged one shoulder, looking almost embarrassed. "I just want to understand you better."

Olivia blinked, feeling as if he was suddenly speaking a language she didn't understand. "Is this… some kind of j-joke?"

Setting the book aside, he rolled up off the sofa with an animalistic power and grace that made her heart race…her chest burn. Muscles coiled and flexed as he stalked toward her, bunching and stretching beneath all that tight golden skin. "You really think I'm making fun of you?"

She nodded, her mouth watering as she watched him move. Feeling the need for retreat, she took a step back, and then another, until she had walked herself right back into the bathroom.

And Aiden just kept coming closer.

"Why do you think I kissed you tonight?" he asked in a husky rasp.

Shaking her head a little, Olivia struggled to concentrate past the deep, rhythmic pulse of desire that was arcing through her body, prickling beneath her skin. "I...I don't know. But it wasn't because you wanted to have s-sex with me."

"'S that right?" He snorted, then muttered, "You know, in some twisted way, this is pretty funny."

"What's so funny about it?"

"It's funny," he said in another low, delicious rumble, "because I've wanted to fuck you since the second I set eyes on you."

Her heart tried to lodge its way into her throat, not only from the shocking claim he'd just made, but from the way he suddenly moved farther into her space, closing in on her with his heat and the tantalizing scent of his body. And God, did it smell good. Warm and musky and male, like something wild and earthy that could be found only in the hidden depths of a dense, dark jungle. Something primal and raw and a little terrifying, it was so damn delicious. "Wh-what are you doing?" she gasped, flattening herself against the wall.

"Making the first of what is no doubt going to be a long list of mistakes where you're concerned." The hard, sensual look on his face was the most erotic thing Olivia had ever seen.

She wished she had the nerve to follow through on the 1,001 fantasies burning through her brain, but all she could manage to choke out was a soft, trembling "Then be smart and d-don't do it."

Bracing his hands against the wall, the Watchman caged her in, his rich, provocative scent hitting her full force now. It filled her head. Covered her body like a second skin, enveloping her in a sensual cloud as it mixed with the warm steam that still lingered from her shower. "Trust me," he rasped. "I would if I could, Liv. But I can't."

She had the strangest urge to laugh and cry at the same time as she stared up into his hypnotic eyes, mesmerized by the swirling, discordant streams of emotion burning inside him. Anger. Hunger. Arrogance. And what she could have sworn was fear. "You really are such a strange man," she whispered, wondering how he could affect her so strongly when she'd known him for nothing more than a handful of hours.

His beautiful mouth twisted into a lopsided smile as he

tucked a damp strand of hair behind her ear. "Believe it or not, I get that a lot."

"I b-believe it."

"You're stuttering again." His voice was soft, seductive, his touch dangerously tender as he trailed one fingertip along the side of her face, painting her skin with his heat. "You scared now, Liv?"

For some reason, Olivia felt as if he was testing her, but she didn't understand what he was after. And she definitely didn't understand the man. "I'm n-not afraid of you, Aiden."

He lowered his hand, pressing his large palm against the center of her chest, his skin fever-warm through the thin cotton of her tank top. "Your heart's beating a mile a minute."

She licked her lower lip, acutely aware of her body thrumming with need, her nipples gathering into hard, tight knots that pressed thickly against her shirt. "You're playing with me. I get that. I just don't know what you expect to get out of it."

Aiden leaned close, enjoying the way her pulse leaped and her eyes went dark. So dark he could see his own intense expression staring back at him in the luminous pools of violet. "Maybe I just want another taste of you," he told her, lowering his head until he could press his mouth against the side of her throat. Her skin was warm and soft, a fragile barrier to the succulent heat that flowed beneath the surface. He pressed his tongue to the seductive rush of her pulse, his body burning at the sexy little catch in her breath. "Ever think of that?" he asked, pulling back just enough that he could gauge her expression.

A small V settled between her brows. "But you don't even like humans."

"True," he admitted with a rough laugh. "But I seem to be liking you just fine. And if you don't believe me, then take a look for yourself." He gestured toward his lower body with a jerk of his chin.

Instead of doing as he said, she squeezed her eyes shut.

He whispered, "Go on, Liv. Look. I dare ya."

Trembling, she opened her eyes, glanced down and gave a hoarse, quiet cry of hunger that just made his dick even harder, the brutal ache pounding through all six and a half feet of him. "Jamie's asleep." He ground the words out past his tight jaw. "We could shut the bathroom door."

She ran her tongue over her bottom lip, a soft tremor shivering through her limbs, the scent of her need so thick in the air he had to mentally claw onto his beast, holding it back from her. "As tempting as that sounds, I'm afraid I'll have to p-pass."

Aiden didn't say anything. He just fought for control as he put his face close to hers and stared, waiting for her to look at him again.

It took awhile, but she finally tore her gaze away from

his crotch and lifted it back to his face. "You seem...surprised," she said with a shaky, nervous kind of laugh.

His chest rose with each hard, slow breath as he studied her from beneath his lashes. "To be honest—" his mouth tilted in another crooked grin "—I'm not used to being turned down."

"Especially by women who look like me, huh?"

"What's that supposed to mean?" he grunted, not liking the insinuation in her tone.

"Come on," she said dryly, rolling her eyes. "I'm a plateful of leftovers compared to what must be the 'usual' for a guy like you."

Aiden stared, not knowing what to make of her. He'd never heard a woman speak of herself in such a way. The ones he'd known, for the most part, had been vain creatures, obsessed with their looks and their ability to seduce. But here was this one, trying to tell him that she was... What? Plain? Something to be passed over? When he knew damn well that she was beautiful—sexy and lush and soft in all the right places, and that was just on the outside. Inside, well, she might have been a relative stranger to him, but he'd already learned so many things about her character. She was obviously brave, as well as compassionate and caring. Not to mention fiercely loyal to those she loved.

She was, in short, completely fascinating.

It didn't matter that she was human. That she was under his protection. Aiden still wanted to lay her down for hours…days, and show her in explicit, intimate detail all the things that he liked about her. He liked her blushes. Liked the way her breath quickened when he said something she considered wicked. It was driving him mad, thinking of the things he could say…the things he could do, that would set that pretty pale skin of hers on fire. He liked the idea of commanding her to keep her eyes on him, steady and wide, while he spread her sex with his thumbs and went down on her. Liked the idea of her convulsing against his tongue…

Want her, that familiar guttural voice snarled inside his mind. *Need her. Now.*

God, this was bad. When she'd showered, he'd damn near hurt himself imagining what she looked like with water dripping down her creamy, petal-soft skin. When she stared at him with her big violet eyes, he had to grit his teeth to keep from coming. And then, when he tried to get things going, she turned him down, making the animal inside him seethe with frustration.

"Face it, Aiden. You…well, you're *way* out of my league. I'm pretty average, and I'm fine with that. Honestly. I don't feel the need to reach beyond, and I'm also fully aware of what kinds of women you *do* go for."

Raising his brows, he pressed even closer, liking the way she pulled that full lower lip through her teeth when he nudged his jeans-covered cock against her belly, the color in her cheeks turning darker. "And exactly what kind would that be?" he asked, enjoying the way she had to struggle to concentrate, her smoky gaze hazy with lust. Enjoyed even more that she didn't pull back, trying to undo the intimate press of their bodies.

"Um, well, easy ones, for a start." She coughed, sounding as if she'd swallowed something scratchy. "And I suspect you also enjoy a fairly wide variety."

He couldn't help but laugh at her assessment, even though she had pretty much nailed it. "That's an awfully judgmental view," he murmured.

"But a true one, I bet. Men like you are easy to peg."

"Honey, you've never known a man like me." To prove his point, he gave her a cocky smile, flashing the pointed tips of his fangs. Then he slowly shook his head. "But my timing probably isn't all that great tonight," he admitted wryly, rubbing the backs of his knuckles against the downy softness of her cheek. "So I'll ease off. For now."

Before Olivia could respond, he took a deep breath and pulled away from her. The soft glow of the bathroom light made his skin gleam like satin, drawing her eyes to the wide, muscled expanse of his shoulders and chest, his body unlike anything she'd ever seen. Perfect and hard and ruggedly sculpted, the occasional scar somehow only heightening his dangerous beauty, while reminding her that this was a male warrior who lived in a world completely different from her own. "If I were to ask what kind of shifter you are," she whispered, "would you tell me?"

He pushed his hands into his front pockets, his powerful muscles rippling with the movement. "Sure I would."

"Well?" she asked, her chest tight as he held her with the dark intensity of his stare.

"I'm the scary kind, Liv."

"That's it? That's all you're going to tell me?"

He gave a low, rusty laugh. "Pretty much."

"You're going to drive me insane, Aiden."

"Then we'll get along great with each other," he drawled around a wide yawn as he took one hand from his pocket, covering his mouth. "My friends all think I'm crazy as a loon."

"Are you?"

"Naw." His mouth twisted, caught between sharp, conflicting emotions. "I just like to live a little on the edge."

She couldn't help but smile at that. "Now, why doesn't that surprise me?"

"I guess you're just perceptive. And since it doesn't look like I'm going to get lucky tonight," he teased, "I say we go ahead and crash."

"When was the last time you slept?" Lifting her hand, she touched the tip of her finger to one of the dark shadows beneath his eyes.

"Few days ago," he rasped, his body going completely still as she touched him.

"What have you been doing every night?" she asked suspiciously.

With one hand across his heart, he gave her another slow, knowing grin. "I wasn't out getting laid, if that's what you're thinking."

She flushed with guilt. "That's not what I mea—"

"I told you we've been searching for the Marker Jamie's wearing," he rumbled, cutting her off as he turned and headed back into the bedroom, while she followed him. "With Kell's and my night vision, we were pretty much able to search through the night, so long as the skies were clear."

She watched as he pulled the gun from the waistband of his jeans, reached up and set it on top of the room's high wardrobe, where Jamie couldn't reach, then lay down, settling his long body out over the sofa. Olivia tried not to wince, knowing he had to be uncomfortable on the short piece of furniture…with his jeans still on, but he didn't complain as he threw one tattooed arm over his eyes, one leg bent at the knee, resting against the back of the sofa.

"Do you want a blanket?" she asked.

"No, thanks." The wryness of his tone was unmistakable as he reached down and rearranged the massive erection trapped inside his jeans. "With the state I'm in, I doubt I'm going to feel the cold anytime soon."

Allowing herself a few moments to simply soak in his beauty, his chest rising and falling with his deep, even breathing, Olivia finally turned out the light and settled into bed beside Jamie. Thinking he was already asleep, she quietly said, "Good night, Aiden."

His deep voice surprised her, reaching through the dark like a physical caress. "Sleep tight, Liv. And try not to dream of me if you can manage it."

"You are so conceited." She gave a soft laugh, knowing instinctively that he was grinning like a jackass.

"Maybe," he rasped with a wicked drawl. "And you're the one who talks in her sleep, honey. So I'll be listening, just in case."

CHAPTER SEVEN

Lennox, Kentucky
Saturday, 2:00 a.m.

JOSEF SCHECTER DIDN'T LIKE to lose. As one of the few Casus permitted within Anthony Calder's inner circle of power, he'd grown accustomed to enjoying the privileges and respect that were his due. And after slowly rotting away within Meridian, the hellhole of a prison that had held the Casus for over a thousand years, Josef figured he was due a hell of a lot.

No one, however, was paying out. Instead, his time was being wasted cleaning up after others' mistakes—a circumstance that a perfectionist like Josef loathed. It was embarrassing to be surrounded by mediocrity and failure. Now the Merrick child was not only gone, she was under Watchman protection, which meant that her capture had just gone from a walk in the park…to deadly.

Staring up at the two-story house where their prey had

been hiding, Josef was furious they'd been allowed to escape, his rage like a thick black toxin scraping through his veins. Curling his lip, he shifted his gaze toward the ominous storm clouds gathering overhead, his eyes burning with hatred as though the grumbling heavens were to blame for the asinine situation. But he knew better. No celestial beings could claim credit for the failures that surrounded him. No, it was his brethren who were to blame. Specifically, Miles Crouch. As the bitter December winds chafed the chiseled face of the body his Casus shade now occupied, whipping the shaggy strands of thick, mahogany-colored hair around his head, Josef slowly flexed his hands at his sides, struggling to control his anger at those under his command.

"To lose control is to lose your focus," he rasped, the low words swallowed by the eerie cry of the wind as it swept through the thrashing treetops. But restraint wasn't easy. After all, he wasn't meant to be standing beneath a Kentucky moon, dealing with a bunch of incompetent idiots. Instead, Josef had been meant to come through in the final wave, when Calder—the Casus who had risen and offered his imprisoned brethren the chance for freedom—finally returned to this world, bringing the flood with him. But a change in the time line had been necessitated by the problem of Gregory DeKreznick. Despite being mortally wounded several weeks ago, Gregory's shade had not returned to Meridian. Somehow he still inhabited this realm—and they needed to know why.

They also needed him dead.

Gregory's brother, Malcolm, had been the first Casus who'd escaped Meridian, and it was Ian Buchanan who had used a Dark Marker to send Malcolm's shade to hell. Now Gregory was obsessed with destroying the Buchanan Merricks in order to avenge his brother's death. He cared nothing for his orders or Calder's authority or even his fellow Casus. In short, he was a loose cannon that Westmore and Calder wanted contained, as well as the Collective Generals, and so Calder had finally sent Josef, one of his best, most ruthless soldiers, to see that the job was completed.

Josef was only too happy to send Gregory back to the pit, if they could actually find the bastard. Westmore had been using all the resources at his disposal to come up with a lead on Gregory's whereabouts, and had even gone so far as to capture Chloe Harcourt, the female Merrick whose awakening had been caused by Gregory's return to this world. According to the rules Calder had established for their returns, her "kill" should have been reserved for no one but Gregory himself, providing him with enough power to pull another shade from Meridian without any help from Calder and his followers. Stealing her was the ultimate insult—and at this point, they were looking to strike out at Gregory with everything they had.

While waiting for Westmore's men to pick up a lead, Josef had contented himself with hunting down his own awakened Merrick, who had just so happened to be Chloe Harcourt's older sister, Monica. It had been the most delicious of surprises when he'd learned that she was not only part Merrick, but a Mallory witch, as well. The witch had been the first of her kind that Josef had ever killed, but she definitely wouldn't be the last. Not when he'd discovered just how intoxicating it could be to sink his teeth into warm, delectable Mallory. Though many of his brethren had hunted the Mallory prior to the Casus's imprisonment, that had been before the clan of witches had been cursed—and it was because of the curse that Monica Harcourt's death had been so…perfect. So addictive that he now wanted the woman's sister and daughter with a hunger that scraped his insides like metal against bone, but they had been decreed off-limits.

He'd have liked to rage at the heavens for that as well, but knew he had no one to blame but himself. If he'd kept his mouth shut, Chloe Harcourt could have already been his. She was in Westmore's custody, hidden away in a place where no one would ever find her. If he'd asked, odds were that she would have been given to him once he'd completed his mission and destroyed Gregory. But Josef's lone mistake had been in telling Westmore about the intense pleasures of his kill when he'd taken the sister's life. Upon hearing Josef's description, Westmore—who remained embarrassingly eager to please Calder—had immediately decided that Chloe Harcourt should be kept for the leader himself, so that Calder might claim the pleasures of her death as his own.

And despite the fact that Monica Harcourt's daughter was too young to wholly satisfy a Casus male's hunger—since they preferred to rape their female victims while they fed upon their flesh—there was always the chance she might give her killer the same kind of kick her mama had provided Josef. Hoping Calder might enjoy killing the child for her Mallory blood alone, Westmore had put out the order that she be brought in, as well. Her capture had been placed in the hands of Miles Crouch, but Josef had been asked to oversee the operation, since Westmore was no longer in the country.

Though Josef was now busy with his search for Gregory, a recent lead in Mississippi taking his full attention, he'd gotten to Lennox as quickly as possible when he'd learned that Monica's daughter and the child's aunt—the human Harcourt stepsister named Olivia—were finally going to be taken that night. Unfortunately, he hadn't arrived until a quarter of an hour ago, and by that time, Miles had not only allowed them to escape…but had also lost most of his unit in the process.

They'd been waiting weeks for this opportunity, and now Miles had blown it. It had been impossible to get to the child when the Harcourt house had been packed to the gills with humans. Too much potential for exposure, and Westmore had demanded they keep a low profile. Josef knew it had been a simple case of waiting them out, but now Miles had delivered them right into the hands of the Watchmen.

Westmore was going to be displeased, to say the least. And Josef was ready to draw blood.

While his own personal unit of Casus searched the surrounding area, Josef knelt and scooped up a handful of grass and dirt from the house's backyard, lifting it to his nose. With a low growl he pulled in a deep breath, his muscles coiling as the scent of the child's aunt slid down his throat. For a human, she smelled deliciously ripe. He'd given Miles specific orders to bring the human bitch and the child to him, so that he could deliver them to Westmore himself. They'd deemed it too dangerous to leave the aunt behind, unsure what she would do once the child was taken. Josef assumed Westmore had something in mind for the woman, and though he considered himself a loyal soldier, he found himself tempted to take Olivia Harcourt for his own. Westmore wouldn't be happy, but Josef considered it a fair exchange, since he wouldn't be allowed to touch the little girl.

Overhead, the sky splintered with a sudden sharp crack of lightning, and from the corner of his vision Josef spotted Miles Crouch stepping out of the shadowed woods, dressed in jeans and a long-sleeved T-shirt. The

Casus looked worried as he moved across the wide lawn, but then he had reason to be. This was the second time that he'd screwed up, the first being when he'd taken it upon himself to try to talk Gregory into being a team player, instead of taking him down when he had the chance in Washington. That mistake had resulted in the loss of too many Casus, and now he'd lost even more, their shades returning to Meridian, where they would have to wait until they could be pulled back across the divide.

Moving to his full height, Josef let his mouth curl into a hard, dangerous smile that stopped the approaching Casus in his tracks. "I see you've failed again," he drawled. "Tell me, Miles. Is this becoming a habit of yours? Because it certainly seems that way from where I'm standing."

"You know the Watchmen are lethal fighters," Miles grunted, the moonlight glinting off the pale skin that covered the shaved head of his human host, while a crimson patch of blood spread out over the shoulder he'd obviously injured during the fight. "And they had a Marker with them."

Josef arched his brows, his voice a slow, cultured drawl as he spread his arms wide and said, "Look around you, Miles. Do you see any burning piles of ashes? No one's been sent to hell. Their possession of the Marker was irrelevant tonight."

Miles's beefy hands flexed at his sides. "The bastards used guns on us, instead of fighting hand-to-hand."

"Then the answer seems simple." Josef fought the urge to shred the idiot's face with the razor-sharp claws prickling at the tips of his fingers. "Get a fucking gun."

"What's the point," the Casus argued with his characteristic stubbornness, "when bullets don't even kill most of the shifter breeds?"

Josef took a step forward, going nose-to-nose with the bald behemoth. "I'm going to offer you a little advice, Miles. And if you're smart, you'll take it. Calder expects you to succeed when you're given a task, and that means adapting your strategy so that you can defeat the enemy. I would have thought that became rather obvious after you got your ass kicked in Washington last month. They weren't worried tonight about sending our brothers to hell. They just wanted to get the human and the child out alive. It stands to reason, then, that a few well-placed bullets, which would certainly slow them down, might have been a good idea. Who gives a damn if it doesn't kill them, so long as it enables us to get our hands on the target!"

"The Watchmen have bought them some time," Miles muttered, sounding like a belligerent child, "but that's all. I won't fail the next time."

"You'd sure as hell better hope you don't. And seeing as how you allowed your Casus unit to get sent back to the pit, you'll be taking Westmore's men with you now."

The Casus's face turned blotchy with rage, and Josef didn't even try to hold back his mocking smile. "I can see the idea doesn't sit well with you," he drawled, "and to be honest, Miles, I really don't give a shit."

"I refuse to work with the Kraven," the Casus snarled. "Aside from Westmore, I don't trust them."

A lock of hair fell across his brow as Josef shook his head. "You can refuse all you like, but it isn't going to matter."

While he gave himself a moment to enjoy the way Miles ground his jaw, no doubt choking on his bitterness, a sound off to their right caught Josef's attention. Turning his head, he found two of the Casus from his own unit coming toward him, a struggling teenage girl trapped between them. They'd gagged her with a strip of cloth, her muffled cries for help too silent to draw anyone's attention from the neighboring houses, though they sent a shiver of anticipation down Josef's spine.

"And what do you have here?" he asked, his blood already heating as he ran his gaze over the girl's scantily clad body, a short nightgown and hoodie the only clothes covering what was clearly a lean, athletic build.

"We caught her creeping away from the house next door," the Casus on her right replied, his long fingers digging into the wriggling girl's biceps. "Said she was sneaking out to meet her boyfriend, but we haven't found any sign of him."

Josef clucked his tongue. "Naughty girl," he murmured, moving toward her. She trembled, tears pouring down her face, the heavy scent of her terror thickening his body with hunger. Others from his unit came their way, drawn no doubt by the girl's fear-thick scent. Addressing two of his men, Josef said, "Search the woods for the boyfriend. If you find him, I want him brought in alive."

"What are you going to do with her?" Miles demanded at his back.

Looking over his shoulder, Josef arched one brow. "Is that really any of your business?"

Miles's voice shook with rage. "You can't kill her. It's forbidden to take a human until Calder says otherwise. We're only allowed to feed from animals, Josef."

"On the contrary," Josef replied with a low, husky laugh. "She's seen our faces, which means she can't be allowed to live. Calder would insist she be taken down."

Miles's ice-blue eyes burned with hatred. "You *can't* feed from her."

"Wrong, Miles. I can do whatever the hell I want." Turning his attention back to the girl, Josef reached out and stroked his hand down the pale, shimmering length of her golden hair. "She must be dealt with immediately."

Miles moved to Josef's right, aggression pumping off his muscular body like a sweltering wave of heat, his meaty hands fisted with frustration. "You're walking a dangerous line, Josef."

Cocking his head a fraction to the side, Josef held the Casus's scornful stare, silently warning him to back off.

When Miles failed to relent, Josef transformed his right hand in a lightning-quick movement, his long claws wrapping around Miles's throat before the Casus could so much as blink. Miles froze, his eyes wide with fear, his clammy skin only a fraction away from being sliced open beneath Josef's lethal grip.

Leaning close, Josef whispered against the other man's cheek. "Do you really want to lecture me, Miles?"

The Casus held perfectly still, not even daring to breathe, and Josef gave a low, arrogant rumble of laughter. "That's what I thought," he drawled, releasing his hold. Miles swallowed convulsively, sucking in a shuddering breath, his expression an entertaining blend of outrage, relief and lingering fear. Josef smirked at how easy it'd been to cow the soldier, then turned his attention back to the girl, whose terrified gaze had latched itself on to his clawed right hand.

"Now, where were we, sweetheart?" Wearing a lop-sided grin, he stepped forward, then hooked his claws at the neckline of her gown, shredding the cloth down the center. She screamed behind the gag, flailing and kicking, but he could see in her glazed eyes that she knew it was too late. Nothing was going to save her now. Not her boyfriend or her sleeping parents or Miles's pathetic protests. And despite what Miles believed, there would be no repercussions for her death. After all, Josef had Calder's permission to take as many of her kind as he needed.

His whole purpose in being there was to take down Gregory, and it was no secret that DeKreznick had been taking human meals. In order to match him in strength, Josef had been given permission to take proper feedings, so long as he was careful to keep control of his hunger, without allowing it to override his reason, as it had done to Gregory's brother.

Without taking his eyes off the girl's twisting body, he spoke to his men. "Secure her on the ground, arms and legs spread as wide as they'll go."

While the Casus followed his orders, Josef removed his clothing, then leaned his head back, soaking in the light mist of rain against his naked flesh as he allowed the full change to overtake him, transforming his body into the ultimate instrument of pain. Thunder bellowed in the distance, echoing the frantic pounding of the girl's heart as Josef positioned his massive, leathery gray body between her thighs. Taking a handful of earth that held the human Harcourt sister's delicious scent, he rubbed it over the girl's trembling body, grinding the dirt into her pale breasts. As he pulled in a deep breath, Josef smiled down into her fear-twisted face. "That's better. Now you smell good enough to eat."

So good, in fact, that for a moment he actually considered keeping her around for seconds. Like leftovers, he could taste her again before making the kill. Tie her up on a bed and have his way with her for as long as he liked.

It was an interesting thought, but then he shook his head, changing his mind. If he was going to put that kind of effort into it, why not wait until he finally got his hands on Olivia Harcourt? Her scent was compelling enough to keep it interesting long after she'd gone numb from fear.

Covering the girl's body with his heavy form, Josef growled with triumph as he took his first bite at her shoulder, burying his fangs hard and deep. God, there was nothing like it, the power that came with the kill. He didn't even mind that they weren't alone. The greedy eyes of those watching only made it sweeter. Made him feel like a god. One whose due was this succulent little piece of flesh beneath him.

Josef only wished he had more time to enjoy her.

Though his ears were roaring with the ecstasy of the kill, a sharp sound caught his attention, and as he turned his wolf-shaped head to the right, he found Miles backing away, the Casus's forearm held over the lower part of his face, as if to block out the intoxicating scent and taste of the girl's blood in the air. Staring into the man's horrified eyes, Josef gave him a slow, bloodied smile.

"And Miles," he called out, the raspy words garbled by the distorted shape of his mouth.

"Yeah?"

"Third time's a charm. Screw up again and I'll be sending you back to Meridian myself. In pieces."

The Casus responded with a curt nod, then turned and quickly disappeared into the darkness, leaving Josef to his feast.

CHAPTER EIGHT

Saturday morning

THE INSTANT OLIVIA OPENED her eyes, the bright streams of sunshine creeping around the edges of the blinds told her that she'd overslept. She was still rubbing her eyes, trying to get her brain working, when Aiden came out of the steam-filled bathroom wearing nothing but his signature smart-ass grin…and a snowy-white towel tied around his sleek waist. She knew she should look away, but it just wasn't going to happen. Not in this lifetime. The guy was nothing short of perfection. Pure animalistic beauty, deadly and dangerous and drop-dead gorgeous. She couldn't stop watching the way his muscles moved beneath all that dark golden skin as he walked across the room, everything cut and tight…and big. She wasn't some shrinking violet, but it was impossible not to feel small and delicate and dainty when he was near. His body was massive...*huge,* the towel leaving far too much firm, mouthwatering flesh for her to ogle.

And you're going to just keep on ogling the poor guy until you make an ass of yourself, aren't you?

She mentally nodded in response to the silent question, knowing it was true. But what hot-blooded woman wouldn't ogle such a prime specimen of rugged, masculine beauty? He truly did remind her of an ancient Celtic warrior. His body wasn't the kind you found in a gym. No, it was a body that had been honed into a lethal weapon, its purpose to destroy its enemies. His shoulders were broad, his muscles ropy and thick, and yet he didn't look overblown. Instead, Aiden Shrader had the sleek, toned look of a deadly predator. One she could easily imagine crouching in the silent darkness of the night with gaping jaws, eyes glowing as it stalked its prey.

Knowing she was going to do something embarrassing if she allowed herself to keep staring, Olivia managed a deep breath and finally forced herself to look away. She figured she would last about a second before her gaze shot right back to him, gorging on the visual feast, but a startled cry broke from her lips the instant she spotted the empty side of the bed. "Where's Jamie?" she demanded, lurching up into a sitting position, her wild gaze flying around the room in a terrified search for her niece.

"Calm down, Liv. She's fine." Her gaze whipped back in Aiden's direction as he picked up a comb off the dresser and began working it through the wet skeins of his hair, his powerful biceps bulging as he raised his arms. "You were out for the count when she woke up, so I helped her pick out some clothes. She dressed herself in the bathroom, brushed her teeth, then claimed she was starving, so Kellan and Noah took her to the restaurant for some pancakes and sausage." With a grin kicking up the corner of his mouth, he laughed as he said, "She's already got those two wrapped around her little finger."

"Oh." She blinked, trying to decide how she felt about that. "Will she be okay with them?" He gave her a look that had her wincing, and she shook her head, trying to get her thoughts in order. "I'm sorry," she murmured, rubbing two fingers against her pounding forehead. "I don't mean to insult anyone, especially after what the three of you did for us last night. It's just that I don't... well, I don't know them."

"Nothing's going to happen to Jamie on our watch, Liv. Kellan and Noah are two of the best guys I've ever known. They're taking good care of her."

Olivia nodded, surprised to find that she actually believed him. The pressure in her chest began to ease a little, allowing her heart to beat a bit more normally, her lungs no longer choked with fear. Of course, the instant she was no longer upset about Jamie, her hormones reminded her that she was alone with a half-naked man. One who just so happened to be the hottest thing she'd ever set eyes on.

And as one minute flowed into the next, Olivia suddenly found herself thinking that if the towel around Shrader's waist was just a *little* smaller, she'd be able to get a glimpse of...well, of *all* of him. And from what she'd seen last night, she knew there'd be nothing "little" about it.

Running her tongue over her lower lip, she did her best not to dwell on that particular thought...or to drool over the hard muscles moving so sinuously beneath his dark skin. But God, she'd had no idea that a man could actually be built like *that.* Of course, the second the thought fired its way through her brain, she realized her mistake. Aiden wasn't a man. He was something *other*...something *more.* And from the looks of the bulge beneath that white cotton, a lot of it appeared to be between his legs.

And there you go obsessing about the guy's crotch again! Get a grip, woman. This is getting ridiculous.

Pressing her hand to her forehead, Olivia coughed, striving to sound normal as she said, "Uh, shouldn't you get dressed?"

"Should I?" His low voice reminded her of a sensual purr, thick and dark and sexy, his hazel eyes heavy lidded as he watched her with a strange, searing intensity that had chills dancing over her skin.

She pulled her brows together as she studied his hypnotic expression. Quietly she said, "Are you trying to seduce me, then?"

The wicked smile that slowly curled across his mouth

did something funny to her pulse, the rushing sound outrageously loud in her ears. "Is that what I'm doing, Liv? Seducing you?"

"I told you before," she said carefully, surprised by the hoarseness of the words, "that I'm not all that impressed with sex."

A deep, husky burst of laughter rumbled up from his chest, the provocative sound making her realize that she'd never really noticed how bone-meltingly sexy a laugh could be. "Yeah, well—" he tossed the comb back onto the dresser and gave a laid-back kind of shrug "—that's probably because you've been having sex with the wrong kind of guys, honey."

Even though she knew she should have been mortified by the conversation, Olivia couldn't help but laugh herself. "I hate to admit it, but you're probably right."

"What happened with the dickhead ex, anyway?" He moved to the foot of the bed, where he must have placed his bag before taking his shower.

Olivia pulled her sheet-covered knees up to her chest and wrapped her arms around them. "Chris was a divorced dad whose son was in my class last year. Turned out he thought I'd make a good stepmom, but wasn't all that interested in 'satisfying himself exclusively' with a woman like me for the rest of his life. His exact words, no less."

"You're kidding me," he grunted, shooting her a dark look from under his brows. "That's some kind of joke, right?"

A bitter laugh broke from her throat. "Trust me, I wish it was."

"What a prick." The masculine look of outrage on his beautiful face did wonders for her wounded pride. "And you actually liked this guy?"

She rolled her lips inward as she turned her attention to tracing the floral pattern on the comforter. "He was my slice of normal."

"Slice of normal? What the hell's that mean?"

Glancing up, she tried to explain. "I'm the lone human in my family, Aiden. Chris was…well, he was where I thought I belonged. The human boyfriend who could offer me a nice little human life. My slice of normal."

He pulled on a pair of boxers under his towel, then tossed the towel onto the end of the bed. "But did you *like* him?"

"We seemed to have a lot in common," she said with another soft laugh, eyeing the discarded towel. She wanted to pull it against her face, where she could have a deeper pull of the Watchman's dark, alluring scent, and she had to force herself not to act on the impulse. "And Chris and I got along well," she added, lifting her gaze to find him pulling a pair of faded jeans out next. "I really wanted to like him."

With his mouth curled in a cocky smile, Aiden gave a sarcastic snort. "That's a telling answer," he drawled as he pulled on the jeans and buttoned the fly.

"Yeah, I guess it is. But it's the truth. His son, Nathan, was adorable, and at first Chris seemed like the perfect guy. It wasn't until I caught him…" She paused, her voice trailing away as she realized what she was doing, pouring out her heart to a guy who could easily run for the King of the Studs. "God, I don't even know why I'm telling you this," she admitted with an embarrassed laugh, hiding her face behind her hands.

"Aw, don't be like that. I'm dying of curiosity over here, Liv."

Peeking at him through her fingers, she watched as he slipped on a dark green T-shirt that did amazing things to his eyes. "Seriously, Aiden. It's not like you're even interested. You're just being…nice."

"Trust me," he muttered under his breath, his attention focused on his bag as he zipped it closed, "I'm not particularly nice to women. And after last night, you should have figured out that you're wrong about the not being interested part, as well."

Tilting her head to the side, she tried to read his expression. "I so don't get you."

"What's not to get?" he asked, shooting her a sideways look as he grabbed his gun from its hiding place on top of the wardrobe.

"It's just…well, I would think human women would be boring for a man like you. Not to mention the fact that you don't like humans to begin with."

Olivia wondered if she kept repeating that particular truth as a way to remind herself to keep her head, or if she just liked the twinge of pain it inflicted. Before she could decide on the answer, he shocked her by saying, "Actually, I prefer them."

Though he'd averted his gaze, Aiden could feel Olivia's confusion as she tried to come up with a logical reason for why he would prefer sleeping with a species that he hated.

"I don't understand." Soft, nearly silent words. "Why would you prefer them?"

"Because they're safe," he muttered, checking the clip on the Glock.

"Safe?"

Rolling his shoulder, he struggled to put the truth into words as he reached behind him and slipped the gun into the waistband of his jeans. "They don't get to me. Don't make me feel anything I don't want to feel. They're just… there."

Her breath sucked in with a shaky gasp, and Aiden knew exactly how she'd taken the telling statement. Knew she was thinking the worst of him—that he was a user, a bastard. Which was pretty much the truth. He wanted to say something to make her understand that she was different, but what could he say that wouldn't make it worse?

Better just to change the subject before he ended up saying something he would really regret. "So this ex." He refused to say the prick's name. "Didn't he mind?"

"Uh, mind what?"

Slipping his wallet into his back pocket, he ran his tongue over his teeth. "The fact that he couldn't get you off."

Her eyes went wide. "How do you know that he didn't?"

Aiden shot her a crooked smile that felt tight on his face. "If he had, you wouldn't keep claiming that sex isn't really your thing."

She frowned, looking for a moment as if she would tell him it was none of his damn business. But then she exhaled a soft breath of air, her irritation seeming to bleed out as she said, "I don't really know if he knew, since we didn't talk about it. But maybe…maybe that's why he felt the need to get his jollies elsewhere."

"So he was an idiot as well as a prick," he snorted, wishing he could have just five minutes alone with the guy. That was all it would take to repay the bastard for hurting her.

"Pretty much." She shrugged, her eyes dark with emotion. "But I tried to make it work. I mean, it wasn't like I didn't…make an effort."

Aiden knew exactly what she was attempting to say. She'd tried to enjoy sex with the worthless prick, and as her soft words melted into him, something hot and thick twisted through his insides, the powerful sensation as foreign as it was disturbing.

That's because for the first time in your life, you're actually jealous.

Whoa. Sagging back against the wall, he scrubbed his hands down his face as he tried to wrap his mind around that stunning realization.

Knowing this was going to spell trouble, Aiden wanted to laugh it off as some kind of cosmic prank, but the truth was hard to deny. And to make it even worse, he wasn't the only one who was dealing with that ugly green monster. No, his beast was suddenly focusing on Olivia with a fierce, possessive purpose, its guttural voice snarling within his head that she was *his.* He forced himself to look away from her, but the damage had already been done. The provocative image of her sitting there in the midst of all that soft white bedding, her hair tousled, cheeks still warm from the heat of her blush, already had his dick as hard as a friggin' spike. His gums burned from the weight of his fangs, the animal in him more than ready to come out and take matters into its own greedy hands.

"Aiden, are you okay?" She sounded concerned, and for some illogical reason the idea made him even harder, the fire in his gums growing hotter. Molten. And yet there was panic there as well, flavoring the sharp, visceral burn of lust. He didn't want this raging desire to *mark* her, damn it. Didn't want to be filled with savage thoughts of possession—of keeping her and owning her forever. Of having the right to break any asshole who tried to put their filthy hands on her. That was a bad, *bad* road, because in the back of his mind burned the ugly truth that once she really clued in to what he was, to the things he'd want from her, to the fact that he was a hell of a lot more animal than man, she wasn't going to be able to run fast enough.

Not to mention what her reaction would be like if she ever learned about his past. Learned where he'd come from. What he'd done to survive. If that didn't have her looking at him with revulsion, nothing would.

"Seriously, say something. Please. You're starting to freak me out."

Worrying his hand over his mouth, he managed to scrape out a husky "We need to get out of here."

"Why? What's wrong?"

"You don't want to know," he muttered, pushing away from the wall.

"Yes, I—"

"Just get dressed." He threw the words over his shoulder, sweating, shaking, knowing he had only seconds before the tiger was out of its cage. Literally. And for the first time in years, Aiden honestly didn't know if he'd be able to control it. Not when her very proximity tempted him to do the unthinkable, binding himself to a woman who would end up cutting his goddamn heart out.

"I'll be waiting outside," he growled, and without looking back, he headed for the door.

CONFUSED BY the Watchman's strange, turbulent mood swings, Olivia rushed through her morning routine, then threw on some jeans and a sweater. When she left the room, she found Aiden smoking a cigarette, his body all but vibrating with a hard, restless energy as he leaned against the outer wall of the hotel. "I didn't know you smoked."

"I usually don't," he muttered, glaring down at the filter pinched between his thumb and forefinger, as if he was almost surprised to find it there in his hand. Dropping the cigarette, he ground it out with his boot. "Come on. They're waiting for us."

The instant they stepped into the brightly lit restaurant they spotted Kellan and Noah at a booth in the back corner, both men a good half a foot taller than any of the other customers, with Jamie's little body wedged protectively between them. Noah sat on her right, carefully cutting up a fluffy stack of pancakes. He was beautiful, in a dark, fallen angel kind of way, a menacing aura of danger and violence flowing around him. But the gentle smile on his face as he talked with Jamie assured Olivia that he wasn't a threat to her niece. Clearly, Jamie was already working her charm on the guys, her face glowing as they gave her their full attention. Then Olivia realized what Jamie was wearing, and she couldn't hold back a choked laugh of surprise. Looking at the gorgeous male standing at her side, she said, "I thought you helped her pick her clothes out."

"I did," Aiden said defensively, sliding her a sideways glance. "She looks adorable."

Olivia rolled her eyes. "She looks like a pink nightmare in that outfit."

His eyes crinkled sexily at the corners as he looked toward Jamie. "What's wrong with it? Everything's pink."

Everything was pink, all right. Her niece was wearing a hot-pink polka-dotted jumper with a magenta-and-periwinkle-striped shirt underneath, topped off by a strawberry-pink hair band. "Never mind." She sighed, knowing he would think she was crazy if she tried to explain that just because something was a "shade" of pink didn't mean that it matched.

Though he was still vibing that hot, strange burn of energy that had come over him in the hotel room, his touch was gentle as he took her elbow and guided her across the crowded restaurant. As they neared the booth, Kellan's head suddenly shot up…and he lifted his nose a little higher in the air, like an animal searching for a scent. A wicked smile slowly curled its way across his mouth, his eyes glittering with humor as he looked at Aiden. "Man, Ade. She really does smell tasty, doesn't she?"

Frowning and feeling acutely self-conscious, Olivia slid into the empty side of the booth. "Isn't there something I can do about…the scent?" she asked Aiden as he slid in beside her.

His mouth hardened, and he shook his head. "'Fraid not. No matter what you do, it's going to bleed through."

"And it's that different?" she asked tightly, though she forced a smile on her face for Jamie's benefit.

He cleared his throat, his gaze shifting away as he said, "Yeah. It's pretty different, all right."

Kellan sent her a sheepish grin from the other side of the table. "Guess I need to learn to keep my mouth shut. I didn't mean to embarrass you."

"No harm done," she murmured just as their server came to the table, her baby blues zeroed in on Aiden as she asked if they were ready to place their orders. Olivia fought to hold her smile in place as Kandy, according to the name tag pinned just to the left of her cleavage, began to flirt with Aiden. Not caring to witness his response, she muttered that she'd take a coffee and croissant, then focused her full attention on the men sitting across from them. Now that she was closer, little details caught her attention, making it obvious that the guys were working hard to project a carefree image for Jamie's sake.

Kellan had an edgy alertness in his odd-colored eyes, as if he was just waiting for something bad to happen.

Noah, on the other hand, looked exhausted. The dark, bruise-colored shadows under his eyes only made the unusual blue seem brighter beneath the ebony wisps of hair that fell over his brow. Though she couldn't explain it, there was something about him that Olivia couldn't quite put her finger on. He hadn't healed as quickly as Kellan, his lip still mending from their fight with the Casus, but she wasn't buying Aiden's claim that the guy was human. There was something deeper to him. Some dark current that ran just beneath his beautiful surface, and yet Olivia didn't sense danger from Noah Winston. Not for her, and certainly not for Jamie.

And Aiden had been right about Jamie having the two warriors wrapped around her little finger. Not only had they obviously been showering her with attention, but her pancakes had been cut into perfect little triangles.

"She said that's how she likes them," Noah murmured, a wry grin on his face as he gestured with his chin toward Jamie's plate.

"They're perfect," she replied, watching as Jamie grinned around a huge bite of pancake and syrup.

"I have a niece who likes them the same way," he told her, taking a drink of his coffee, "so I've had my share of practice."

Looking from Noah to Kellan, she said, "Thank you for bringing Jamie over."

"We figured you could use a little time to yourself," Kellan rumbled, and from the corner of her eye she caught the look of warning that Aiden shot the grinning Watchman.

Kandy returned with their coffees and her croissant, her eyes focused on Aiden with almost worshipful attention as she told him she'd have his order to him right away, then asked if there was anything else she could get for him. Liv had the ridiculous impulse to defend her territory, the white-hot burn of jealousy actually hurting as it rolled through her system. She frowned with confusion, wondering what was wrong with her. After so many careful years of control, she was letting this man get to her, allowing her emotions to get the better of her. Taking a deep breath, she reminded herself that the dumbest thing she could do was get twisted up about a guy like Aiden. It would be a disaster in the making, because she could see just how it would pan out, with her falling hard…and him walking away without a backward glance.

That's the last thing you need, Liv. No matter how freaking gorgeous and sexy and protective he is.

"So what's our plan for heading home?" Kellan asked as soon as Kandy had swished her tiny little backside away again. Aiden began talking, and as he explained about the alternative routes they could take and how they could loop back on themselves to throw off the Casus, Olivia doctored her coffee with cream and sugar. Sweeping her gaze over the restaurant, she noticed that more than one pair of interested female eyes were zeroed in on their table…and the devastatingly attractive shape-shifter sitting at her side, his provocative air of danger serving only to draw them closer, like flies to honey.

Her fingers tightened on her mug, her throat burning from the possessive words she knew she couldn't say. *Let it go,* she silently muttered. *If you don't, you're going to make a complete fool of yourself. Then you're really going to be embarrassed.*

No sooner had she finished the thought than Kandy came strolling back, this time with Aiden's breakfast… and a perky brunette who refilled his coffee, her smile as flirtatious as her friend's. At least Aiden had the sense to look annoyed with the attention, and Olivia could have sworn he muttered something foul under his breath when they finally left the table.

"Aren't you eating?" she asked Noah and Kellan, while Aiden dug into his food.

Kellan laughed. "We already did. This is Jamie's second helping of pancakes."

Jamie giggled and made a snorting sound like a pig, which had them all laughing. "For such a little thing," Noah drawled, "she can really pack it away."

Jamie smiled proudly, and while Aiden finished his breakfast, Olivia talked to her niece about the trip they would be taking to Colorado, answering her questions, along with help from Kellan and Noah. Aiden had just taken his last bite of scrambled eggs when Kellan said, "So I got a call from Kierland on our way over here."

"Everything okay?" Aiden asked, wiping his mouth with a napkin.

Kellan shrugged and pushed his empty coffee cup away. "I don't know. He sounded kinda weirded out, but said he couldn't go into any details. Just that we should be 'ready for trouble.' You know how he is. One of those 'expect the unexpected' lectures he loves to give, but he didn't back it up with any meat. Said he had some research to do and was going to call back this afternoon."

Aiden leaned back in the booth, his right arm brushing against Olivia's side with a tingling rush of warmth that she did her best to ignore. "Huh. Wonder what's going down."

"Me, too," Kellan murmured. "Before he hung up, he did say that he'd try to get an update on the search for Chloe."

"Speaking of your sister," Noah said, his pale blue eyes snagging Olivia's gaze, "does she look like you?"

Olivia shook her head. "We're only stepsisters. Chloe is…well, she's beautiful. Here," she told him, digging in her purse for her wallet, "I have a picture."

"Nice," Noah murmured as she handed over the snapshot. Kellan simply stared at the photograph, his gaze shadowed by his lowered lashes, concealing his own reaction.

"How did they pick her up?" Aiden asked, leaning forward so that he could see the photo, too.

Olivia fought to keep her voice even, not wanting to upset Jamie, who was happily finishing off the last of her pancakes. "She'd taken a trip down to Florida to visit some friends she went to college with. When she left to come home, she went missing and never made it back to Kentucky. That was a little more than five weeks ago."

"You mind if I keep this?" Kellan asked in a low voice,

already reaching over and snagging the photo from Noah's fingers.

"Uh, no, not at all," she told him, though she had a strange feeling the Watchman would have kept the photo regardless of what she'd said. She had so many questions about the search for her sister, but before she could say anything, Kandy came back to the table. As the flirty blonde slid Aiden the bill, Olivia saw that she'd written her phone number on the bottom. Rolling her eyes again, she was about to ask Kellan and Noah if this kind of thing happened to Aiden all the time when a group of pretty, tanned, long-legged coeds who had been staring at him from one of the nearby tables walked over and started commenting on his "wicked tats." Then they asked if he was going to be in town long.

Across the booth, both guys snickered under their breath, and Olivia locked her jaw, determined not to say anything—not to *feel* anything. Honestly, it was like a bad joke, the way the women kept coming on to him right in front of her, as if it was a given that they weren't a couple.

Either that or they simply didn't care that he was there with another woman.

At least Aiden managed to get rid of the girls quickly. The instant they walked away, he slid a suspicious look toward Kellan. "Are you behind this?"

Kellan lifted his hands. "Hey, don't blame me. I'm innocent."

Aiden made a snide, sarcastic sound of disbelief in the back of his throat, looking as if he wanted to throttle the grinning Watchman.

"Aw, don't take it out on Kell. We can't help it if you're already gathering another fan club," Noah drawled with a low rumble of laughter.

Ouch. Olivia really didn't like the sound of *that*. But she couldn't say she was surprised. Using everything she had to control her wayward emotions, she took a deep breath and wiped the croissant crumbs from her fingers, aware of Aiden studying her profile. "Another fan club?" she asked as she set down her napkin, pleased that the question sounded like nothing more than casual interest.

Kellan leaned back in the booth and spread his arms along the back, an easy grin on his mouth as he explained. "Not that Noah and I are slouches, but Aiden here is like a babe magnet. I swear women go a little gaga whenever the guy's around. We barely even get noticed."

"Enough of this sh—crap," Aiden muttered, his rough tone cut with anger and impatience. Taking Olivia's hand in a strong hold, he slid from the booth, pulling her along with him. If he hadn't known better, he would have sworn he was being punked by his friends, but he couldn't say this was the first time something like this had happened. It was, however, the first time he'd ever been embarrassed, not to mention irritated as hell by the kind of female attention he often received, knowing it was going to make things more difficult with Olivia. "Jamie, I need to talk to your aunt for a second outside. You okay with that, sweetheart?"

The little girl nodded, giving him a shy grin, and Aiden headed for the nearest exit, tugging Olivia along behind him.

"What's going on?" she asked.

Aiden grunted in response, his jaw clenched as he heard Kellan and Noah laughing back at the table. Taking hold of her elbow, he guided her through a side door and toward the back parking lot, where Noah had parked his truck. He felt antsy, on edge, a combustible combination of too many irritating emotions itching beneath his skin. Her scent and nearness still had his beast on the prowl and he put a mental lock on it, knowing he needed to calm down. When they reached the truck, he pushed her against the passenger door, his hands wrapped around her biceps, holding her in place. "I wouldn't have." He ground out the words, his tone guttural and sharp with frustration. "I mean, I didn't even want to."

She blinked up at him, looking completely confused. "Didn't want to what?"

"I didn't want to take them up on their offers," he muttered. "Any of them."

Her cheeks flushed with color, but she appeared perfectly calm as she shrugged her shoulders. "You don't owe me any explanations, Aiden. It's none of my business."

Her offhand tone had him grinding his teeth. "Yeah, well. I just wanted you to know."

She shrugged again, turning her face to the side as she stared into the woods that bordered the back of the parking lot. "Fine. If it makes you feel better."

"Damn it," he growled, giving her a little shake. "I'm trying to make *you* feel better."

"Me?" Her brows nearly arched to her hairline, her gaze whipping back to his with a wide-eyed look of incredulity, as if he wasn't making any sense. "What do *I* have to do with anything?"

Aiden opened his mouth, but what could he say? For all intents and purposes, they were strangers. Twenty-four hours ago they hadn't even known each other. And yet, with each second he spent with her...watching the way she was with Jamie, pulling in her intoxicating scent, listening to the husky sound of her voice, she was slipping into him. Digging into him, deeper...and deeper, until he knew it was going to sting like a bitch when he walked away from her.

It shouldn't have mattered what she thought. But it did. And damn it, though it didn't make any sense, considering he was after a short-term score and nothing more, he wanted his actions and intentions to mean something to her, as well. He'd been expecting at least a little jealousy on her part, but she looked as if she couldn't have cared less that those women had been pouring themselves over him. "I don't get it, Liv. Why are you acting like it doesn't bother you?"

"Like *what* doesn't bother me?"

A thick sound of frustration vibrated in the back of his throat. "The way those women were flirting with me."

"Because it doesn't," she said flatly.

He stared down at her with his eyes at half-mast, wishing he could get inside her head. There was something different about her, as if someone had flipped a switch and shut her down, leaving nothing but a pretty, decorative shell behind. Releasing his hold on her arms, he quietly asked, "Where'd Olivia go?"

A little groove formed between her brows. "What do you mean?"

"I mean you were different before we went into the restaurant. Now it's like you're all closed down."

"There's no great mystery, Aiden. I'm just…back to my usual self."

She might have sounded sincere, but he wasn't buying it. "Bullshit. This isn't you."

"Yesterday was a fairly big shock to my system," she murmured, "and I was obviously reacting to it. But I'm usually much better at keeping myself even."

"Even?"

She squinted up at him, the butter-yellow sunshine doing mesmerizing things to her fiery hair, as if it were streaked with crimson and gold. Aiden was fighting the urge to reach out and touch it, digging his fingers into the silken mass, when she asked, "Have you ever been around a Mallory witch before?"

He thought for a moment, then shook his head, realizing the answer was no. He'd known some Reavess, and even some Bailey witches, but never a Mallory. "Can't say that I have."

"Well, if you had," she explained in that same odd monotone that was really starting to get on his nerves, "then you'd understand."

Pushing one hand back through his hair, Aiden searched his mind for anything he might have heard about the Mallory. "Because of their curse, they affect emotions, right?"

Olivia nodded, her gaze sliding away again as she said, "If I wanted to keep my sanity, I had to learn to keep myself on an even keel. Any strong emotion gets blown out of proportion when you're around a Mallory witch."

"Well, for what it's worth," he muttered, "I liked you better the other way."

Her gaze snapped back to his, and he couldn't help but welcome the flash of temper that flared in her eyes. "I'm human, Aiden. Remember? You shouldn't like me at all."

It was his turn to break eye contact, and he shoved his hands into his front pockets, not trusting the hunger itching beneath his skin, pushing him to act on impulse and just take what he wanted. "I have good reasons for the way I feel, Liv."

"Honestly, what is it with you?" The low words were flavored with anger and accusation. "I mean, I keep trying to figure out what you're after, but you're making my head spin. One second you're pushing, then you're pulling back. You're flirting, then you're running from the room. It's like a freaking roller coaster. What in God's name do you want from me?"

A muscle ticked below his right eye, his muscles coiling for action, though he refused to move. "I want more than you could ever imagine," he bit out, wondering if she had any idea how much it had cost him to pull away from her last night. To give her the space that she'd needed. How much it'd cost him not to lay himself down on her when she'd been lying in bed that morning, all soft and warm and more tempting than any other woman he could ever remember having beneath him. "And I want it a hell of a lot more than I should."

Her eyes were huge, the smoky violet burning with heat, luminous and bright, like stained glass backlit by the sun. Her mouth trembled with all the sharp emotion she'd been trying so hard to hold inside. "You're crazy."

"Crazy or not," he countered in a deep voice roughened by need, crackling like a bed of autumn leaves, "it's going to happen between us."

"It isn't."

"It *is*. You might as well stop fighting it."

"It doesn't make any sense for you to want me!" she

burst out, that smooth shell of control cracking even further. "I'm a sexually repressed kindergarten teacher and you're a womanizing tomcat! We're completely wrong for each other!"

"What the hell does that matter?" he shot back, his own gnawing frustration getting the better of him. "God, Liv, it's not like I said I want you forever!"

CHAPTER NINE

IT'S NOT LIKE I SAID I want you forever....

Whoa. Jesus. Had he honestly just said that to a woman? To Olivia?

Nice one, man. You might as well have gone ahead and told her you want to fuck her a few times, then walk away, leaving her behind with your buddies while you go off and find someone else to screw around with.

Popping his jaw, Aiden wished he could turn around and kick his own ass for sounding like such a prick. At the same time he wondered what it was about this woman that made him act like such a jackass. He hated the way she reacted to the callous words, that beautiful heat in her eyes quickly fading to something brittle and cold. Or maybe that was simply the bleakness of his own emotional wasteland reflecting back at him. Either way, Aiden knew he'd messed up, and he fought hard to undo the damage. "But there's no doubt that I want you, Liv."

He'd left some significant parts of that statement unspoken, but she'd heard them anyway.

"You mean you want me for sex." A wry, crooked smile played at the corner of her mouth. "And that's supposed to be enough?"

He took a deep breath, then slowly let it out. "It could be, if you let it."

She shook her head, looking as if she was trying hard to close down again. "Even if that was a sane idea, I'd be an absolute fool to trust you."

"For a relationship, yeah." He pulled back his shoulders, instinctively fighting against the guilt. God, it wasn't as if she was still going to want him around anyway, once she finally clued in to the differences between them. Sooner or later she would come to think of him as an animal—one who had been bought and used in the basest, vilest of ways—and then those hot looks of lust would change, replaced by disgust. Or worse.

Yeah, it might be selfish, but Aiden knew he'd rather not be around when it happened.

"But you could trust me for an affair." He tried to smile, but couldn't really pull it off. "I'm great affair material, Liv."

She started to laugh, but the sound was hollow, and they both winced. "Affairs can be just as painful as relationships, Aiden. I have no desire to be used and tossed aside."

"You can't be worried that I'll use you, if you're the

one using me." He knew he sounded close to begging, but he couldn't stop. Couldn't stand the thought of simply turning away from her, going back inside the restaurant and finding some other woman to scratch the itch that she'd started. What was the point, when he knew he'd walk away from whoever he chose with this same raw, scraping need eating away at his gut, burning under his skin?

No, the woman he wanted was standing right in front of him, and in that moment he honestly didn't give a damn that she was human.

He just wanted her.

"I'll make you feel good, Liv. Seriously, this can be all about you, if that's the way you want to play it. Just me giving you whatever you want, making you come like crazy, however many times you can take it." He finally allowed himself to move in, crowding her against the truck. "Just…let me get close to you."

"I can't." She wet her lips as she tilted her head back, holding his stare. "It would be a mistake, and I need to focus on Jamie right now. I can't afford to get involved with you, even if it is just for sex."

"Sure you can." Forcing an easy, boyish grin to his lips, he shifted even closer, trapping her between his body and the truck. And damn, but it felt good. Better than good. The intimate press of her lush breasts against the wall of his chest, of her smaller body crushed against his larger frame, was just about the best damn thing that he'd ever experienced.

"Take my word for it, Liv." Lust gave a guttural edge to his teasing tone. "I promise I'll be cheap."

She was still snuffling a soft burst of laughter under her breath when Aiden lowered his head, pressing his mouth against the tender side of her throat, his nose buried in the thick mass of her hair. The heady, provocative taste of her skin sent a deep, pulsing burst of pleasure sliding up his spine, curling around the backs of his ears, sharpening his breath. As he braced his hands against the cold surface of the truck, caging her in, a low growl vibrated in the back of his throat, the feel and scent and taste of her burning through him like a blistering wave of heat. It seemed like some kind of madness, how badly he wanted her, as if he'd been years without a woman, rather than a mere matter of weeks. "You smell so good," he groaned, his hands fisting against the window in hard, tight knots. "Taste good. Feel good."

For a moment her body remained rigid with tension and remnants of anger, her breath panting and sharp against the soft sounds of the morning. Her fingers danced along the bare skin of his arms, as if she wanted to grab hold of him but was struggling to fight the temptation. Then she trembled as he ran his tongue around the tender shell of her ear, nipping the delicate lobe with his teeth, and the stiffness flowed out of her on a soft groan, her head tilting to the side to give him better access as she whispered his name.

"Don't fight it." The order was thick, husky…raw hunger pouring through his veins in a heavy, visceral surge. Gripping her hip with one hand, Aiden quickly shoved the other under her hair, his long fingers holding her in place as he kissed his way across her jaw, until he found the lush, petal-like softness of her mouth. The wind rushed against their bodies, pulling at the long strands of their hair…whipping at their clothes as he ate his way past those soft, strawberry-flavored lips, his tongue rubbing against hers, urging her to kiss him back. Her taste melted through his body until he could feel it all the way down in his bones, and he growled from the heady sweetness, deepening the kiss.

"Aiden," she cried breathlessly, her tender lips moving against his, creating a slick, delicious friction, her nails digging into his biceps. "We're outside. In broad daylight. We could be seen."

"I'll hear anyone who comes back here. I promise I won't let anyone see us," he choked out, the clipped, rough sound of his voice proof that the predator in him was gaining the upper hand. Again he was caught by how strange it was…the fact that he was actually getting off on kissing her. In the grand scheme of things, it was such an innocent act compared to what he usually did with women, and yet he couldn't get enough of it.

Then again, there wasn't anything all that innocent about the way their mouths were sealed together, the kiss turning hotter, slicker…hungrier, more devastating with each second that ticked by.

"Gotta touch you," he growled, no longer sounding human as he pushed his hand between her legs. He cupped her sex in a hard, possessive hold, and even through her jeans he could feel her heat, the scent of her need growing stronger, rich and warm and sweetly spiced. It made him want to release his fangs and sink them into her shoulder, marking her…holding her in his grip as he tore off her clothes, lifted her against the truck and shoved himself into her with a hard, hammering, throw-your-head-back-and-scream kind of drive.

"I can't think," she whispered, arching against him, and Aiden could feel the rise of pleasure twisting through her, rushing for release. "Aiden, I'm not sure I—"

"Just let me," he groaned, shaking, his body tight… slick with sweat. Warnings roared through his brain like shots from a cannon, but he beat them back, shutting them out.

It's okay. You can handle it. Just take what you need.

In the rational part of his mind, Aiden knew he was only telling himself what he wanted to hear so that he could get her against him. Get more of her taste in his mouth. He'd convince himself that she was as harmless as any other woman, if it meant he could have more of *this*. He needed it too badly. Needed her softness under his hands, that enticing scent filling his head, sinking into his skin. Needed to take in the sumptuous, delicate details and know firsthand just how she felt. How she tasted in all those secret, intimate places.

And really, wasn't he worrying for nothing? Keep his emotions under control, and there wouldn't be any danger. Just a physical, carnal exchange of pleasure.

Except that his heart was pounding like a damn jackhammer.

If you let her, she'll betray you. You know how fickle humans can be. How quickly they can turn on you. The words were whispered in his mind, but they weren't his beast's. No, the animal wanted her just as badly as Aiden did. This was his fear speaking, its chilling voice scratchy and thin, like a hiss. *She'll cut you deeper than any blade ever could. Bleed you out until there's nothing left but meat and bones.*

He didn't need the internal lecture. He knew the kind of threat she posed. But he didn't give a damn. Before she could tell him no, he flicked the top button on her jeans and shoved his hand inside the top of her panties, not even bothering with the zipper. He swallowed her hoarse cry of surprise with his mouth, thrusting deep with his tongue as he pushed his hand deeper, past the soft hair on her mound, not stopping until he'd found the smooth, moist flesh buried there between her quivering thighs. Until he'd delved into that hot, humid paradise.

He gasped her name, forcing her legs farther apart with his knee so that he could reach more of her, the tender folds of her sex like warm, drenched silk as he spread her open, circling one blunt fingertip around the delicate opening. "You're melting for me," he whispered against her mouth, her breath panting and sweet as it pelted against his lips. "Like honey, Liv. I bet you taste incredible."

She shivered in response, arching against him, her nipples deliciously thick and tight against his chest. Her hips moved the barest fraction, rubbing those velvety folds against his hand. His body reacted with a thick surge of lust, and he locked his jaw, wondering if he could actually get so hard that he caused himself bodily harm.

Just go easy, he cautioned himself, since he didn't know how small she was built—but it seemed he was too jacked up for tenderness or finesse. With a low growl tearing up from the deepest reaches of his chest, Aiden plunged two long fingers inside her, thrusting them deep. Hard.

And damn near died from the feel of her closing in on him.

Burying his damp forehead against hers, he made a feral sound that should have scared the hell out of her, but only had her clenching around him, the soft, tender tissues burning hotter…slicker, drenching his hand. She had the tightest little piece he'd ever known, those lush, cushiony muscles clasping him in a greedy hold as he began to move his fingers in and out, working her with his hand the way he wanted to take her with his cock. Or his…tongue. An odd thought for him, and yet Aiden couldn't deny that he wanted to drop to his knees, rip her jeans away and bury his face in those melting folds. He'd lick her with long, ravenous strokes, starved for the taste of her. Thrust his tongue inside and eat her from the inside out, taking all of that hot melting sugar into his mouth and swallowing it down.

Touching her like this was heaven, as well as hell. And if he wasn't careful, Aiden knew he was going to lose a lot more than his sanity to this woman.

"So beautiful," he grunted, sounding like a friggin' caveman as he watched the way her eyes grew heavy with pleasure, unfocused and dazed, her fair skin burning with bright splotches of color. He liked the way her breath caught as he pushed the aching, rigid length of his cock against her hip, grinding against her while he withdrew his fingers. He teased them around the small, slick opening, his mind seared by thoughts of how good it was going to feel when he was kneeling between her splayed thighs. She writhed, watching him through the thick fringe of her lashes as she pushed against his hand, silently begging him to fill her up again.

And then not so silently as she groaned, "Aiden… please. *More.*"

With a low, wicked rumble of laughter, he plunged his

fingers back inside, forcing her to take them deeper just as he caught her clit with his thumb. Torturing the swollen, tiny knot with wet, circular strokes, he moved his fingers faster…harder, positive that her shyness would get the better of her and she'd close her eyes when she came. But she didn't. No, she stared right back at him, every naked emotion and dazzling shock of pleasure burning right there in her wide gaze as it crashed through her, the most breathtaking thing he'd ever seen. Her head tilted back into his hand, her pink face covered with a fine sheen of sweat as she sank her teeth into her lower lip to keep from crying out, and he realized in that moment that making Olivia Harcourt come apart in his arms was something he could easily get addicted to.

Something he could come to need again. And again.

"I mean it, Liv. You're so damn beautiful." He fisted his hand in her hair as he covered her mouth with his. He nipped at her bottom lip, unable to resist that plump, succulent flesh. Then he went deep, ravaging the sweet, moist well that lay within, all the while fighting for control. But it wasn't easy. Explicit images were firing through his brain, pushing him…daring him to take what he wanted. What the savage predator prowling within his body demanded.

Want it, the animal snarled. *Need it. Now.*

Shoving himself against her hip, *hard,* Aiden struggled to stay in control…while doing his best to calculate how quickly he could get them back to the room, where they could finish what they'd started. As the last tremors of her orgasm slowly fluttered around his fingers, he pulled his other hand from her hair, ready to sweep her up into his arms and run for the room, when an eerie chill swept over his back. Reacting instantly to the possible threat of danger, Aiden quickly pulled his hand from her jeans, a deep, guttural snarl on his lips as he spun around, both the animal and man ready to launch an attack and protect her with his body. With his life.

But there was nothing there.

"What is it?" she whispered from behind him, the rustling sounds telling him that she was buttoning her jeans. "The C-Casus?"

"I don't think so." Soft. Savage. The huskily spoken words were almost silent as he took a step toward the woods, his eyes narrowed on the thick line of trees. He couldn't see what was there, but he could smell the rank stench of its rotting flesh. Knowing something bad was about to happen, Aiden started to order Olivia to run—but he was already too late. Before the first word had even left his mouth, a powerful blow to his chest threw him backward, the heavy weight of his body slamming her against the side of the truck. His assailant was nothing more than a pale blur as it flew through the air, moving with lightning speed, impossible to follow. Within seconds he was hit with a rapid sequence of strikes, the blows slamming into his stomach and chest, and he spun around, leaving his back exposed to the attack so that he could shove Olivia away from him. She stumbled, but quickly righted herself, turning to stare with wide, terrified eyes.

"Run!" he roared, growling as claws scraped along his right side.

She shook her head, fiery strands of hair flying around her pale face. "No way. I'm not leaving you!"

"Get the hell out of here!" He shouted the warning as he whipped around, determined to take out whatever was after them before the fool woman got herself killed. The air ahead of him blurred, as if something moving at high speed was coming at him again, and then a lethal set of claws slashed across the top of his right thigh, ripping through the denim and flesh, cutting all the way down to the bone. He snarled, lashing out with a hard side kick that should have knocked whatever was attacking him on its ass, but his foot went right through it. Wondering what the hell he was up against, Aiden tried to punch the thing as it sped past, but it was like shoving his fist through a thick, sticky mist.

The air filled with a high, demonic sound of laughter, and then something began to take shape about five feet in front of him, hovering just above the ground, the figure hazy…but visible, as if the creature were pulling itself into a tangible form. It stood as tall as Aiden, with pale white skin like a cadaver, every inch of its skeletal form covered with what appeared to be vicious bite marks, chunks of skin actually missing in some places, though the wounds no longer bled. Its head was smooth, hairless, with only two small horns protruding from its temples, its eyes burning within its white face like two gleaming yellow orbs, its mouth filled with sharp, jagged fangs.

Leaning its head back, it sniffed at the morning air. "You don't smell as good as a Kenly, but you'll do, Watchman. You'll do."

A Kenly? They were one of the ancient clans that had been hunted nearly to extinction by a rival clan known as the Regan. Aiden had come into contact with a few Regan over the years, but he knew they didn't look like this son of a bitch. And yet he could see traces of the Regan's characteristics in the creature's grisly face. Pointed ears. Long nose. Deeply dimpled chin.

His fingers itched with the impulse to release his lethal claws, but he held back, unsure how Olivia would react.

Stupid to worry about it. She's going to see you go "animal" sooner or later. Might as well be now.

Popping his jaw, he flexed his fingers at his sides, his eyes narrowed as he searched for its weakness…a way he could take it apart. Just off to its right he spotted Olivia creeping up behind it, a fallen tree limb that the wind had blown into the parking lot clutched tight in her grasp. Fury welled within him like a volcanic blast, mixing dangerously with his fear for her safety, the thunderous roar of his heart banging inside his head. She thought she was sneaking up on the creature, but Aiden could tell from the look in its yellow eyes that it knew she was there.

"Goddamn it, I said to get your ass out of here!" he snarled, but the bastard was already whipping toward her, cracking her against the side of her head with the flat of its palm. She hit the ground hard, going down on her side, and Aiden exploded with rage, his claws instantly spearing through the tips of his fingers as he charged. But it was on the move again, rushing through the air like a bullet, nearly impossible to track.

Groaning, Olivia managed to get herself up on her hands and knees. Aiden made a move toward her, but the thing cut him off, hovering in front of him like a specter. It hit him with a backhanded smack that snapped his head to the side, busting his lip, then kicked him dead center in his chest again, knocking him back on his ass. "I shouldn't be here," it hissed in a soft, lisping voice as it floated close to his face, its rank breath making him gag. "Not strong enough yet to do what needs to be done. But I just wanted to get close. See for myself what the Watchmen are like now."

"Why me?" he snarled, hoping that if he could keep its attention focused on him, then Olivia would wise up and finally get herself out of there.

"I've been looking for you. Looking and looking and looking," it sang in that eerie voice that made chills break out over his skin. "See, I've been assigned to your breed. Which means that you and I are going to have a little fun together."

"I doubt that." Aiden gave it a mocking smile. "I make it a point not to screw around with things that smell like you."

Hatred hardened its expression, its yellow eyes slitting like a serpent's. "You think you know so much, but you know nothing. Nothing at all about what's going to happen to you."

"Yeah?" He slowly moved to his feet. "Then explain it to me. I'm dying of curiosity over here."

It licked its lips, snickering softly under its breath. "Be careful, Watchman. You know what they say about how curiosity killed the cat."

"I'm willing to take my chances," he muttered, waiting for the moment to strike, the creature growing more solid with each second that passed. Aware of Olivia now standing a few feet behind him, Aiden accepted the fact that she obviously wasn't going to run so long as she thought he was in danger. His only hope was to attack while the thing was in this semisolid form, and hope that he was able to hurt it.

Just a little more, he thought, flexing his long, razor-sharp claws at his sides, his muscles coiling for action. *A little more...*

Launching his assault, Aiden burst forward, his right

arm swinging in a wide arc that tore his claws across the creature's white stomach, drawing a spray of slick black ooze that seemed too thick to be blood, the noxious odor burning his nose. Its clawed hands pressed against the wound as it stumbled back, and Aiden was able to get in another strike across its pale chest before it levitated, settling onto one of the high branches of an ancient oak tree. Craning his neck, he watched with a raw, deadly rage as it curled its long body in on itself, a low, mewling sound scraping from its throat. Then, without warning, it shot from the branch, heading straight toward him.

Aiden braced his feet for the blow. He didn't dare move, unwilling to take the risk that he might draw its attention back to Olivia. He flexed his claws again, planning to go for its throat the moment it struck, when Noah suddenly came out of nowhere and slammed into its side, taking it to the ground. It screeched like a wet cat as they tumbled across the gritty asphalt. Noah came out on top, pinning it beneath his body as the twin knives he always carried slashed toward its abdomen and chest. The human held the blades in his clenched fists, with his thumbs at the end of the hilts, slicing from one side to the other—though he had no better luck than Aiden in killing the thing. It snarled, then smashed its fist upward, punching Noah's head back with a sharp crack to the jaw, stunning him. The next hit caught Noah in the chest, the blow so powerful it sent him flying through the air, until he crashed against the side of a nearby minivan, one of his knives skidding across the pavement.

From the corner of his eye Aiden could see Kellan cautiously approaching between two parked cars. The Lycan took hold of Olivia's arm, jerking her behind the shelter of his body, while he clutched a pale-faced Jamie in his arms, the Marker still hanging around her neck, glinting in the morning sunlight.

As if sensing the focus of Aiden's attention, the creature turned its pale head toward the group. At first it curled its lip, snarling at Kellan as he slowly backed away, but then it went silent, its eyes widening as it caught sight of the ornate cross. But it didn't make a move to go toward it…or them. Instead, it cocked its head a little to the side, a sickening smile curling across the thin line of its mouth as it stared with a dazzled absorption. With its attention distracted by the Marker, Aiden retracted his claws, pulled his gun from behind his back and fired off a head shot just as a semi out on the highway conveniently blared its horn, covering the blast.

The bullet ripped straight into the creature's temple.

But it still didn't go down.

Instead, it slowly turned its head, its yellow eyes burning with hatred. It started toward him again, this time in a slow, weaving glide, more of that black liquid oozing from its temple, dripping like a dark river down its mutilated, cadaverous skin. "Get them out of here!" he roared at Kellan, while Noah staggered to his side, ready to help him, though Aiden feared they were fighting a losing battle. No matter what they did, the son of a bitch just kept on coming. And it was only by the grace of God that no other hotel guests had wandered into the back parking lot during the fight. A fact he was all too aware could change at any moment.

"I'll try to get hold of it, then you go for its throat," he rasped, thinking that maybe between the two of them they could manage to decapitate the thing, and possibly even kill it. Noah nodded, his expression one of grim determination that Aiden knew matched his own.

"Get ready," he muttered, tucking his gun behind his back to free up his hands, a murderous glint in the creature's yellow eyes as it drew closer…closer. Then the loud revving of motorcycle engines stopped the thing in its tracks as two bikes pulled around the side of the hotel. Hissing, the creature whirled into the woods, hovering just inside the shadow of the trees. Three more bikes followed the first two, all of them gathering at the other end of the lot, and Aiden had never been so happy to see a group of humans in his life.

"Too weak to take on all of you," it seethed, pulling farther into the shadows. "But not for long. I'll be back… and next time I won't be alone. You're going to have your hands full, Watchman."

Aiden shot it a cocky smile. "Keep 'em coming."

"Oh, we will. Thanks to you and your friends." Then it was gone as quickly as it had come, the air clearing of its rank stench as the wind swept through the parking lot.

Scraping his bloodied fingers through his hair, Aiden surveyed the damage. Noah was rubbing his right shoulder, a grimace twisting his features, though Aiden could tell he wasn't seriously injured. Just banged up, and no doubt bruised as hell. Jerking his chin toward the human, he thanked him for his help.

Noah reached down for his other knife, grunting, "Any time."

"Okay. Anyone else weirded out by Mr. Creepy, or is it just me?" Kellan muttered, moving to join them, Jamie's arms still wound tightly around his neck.

Not trusting himself to look at Olivia without bending her over his knee for refusing to listen to a single word that he'd said, Aiden kept his gaze on his fellow Watchman. "I think it was a Regan. Or at least it used to be."

"I thought they'd all but died out."

"Yeah, well, that thing smelled like it's been dead for a while now," Noah offered with a gritty laugh.

Kellan's odd-colored eyes darkened as he stared into the woods. "Do you think this was what Kierland was talking about when he told us to be ready?"

"With our luck? I wouldn't be surprised."

"What do you think that 'thanks to you and your friends' was about?" Noah asked.

Aiden shrugged, his voice tight with frustration. "I guess it could have been nonsense, considering that thing seemed whacked out of its skull. But my gut tells me that it was trying to tell us something."

"Did it make a go for Liv?" This question came from Kellan, his arms still wrapped around Jamie in a strong, protective hold.

"I don't think it was here for either of the girls." His mouth was still bleeding from one of the hits he'd taken, and he turned his head, spitting out a mouthful of blood that joined the small, dark pool collecting beneath his right leg. Though he could feel the wound already beginning to heal, it still hurt like a bitch, and he knew he'd have to bind it before they headed out. Looking back at Kellan, he added, "It only seemed interested in coming after me."

"I'd feel a hell of a lot better if we knew what it was." Noah wiped the back of his wrist over his own battered mouth. "And what it was after."

"Did you see the way it looked at the Marker?" Olivia asked, speaking up for the first time since the creature had disappeared. "It knew what it was."

"And it didn't look afraid of it," Kellan murmured. "Its look was almost greedy. As if it wanted it."

"But it didn't even try to take it," she pointed out, and Aiden couldn't resist looking at her any longer. She had one hand raised, stroking Jamie's back in a soothing rhythm, her big eyes staring right back at him, filled with concern. He could tell from her expression that she expected him to be furious with her. And he was. But even more than that, he was nearly staggered by his relief that she was okay...that she hadn't been hurt by that psychotic asshole.

He cleared his throat. Shoved his hands into his pockets. Fought to make sense of the strange warmth in his chest as their gazes held. "What brought you guys out here anyway?" he asked, finally tearing away from those violet eyes as he looked toward Kellan again.

"We got a call from Molly saying you were in trouble," the Lycan explained, the corner of Kell's mouth kicking up in a smart-ass grin. "I was worried we'd be breaking up something hot and heavy, but she was right. You were getting your ass kicked."

Aiden ignored the taunt, more interested in how Molly had known he needed help. "She hear from the source?" he asked, his look warning Kellan not to say anything about Monica. Last thing in the world he wanted to do was upset Jamie right now, her little face still buried in Kellan's shoulder.

Kellan nodded, all traces of humor vanishing from his expression, the look in his eyes warning Aiden that he wasn't going to like the answer. "Yeah, she heard from her."

"And?" he bit out, the single word thick with frustration as well as dread. "What did she say?"

"Death." The low word echoed in his ears, and he looked toward Olivia, holding her terrified gaze as the Watchman continued. "That was the message, Ade. According to the source, Death was coming."

CHAPTER TEN

Indiana
Saturday afternoon

"DO YOU HAVE THEM YET?"

Closing his eyes, Miles Crouch leaned back in the driver's seat of his parked Jeep, his thick fingers clenching around the cell phone jammed against his ear. Despite his tension, his mouth curled in a slow smile while he fantasized about how good it would feel to rip Schecter's heart from his chest, squeezing it in his fist like a sunripened peach. Though he'd always believed that it paid to be loyal to those who ruled, he was beginning to have his doubts. Wasn't Schecter's irritating presence in this world proof that some orders were better left ignored? He'd killed his Merrick, and had pulled Josef across, just as Westmore had told him to do—but now he wished he'd listened to the little voice in his head instead. The one that had warned him he was going to be sorry.

"I don't have all day, Crouch. What the hell have you found?"

"Nothing yet," he muttered, tuning out the sounds of the bustling strip mall where they'd stopped for lunch. The Kraven traveling with him had gone inside one of the fast-food restaurants—their vampire halves requiring them to take regular meals, as well as the occasional blood feeding—while Miles waited in his car at the far edge of the parking lot, having claimed he wasn't hungry. "We've been one step behind them all afternoon," he went on to say, "but they're not stupid. They made a strange turn near Indianapolis and we lost them."

Silence settled heavily over the line, then Schecter slowly exhaled. "How unfortunate."

Working his jaw, Miles focused on the way the sunlight burned colors through his lowered eyelids, bright splashes of crimson and orange and yellow, doing his best to control his temper. "These Kraven are useless at tracking the human's scent. And the child's Merrick signal is almost too faint to follow. If you sent me some Casus, it would improve our chances of staying on their trail."

Schecter's tone was dry. "That would be easier to do if you hadn't allowed the shifters to send half our unit back to Meridian. And that's *after* the heavy losses we suffered in Washington, thanks to your incompetence."

Frustration prickled beneath Miles's skin, making him sweat despite the chill in the air. He wanted to argue, but what could he say? He *was* to blame for Gregory's escape, damn it. Westmore had sent him to Washington to help track Gregory down, but when he'd found him, he hadn't made the kill or even taken the Casus into custody. Like an idiot, Miles had hoped to appeal to the guy's sense of reason, but unfortunately Gregory didn't have any. The bastard had gone after Riley Buchanan anyway, and Miles had been left looking like an asshole.

Yeah, he knew he'd screwed up. But that didn't mean he was going to sit there and take this crap from a prick like Schecter. "Look, you got anything important to say? 'Cause I gotta go."

"Actually, I have news from Westmore."

At the mention of the Kraven's name, the man's image filled Miles's mind, making him shake his head. It still amazed him that Westmore had managed to pass for human when he'd first approached the Collective Generals. If you knew what you were looking for, it was easy to recognize a Kraven. But then, that was the problem. Very few knew what to look for…and those who did seldom revealed the secret. "And?" he muttered, his impatience getting the better of him when Schecter fell silent again.

"And it seems that you're going to have some company."

Opening his eyes, Miles glared at the sliver of pale gray sky visible through the Jeep's sunroof. "What kind of company?"

"Nothing that should interfere with your hunt. But you'll want to be careful all the same. It looks as if our suspicions about the Markers have proven true."

His eyes went wide with shock. "Are you telling me that the Death-Walkers are here?"

"We haven't made contact yet, but Westmore has men working on it. Just hurry up and get your hands on the girl. They seem to be targeting the Watchmen, which works into our plans perfectly. If our newest intel is correct, they've already taken one shifter down in Russia, and another's been killed in New Zealand. They've shown no signs of going for the Merrick or the Markers, but if for some reason that were to change, you'll be expected to deal with them."

Miles snorted. "Yeah? And exactly how am I supposed to do that?"

"You've got a half-decent brain on you. Or at least that's what Calder keeps claiming. Let's see if you can figure it out for yourself."

Bastard, he thought. And in that moment, his vision of squeezing Schecter's heart in his fist morphed into something much darker…and far more satisfying. In his Casus form, Miles would have the power to shove his muzzle right into the prick's chest and eat his heart out with a single snap of his jaws.

Only problem was, he didn't like the taste of self-righteous jackass.

Without bothering to say goodbye or any of the other

snarled phrases burning on the tip of his tongue, Miles pulled the phone away from his ear and jammed his thumb down on the end button. Cursing under his breath, he tossed the phone into the passenger seat, then rested his hand on his churning stomach, his skin covered in a clammy film of sweat.

Had he honestly claimed he wasn't hungry? Christ, he was so empty inside he could barely see straight. In truth, he was *starved,* the need to take a proper feeding burning through his veins like acid, stripping him raw. But he knew better than to allow himself to fall the way Gregory had done.

If he could just hold strong, Calder had promised them that the feeding restrictions would be lifted once the flood came. Only then would they be free to do as they pleased, living like gods in this world. But if he gave in, he'd become a slave to the hunger too soon, and before he knew it, someone would be tracking *him* down with orders to send him back to the pit.

He couldn't let that happen. Would rather waste away to nothing before he found himself rotting away in the stench of Meridian again.

Still, his gut ached with a hollow, grinding pain, and he gnashed his teeth. Though Miles had made his share of animal kills since his release, it simply wasn't the same. Like comparing water to the most succulent wine, animals didn't have the kick that came with devouring human flesh. And while he could get a good meal out of a man, it was the women who truly gave the males of his kind what they needed. He craved a proper feeding, like the one Schecter had taken from the little Kentucky teenager, and with each day that crept by, the craving thickened within his blood and his bones. In the very substance of his being.

His hands curled into fists as he thought of the moment when Schecter had taken the girl's body beneath his. Miles's own body shook as the visceral, intoxicating images flooded his mind. Her smooth, pale skin bathed in silver moonlight. The heady, delectable scent of her blood. The dazzling beauty of her fear. Losing control, his fangs slipped heavily from his gums just as his claws began to pierce the tips of his fingers, lacerating the palms of his fisted hands. The scent of fresh blood drifted to his nose, and he knew what he was going to have to do. Again. His weakness disgusted him, but there was no other choice.

Just once more, he thought, uncurling his clenched fists. *Once more, and then you'll be back in control.*

Undoing the cuff at the end of his sleeve, he saw that his hands continued to shake as he rolled back the dark cotton, slowly revealing his bandaged forearm. Beads of sweat slipped from his shaved head, sliding down the sides of his face. His mouth watered with anticipation.

Miles began to unwrap the stained bandages with slow, methodical precision.

"Once more," he chanted beneath his breath. "Just once…"

As if drawn by an invisible wire, his gaze rose to the photograph of Olivia Harcourt that he'd attached to the sun visor. Her smoky eyes stared right back at him, *into him,* causing his pulse to pick up speed, his heart banging violently against his ribs. He shifted restlessly in his seat. She was breathtaking, really. And that scent, mouth-watering. It filled the Jeep, emanating from the sweater he'd stolen from her home back in Lennox, the sweater now draped over the back of the passenger seat.

His eyes began to burn, but he refused to blink. He couldn't, held transfixed by the violet eyes watching him. They tempted him to do the unthinkable. To hunt her down and take what he so desperately needed, truly satisfying the hunger ripping his insides to shreds.

"Too dangerous," he whispered, shaking so hard that his teeth chattered.

Keeping his gaze focused on the image of her face, he reached down, grasping the lever for the seat, and pressed back until he was nearly lying down, low enough that he wouldn't be seen by anyone who happened to walk near the car. Not that he wouldn't hear their approach well before they could see anything. He was safe from view there. Safe to do as he pleased.

Still, he waited, letting the anticipation build. Letting it spread through his body, his cock hardening to the point that it pulsed with a dull, throbbing pain.

A breathless cry trembled on his wet lips…and he broke. Lifting his arm to his mouth, Miles finally sank his fangs deep, biting through muscle and sinew. *So good…so hot…*

As the warm blood flowed over his tongue, his mind filled with an image of Olivia Harcourt spread beneath him, screaming with terror. Closing his eyes, Miles embraced the image, letting it bloom, the fantasy spreading like a drug through his veins. He drank deep, going light-headed as the dark spill of pleasure grew stronger, fired by the fantasy, until he finally threw back his head, his mouth opened wide for a harsh, primal roar.

It seemed forever that his lungs jerked for air, the inside of the Jeep smelling of sweat and blood and come. Cracking his eyelids, he struggled to focus his swimming vision on the photograph, his muscles twitching. He cringed at the thought of what the others would say if they ever learned what he'd done, feeding from his own flesh in a pathetic moment of weakness. But what choice did he have? If he fed the hunger the way Schecter had done, there could be consequences.

No, it would be madness to take such a dangerous risk.

He could be strong, damn it. He could fight it.

But as the last devastating pulses of pleasure swept through him, he reached up, grasping the photograph in his bloodied fingers, and brought it closer, studying the shape of her mouth. Her eyes. The silken fire of her hair.

Beautiful.

He drew in a deep, shuddering breath, her scent filling his head, and felt a sudden mental *snap* popping inside his mind. Another snap followed…and then another, like firecrackers bursting behind his eyes, the echoes ricocheting through his skull.

As the tension eased from his muscles, Miles was vaguely aware of what was happening, the strained bands of his will finally giving way like stressed elastic. As they continued to break, a slow, easy smile curled across his damp mouth, the inevitability of what was to come freeing him from his torment. No more resistance. No more fighting against what would be.

His thumb caressed the photograph, stroking the human's cheek, her name lingering on his blood-covered lips like a vow.

Or a promise of something to come.

CHAPTER ELEVEN

Saturday, 5:00 p.m.

Returning his cell phone to its case, Aiden quietly opened the driver's door of his truck and climbed into the cab, easing back behind the wheel. They'd been driving all day, almost nonstop—except for the occasional need for a bathroom or fuel—and had finally pulled into the parking lot of a McDonald's for some food. Kellan and Noah, who were driving Liv's car, had run inside to order, while Aiden used the time to make a few phone calls. He'd stood outside the truck as he talked, not wanting to wake Olivia and Jamie, who had managed to nod off an hour ago. He envied them the peaceful moments of oblivion, considering what the day had been like.

After dropping the "Death" bomb on them that morning, Kellan had quickly reverted back to his typical smartass sense of humor. "Not that I want to sound like a wuss or anything, but why do we always get the nasties coming after us? I mean, why couldn't it be something fun, like a flock of rabid nymphs? Death just sounds like such a downer," the Lycan had drawled, prompting Jamie to lift her head and ask what a nymph was. Olivia had smothered a laugh under her breath, then taken the little girl into her arms and told her that they were mythological creatures who could turn into trees. Jamie had cast a curious look toward Kellan, as if wondering why he'd want an entire flock of them. But she hadn't asked. She'd simply fallen silent again, just watching them all with her big brown eyes, retreating back into her own little world, as she had after the fight with the Casus.

Shaking his head, Aiden wondered what they'd have to face next. First the Casus. Then the crazy-assed freak from that morning. He honestly hadn't thought their situation could get any worse, but it had. As if having one group of monsters after them wasn't bad enough, they now had to be on the lookout for that foul-smelling thing to return…with more of its kind. He'd been on edge every second of the day, eyeing the other cars on the road, trying to make sure they weren't being followed. But there was only so much he could do. Though they'd had the odd rain shower, which would help slow anyone tracking Olivia's scent, they still didn't know if the Casus were able to track Jamie's Merrick blood.

In fact, it seemed as if they were still gathering a lot more questions than answers.

And the clock was ticking.

Tilting his head back, Aiden rested it against the seat, while his mind wandered onto the long list of questions Olivia had fired his way throughout the day, increasing the tension of the drive. Not that he didn't enjoy being near her, because he did. More than was wise. But their conversations hadn't been light…or easy. She'd plied him with questions about what had happened in the parking lot, though there wasn't much he could tell her. He didn't know what that thing had been or what it wanted from him…or why Monica had referred to it as "Death." She'd also asked about Noah, wondering where he'd learned to fight the way he had, handling knives like some kind of martial arts guru. In that at least Aiden had been able to give her some answers, explaining a little about Noah's rather unconventional upbringing, though he was careful not to reveal too much. She trusted Noah, and he didn't want that to change.

And face it, man. You want her to trust you, too.

Surprised, he ran the unspoken, unfamiliar words over his tongue, studying their flavor. Something pulled tight in his chest, and he lifted his hand, rubbing at the odd ache burning just behind his sternum.

Though he'd have loved to deny it, the words were true. Despite knowing it was an asinine, doomed-to-fail kind of idea, he really did want Liv to trust him. Not just to keep her safe or to protect her, but…well, in all ways. All the ones that mattered between a man and a woman.

Fool. Idiot. Jackass.

Ignoring the irritating chorus of voices, he shifted in his seat, positioning his body so that he could simply watch her like some kind of lovesick lapdog. The idea made Aiden's lip curl, but he didn't turn away. He couldn't, too riveted by the sight of her. The passenger seat had been lowered a little, and she lay on her side, facing him, her cheek resting on her hands. He enjoyed the unguarded moment that allowed him to simply stare, soaking in the little details that he found so fascinating. The graceful shape of her brows. The thickness of her lashes. The fullness of her bottom lip and the smooth curve of her cheek. She didn't wear any makeup today, other than a light sheen of gloss on her bee-stung lips that just made him want to nibble on them, licking and sucking and kissing. But then, she didn't need to wear makeup. Her complexion was flawless.

"Aiden," she whispered, and for a moment he thought she was talking to him. He'd already started to respond when he lifted his gaze from her mouth and found her eyes still closed, her lids twitching. Obviously dreaming, she moaned, whispering his name again, and his breath got all jammed up in his throat, his heart damn near beating its way out of his chest.

She was talking in her sleep.

And she was talking about *him.*

Scrubbing his hands down his face, Aiden choked back

the thick animal sound that tried to crawl its way out of him. He was so jacked up after touching her that morning, he felt as if he could go off at the slightest provocation. And hearing her moan his name in her sleep was provocative as hell. The animal in him wanted to scoop her up and run for the trees that lined the back of the parking lot, where it could have her to itself. Strip her, take her to the ground and go all kitty on her. Place its scratchy tongue against the downy softness of her skin. Lick her from head to toe, lingering on all her sweet spots.

Come to think of it, the man in him thought it sounded like a hell of a plan, as well.

Like she'd let you, a bitter voice suddenly muttered inside his head, jarring him out of his fantasy.

Think about it. Who said she was dreaming anything "nice" about you?

Scowling, Aiden narrowed his eyes. He studied her expression, searching for clues. She looked flushed, turned on, but who knew? After what she'd seen that morning, maybe he'd become her worst nightmare. Maybe he *was* just projecting his own desperate fantasies onto her. Maybe all she wanted was to get away from him. Ditch his ass and never set eyes on him again.

A loud, furious roar filled his head, and he winced, grimacing from the pain. *Ouch.* Obviously the tiger wasn't any happier with that idea than he was.

Under the watchful intensity of his gaze, she shifted,

restless, her lips parting. Aiden felt himself drawn forward, poised on a sharp edge of anticipation as he waited to see what she would say next.

A second passed. His muscles coiled, tension drawing him tight...tighter.

Another second. He held his breath.

She sighed, her lips moving as she started to say—

Tap...tap...tap.

The quiet rapping of knuckles against the window at his back caught him completely off guard. Startled, Aiden lurched in his seat, smacking his head on the roof of the truck. *What the...?* Feeling like an idiot, he slid a cautious glance toward Olivia, thankful to see that she was still sleeping.

Unfortunately, the low rumble of laughter coming from outside the truck told him that Kellan and Noah had thought it was funny as hell. Whipping around, he gave a soft growl at the sight of Kellan bent forward, one hand clutched around two large bags of food, the other crossed over his stomach, as if he had to hold himself together. Noah stood beside the laughing werewolf, his broad shoulders shaking with humor as well, while he balanced two trays of supersized drinks in his hands.

Reminding himself that it wasn't going to help his case with Liv if she caught him clobbering his friends, Aiden climbed out of the truck, quietly shut the door behind him, then shoved his hands into his pockets, where they couldn't get him into trouble. He scowled at Kell's good-natured ribbing, their laughter dying away as he brought them up to speed, relaying what he'd learned from his calls. They decided they would go ahead and set out again, eating as they drove, and after handing over a bag of food, as well as a tray of drinks, Kellan and Noah headed back to Liv's compact.

Balancing the bag under one arm, Aiden opened the truck door and found Olivia sitting up in her seat, rubbing her eyes. She gave him a soft smile as he handed everything over, then climbed behind the wheel.

"What were you guys talking about?" she asked as he started the engine, reversed out of the parking space and followed Kellan back out onto the highway. "The three of you looked tense. Did something happen while I was asleep?"

"I made a few calls when we stopped. Talked to Quinn again—" he'd already talked to Michael Quinn, the Watchman who was now engaged to Saige Buchanan, earlier that morning, and asked him to inform everyone at Ravenswing about the strange attack at the hotel "—then managed to get in touch with Kierland."

"And?" she asked, pulling a Happy Meal for Jamie out of the bag.

"It sounds like he could be on to something that might actually explain what went down this morning. Last night he was approached by a Deschanel." He slid her a curious look. "You heard of them before?"

"Vampires, right?"

"Yeah. It seems there was a Watchman killed in Russia a few days ago, the body drained completely of blood, which doesn't mesh with a Casus feeding. When those bastards feed, they take as much flesh as they can."

She flinched, and he suddenly realized what he'd said. Monica had been killed by a Casus, and here he was spouting his mouth off. Christ, he couldn't have been more callous if he'd tried. "Damn, I'm sorry, Liv. I, uh, wasn't thinking."

She nodded, took a deep breath, then moved the conversation along. "If not a Casus who killed the Watchman, then what?"

"That's the thing. We don't know." He hit his signal to change lanes, pushing the speed limit as far as he dared. "Rumors are going around that it was a Deschanel kill, but the vamp who approached Kierland denied it. Said they want to make a deal with us. Trade information about some new threat to the Watchmen in exchange for Westmore."

"He's the one who's working to bring back the Casus, right?"

"Yeah, that's him." Aiden explained why the Deschanel wanted to get their hands on Westmore, as well as Kierland's suspicion that the murder in Russia could be connected to that morning's attack at the hotel. He also told her that another Watchman murder had been reported in New Zealand, keeping the gory details to himself. While he talked, Olivia listened as she woke Jamie up from her nap and set about unpacking their food.

"So what exactly is Kierland doing in Prague anyway?" she asked, handing him his Double Quarter Pounder with Cheese.

With the burger in one hand, Aiden steered with the other. "He's still trying to convince the Consortium that the clans need to make a unified stand against the Casus."

Nibbling on her fries, she said, "Why does he want the Consortium involved?"

"Because an operation this size needs central leadership if it's going to work. Kierland not only wants all the clans working together, but he wants a system set up that will allow the Markers to be shared among the different Watchmen units, who would then make sure they were available to any Merrick who needed them."

"But isn't that dangerous?" she asked, taking a sip of her soda. "I mean, obviously the Merrick need them in order to fight the Casus, but what if the Markers fell into the wrong hands?"

"One already has," he muttered, and quickly explained how Westmore had already gained possession of one cross, making the current tally, as far as they were aware, four to one. "In the beginning, we just wanted to hoard the crosses to keep them safe," he went on, finishing the last of his fries. "But too many Merrick started falling. It became clear, pretty quickly, that the only way to deal with this thing is to get the Markers out there in the field, where the Merrick can use them."

"And you have no idea how many Markers are still out there, waiting to be found?"

"Not yet. But Saige is starting to decipher the maps faster and faster, so hopefully we'll have a count before too long." Nodding toward her soda, which she was trying to balance between her knees while she ate her food, he said, "If you open up the glove box you can sit your drink in the cup holder."

"Thanks." She popped the glove box open, then immediately slid him a startled, wide-eyed look. Taking another bite of his burger, Aiden hoped he'd remembered to move the stash of condoms he usually kept in there.

"Something wrong?" he asked after he'd swallowed the bite.

She tilted her head toward the open glove box. "Did you know you have a bunch of wooden stakes in here?"

He laughed under his breath, feeling as if he'd just dodged a bullet. "You remember the Kraven I told you about?" he asked, relieved to be talking about weapons instead of his sex life. "Well, the only way to kill them is to stake them through the heart with wood."

She gave a soft, feminine snort. "You're kidding."

Aiden flashed her a wry grin. "I wish I was."

"How…gross."

"It isn't pretty, I'll give you that." He wadded up the wrapper from his burger, cleared his throat and forced himself to say, "And, uh, speaking of other things that aren't pretty, I'm sorry about earlier." He'd been too chicken to bring it up until now, but knew it needed to be said.

"What do you mean?" she asked, opening the bag for him to toss his wrapper into.

Heat crawled its way up his chest. "I'm sorry you had to see that."

"That?" Her voice held a quiet note of confusion, her attention on Jamie as she twisted around to check on her.

"The way my claws released during the fight," he grunted, forcing the words from his tight throat.

He could feel her surprise as she swung her gaze back to him, staring at his profile. "Don't be ridiculous, Aiden. You were fighting to protect me. There's nothing to apologize for."

He raked his hair back from his face, a restless energy thrumming beneath his skin. "Yeah, you see…I, uh, I just don't want you to be afraid of me."

"Don't worry." Another feminine snort. "It'll take more than some fancy claws to scare me off."

His chest vibrated with a deep, gritty bark of laughter as relief flooded his system, easing his tension, making him feel mellow for the first time since the attack. Reaching down, he turned the radio on low, then jerked his chin toward the backseat. "Since we're on the topic, have you told her what I am?"

She spoke quietly enough that Jamie wouldn't overhear. "She knows you're a shifter, but not what kind. And in case you've forgotten, you still haven't told me what kind, either."

"Curious?" he murmured, sliding her a quick grin, a strange feeling of lightness in his chest now, as if he'd swallowed a balloon.

Her gaze slid away. "After seeing you this morning, I'd be lying if I said I wasn't."

She looked…nervous, and his easiness began to fade. "I would never hurt you, Liv."

"I know that. It was just…you were one serious badass, Aiden. Even when trying to fight something that was more mist than substance. It's just that…well, I wish *I* could be like that." She lifted her gaze, giving him another one of those soft, tender smiles. "Jamie deserves a champion like you to look after her."

"And what about you?"

"Me?" More nerves were revealed in that single shaky word. Or maybe shyness. Either way, it was clear she didn't like being the focus of the conversation, but he wasn't going to let it drop.

"What do you deserve, Liv?"

"I don't understand," she hedged, busying herself with cleaning up the rest of their trash.

"Yeah, you do." Keeping one hand on the wheel, he reached out and caught her chin, pulling her face back around. A glance revealed rosy splotches on her cheeks, burning beneath the pale skin. If he hadn't been driving, Aiden knew he wouldn't have been able to stop himself from leaning over and touching his lips to those bright patches, tasting the heat of her blush. "Come on, Liv. Talk to me."

"All done!" Jamie's little voice suddenly called out from the backseat, breaking the spell. "That was yummy!"

"Saved by the munchkin," he drawled, pulling his hand back from her face. Liv shook her head in one of those I-need-to-collect-my-wits kind of moves, then turned to collect Jamie's wrappers.

"Can we play a game?" Jamie asked, and after turning off the radio, Aiden quickly found himself joining in a game of "I Spy." Afterward, Liv and Jamie sang silly songs that had him laughing out loud, while inside his freaking head was spinning. He didn't know who this man was, driving the truck down the highway, enjoying the company of a human female and a little girl, as if they were *his* to enjoy. As if they belonged to him.

As if they were one big happy family.

He should have been going out of his skull—but the truth was that he couldn't get enough of it. Was eating up each moment like a fly with honey.

When Jamie decided she'd had enough of the games

and songs, Liv set her up with the iPod again to watch another Disney movie, and Aiden reached down to turn the radio back on. He scanned the channels until he found a classic rock station playing Van Morrison, then set the volume low enough that they could still talk.

"God, I shouldn't have eaten all that," Olivia groaned, nudging the McDonald's bag with the toe of her shoe. "Every single one of those calories is headed straight for my backside."

He snorted, shaking his head. "I'll never understand why women worry about their bodies like they do. Men like women with a little meat on their bones."

"I have more than a little," she snickered.

Aiden slid her a crooked smile. "You're damn near scrawny, Liv."

"Yeah? Well, you obviously need glasses, Watchman."

"Perfect eyesight, actually," he shot back, enjoying their easy banter. "Better than a human's."

"Then you know damn well that I'm…plump." Her voice was light, and yet there was something edging the words that caught his attention. Made him wonder if some jackass had actually said something to give her a complex about her weight.

"In some places, yeah," he grunted, his fingers flexing around the wheel as he thought about how good it would feel to wring said jackass's neck. "The right ones. I mean, you *are* top-heavy."

She covered her mouth with her hand as if to hold back the soft spill of her laughter. "That's not what I meant and you know it."

"Face it, Liv. You're tiny compared to me," he offered with a shrug, dragging his heavy-lidded gaze down her body for a quick once-over before looking back at the road. Another light rain began to fall, the sky darkening with thick, swollen clouds.

"Anyone is tiny compared to you," she said dryly, rolling her eyes. "Your mother must have had a heck of a time keeping you in clothes when you were a kid."

The *M* word hit him low in the gut, his stomach going sour at the thought of the woman who'd birthed him, while a familiar burn of rage swept through his system. He locked his jaw. Kept his gaze glued to the road, taking slow, easy breaths as he watched the streams of rain meander their way in jagged lines across the windshield.

"Did I, uh, say something wrong?" she murmured.

"Naw." He rolled his shoulder. Shifted in the seat to get more comfortable. Chewed on the inside of his cheek, thinking that he'd kill for a friggin' cigarette. "I just don't talk about my mother. Ever."

He didn't even realize he'd started to rub his right wrist, until she reached over and touched her fingertips to his skin, making him jump. The sensation slipped down his spine. Climbed back up with a surge of heat that struggled against the knot of cold still sitting in his gut like a lump of metal.

"When did you get these?" she asked, tracing the tip of her finger along one of the intricate designs. Though he knew she could feel the scar tissue that encircled his wrist, she didn't say anything. Simply followed the patterns of his tattoos with that light, easy touch that was creating all kinds of havoc in his body.

Aiden cleared his throat. Reached down and rearranged his dick to keep it from strangling. Fought to make sense of the strange emotions crawling through him, prickling beneath his skin. "I got the tats when I was fourteen."

"So young," she said with a soft note of surprise, returning her hand to her lap. Part of him was relieved she was no longer touching the tattoos, while another part wanted to shout, *Put it back! Touch me again!* The gentle press of her fingers had been so different from the way women normally touched him. There was no sexual intent in it. Just a tender, gentle caring that rattled something inside him loose. He didn't know what it was, but could feel it banging around inside his chest, probably causing all kinds of damage. Not that he cared. "You were still just a kid."

"Naw, I was old by then," he muttered, pulling his hand down his face.

He could feel her unspoken questions blasting against him, crowding the inside of the truck, and he ground his jaw, wishing he wasn't so screwed up inside. That he could be just a little bit closer to the "normal" that she wanted for her life.

"Are they protection spells?"

He barked a gruff burst of laughter. "Not likely."

"Okay. What, then?"

For a moment he almost considered telling her what they were, then regained his hold on sanity and shoved the idiotic idea aside. No sense scaring her off any more than he already had. Or would. Sooner or later, he knew she was going to look at him as something that wasn't good enough to wipe her feet on, much less to lie down with. He just hoped he'd have gotten his fill of her by the time it happened.

"Oh, my God," she gasped, suddenly grabbing his arm.

"What? What is it?" A quick glance showed her wide-eyed gaze zeroed in on his thigh—the one that bastard had clawed open. His jeans were dark with wet, sticky blood, and he winced, hoping she wasn't going to freak. He'd changed his clothes and bandaged the wound as best as he could with the first aid kit he carried in the truck, but it had obviously pulled open and bled through its wrapping.

"You were lying about how quickly it would heal," she said unsteadily, settling that smoky gaze on his face. "When I asked you this morning, you said you didn't need stitches because it would close up in a few hours."

When they'd headed back to the hotel room that morning and he'd stripped down to his boxers, she'd freaked when she'd seen his injured leg. He'd finally calmed her down by explaining that the wound was nothing…that it would heal quickly and she'd never even know it had been there. And by tomorrow that would be true. He'd just exaggerated a bit about how long it would take.

"You need to see a doctor, Aiden."

He shrugged. "Naw, it'll be closed up soon. Trust me, Liv—I've had worse."

She crossed her arms, her quiet voice rough with tension as she said, "I still think we should get you some stitches. It's ridiculous just to let it bleed like that. Not to mention the fact that you must be in pain."

"Seriously, I'm okay," he grunted, his stomach muscles knotted by the fact that she actually sounded as if she cared that he'd been hurt. As if it actually mattered to her. "I'll pick up some more bandages before we stop tonight. But it'll probably be healed by then, anyway. I doubt it'll even leave a scar."

Without any warning she reached out and touched her hand to one of the smooth scars that marred his wrists beneath the dark tats. "If that's true, then why didn't these heal?"

"I was too young when they were made."

"Someone hurt you when you were little?" Shock, as well as a healthy dose of outrage.

He shifted again. Rubbed his palm against the scratchy edge of his jaw. "Yeah, but they paid for it when I got bigger."

"Paid for it how?" Soft words, little more than a whisper.

He cut her a dark look, arching his right brow. "How do you think?"

She didn't flinch away from his look. Just stared right back at him, violet eyes wide and clear. "You killed them?"

"Christ. This isn't good conversation material," he muttered, reaching up to rub at the knotted muscles in the back of his neck. "Trust me."

"So let me see if I've got this straight. You don't talk about your mother. Don't talk about your scars. And you don't even talk about your tattoos. Is that right?"

"That's about it." He ground out the words.

"So I spill my secrets, but you get to keep yours?" He'd have had to be an idiot to miss the rising temper in her words. Not that he blamed her.

"You should thank me," he rasped. "There are some things you don't want to know."

"Or maybe they're just things *you* don't want me to know."

He nodded. "That, too."

"Fine, but don't expect me to keep spilling my guts to you. I—"

"Jesus," he growled, cutting her off. "There's no reason to get pissy. My past would probably bore you, Liv, so think of it as me doing you a favor, okay?"

"Whatever, Aiden."

A muscle ticked in his jaw, but he struggled to keep his voice calm. "I'm telling you, it's no big deal."

Clearly the woman didn't know when to give up, reminding him of a pit bull with a bone. "And I'm telling you that I know you're lying."

"Drop it," he grunted, forcing the words through the clenched wall of his teeth.

"You know," she said tightly, looking away as she wrapped her arms over her front, one hand resting on her shoulder, the other on her rib cage. "You could try trusting me. But you won't."

A dark sound tore from his throat, thick with frustration.

Silence stretched out. Thick. Heavy. Punctuated only by the rhythmic slapping of the windshield wipers.

"Just tell me one thing," she said, her voice muted.

"Christ, what?" He sighed, pulling his hand down his face again.

She turned her head so that she could look at him. "*Did you kill them?*"

Aiden didn't answer at first, but he could feel her gaze burning against the side of his face and knew she wasn't going to let it go. "Every last one of them," he finally admitted in a low voice, wishing he could get the visions out of his head. But they were a stain he couldn't wash out. A blotch on his soul that he knew would always be there.

Not that he regretted the killings. But he couldn't forget the way he'd done it. The sheer savagery of the act. Or the consequences that had followed.

She shivered, tightening her arms around her body.

Aiden had expected her to be disgusted by the revelation, or at least horrified by his ruthlessness, but as she turned her head to stare out her rain-spattered window, he could have sworn she whispered, "Good."

CHAPTER TWELVE

Southern Illinois
Saturday night

PEEKING AROUND THE CORNER of Aiden's bedroom door, Olivia peered into the small hotel room, fully aware that she was making a mistake. After driving late into the evening, they'd finally stopped for the night and taken a family suite with two connecting bedrooms. Because Kellan had his handmade alarms with him, Aiden had agreed that she and Jamie could have their own room. He'd taken the other one, leaving Kellan and Noah with the two sofa beds in the living room, though the men had agreed they'd take shifts pulling guard duty during the night, their level of caution elevated even higher after the events of the morning.

If she'd been smart, she would have been using the time to get some rest. God only knew when things were going to get crazy again. The Casus could find them. Or another of those creepy things from that morning, and yet there she was, acting like a Peeping Tom. Olivia had intended to simply knock and ask how he was feeling, but when she'd found the door ajar, she hadn't been able to resist a look inside.

Hoping to catch a glimpse of something you shouldn't...hmm?

"Shut up," she muttered under her breath, both bemused and irritated by the fact that she was talking to herself.

Her gaze found him instantly, her tummy doing another one of those nervous little flips at the decadent sight he made. No matter how she looked at it, the odds were strong that this wasn't a good idea. A stupid one, more than likely. But she didn't care. She was all too aware of the terrifying fact that he could have died that morning. That she could have lost him. She needed to see with her own eyes that he was okay. That the injury to his leg wasn't causing any lingering pain.

Needed simply to be near him, which told her just how much trouble she was really in.

He was lying diagonally across the bed, on his stomach, with nothing more than a small hotel towel wrapped around his lean hips, humming softly to himself. Since he faced away from the door, Olivia couldn't see his expression, just the back of his head and one side of his long, golden body. He'd showered, washing away the blood

that must have covered his leg, and she shivered as she remembered his blood-soaked jeans, then immediately
shoved the chilling image away.

No, she wouldn't think of that now. Instead, she would
give herself this moment to simply enjoy the eye-dazzling
view. She started at one end of his mouthwatering body,
moving her avid gaze over his long feet, up along the
strong muscles of his legs, relieved to see that he hadn't
needed to rebandage his thigh. From there, Olivia followed the naked line of flesh up to the hem of the white
cotton, then over the firm, towel-covered muscles of his
backside until she reached the breathtaking expanse of his
golden back. He had his right arm folded beneath his
head, the tattooed fingers of his left hand moving
smoothly against the snowy white of the top sheet.

A low hum of music drifted softly from his lips. Beautiful. Dark. Enthralling.

Before she could say anything to announce her
presence, he drew in a deep breath, and his long fingers—
fingers that had been inside her body just that morning—
stilled, telling her that he'd scented her presence. Her
cheeks flushed as he rose to his elbows and turned his
head, looking at her over his broad, gleaming shoulder, his
long hair still damp from his shower.

In that moment Olivia felt the same sense of danger that
had come over her that morning when he'd pulled her out
of the restaurant and into the hotel parking lot. She

recalled flinching from the brightness of the sun. Recalled the feel of its heat against her skin.

And she recalled the way in which the reality of their situation had slammed back into her with stunning force. The fact that they were being hunted. That monsters were coming for them. That their lives were in danger. *Run. Hide. Take cover,* a chorus of voices had whispered through her mind.

She'd known it was wrong, but she'd ignored them, and stayed there with him. Allowed him to kiss her. Touch her. Make her come.

And here she was again, flirting with danger. Literally. Olivia knew she should turn around and leave, but for some reason she did the opposite. Taking a shaky breath, she moved a little way into the room, standing just to the side of the partly opened door. "What were you d-doing just now?" she asked, the words stumbling over themselves in her nervousness, her face no doubt burning with a ridiculous flood of color. She didn't know what she was doing, slipping into his room uninvited, invading his personal space. But she couldn't make herself turn and leave, her muscles locked in place, her body holding her prisoner.

"I was just thinking about a piece of music I've been working on." He gave a low, almost embarrassed laugh, his eyes heavy lidded…curious. Probably wondering what she wanted.

"For the piano?"

"Yeah." He shifted, using his right hand to push the damp strands of his hair back from his face, the light catching against the golden bristles that covered his jaw and chin. "It helps me think. Even mellows me out."

Studying his expression, Olivia realized that he looked more relaxed now than he had when they'd stopped for the night. "Do you do that a lot?" she asked, leaning back against the wall. "Think about your music?"

"I guess I do," he replied in a low drawl, and without fail the corner of his mouth kicked up in another of those sexy, crooked grins that she could never get enough of. That she was actually starting to crave. "Hell, there were times when I was younger that the music in my head was the only thing that kept me going."

Olivia wanted desperately to ask what he meant by the strange comment, to ask about his childhood, but bit back the intrusive questions, knowing he would refuse to give her any answers. That had been made painfully clear during their earlier conversation about his tattoos and his scars, as well as his mother. Instead, she was just going to have to glean every little bit that he revealed, and try to piece together the story on her own.

The only problem was that he gave away so little.

Even though the shadows had left his eyes, it was still difficult to read his mood as he watched her from the bed, his dark body in sharp contrast against the bleached white linens. As the silence stretched out to an uncomfortable level, she started to edge back toward the door, ready to mumble something about letting him get some rest, when he said, "Where's Jamie?"

"Kellan and Noah are with her. In fact, I think they've been sucked into *Hercules* right along with her. All three of them, brainwashed by Disney," she told him with a soft laugh. "We should get a picture. Blackmail them with it some day."

Though it sounded as if it hurt, his own low burst of laughter rumbled up as he rolled onto his side. A cocky smile played at the corners of his mouth as he braced his upper body on his left elbow, the heavy slabs of his muscled chest the most drool-worthy sight she'd ever seen. "So what brings you in here, Liv? You come to kiss me good-night?"

Blinking, she struggled to concentrate on his huskily spoken words, but it wasn't easy. Not when that damn towel was barely hanging together around his lean hips. When so much of that hard, powerful body was just lounging there, begging to be ogled. The wounds on his arms and side were already pale lines of color, barely visible in the soft glow of lamplight spreading out from the bedside table. His leg, however, was a different story. An angry-looking weal darkened his hair-dusted skin, but at least the cut was closed and no longer bleeding.

And it wasn't as if the battle wounds detracted from his

beauty. Call her a savage, but she thought he looked sexy as hell sporting the scratches and scars. She only hated the pain they'd caused, knowing they'd had to hurt when they were made, no matter how tough he was.

Clearing her throat, she gave herself a little shake and finally managed to say, "Actually, I, uh, just w-wanted to check that you were okay."

"Yeah?" There was something beautifully animalistic about the way he slowly rolled to his back and pushed his way up the bed, until his upper body was braced against the mountain of pillows, his right leg bent a little at the knee. The towel gaped, revealing a dark, provocative shadow of pubic hair and his heavy testicles, as well as the impossibly broad base of his cock.

Olivia's mouth went dry, and although she knew damn well that she should look away…she couldn't. And the arrogant bastard knew it, his voice a low, seductive rumble as he bent his right leg a little higher. "You should probably come closer if you're going to do a thorough job," he drawled in a low, wicked slide of words. He bent his left knee a little, then let his leg fall open, dropping to the bed, the entire length of his dark, massive erection suddenly on bold display. "You know, of making sure I'm all right and everything."

She would have rolled her eyes if she could have looked away from the decadent sight, her mind boggling at the idea of taking something that size inside her body. It was both exciting…and more than a little worrying. "Obviously you're f-fine," she stammered, hating that her nerves betrayed her so easily.

His eyelids lowered to half-mast. "Have I told you yet how hot it makes me when you stutter?" He lowered his hand, and she nearly drooled as she watched him lightly touch his fingertips to the dark, vein-ridden flesh.

A soft, nervous rush of laughter fell from her lips. She wondered if his expression was teasing, but couldn't seem to steal a glance at his face to see.

"Really, it's sexy as hell," he murmured, still talking about her stammer. "Because whenever I hear it, I know it means you're getting all wound up inside."

Her shyness urged her to look away, but she refused, watching as he curled his big hand around the wide root nestled in that dense patch of caramel hair. The shaft was as thick as her wrist, and she couldn't stop the erotic images from playing across her mind. Breathtaking fantasies of what it would be like if it were *her* hands touching him…stroking him.

"You wanna know why I was hoping you'd come in here?" he asked, rolling up into a sitting position as he swung his legs over the side of the bed.

She nodded, unable to get any words out. The moment felt so fragile, so intense. Thick. Viscous. It was almost difficult to breathe through the excitement, the air steamy against her skin, her face flushed with heat. Her mouth trembled, fingers fluttering with little twitches that she couldn't control. She felt like a neon sign blasting out her helpless longing for something she knew she could never have. That could never truly be hers.

"I was hoping you'd come to take me up on my offer," he drawled, his slow, sin-tipped smile doubling her heart rate as he stood and took a step toward her.

"You m-mean for an affair?" she asked, dazed by the sight of his stomach, the muscles cut in a way no human male could ever hope to achieve, no matter how many grueling hours he spent in the gym. And the way he moved. It was beautiful. He didn't walk, *he stalked... prowled,* those ripped muscles moving with a raw, animalistic grace that completely betrayed the fact that he was something so much more than human.

Oh yeah, she could so easily see him as the dangerous predator. As something that would stalk the shadowed jungle, taking down its prey with a deadly set of jaws.

"Why do we have to call it anything, Liv?" He cocked his head a little to the side, hazel gaze bleeding to warm, rich amber. "Why not just enjoy it?"

She closed her eyes, took a deep breath, then slowly opened them again. "B-because I'm afraid to."

Wanting nothing more than to kiss the frown from her lips, Aiden took another step toward her, and the knot on his towel finally gave way. As the damp cotton fell to the floor, he didn't try to catch it. He figured he could have played the gentleman and covered up, but what the hell. He'd already spread his legs on the bed and flashed her his monster-sized hard-on. She made him feel like a freaking caveman, so why shouldn't he go ahead and act the part?

And though he knew no one would ever have believed it, he wasn't in the habit of showing off his body in front of his lovers. He'd gone through enough of that during his years at Mueller's, and had never really gotten into the whole admiration for his "size" when he'd become a man.

But…it was different with Liv. It jarred him just *how* different she made him feel, though he knew he shouldn't be surprised. She made everything seem new to him, so why should sex be any different? He might be as jaded and as used as they came, but Liv made him feel… fresh, in some whacked-out, weird kind of way. He wanted to show himself to her in an earthy, animalistic act of seduction. Watch her pale skin go warm as he flaunted his iron-hard cock before her, giving her proof of just how badly he wanted to be inside her.

And maybe, just maybe, it would ease the ache. Make sense of some of the madness that had been tearing him up inside since he'd met her. That had only grown worse with each second that he spent with her.

And maybe it will just make it worse, jackass.

That was certainly a possibility. And yet, did he really care?

You had better care. Because if you don't, everything's gonna blow up right in your face.

No, he could control it. If it meant being able to touch her, he would find some way to master the beast and beat the bloody thing into submission.

Wanna bet?

Damn. He was looping so many lines of bullshit, he didn't know what he was doing anymore—didn't know which voices to listen to. To believe. All he knew was that he couldn't be close to her and not touch her. Not when he was enjoying being around her as much as he was, something that *never* happened to him with women. Not to mention human ones.

And then there was the head-spinning attraction. The I've-got-to-have-you-or-I'm-going-to-die burn of hunger. Her scent was like something that he could taste in his throat, through his skin. It was thick…warm. Delicious. His chest expanded as he pulled it into his lungs, savoring it, his awareness of her spreading out like a net. He wanted to throw it out and snare her in its grip. Wanted to take her into his arms and drag her away to his cave and…keep her, to hell with the consequences. To hell with "the Eve effect" and her hope for a normal life. To hell with his past and his fears and the fact she was human. To hell with all of it.

At least for as long as it would take him to get what he needed.

Aiden half expected her to shriek as he prowled toward her, but she surprised him, going perfectly still instead, her smoky gaze locked in tight on his cock again. She cleared her throat, her voice shaking with nerves. "You, uh, really shouldn't d-do that."

A quick arch of his brows. "Do what?"

"Walk around…like that."

Aiden stopped just a few feet in front of her, careful to keep his body positioned so that he wouldn't be seen through the open door, and braced his feet. Hooking his thumb around the base of his cock, he pushed the shaft away from his body, imagining what it would be like if she sank to her knees, her parted lips begging for him to come closer. The swollen head was already slick, practically drooling with eagerness. "Tempted?" he rasped, gripping himself in a tight fist, the thick knotwork of veins going dark as he squeezed.

"Yes," she whispered, flicking her tongue against her upper lip in a quick, shy swipe, as if she was already licking the head of his cock, taking the salty bead there at the tip into her mouth.

Her honesty caught him off guard, but only for a moment. "Ah, that's good to hear, Liv. I was beginning to think I'd lost my touch."

She swept her gaze up to his lopsided grin, her brows drawn together in a V. Uncertainty flickered in her gaze.

As well as caution. "Seriously, Aiden. Is this all some kind of game to you?"

He'd started to take another step toward her, but stopped, the raw vulnerability of her expression hitting him low in his stomach. He hated that she could disarm him so easily. Make him feel things he didn't want to feel, as if his emotions were suddenly hers to manipulate at will.

"No. No game." He ran his tongue over his teeth. "I want you, Liv. More than I should," he added, fully aware that he was repeating words he'd said to her before. He shook his head, his hands aching as he fisted them at his sides, struggling to hold himself back from her. "But no matter what happens between us—" the gravelly words scraped against his throat "—I'm staying. Sex isn't a condition of your and Jamie's protection. I just want to make sure that's clear."

She blinked up at him. Took a shaky breath. "You're going to drive me out of my mind," she said in a soft voice, "but you're a good man, Aiden."

He snorted. "I thought you said I was a tomcat."

"You'd never be a good husband or boyfriend," she offered with a wry laugh, "but I have a feeling you would make a great friend."

Something pulled tight in his chest, but he didn't argue. "Then I'll be your friend, Liv." *Until you're ready to ask me to be more.*

Whoa. Taking a mental step back, he wondered where those strange words had come from. Damn it, he didn't want her to ask for more, and even if he did, there wasn't a chance that she would ever do it.

Forcing himself back on track, he said, "I'll be your friend, and if you'd give me the chance, I could be a hell of a lover."

She shook her head, pressing herself tighter against the wall. "God, Aiden. Do you enjoy torturing me? Tempting me to m-make an idiot of myself?"

"You forget that you're the one who came in here to me, Liv?" A sliver of his desperation suddenly bled through in his tone, his voice going gritty and hard. "And it wouldn't be torture if you'd stop fighting the inevitable and just give in."

"Why? *Why* do you want this to happen? And for once just tell me the truth!"

His gaze slid to the side, and he caught a flash of his reflection in the mirror above the dresser. Immediately he looked away, not recognizing the man who'd briefly stared back at him. There'd been too much intensity in his golden eyes. Too much need etched into the hard angles of his face. He felt too raw, too exposed, as if he'd been stripped down and everything laid out for the world to see.

Which was pretty funny, really. Considering he was standing there in front of her bare-assed naked.

Rolling his shoulder, Aiden locked his gaze on the white nothingness of the wall behind her head. "You want the truth, Liv? Well, here it is." The words were low, guttural, all but ripping their way out of him. "The truth is that I should stay away from you, but I can't." He lifted his right hand, worrying three fingers against the edge of his jaw. "You make me smile. Make me laugh. Every time you walk into a room, my cock goes hard and my heart starts pounding like it wants to bust its way through my chest. My ears roar and my mouth waters." Taking a deep breath, he lowered his gaze, locking onto the violet smoke of her eyes. "You want the truth? The truth is that I hate the way you keep pulling away from me. And the truth is that I don't like being this out of control, but I can't stop it."

"Then leave." She broke eye contact with him as she sidled to the side, as if she was planning on slinking out the door and running away. "Let Kellan and Noah take over and just go."

Aiden reached out, smacking his right hand against the door. It slammed shut, the sharp sound making her jump. He moved closer, crowding her against the wall, caging her in. "Is that what you want? You want me gone?"

She kept her eyes on his throat. Pulled her lower lip through her teeth. "We're talking about you, not me."

"Don't play games with me," he growled, forcing the words through his clenched teeth as he smacked the flat of his palm against the door. "I'm not in the mood."

She trembled, closing her eyes, and Aiden forced another deep breath into his lungs, mentally shaking his head at himself. Christ, so much for keeping it light and easy.

Smooth, asshole.

The color in her face was burning brighter as she dared a quick look up at his face. "I tried to explain it to you before," she whispered. "I don't know the first thing about having casual sex, and I've never had a one-night stand in my life."

With one hand braced against the door, the other against the wall, Aiden lowered his head and buried his nose in the tender curve of her throat, torturing himself with her scent. "Who said anything about one night?" he muttered. "It's going to take a hell of a lot longer than that for me to get my fill of you. And I can guarantee there won't be anything casual about it."

Lifting his head, he trapped her with the burning intensity of his stare. "And if you keep telling me that you can't," he grunted, driven by the powerful urge to see her smiling up at him again, "it's gonna give me a complex. I'm liable to start thinking that you just don't want me. It'll be pathetic, Liv, and you'll have no one to blame but yourself."

Something soft and shaky slipped from her lips, like a fairy's laugh, the light sound filling him with an almost visceral satisfaction. "Oh, God. Honestly, Aiden. I'd have to be out of my mind not to want you. You know that's not it."

He cupped her jaw with his right hand, pressing his thumb into her lower lip. "Good."

"But that doesn't mean that I can be reckless and just do whatever I want."

"Wrong, Liv," he argued, swiping his thumb along the inside edge of her lip, feeling the damp heat of her mouth. "You're a grown woman. You can do whatever you want."

"But it's a mistake."

He snorted, shaking his head. "Welcome to the club, honey. People make mistakes every day of their lives. Might as well be one that we can enjoy."

She stared so deeply into his eyes that he fought not to squirm. "Is it really that simple to you? Don't you ever worry about getting hurt?"

"I told you before, I won't hurt you."

"Aiden," she said unsteadily, her mouth trembling, "you'll do it without even trying."

A muscle ticked in his jaw, no doubt betraying how wound up he was inside. "You're just going to have to take that risk."

"Risks aren't smart." A soft, breathless whisper that made him want to roar with frustration.

"Screw smart. Go with instinct for once in your life, Liv. Be selfish and look at it as using me for pleasure, just like I told you to do this morning. You can settle for your boring little slice of normal later on. But right now you should—"

"Aiden," she murmured, cutting him off as she pressed her hands to the burning heat of his chest, "I—"

He didn't wait to hear what she had to say, too afraid it was going to be another rejection. Instead, he grabbed her cool, slender hand...and flattened it against his cock. "Damn it, Liv. I *need* to get you under me." He ground out the words, his breath hissing through his teeth as her fingers curled around him in a tight, greedy hold. "And it needs to happen *now.*"

CHAPTER THIRTEEN

THE WORDS WEREN'T SHOUTED, but Olivia could feel Aiden's control slipping. See the raw desire shaking him apart inside. She didn't understand *why* he wanted her physically, considering he could have any woman he chose. It didn't make any logical sense for him to want *her,* the sexually inept kindergarten teacher who had never really been wanted by anyone. At least not like this, as if she were actually something worth wanting. But she could feel his need pulsing against her hand, hard and hot and urgent. See it glowing in his eyes, the smoldering amber reminding her of how he'd looked that morning, when he'd had his fingers buried inside her body, urging her to come for him.

She was acutely aware of the fact that this was the moment she would normally have shied away from such mouthwatering temptation and shut herself down, falling back on old habits that were hard to give up. But she turned away from them, slamming a metaphorical door in their startled faces. And with that uncharacteristic act of defiance came a sharp, electrifying surge of anticipation. One that grew, swelling, until it was something she could feel pulsing inside her, like a living thing.

Now, for the first time in what felt like forever, she chose to give free rein to her emotions and simply enjoy the moment. Enjoy everything she could from the complicated Watchman, for as long as it lasted. She could shut down again later, when it was time to slink away and lick her wounds. But for now she wanted to feel the fire. The heat and the burn and the blistering passion. She wanted to feel Aiden. All of him. Everything.

Which was kind of convenient, seeing as how her hand was fisted around his vein-ridden cock, the suede-soft skin a sensual contrast to the raw, primal power pulsing beneath its surface. She tightened her grip, squeezing as much of him as she could, though her fingers didn't even fit all the way around. He grunted, thrusting against her in a hard, reflexive move, pushing the broad shaft through her fingers. His tall frame shuddered, every stark, powerful muscle rigid beneath the tight stretch of his dark, silk-textured skin.

Loving the wild, I'm-going-to-do-things-to-you-that-you-can't-even-imagine look in his eyes, Olivia squeezed him again, this time in a long, slow pull that ripped some kind of thick animal sound up from his chest.

And she liked that sound so much that she did it again.

Then she watched breathlessly as a feral glow flashed in his gaze, almost as if something *else* was staring back at her. Something predatory and savage and dangerous. Something that was Aiden...but different. Other.

One second he was shuddering against her, and in the next his lips pulled back over his teeth...and he ripped her hand away. "No more," he growled between deep, ragged pulls of air. Taking hold of her hands, he lifted them both above her head and pressed them against the wall, trapping them there. "I'm too on edge. You're about to make me come."

Olivia wet her lips, her breath quickening as need-drenched desire spilled through her system in a warm, succulent wave. It sent her head spinning, her body all but melting against him, readying itself for whatever he wanted to do to her. "Isn't that what you wanted?"

"Not yet." Each word was formed with hard, guttural precision. "Not until I've made you come first." He got close, right in her face, his breath warm and sweet and tempting. "You're small, Liv. And I'm built like a bloody horse. The more times I can get you off, the easier it's gonna be for you to take me."

"That's hardly fair, Aiden. I want to be able to touch you—"

"You will," he broke in, cutting her off. "But right now I just need you to trust me on this, okay? That's all I'm asking."

She shivered as his thumbs found the damp hollows of

her palms, stroking the sensitive skin. Chills raced after prickles of heat, her own hunger twisting inside her like a sinuous animal thing that was starved for pleasure. "One of the first things you said to me last night," she whispered, "was that you didn't care if I trusted you."

"Yeah, well." A crooked, boyish smile flirted at the corner of his mouth, his eyes still flickering with that sharp, feral glow. "I've been known to lie a time or two."

Her own smile was wry. "Make a mental note, Aiden. You should never admit to being a liar when asking for a woman's trust. Kinda defeats the purpose."

His chest vibrated with a deep, sexy bark of laughter, and he grasped her waist, lifting her effortlessly off the floor. He pinned her against the wall, his heavy-lidded stare never leaving her face as he guided her legs around his hips, his cock lodged heavily against the sensitive core of her body. "Seriously, Liv. You *can* trust me." A low, solemn tone, like a vow. "And I swear nothing's gonna happen here that you don't want to happen."

"That could, um, actually be a problem," she groaned, dropping her head back against the wall.

Catching the teasing note in her voice, he arched one golden, arrogant brow. "Why's it a problem?"

"Because you make me feel greedy," she whispered. "I have a feeling I'm going to want it all."

His grin was downright wicked, wreaking all kinds of havoc inside her body. Heat. Nerves. Rushing pulse and churning, almost painful anticipation. "Saying things like that is gonna get you into trouble, Liv."

"Not to point out the obvious," she murmured, unable to stop the needy roll of her hips that pressed her tighter against his erection, his low growl and the tightening grasp of his hands telling her how much he liked it. "But I have a feeling I'm already *in* trouble."

With another sexy rumble of laughter, Aiden lowered his head. The thick silk of his hair fell forward, brushing against her face as he ran the damp heat of his mouth along the edge of her jaw. "You might be right, honey."

"I know I'm right." A soft, breathless rush of words, while her hands stayed busy exploring the hard, mouth-watering muscles in his shoulders and arms, his skin hot and slick to the touch, as if he were burning with fever. "And seeing as how I'm not very good at this, maybe you should tell me what's going to happen first. You know... so I can be p-prepared."

She could hear the smile in his voice as he kissed his way down the side of her throat. "You know in that book of yours where the duke ties the chick up to the bed and licks her from head to toe?"

Olivia nearly choked on a shy, shocked burst of giggles. "We d-don't have time for that. Jamie might need me." Not to mention the fact that she'd die of embarrassment if Aiden tried to do something like *that* to her less-than-perfect body. In her mind, she was thinking more of sliding beneath the covers, under a comforting shadow of darkness, so that the differences between them wouldn't be quite so obvious.

"If you won't let me tie you up," he rasped within the sensitive hollow of her ear, handling her weight with ridiculous ease as he held her against him, carrying her toward the bed, "then I guess I'll just have to improvise and hold you down instead."

The next thing Olivia knew, he was tossing her onto the soft, Aiden-scented sheets. He stood there for a moment, just staring down at her, the most provocative look she'd ever seen on any man's face carved into the rugged lines of his expression, the sexy creases beside his eyes only adding to his devastating good looks. Then he crawled over her, his parted lips hovering just above hers as he slid one hand between her legs. He palmed her sex through her jeans, holding it as if he owned it, or wanted to, and her heart flipped over in her chest, reminding her that she was playing a dangerous game, fooling around with a man who wanted her only for sex.

A man she'd only known for little more than a day, though it felt as if she'd been wanting him, craving him forever. For a lifetime.

"Touching you this morning was incredible, but I need…I need this in my mouth, Liv." He rubbed the heel of his palm against the top of her cleft, making her tremble. "Need to feel you against my tongue."

She covered her hot face with her hands as he suddenly stood up again and practically ripped off her jeans. His hands were hot against her knees as he pushed them apart, the tiny pair of white cotton panties that she'd put on that morning the only thing shielding that most private part of her from his gaze. Desire pulsed its way through her body, potent and sharp—but there was fear there, as well. Fear that she wouldn't please him. Fear that she'd lock up, close down and end up lying there like a dead fish, boring the hell out of him. She couldn't help the burning twinges of self-consciousness and doubt, when he was standing there looking like a freaking god, his body nothing short of luscious perfection, with muscles poured over muscles, and a face that any man would die to possess. "Aiden. I, um, I know I said I wanted it all. But I…I don't know if I can do this. I mean, maybe we should skip the…um, oral part, and just get to the other stuff."

"Stop worrying, Liv. All you have to do is lie there and come." Aiden worked to keep his voice soothing, which wasn't easy, considering all he wanted to do was growl and snarl and roar like a bloody madman, his beast so worked up it was a miracle he was managing to speak at all.

Just calm down, damn it. Or you're going to scare her off. And there'll be no one to blame but yourself.

The tiger chuffed with frustration, tossing its head, then

went back to prowling the confines of his body, lurking just beneath the surface of his skin, seething with hunger.

Taking a deep breath, Aiden slid his hands up her legs, gripped her thighs and pinned them against the mattress. He crawled back onto the bed and leaned forward, his mouth watering as he pressed his nose against the damp panel of her panties. She groaned, sounding embarrassed and aroused all at once, and he had to fight the primal urge to rip the cotton away with his teeth, so that he could get to the sweetness that lay shielded beneath. Her thighs strained against his hold as she reflexively tried to pull them closed, the arch in her back the most sensual thing he'd ever seen, her nipples hard and thick beneath the soft cotton of her sweater. He wanted to remove every stitch of her clothing, but didn't trust himself. Knew the sight of her flushed, feminine little body would push him over the edge, shattering his control.

And God only knew he would need every ounce of control that he had if he was going to keep it together long enough to make this work. It was the given truth that oral sex had never been his thing, after his years at Mueller's, but he had no doubt that he was going to enjoy going down on Liv.

Probably even love it, he thought, rubbing his tongue against the roof of his mouth. Become addicted to it, if she tasted even half as good as she smelled. His instincts were purring for *this*. For *her.*

And Aiden had always been a man who trusted his instincts.

Touching his open mouth to the pale, tender skin of her hip, he rubbed his fingers against the drenched cotton. "I'm going to put my tongue right here," he told her, slipping his finger beneath the elastic leg band and stroking the small, tender opening. "Push it inside you. Lick you until you come in my mouth, all hot and slick and sweet."

Bracing himself on his left arm, Aiden thrust two thick fingers up inside her, and watched as her hands fell away from her face, to her sides, clutching handfuls of the sheets as if she needed to anchor herself. Thick, savage satisfaction spilled through his veins at the dazed look of lust darkening her violet eyes as she stared back at him, her lips parted for the shallow, jagged rhythm of her breathing. She was thinking about it, imagining what he'd described, and he could scent the rise of her need, that provocative perfume seeping into him, making him drunk with craving.

"This is, um, a little embarrassing," she whispered, flicking her tongue against her lower lip. Damp ringlets curled at her temples, one fiery strand draped across her warm cheek. "I mean, I'm not really comfortable doing this kind of thing with the l-lights on."

Choking back a low growl, Aiden nuzzled the hem of her sweater above her navel, then buried his face against the gentle swell of her belly. No way was he going to let her hide from him. "You don't have anything to be embarrassed about, Liv." He pulled his fingers back, then shoved them deep again, nearly dying as her lush sheath clasped him in a tight, greedy hold. "You're perfect. We're talking the *blow my mind, make me dizzy* kind of perfect."

He licked the soft patch of skin just beneath her navel, slowly working his way toward the edge of her panties. He could feel how shy she was, but it didn't turn him off. If anything, Liv's shyness just turned him on. A lot. Hell, he even got off on the way she breathed. The way she blinked. She could probably recite the bloody alphabet and make him hard as nails. The woman was just too tempting to resist.

"Can't wait any longer," he growled, pulling his fingers from the soft, liquid clutch of her body. She gave a shocked cry as he fisted his hand in the front of her panties, ripping the cotton with ridiculous ease, then tossed them over the side of the bed. Leaning forward, he wedged his shoulders between her legs, forcing them to part a little wider for him. He wanted to tell her how beautiful she was, but the words were all jammed up in his throat, his head thick with hunger and craving as he rubbed his thumbs along the silken inner surface of her thighs. His gaze locked with a visceral force of need on the exquisite flesh nestled there between her legs, his eyes burning as he stared at that tender, private part of her.

Private.

Until that moment, Aiden had never really thought there was anything particularly private about a woman's sex. The females he normally took to bed weren't innocent or shy. They tended to strip easily, lie back, spread their legs and show him what they knew he was after. He didn't think badly of them for it. In fact, he'd always appreciated the fact that they understood what he wanted from them, as callous as that sounded, and didn't waste his time making him work for it.

But there was something wonderfully intimate about coaxing Olivia to spread her legs wider for him, so that he could open her up like a gift, revealing all the pink, slippery details. He exerted gentle pressure with his hands as he pressed his nose against the silky, strawberry curls that lay in a soft patch against the top of her mound.

"The light," she gasped, shivering beneath his mouth.

"I'm not turning it out," he muttered, the guttural edge of the animal's voice bleeding through the human words. Unable to wait any longer, Aiden used his strength to position her legs the way he wanted them, pushing them out high and wide. "I want it bright. Need to be able to see every part of you."

She stiffened, reaching down to cover herself, but he stopped her with a single word. "Don't," he growled, making her jump. "Sorry, just…don't cover yourself, Liv. Don't move." He took a deep breath, forced out a gritty, desperate *"Please."* Then nearly cried with relief when she shifted her hands to his hair, soothing him with tender strokes of her fingers, as if she were gentling some wild, out-of-control creature. It made him feel raw. Exposed. Though he'd have cut his own tongue out before telling her to stop, the touch of her hands against his hair too blissful and sweet.

Using his thumbs, Aiden spread her open until he could see all the slick, tender bits that lay inside. He was mesmerized, dazed by the sheer perfection of her. Smooth, pale thighs, and then that blushing, candy-pink center, all vivid and wet and pretty. It was like opening the lid of a treasure chest to find the jewels hidden inside. Like discovering an exotic hothouse flower, its succulent scent like no other in the world.

That was how it felt with her. He might have had more than any man's fair share of women, but staring down at Olivia with rapt fascination, he knew he'd never seen anything like her. Nothing this perfect. This sweet. This…private. In that moment, Aiden finally understood the deeper meaning of that word. One that burned in his chest, hot and vital and violently strong. Yes, that was how he felt. This *was* private. Something that no one should ever have the right to see but him. That no one else should ever be allowed to touch. Or taste.

Dangerous thoughts. But impossible ones to ignore. Not that he knew what to do about them.

"You're staring at me," she whispered, her breath hitching as she lifted herself on her elbows, staring at him over the trembling line of her body. "And you have the strangest look on your face."

"Not strange," he rasped, the corner of his mouth twisting with a tight, wry smile. "Believe it or not, honey, that's just my happy look. Feel kinda like I've died and gone to heaven."

She fell back against the bed again as she gave a soft laugh, her hands clutching back onto handfuls of the sheet. "You're a madman, Aiden."

Yeah. Probably. God only knew that he must look like one. Sweat covered his face, his chest, the craving twisting him up inside, scraping and raw, no doubt etched into his expression. He wanted to mark her, branding her body in ways that would let every other male out there know they had no claim on her.

That she was *his* and no one else's.

For the moment, sneered an all-too-human voice in his head. *Only for the moment.*

He snarled the bastard back into hiding, unwilling to listen to his bullshit. Not now. Not when he really was about to experience the closest thing to heaven he knew he'd ever get.

"You're so beautiful," he groaned, lowering his face, unable to fight the urgent need to get his mouth on her. He'd feared that panic might take hold of him when he got to this point, but he shouldn't have worried. There was no reminder from his past. No unwanted memories or emotions. There was just Liv, the intoxicating feel and taste of her exploding through his body, drenching his senses in pleasure.

"So good," he growled, licking her, his tongue in ecstasy as it lapped at her glistening flesh, then thrust inside the tiny opening, going deep. She didn't taste as good as she smelled. She tasted *better.* Like strawberries and sugar and heaven. Yum.

She writhed beneath him as he whispered hoarse, broken phrases, telling her how gorgeous she was, how incredible she tasted, using carnal words that had her pale skin burning with heat, her entire body covered in a dark, brilliant blush. Aiden couldn't get enough of the taste of her skin, her flavor, nearly dying when her back arched, a throaty cry spilling from her lips as she crashed over the edge, pulsing against his mouth in a sweet, melting rush of pleasure.

"That was…I didn't know how it would…that I could actually…" She struggled to get the husky words out between her panting breaths, her voice blissed-out and dreamy.

Aiden licked his lips, starving for her. "Yeah, it was. I want *more.*"

"No, wait. I want to be able to touch you, too."

His beast roared at the idea, and Aiden knew he was pushing it. He'd known that going down on her would whip the animal into a frenzy, but he hadn't been able to deny himself a taste of her. And now that he'd had one, he *needed* another.

"You can touch me after," he groaned, flicking his tongue against the swollen knot of her clit. "Right now I just need to keep doing this."

And boy did he do it well. Taking a deep breath, Olivia lifted her head, needing to see it. Aiden. Between her legs. His pink tongue lapping at her, licking her. Those hard, beautiful features pulled into an expression of pure, breathtaking lust. Need. Hunger.

She moved her gaze down his body, his weight balanced on his left arm and his knees, and almost came again when she saw him stroking his cock in a hard, brutal-looking grip with his right hand. She blinked, wetting her lips, thinking it was incredibly erotic, not to mention sexy as hell, that going down on her made him want to touch himself.

He flicked his golden eyes up to her face and found her staring at him. "The beast," he growled, his mouth slick with her juices. "If I don't take care of this, I'm going to…" His voice broke, his eyes flashing…the sharp points of his teeth edging beneath the sensual curve of his upper lip, and she realized his fangs were descending. That he was…changing, at least partly. The hard, hungry look on his face as he started to crawl his way over her—his body moving like a sleek, powerful predator—should have scared the hell out of her, but it didn't. It just made her hotter, needier…everything inside her screaming to get as much of this man as she could.

You're losing your mind, woman. We're talking grade A certifiable.

Maybe. But in that moment she honestly didn't give a damn.

"Aiden." She cleared her throat, trying to talk past the twisted knot of lust and emotion that was choking her. "Come closer."

When his face was just above hers, he stopped, his sweet breath warm against her mouth as he stared down into her eyes with a dark, hypnotic look that made her burn with heat. He lifted his right hand, laying it against the curve of her cheek, his thumb stroking the corner of her mouth. His gaze fell, following the lazy movement of his thumb as he swept it across her lower lip, his breathing loud against the heavy silence of the room. Flicking her tongue out, Olivia licked the tip of his thumb, and his gaze flew up, locking with her own.

A rough, guttural sound vibrated in his throat. And then he was kissing her. Or rather, consuming her. His tongue swept past her lips, claiming...seducing, with bone-melting, heart-pounding skill.

"Touch me, damn it." The low growl blasted against her mouth, and then he was kissing her again, harder, wetter, his head angling to the side for a deeper connection as she reached between them, wrapping her fingers around his heavy cock. She squeezed, milking him, and he broke the kiss, chanting a breathless, sexy string of swearwords against her cheek, her temple, his lips moving against her skin in a soft, sensual brush.

Knowing she'd go crazy if she didn't get him inside her, Olivia arched her hips. She was angling his cock toward that part of her that so desperately needed to be filled, Aiden's right hand roughly shoving up her sweater, when the first knock sounded against the bedroom door. They both froze, her eyes wide, his narrowed with fury.

"What?" he snarled, dropping to his side as a second knock came, this one louder than the first.

"Sorry to, uh, interrupt," Kellan called through the door, "but Jamie nodded off during the movie and we think she must have had a bad dream. She woke up asking for Liv, and she's starting to get a little anxious."

Olivia scrambled to her feet, quickly pulling her jeans back on, while Aiden remained on the bed, one arm thrown over his eyes, his cock rising high against his ridged stomach, so hard it looked painful. His chest rose and fell as he took a series of slow, deep breaths. "Sorry," she whispered, biting the corner of her lip. She hated that she had to leave him like that, knowing damn well he didn't deserve it after everything he'd done to her. *For her.* "I…you know I have to go."

"You don't need to apologize," he rasped, still covering his eyes. "She needs you, and it's not like a hard-on is gonna kill me." Another deep breath lifted his chest, the light glinting against the tip of a fang just beneath his upper lip. "It's probably better this way. I seem to be a little low on control tonight."

"Is control so important?"

A gritty, bitter laugh. "Honey, you have no idea."

Wondering what he was hiding, she turned away, her heart still beating like a trapped bird within her chest. Somehow she managed to make her way toward the door, even though her legs felt like overcooked linguini.

"Liv."

With one hand on the door, she looked at him over her shoulder.

He'd lifted his head, his gaze shadowed by the thick, golden fringe of his lashes. "Just so you know, that's how it'll be between us every time. You won't ever have to fake it or pretend something you don't feel."

She gave him a tremulous smile, painfully aware that she was feeling so much more than she should. Certain, now, that there was nothing she could do to stop it.

You're gonna be sorry. And then you're gonna feel like a fool.

"Try to get some rest," she told him, turning a deaf ear to the words being whispered through her mind. Then she hurried through the door, leaving the ultimate temptation behind her.

CHAPTER FOURTEEN

Iowa
Late Sunday afternoon

IT'D BEEN A BITCH OF A DAY, the traveling taking its toll on each and every one of them. Not to mention the stress. Aiden had wanted to say to hell with the tedious way of traveling—the constant backtracking to throw off any Casus who might be on their trail—and make a fast, straight run for Colorado. But Kierland had cautioned him against it, claiming that the safest place for them right now might very well be out in the middle of nowhere. At least until they had a better understanding of what they were up against. When he'd talked to Kierland that morning, he'd learned that another Watchman had been killed, this one in South Africa. Compounds were going on high alert all around the world, and Quinn was keeping a close eye on things back at Ravenswing. They had the most high-tech security available at the Colorado compound, but there was no way of telling how it would hold up against this strange new threat that was targeting the shifters.

Determined to offer Liv and Jamie as much protection as possible, Aiden had called in one of their colleagues, Morgan Cantrell, from the Watchmen compound in Reno. Morgan had been on the road for hours, after flying in to Des Moines, and was set to catch up with them any time now. They'd pulled into a populated rest stop about ten minutes ago to wait for her, giving everyone a chance to get out and stretch their legs for a bit.

While Kellan and Noah were grabbing sodas from the small shop set up at the far end of the parking strip, Aiden stood beside the truck and smoked a cigarette, the late-afternoon breeze whipping at the shoulder-length strands of his hair. Liv was still sitting in the truck with Jamie, who hadn't woken up from her nap yet, the engine left on so that they could have the heater running on low.

Leaning back against the driver's door, Aiden tilted his head back and stared up at the dark blue of the sky, trying to find a moment of stillness…of peace. But his head just kept spinning around and around.

Something had changed between him and Olivia during those minutes they'd spent in his hotel room the night before, the stakes even higher now than he'd imagined they'd be. The rational part of his brain knew he should cut his losses while he still could, but being with her just felt too good.

Better than good. Damn it, being with her felt *right*.

He'd been sucked in, and now he just wanted to wallow for as long as he could, soaking in the warmth and sweetness before he found himself shoved back out into the bitter, biting cold. And he had no doubt that the cold front would hit, leaving him right back where he'd started, fucking his way through an endless stream of women who didn't mean jack to him. Who never reached beneath his skin. Never made him think about impossible things he knew he had no business thinking about. Especially with a human.

It had been dangerous enough getting involved with her when the only thing drawing him to her was that lush, evocative scent. That brutal, intense physical pull. Then he'd had to go and get to know her, discovering that he actually liked her. A lot. Enough to make every moment he spent with her a monumental kind of mistake, for the simple fact that Olivia Harcourt was not the kind of woman he could keep.

Hell, even if he ignored his messed-up past and the fact that he would never truly trust her not to betray him, there was still the fact that she wanted that nice little slice of normal for her life. And God only knew that he was anything but. Even in the bizarre world of the clans, Aiden was something screwed up and different.

And yet, despite the fact that he couldn't have been further from what she wanted for a serious relationship, there was no denying that she was attracted to him sexually. They had lust, and Aiden was desperate enough to use it. He just had to figure out a way to touch her without almost losing it, as he had last night.

And if you can't? What then?

Before he could start another internal debate over his pathetic lack of control, the door opened on the opposite side of the truck, her scent hitting him like a physical punch as the wind whipped it around his head, making his mouth water. Gritting his teeth, he waited for the verbal lashing he expected she'd been itching to deliver, considering he'd been acting like a prick for most of the day.

From the corner of his eye he watched as she came around the back of the truck then leaned against its side, leaving a few feet between them, as if they needed the buffer zone. "Are you okay?" she asked.

A low, gritty laugh rumbled up from his chest, and Aiden shook his head, still staring up at the fiery blue of the sky, thinking that this woman would never cease to surprise him. Here he'd been expecting her to lay into him like a shrew, and instead her soft voice held only the tender, resonating notes of concern.

Taking a deep drag on the cigarette, he slowly exhaled, watching the billowing thread of smoke fade to blue. "I'm fine, Liv."

"You look as if you're a million miles away."

"I've just got a lot on my mind. Molly called a few minutes ago."

"Did she hear from Monica again?"

"Yeah." He took another deep drag on the cigarette, letting the smoke burn his lungs. Exhaled with a hard breath that revealed his frustration. "But I don't know what to believe."

"Why? What did Monica say?"

"Not much." Lifting his free hand, he worried two fingers against the hard set of his jaw. "She can't give us anything solid about that bastard that attacked us, or the other Watchmen murders. But it sounds as if she agrees with Kierland."

"You mean about us staying on the road right now?" she asked with a soft note of surprise.

He responded with a sharp nod, took another drag, then flicked the cigarette onto the asphalt and ground it out with the bottom of his boot. "But it doesn't make any sense. I can surround you with protection at Ravenswing. But the longer we wander around out here, their chances of getting to us are only gonna get better."

She was quiet for a moment, the heat of her gaze burning against his profile, and then she asked, "Did Monica have any information about Chloe?"

Aiden shook his head again, shoving his hands into the pockets of his jeans. "No, but Mols told me that a teenager's been reported missing back in Lennox. The girl lived next door to your friend's house." Turning his head, he met the wide-eyed surprise of her stare. "We don't have any proof, but I'd be willing to bet my ass that more Casus must have arrived after we left on Friday night."

"Oh, God," she gasped, her face completely draining of color as she pressed one slender hand to her mouth.

Knowing damn well what she was thinking, he said, "It's not your fault, Liv."

"You…you said that she's missing," she whispered unsteadily. "So…they haven't found a body. Couldn't… couldn't she have maybe run away?"

"I doubt it." He cut his gaze toward the tall woods that edged the rest stop, hating that shattered look on her face. The watery sheen of tears in her violet eyes. "We wouldn't have expected there to be a body. They probably took her somewhere and charred it."

"Ch-charred it?"

A muscle ticked in the side of his jaw, his hands itching with the need to reach out and grab her, pulling her against his chest, where he could just hold on to her. Do his best to offer what comfort he could, though he didn't have a clue how to do it.

Clearing his throat, he answered her question. "For the most part, the Collective have been using a chemical compound to cover the evidence of any Casus kills. It's one that they bioengineered to burn a body down without any flames, making it impossible to determine how the kill was made."

"But Monica's body wasn't burned."

"There have been a few cases where the compound wasn't used. Monica was one of them. We think they were probably scared off and her body discovered before they were able to come back and destroy it."

Though she didn't say anything, Aiden could feel the force of her anguish blasting against him as she thought about her sister and the teenage girl. He was usually clueless at reading a woman's emotions, unless she happened to be pissed off at him. But for some reason, he felt completely attuned to Liv, sensing her pain as if it were his own, which just set him even further on edge, cranking up his tension.

Silence settled between them, as heavy as the clouds that were rolling in from the east. He was about to suggest they wake Jamie up, so that she could get out and run around for a bit, when Liv finally spoke up. "Are you sure there isn't something else that's bothering you?" she asked, the change in subject not one Aiden would have chosen. But he figured he might as well go ahead and get it over with.

"I can tell you're hankering to bitch about something." He slid her a wary look, knowing that he sounded like a jackass. "So why don't you go ahead and just spit it out?"

For a moment she looked as if he'd slapped her, but then she shook it off, saying, "You could have just stopped."

Aiden arched his right brow. "Stopped what?"

"Last night."

"Yeah." Another low, gritty bark of laughter scratched his throat, and he rolled his eyes. "Like that would have ever happened. You really don't understand much about guys and sex, do you?"

She blanched, spinning around with the obvious intent of getting away from him. Quietly cursing himself for acting like such a jerk, Aiden reached out and grabbed her arm, stopping her before she could walk away. "Liv," he said softly, "look at me."

She took a deep breath, cast a cautious look over her shoulder.

"I'm in a shitty mood today," he told her, reaching out with his free hand to catch loose strands of her hair, tucking the fiery curls behind her ear. "But that doesn't mean I regret what happened between us."

She narrowed her eyes, obviously trying to decide whether or not she ought to believe him. "If that's true, then what's your problem? You've been acting pissy all day. "

"First of all, guys don't act *pissy,*" he snorted, his mouth twisting with a wry grin. "And secondly, I'm in a shitty mood because I'm a selfish son of a bitch who wishes the goddamn day would go ahead and be over with so that we can find a hotel and finally finish what we started."

She ran her tongue over her bottom lip, her eyes darkening to a smoky violet as she studied his expression. Quietly she said, "There's more to it than that."

"Yeah? What, then?"

Turning back around, she pulled out of his hold, and Aiden forced himself to drop his hand back to his side, when all he really wanted to do was pull her closer. She crossed her arms, her head tilted at a thoughtful angle as she held his stare. "You don't like wanting me."

"Oh, Christ." Aiden pulled his hand down his face, then propped his shoulder against the side of the truck. "Don't start on your looks again," he groaned, raising his voice so that he could be heard over the roaring engine of a passing semi out on the highway, "because you're only going to piss me off."

"I don't mean that. Though it still doesn't make any sense—the you-wanting-me part. But it's not sitting well with you, and to be honest, I'm not even sure anymore that it's just because I'm a human. I think there's something more. Something you're not telling me. But whatever the reason, you don't *want* to want me, Aiden."

He knew he should argue, but damn it, she was right. He didn't want to feel this way about her. He didn't want to feel *anything* about her. She was human. One who, because of "the Eve effect," could turn his life into a living nightmare. One slip of that teeth-grinding hold he had on his body and his emotions, and he'd make that bite—the one that could never be undone. The one that would forever bind him to a woman who would sooner or later decide he wasn't worth her contempt, much less her faith and trust and love.

No, to feel anything at all for her was a mistake, and for a moment he actually considered just saying to hell with it and coming clean. Tell her the truth. Open his veins and confess the ugliness of his past. Admit that part of the reason he was in such a foul mood was that he'd almost lost control with her last night. Almost allowed too much of his beast to break free. But he held his tongue, knowing that any talk about the animal side of his nature could very well lead into territory he didn't plan on touching with a ten-foot pole.

While he stood there lost in thought, she simply watched him, her solemn, smoke-colored gaze making him feel as if she was seeing past the aggressive, smart-ass attitude he'd always used to shield himself. To keep people away. As if she could see right inside him, down to all the black, toxic grime that coated his soul.

Finally she took a deep breath and slowly shook her head. "I know you'll probably think I sound like a fool. And I'm not saying that everyone in the world should be in love before going to bed together. But…lovers should at least be comfortable with their attraction. They should at least like each other." Soft, husky words that slipped down his spine, melting beneath his skin. "Even if it *is* nothing more than an affair."

"Damn it, Liv. I *do* like you," he muttered, feeling intensely awkward. He wasn't used to admitting his feelings to himself, much less out loud…for others to hear. His gaze shifted away, focusing on the highway, and he scraped his fingers back through his hair. "And let's face it. It's not like you'd ever want me for anything more than an affair anyway."

He could sense the surprise his words caused, but before she could ask what he meant, Kellan called out as he and Noah came walking toward the truck, their arms filled with packs of chips, candy bars and plastic soda bottles. "Morgan just called," Kell told them, his auburn hair hanging over his brow. "She hit some traffic and is running a little late. Probably won't be here for another twenty minutes or so."

Noah lowered the truck's tailgate, and he and Kellan set down the drinks and snacks, inviting them to help themselves. Aiden walked over and grabbed two sodas, then handed one to Liv. She murmured a quiet thank-you and said, "Since we're going to be waiting for a bit, I'm going to wake up Jamie and take her over to the playground."

"I'll come with you," he grunted, sliding a dark look toward the grass-covered, brightly colored play area. It was only about twenty yards away, wedged between the narrow parking lot and the surrounding woods, but he didn't like the idea of them going alone.

"No." She took a step back, her face lowered as she

twisted the cap off her drink, making her expression difficult to read. "That's okay. I think it'll be good if we just give each other some breathing room for a while."

"It isn't safe for you to go off on your own, Liv." He took a drink of his soda, then wiped the back of his wrist over his mouth. "There are cars all over the place here. No telling who's in them. The Casus could be anywhere."

"We'll be right over there, Aiden." She flicked a quick glance up at his face, then looked away again. "You'll be able to see us the entire time. It's not like I'm going to go wandering off anywhere without you. I'm not an idiot. I would never risk Jamie's safety that way."

Obviously sensing the tension between them, Noah spoke up, saying, "If you want, I'll head over with you."

It chafed to see how quickly Liv agreed. "Thanks, Noah. I'll get Jamie," she murmured, while Aiden just stood there, gritting his teeth.

"Don't let them out of your sight," he muttered, cutting a hard look toward the human.

"Don't worry," Noah told him. "I'll stay close."

Aiden gave a grim nod, and the three of them headed over to the playground together, Jamie chattering away to Noah as she held Olivia's hand, the pink ball Aiden had bought her that morning clutched under her arm. The child was obviously thrilled by the idea of some playtime, and as he gazed toward the playground, he watched as Liv pushed Jamie on one of the swings for a few minutes, then helped her make her way across the metal jungle gym. He watched...and watched, and even though he knew he was staring, he couldn't look away. Everything about Olivia Harcourt fascinated him. All those lush, feminine details. The thick, silken fall of her beautiful hair. The delicate angle of her jaw and the glossy, petal-like softness of her mouth. That luminous sparkle in her eyes when she smiled.

He was like an addict, starved for the sight of her. And he wasn't the only one who'd noticed.

Hopping up onto the tailgate, Kellan snickered under his breath. "Dude, you are so obvious."

"Shut up, Kell."

"Seriously," the Lycan drawled, and Aiden could hear the smile in the jackass's voice. "Look at you, man. You can't even take your eyes off her. All you can do is stand there drooling, watching her with those sad kitten eyes."

Aiden ran his tongue over his teeth, reminding himself that it wasn't going to help the situation if he broke Kellan's nose. No matter how bloody tempting it was.

Kellan clucked his tongue. "She's getting to you, isn't she?"

"You not hear me the first time?" Aiden snapped, cutting a furious scowl in Kell's direction. "Mind your own damn business and let it go."

Instead of taking offense, Kellan just grinned back, sitting there with his elbows resting on his knees. "Yeah, let it go," he murmured, a wistful edge to his gritty laughter that couldn't be missed. "It's funny, but I don't think any of us are very good at that sort of thing. I used to think you and the others were sorta pathetic, with all the worrying that you guys do. All the stress and tension and angst. But now I'm as bad as the rest of you." The Lycan looked toward Olivia, who had started playing a game of catch with Jamie and Noah. "I'm also jealous as hell."

Knowing he wasn't going to like the answer, Aiden couldn't stop himself from asking why.

A wry smile twisted Kellan's mouth as he met Aiden's stare. "Look at Ian and Riley. At Quinn. You've got the magic cure now, too, Ade. Someone who not only gives a shit if you live or die, but if you're happy. Sad. Someone who would rather see a smile on your face more than anything else in the world."

"What the hell are you talking about?" he snarled, feeling as if he was being shoved out to the edge of a cliff, the ground crumbling beneath his feet. Any second now, he was going to be in free fall, with nowhere to go but down.

The Lycan gave another husky laugh as Liv overthrew Jamie's head by about five feet, the ball rolling into the parking lot and under a car. Then he looked back toward Aiden, saying, "I'm talking about—"

Aiden struggled to hear the rest of his explanation, but the sound of Kellan's voice was suddenly drowned out by the heavy chugging of diesel engines as a trio of semis pulled into the rest stop, the acrid scent of their exhaust so strong, it nearly made him gag. Looking around, he felt an uneasy feeling settle heavily in his gut as he realized the trucks had separated Noah, who had gone to retrieve the ball, from the girls. With a sharp curse, Aiden started running, fully aware that he was probably overreacting. But he couldn't stop the thundering beat of his heart, or the nauseating spill of fear that was quickly working its way through his system.

The second eighteen-wheeler had stopped right in front of them, waiting for the one in front to park, and with Kellan right on his heels, Aiden quickly made his way toward the back of the truck. "It's going to be fine," he muttered under his breath, his beast prowling beneath his skin, as agitated as the man. "Nothing's going to happen. She's going to be okay. Both of them are."

But the instant he made his way around the end of the trailer, getting a clear view of the other side, he let out a bloodthirsty roar of fury, the savage sound echoing over the engines, torn up from the very depths of his soul. A panic-induced, surreal sense of time and space flooded his system, skewing his sense of perception, as if everything around him was happening in excruciatingly slow motion. A thick, crackling static of white noise filled his head, blotting out all other sound, his legs pumping as he powered himself forward through air that felt as viscous as honey, his right arm already reaching behind him, his fingers grasping for his gun.

The playground was silent.

Still.

Empty.

And neither Liv nor Jamie was anywhere in sight.

CHAPTER FIFTEEN

IT'D HAPPENED SO QUICKLY, there'd been no time to react. One second Olivia had been watching Noah run after Jamie's ball, and in the next, she and Jamie were being abducted, carried beneath the arms of their captor as he ran through the woods, spiriting them away from the rest stop. She couldn't see his face clearly, the shadows thickening as he moved farther into the dense wood, but she had no doubt that he was one of the enemy. A Casus. A monster. One who would kill them both if given half the chance. Though his face appeared human, the hands clutching their bodies had been transformed into gnarled, long-fingered claws that could slice open flesh with nothing more than an easy flick of his wrist.

It seemed unthinkable that they'd ended up in such a deadly situation because of a toy. Because of a pretty little pink ball, and the pathetic fact that she threw like a friggin' girl.

But it was true.

Their only hope was Aiden and his friends. Olivia knew the men would be coming for them, no doubt following her scent, but she screamed as well, while Jamie cried at the top of her lungs. Between the two of them, they were making enough racket to lead the others to their location. If they could manage to catch up. The man holding them moved with preternatural speed, the trees flashing by so quickly that they were nothing more than a blur of branches and leaves. She didn't know how far they'd traveled, but it was obvious that she needed to do something to slow him down. That she had to find a way to buy Aiden enough time to reach them.

And what if he doesn't? What then?

With a violent shake of her head, she refused to go there. She'd think of a way to give Aiden his chance. And for the moment, Jamie still wore the cross, which would offer her niece a measure of protection, though Olivia didn't doubt that the man—the Casus—would try to take it from Jamie if he could.

She didn't know how long she'd been screaming, but eventually her voice grew too hoarse to be effective, her lungs burning from lack of sufficient air, her body aching from the jarring force of being trapped beneath the man's arm as he ran over the rugged terrain. Jamie's cries had drained to broken whimpers, and Olivia did her best to reassure her, shouting that she loved her, that everything was going to be okay, until her voice faded to a croak. She tried to twist her head around so that she could see her niece, but they were being held with their backs to his sides, so all she could manage was a view of the back of Jamie's dark head, her small hands pounding against the man's hard-muscled arm.

"'Bout time you stopped that bloody screeching," he grunted, still running at a hard, steady pace, his clothes wet with sweat, sticking to his skin. Olivia craned her neck, struggling to see his face, but the poor lighting and constant motion made it difficult to focus, her stomach roiling. She had a vague impression of a square, brutish-looking jaw and bald head, his chest and shoulders huge, his height easily over six feet, though she didn't think he was quite as tall as Aiden.

"I can smell it, human." His lip curled, the guttural words thick with things she didn't want to think about. Rage. Lust. Hunger. "Smell that hot blood pumping through your veins."

Olivia had been racking her brain for something she could do—for some way that she could stall him—and she suddenly realized that the Casus had just given her the answer.

Her scent. Her blood.

Her stomach churned at the thought of what she had to do, but she forced the fear away, determination and adrenaline fueling her actions. No matter what happened to her, she *had* to give Jamie a chance to escape. Had to give Aiden the opportunity to rescue the precious little girl.

Taking a deep breath, she bit her lip, closed her eyes…and jabbed her forearm against the tip of one of the scalpel-sharp claws wrapped around her waist. Then she tugged, sweater and skin ripping open as the claw sliced through her arm like a knife through butter. Choking back an agonized cry of pain, she cracked her eyes open and inspected the damage, stunned by how much blood had already spilled out of the wound, drenching the torn sleeve of her sweater.

His nostrils flared as he sucked in a deep, snarling breath, then stumbled…his pace slowing enough that the trees around them began to take shape. He weaved, almost as if he was drunk, as they entered a small clearing. But he wasn't weakening. If anything, Olivia could feel the power in his body growing…building, like a volcano that was getting ready to erupt in a thundering act of violence.

Throwing back his head, he bellowed a stark, guttural cry, then shifted his arm, throwing her to the ground. She landed on her hip, the impact momentarily knocking the air from her lungs. Scrambling back on her hands and knees, her fingers digging into the fallen leaves and cold earth, Olivia stared up at the ravenous, lust-glazed look on his sweating face. With a sharp pang of relief she realized she had his full attention, his ice-blue gaze fixed on the crimson spill of blood pouring down her arm, soaking into the leaf-covered floor of the forest. Licking his bottom lip, he carelessly dropped Jamie's small body to the ground and took a step toward Olivia.

It was nearly impossible to keep her worried gaze from seeking out Jamie, but she was determined not to draw his attention back to the child. Instead, Olivia prayed Jamie would run for help, getting herself to safety.

"Who are you?" she croaked, hoping to distract him with questions. Every second she could keep him talking bought them time. "Why are you doing this? You know they'll find us. The Watchmen can track us anywhere!"

"I know that, you little bitch!" His lips pulled back over his teeth, his face dripping with sweat as he paced at her feet, his shoulders hunched, thick muscles hard with aggression. "You think I'm stupid?"

"I think you're going to be dead if you don't run."

"Shut up!" he roared. The vicious sound bled into a low, keening groan, and he curled his arms over his head, every muscle bulging beneath his skin. He was clearly fighting an internal battle with himself, his pale blue eyes bright with madness as he stared at her blood-covered arm with almost worshipful intensity. "I don't have time for this," he hissed as he began to prowl around her body in a tight circle, his movements becoming less human and more like that of an animal. His nostrils flared wider as he sucked in deep, ragged pulls of air. "But that smell. It's too good." Thick, guttural words that shook with need. "Good enough to make me think you'll be worth the consequences."

Her first instinct was to get up and run, but she'd seen

how fast he could move. "Are you not supposed to kill me, then?" she asked, watching from the corner of her eye as Jamie began to creep away from the small clearing on her hands and knees. Olivia silently urged the little girl to move faster, wanting her as far away from the monster as possible.

"We've been warned about feeding." His corded throat twisted, jerking at an unusual angle, as if something inside him was trying to fight its way out. "Warned about not… not taking the things we need." A slow, evil grin spread across his wide mouth. "You wanna know what I need? You under me. Screaming. Bleeding. Just like that sister of yours bled for Josef."

Closing her eyes, Olivia fought a rising wave of nausea. Her relief that he'd forgotten about Jamie in his blood-frenzy was sharp—and yet she couldn't help but be terrified by his words. "How did you find me?" She finally managed to scrape out the words, forcing her lids to crack open. Better to keep an eye on him, since she didn't have any idea when he would lose control and attack.

A low, arrogant laugh rumbled up from his chest. "I've been on your trail for hours. Just waiting. Biding my time." He lifted one clawed hand, wiping the back of his wrist over his damp mouth. "When those trucks pulled in, the opportunity was too good to resist."

"So you came by yourself, then?"

"There's no one else," he muttered, his claws making

a clicking sound as he flexed his fingers. "Only me. I didn't want to risk anyone else getting in my way."

A flash of movement just to his left caught her eye, and to her horror she spotted Jamie peeking out from behind the nearest oak tree. *No!* Instead of running away, the little girl had stayed, probably afraid to leave Olivia alone with the monster.

As if fate was determined to conspire against her, the wind suddenly surged from the east, brushing past Jamie's dark curls, and the Casus froze, his eyes narrowing as he whipped his head in Jamie's direction. "Where do you think you're going? Get over here, you little brat. I didn't say you could go anywhere."

"Jamie, run!" she screamed, reaching out and wrapping her arms around his left leg. Olivia knew, in the back of her mind, that she wasn't strong enough to hold him, but that didn't mean she wasn't going to try. She'd bite and scratch and kick if she had to. She was more than willing to let the bastard rip her to shreds, so long as it meant Jamie could get away. Her heart twisted as she thought of never seeing Aiden again, but she knew he would understand. That he would have done the same thing if it meant protecting a child. "Get out of here! Run back to Aiden!"

"Shut up," the Casus snarled, reaching down and twisting his gnarled, claw-tipped fingers in Olivia's hair. He wrenched her to her feet, pulling a low groan from her throat. Jamie screamed, running toward them, only to be stopped when Noah suddenly burst through the trees, putting his tall body in front of the little girl as he leveled a gun at the Casus's chest. Olivia nearly sagged with relief, her wild gaze scanning the trees, searching for the others. Where was Aiden? Kellan?

"Jamie," Noah said in a low, easy voice, "I want you to stay behind me. You got that, honey?"

The Casus curled his lip, eyeing Noah with a hot, malevolent stare. "Well, look who it is. You're like a bad penny, Winston. You just keep turning up. First Washington. Now here. If I didn't know better, I'd think you had a thing for me."

"We have you surrounded." Noah's deep voice rang with cool, steady confidence. "Let the woman go."

"I don't think so," the Casus drawled, bringing her closer to his body. "I like her right where she is." His voice sank to a sneer. "I gotta tell ya, Calder has big things planned for your family, half-breed."

Noah lifted his brows, looking for all the world as if he was discussing nothing more interesting than the weather. "Calder? Oh…yeah, I remember. From what the other Casus have said, we figure he's some kind of chicken-shit leader who's still hiding out in Meridian, too afraid to show his face."

The Casus snorted. "Be cocky now, human. But when Calder finally comes across, maybe it'll be your pretty little face he's wearing."

Olivia reeled, unable to believe what she was hearing.

Looking between Noah and the Casus, there was no denying that their eyes were the exact same icy, piercing shade of blue. Understanding slowly dawned, and she swallowed the bile that rose in her throat, a new flavor to the panic that had seized her body and her mind. She got it now—why Noah had always seemed a little something *more* than human. He was descended from a human female who had been raped by one of the Casus monsters before they'd been imprisoned, which meant that his family could act as hosts to the escaping Casus shades.

Her thoughts spun as she tried to wrap her mind around it—the fact that one of Aiden's friends could actually become one of the bad guys. That Noah was a walking human shell for the monsters. Hysterical, she struggled in the Casus's hold, her eyes tearing from the pain as he pulled her hair even tighter, the tips of her toes only just brushing the ground. She fought harder, driven by the knowledge that she had to reach Jamie. Had to get her out of there, away from the madness and the danger.

"I told you to shut up," the Casus snarled in her face, shaking her, and she realized the screams filling her head were her own. "Stop the bloody screaming or I'll—"

"You won't be doing anything," Kellan barked in a hard, deep voice, "except what I tell you to do."

Kellan! Olivia's eyes went wide when she spotted the auburn-haired Lycan moving in from the Casus's right side with his gun held in front of him, the barrel pointed directly at the monster's chest, same as Noah's. The Casus turned his head, a low, gritty bark of laughter slipping from his lips, as if he thought the situation was funny. "You shoot me," he drawled, scraping the claws of his other hand lightly across her throat, "and there's no telling what will happen to Olivia here."

The monster took a step back, dragging her with him, and from the corner of her eye she saw Noah take a step toward Jamie, who had moved off to his left so that she could see what was happening. The rational part of Olivia's brain knew he just wanted to put himself between her niece and the Casus, but she couldn't stifle the scream that stopped him in his tracks, the words ripping up out of her, unstoppable and cruel. "Don't touch her! Just… just stay away from her!"

Noah's face pulled tight, but he didn't argue. He simply raised his free hand in a sign of consent, letting her know he wouldn't move any closer to Jamie.

The Casus barked another low laugh and shook his head. "So judgmental," he drawled, the truth of his words only intensifying the guilty, sour feeling in her stomach. She blinked away the tears blurring her vision, still scanning the edges of the clearing, searching for Aiden. Why wasn't he there? Had something happened to him? Had he decided she wasn't worth the trouble?

A sharp pain twisted through her middle—this one born completely from emotion, rather than a physical wound—and she swallowed, silently praying that he would appear with the next heavy beat of her heart. She took a deep, shuddering breath, and then she felt it, as if there was something electric in the air. She could taste it on her tongue. Feel it shivering across her skin. A heavy, pervasive sense of something powerful watching from the shadowed woods, silently waiting. Was it Aiden? Or someone else? Friend…or enemy?

Kellan still had his gun trained on the Casus, and he lifted the barrel, aiming it right at the monster's temple. "Where are your Kraven buddies? The Collective soldiers who follow you guys around, cleaning up your messes?"

"I left them behind." The claws at her throat made a sickening pass down the front of her body, sweeping low across her pelvis, and she sucked in her breath, wondering if Kellan would take his shot. But he waited, obviously too afraid of the Casus cutting her open.

"Not very smart of you to come without your pals," Kellan drawled, arching one auburn brow.

"I'm not afraid of a few Watchmen," he claimed with cocky arrogance. "And I wanted to make sure I had the human bitch to myself before handing over the kid. Me and her are gonna have a real special time together," he added, snickering under his breath.

A deep, chilling snarl suddenly rumbled in the branches above their heads, the thick sound reminding Olivia of some kind of predatory jungle cat, feral and wild and deadly. As the Casus's gaze swung upward, toward the lofty branches, she twisted to her right, bringing her left knee up and slamming it into the bastard's groin. He grunted in pain, his hold on her hair loosening as he hunched forward, and she was able to drop to the ground. She'd just rolled to her back when he let out a blood-curdling roar, pulling back one claw-tipped arm as he prepared to swipe at her, his face twisted into a grotesque expression of hatred and rage. Opening her mouth, Olivia was ready to scream for Kellan to shoot, when Aiden's body went soaring over her head, as if he'd launched himself from one of the trees. Her mouth fell open in shock as she realized he must have been hiding among the highest branches, waiting for the perfect moment to strike. His trajectory should have had him crashing straight into the Casus, but he twisted at the last second in a sinuous, catlike move, swiping a lethal-looking set of claws across the monster's gut before landing with perfect balance on the balls of his feet.

"Well, if it isn't the kitty," the Casus sneered, clutching one clawed hand against his shredded stomach. Blood oozed through his fingers, dripping onto the leaf-covered ground. "I was wondering when you were going to show up."

"Get away from him, Liv." Aiden didn't take his glittering amber gaze off the Casus as he spoke to her, his claws battle-ready at his sides, long fangs glistening beneath the curve of his upper lip.

"She can run, but you can't protect her," the monster drawled, stepping to the side.

"Like hell I can't." Aiden's mouth curled in a mean smile, the hungry glint in his golden eyes giving the impression that he couldn't wait for the fight to begin as he countered the Casus's move. Pushing herself to her feet, Olivia ran for Jamie, while keeping one eye on Aiden. She was mesmerized by the sight of him. By the raw, animal intensity of his rage.

"You kill me," the Casus rasped, "and something so much worse is going to come for her. He'll tear her apart, piece by piece, and laugh while he's doing it."

Aiden flexed his claws, his muscles bulging beneath the dark sheen of his skin. "He'll have to get through us first, and that's not gonna happen."

"You won't be able to stop him." His skin began to ripple, as if something was moving around inside him, and Olivia shoved Jamie behind her, knowing he was getting ready to change into his Casus form. "He'll find her, take her and then she's gonna bleed for him like a stuck pig," he added, his voice turning deeper, grittier, the shape of his mouth changing as bones began to pop and crack, reshaping themselves into something monstrous. "And knowing Josef, he'll make sure the kid is there to see the whole show. Hell, he might even decide to take the little witch for himself."

Aiden went deathly still, sliding a dark, tortured look

toward her and Jamie. Then, in the blink of an eye, he was across the clearing and yanking the Casus off his feet. Stunned, Olivia watched him drag the monster into the trees, both of them disappearing from sight.

"Aiden!" she cried out, lifting Jamie into her arms and covering her little ears so that the child couldn't hear the horrific sounds tearing through the woods. There were low, gritty words that she couldn't understand, followed by vicious snarls and stark, screaming cries of pain. "What's happening?" she gasped, taking a step forward, terrified that Aiden was going to be hurt. "What is he doing?"

"Leave him," Kellan muttered, grabbing hold of her arm.

"What?" She whipped around, thinking the Watchman must have lost his mind. "Leave him? Are you crazy? That thing was already changing form!"

Another high-pitched cry cut through the forest, followed by a deep, menacing growl. "Aiden's got it under control," Kellan grunted, slanting a meaningful look toward Jamie. She understood what he didn't want to say in front of the little girl. That Aiden wouldn't be coming back until he'd destroyed the Casus, sending its shade back to Meridian.

"Oh, God," she whispered, feeling as if her knees were going to give out. She didn't know if she was going into shock, but she was acutely aware of her body slipping away from her. *Or maybe it's simply the ground slipping away,* she thought fuzzily, tightening her arms around Jamie's body just as Kellan caught hold of her shoulders.

"I'll get them back to the car," he said in a low voice, glancing at Noah. "You stay here. Try to get Morgan on the phone and let her know what's happened. Then wait for him to finish."

As more guttural roars ripped through the forest, Kellan lifted her and Jamie into his arms…then got them the hell out of there.

CHAPTER SIXTEEN

Iowa
Sunday night

STRANGE HOW ONE SMALL, innocuous event, like over-throwing a ball, could lead to such terror. Olivia had never known fear like she had in those minutes that she'd spent with the Casus—and she still hadn't managed to get over it. Even now, hours later, her hands continued to shake.

By the time Kellan had carried her and Jamie through the forest and back to the rest stop, Morgan Cantrell had arrived and was waiting for them, having already spoken to Noah on her phone. She'd parked in the far corner of the parking lot, and the falling twilight had offered a measure of privacy as she'd used her well-stocked first aid kit to tend to Olivia's bleeding arm. After giving her a shot of antibiotics, the slender shape-shifter had cleansed the wound, then used a row of small, neat stitches to hold it together. Olivia had sat through the entire process in a numb state of shock, while Kellan talked to Jamie, promising her that Aiden was going to make it back safe and sound.

The instant Morgan was finished bandaging her arm, they had quickly taken to the road. Olivia and Jamie had ridden with Kellan in her car, and Morgan followed in a rental. When Noah finally called Kellan's cell phone, letting them know that the Casus was dead and that he and Aiden were heading back to the truck, Olivia had nearly sobbed with relief. She'd spent the next hour of the drive just talking to Jamie, and was immeasurably thankful, if not a little surprised, to find that her niece was handling the aftermath better than she was. Olivia didn't know if it was Jamie's Mallory blood that enabled her to process the terrifying event so quickly and put it behind her, or if the little girl was simply burying the trauma, but she couldn't argue the fact that Jamie appeared to feel safe and secure. When Jamie had finally asked to watch a movie, Kellan had done his best to keep Olivia occupied with conversation, probably so that she wouldn't have time to think about what had happened and freak out on him. But she'd been able to learn a lot from their talks.

The first thing Kellan had done was explain about Noah, and she'd winced every time she recalled how she'd reacted when the Casus had revealed the truth about Noah's bloodline. She'd asked questions about his family, and had learned that he had several siblings back at home in California. When he'd joined forces with their Watchmen unit and the Buchanans to fight against the Casus, he'd left the running of his Bay Area bar in the hands of his youngest brother, and had quickly proven himself a valuable addition to their team. According to Kellan, Noah was determined to keep his family from being used as "meat puppets" by the Casus, and Olivia didn't blame him.

They'd also talked about the search for the Markers, and Kellan had explained why they couldn't just use modern equipment, such as metal detectors, to locate a cross once they had an idea of its location. Apparently they'd run extensive tests back at Ravenswing on the first Marker that Saige had found, and discovered that the crosses were made of some kind of strange alloy they hadn't been able to identify, almost as if the materials used in their composition were "not of this earth." In each of their tests, technology had proven useless in the recovery of the crosses—which meant they would just have to keep on digging for them the old-fashioned way.

Olivia had also asked about the mysterious maps Saige Buchanan had found, and had been given a quick explanation regarding the unusual powers that the Buchanan siblings possessed. She'd learned that Ian sometimes had instances of precognition in his dreams, while Riley's telekinetic powers enabled him to control physical objects with his mind, and Saige's power made it possible for her to "hear" objects when she touched them.

Then Kellan had gone back to the topic of the maps, explaining that Westmore had actually managed to steal them during Saige's awakening, though Aiden and his friends had eventually gotten them back. And even though the Watchmen were sure that Westmore had made copies of the maps while they were in his possession, they were holding on to the hope that it would take him a long time to crack the complicated code they were written in, the way Saige had done with the use of her power. But Kellan also admitted that there was something more about the situation that bothered them. According to the Watchman, Westmore had actually tried to kidnap him while they were searching for the third Marker in Washington, in hopes that he could exchange Kellan for the key to the code. But since that time, no other attempts had been made to take any hostages from their unit, which raised the question of why. One of the obvious conclusions was that Westmore no longer felt he needed to make the exchange, which meant that he was more than likely on to the way to decoding the maps himself.

The last question she'd asked the Watchman, just before they'd stopped for the night, was why he hadn't shot the Casus when he'd had the chance, and Kellan had responded with a wry, gruff bark of laughter, saying, "I wanted to drill the ugly son of a bitch with a bullet so bad

I could taste it, but Aiden had made it clear that he wanted the bastard for himself. Still, I'd have taken the shot there at the end, if Ade hadn't been about to make his move."

It was after ten now, and Olivia found herself sitting at a kitchen table in yet another hotel suite, surrounded by calming shades of blue and cream, while inside her head everything was still flashing with bright, chaotic streaks of orange and red and yellow. Noah and Aiden had arrived not long after them, but she hadn't had a chance to talk to Aiden. He'd headed straight for one of the rooms, not even making eye contact with her, though he'd stopped long enough to lean down and give Jamie a fierce hug that had nearly brought tears to Olivia's eyes.

After Aiden had locked himself away, Olivia had pulled Noah aside and apologized profusely for her earlier behavior, admitting that she had no excuse for reacting the way she had. He'd accepted her apology with an easy smile and told her not to worry about it, claiming he would have done the same in her situation. Undone by his kindness, Olivia had started crying again as she argued that he was letting her off far too easily, and he'd laughed as he'd given her a brotherly hug, promising her that his feelings weren't hurt—then teasingly accused her of trying to ruin his tough-guy reputation by insinuating that he had feelings to begin with.

Seeing as it had been hours since any of them had eaten, they'd ordered in room service, no one up to heading over to the hotel's restaurant, and then Jamie had cuddled up on the sofa and quickly fallen asleep. Despite the stormy weather, Kellan and Noah had gone out to run patrol, and Olivia had a feeling they'd asked the female Watchman to keep an eye on her while they were gone. Not that she minded. She actually liked Morgan, and found her easy to get along with. Though the woman was incredibly beautiful—tall and slender, with shadowy gray eyes and a heart-shaped face—she had a friendly, comfortable way about her that made her seem like one of those people you'd known forever, even when you'd only just met.

They'd been sharing some quiet conversation about little things, from movies to music to their favorite drinks at Starbucks, but no matter how hard Olivia tried, she couldn't keep her eyes off Aiden's bedroom door. Couldn't stop remembering how he'd looked when he'd faced off against the Casus that afternoon. He'd been vicious and violent in his fury, but breathtaking, too, in a beautiful, visceral way. She desperately wanted to go to him, but feared his rejection. He hadn't even spared her a glance when he'd come in, making it clear that he wanted nothing to do with her. When Kellan had caught her shattered expression, he'd told her not to worry about it, claiming that Aiden was just crashing after the adrenaline high. But she wasn't convinced.

She hadn't forgotten the look in his eyes when he'd slid that last dark glance toward her and Jamie, before dragging the Casus away to kill him. There'd been fury there, as well as something *more*. Something that had reached into her chest and fisted around her heart like a physical pain.

And it was still hurting. Aching.

Carefully lifting the mug that Morgan had set in front of her, Olivia took a sip of tea and winced from the throbbing in her wounded arm...then winced again as a muted crash came from behind Aiden's door, a strange, almost animal-like sound bleeding through the walls. "Something's wrong with him," she whispered, tightening her fingers around the warm mug.

Morgan gave a delicate snort. "Yeah. He had the crap scared out of him today. As far as wake-up calls go, this one was probably like a knife in the ribs."

Olivia chewed on the corner of her mouth as another strange sound reached their ears, this one pitched low, as if something were in pain. She couldn't help but wonder what had happened when he'd been alone with the Casus. Had something been said that upset him? Something about her sisters? Or Jamie?

Morgan leaned forward in her chair, bracing her crossed arms on the pine tabletop. "You should go to him, Liv. I'm sure today was rough on him. Ade doesn't handle things very well that have to do with kids."

Her gaze flew toward the other woman, wide with curiosity. "What do you mean?"

"He tends to lose it when he sees a child hurt or in

danger. I know any sane person would, but it gets to him in a way that's hard to explain."

Olivia recalled touching his scarred wrist in the truck and how he'd said the marks were made when he was young, as well as his claim to have killed the ones responsible, and though she'd been doing her best to fight it, an idea began to take form in her mind. One that was too horrific to even contemplate. But she couldn't stop herself from asking, "What happened to him?"

Morgan leaned back in her chair, clutching her tea against her chest, her eyes sad as she stared at the red poppies decorating the mug's surface. "It's Aiden's story to tell. But he's more than just a pretty face and a smart-ass attitude." She lifted her gaze, her mouth curling in a lopsided smile. "If you want my opinion, he's used a long list of nameless bimbos over the years to try and help him forget, but it hasn't worked. He locks it down, but eventually something happens that makes it all come bubbling back to the surface. Something like today."

"Used them? You mean for sex?"

Morgan gave another soft, feminine snort. "You know how guys think, as if the answer to everything is hanging between their legs. And for a Prime, like Aiden, it's even worse. Their sex drives are legendary among the clans, rivaling even that of the Merrick and the Deschanel."

So many questions rushed through her mind, tripping over themselves in their eagerness to be answered. What was a Prime? Why did it make his sexual needs so intense? But the one Olivia found herself asking was "Are you saying that he needs sex tonight?" The words came out shaky and low, her mind suddenly filling with the memory of how easily he'd dragged the Casus out of the clearing that afternoon. Shuddering, she broke out in a piercing wave of chills. She knew that Aiden would never hurt her, but she couldn't help wondering what it would be like to experience even a fraction of the power he was capable of.

"I'm saying that he needs *you.*"

Knowing Morgan could probably read every ounce of longing on her face, she looked toward his door again, then back toward the sofa where Jamie was cuddled up sucking her thumb, her small arm strangling the teddy bear Aiden had bought for her.

"Go on," Morgan said in a soft voice. "I'll stay here and keep an eye on Jamie for you."

"Thanks," she whispered, her heart beating like a hummingbird's wings as she pushed back her chair and stood up. One more question lingered on the tip of her tongue, since she still wasn't sure exactly what kind of animal Aiden carried inside him. But she was too nervous to get the words out. The Casus had called him "kitty," but that still left open a world of head-spinning possibilities. Lions. Tigers. Leopards. Jaguars and pumas and panthers.

As if reading her mind, Morgan said, "Whatever you find in there, don't be scared. Sometimes, after a fight, it's necessary for our kind to unwind a bit. But it's still Aiden, and you know he'd rather die than hurt you."

Olivia gave a slow nod as she moved across the room on trembling legs, wondering exactly what Morgan meant by "unwind." Without giving herself time to worry about it, she took hold of the doorknob, twisted and walked into his room. Darkness stole her sight, but she pushed the door shut behind her. Pale slivers of moonlight peeked from around the edges of the drapes, and as she waited, her eyes slowly began to make sense of the shadows. She could hear the harsh, heavy staccato of Aiden's breathing on the other side of the room, but couldn't see him. Not yet. Then he stalked forward, moving into one of the milky streams of light, and a massive orange-and-black-striped tiger filled her vision, its huge paws padding silently over the carpeted floor.

It came to a stop in the center of the room, and all Olivia could think was *Oh, my God. Ohmygod... Ohmygod...Ohmygod...*

The animal's massive head was cocked a little to the side, and its bright amber eyes stared back at her, sharp with intelligence, glittering with awareness. As he stood there in the pale glow of light, she had the strangest sense that he wanted to come closer, but was wary of how she would respond. Of frightening her away.

It took a moment to find her voice, but she finally managed to say, "So I g-guess I was more right than I'd realized when I c-called you a tomcat, huh?"

He chuffed a rough sound under his breath, almost as if he was laughing. But there was a shadow of something dark hanging over him, the intensity of his emotions blasting against her like a physical force. She could see the longing in his eyes. Could sense how badly he needed comfort, someone to hold on to him, and her fear melted away like snowflakes beneath the burning warmth of the sun.

With her back braced against the door, Olivia slid down to the floor and stretched out one hand, calling him to her with the silent offering. He came forward slowly...cautiously, until his fur-covered head nuzzled against her chest. She funneled her fingers through the soft, thick fur on the back of his strong neck, feeling the powerful shift of muscle beneath his hot skin as he drew in a series of deep, ragged breaths. And then, like a dam cracking apart, allowing the rushing waters to flood through, she began to cry. Fat, salty tears that she had no hope of stopping or controlling. She wasn't even sure she could explain what the tears were for, understanding only that they were as essential as the air shuddering in her lungs, the blood coursing through her veins.

Then the unthinkable happened, and Olivia could have sworn that he started to cry, too. The sounds were rougher than human tears, rawer, like something angry and hard being shredded inside him, and her heart softened in a warm, breathtaking wave of tenderness, until it was nothing more than a hot, burning glow in her chest. "It's okay," she whispered, stroking his fur as she curved herself over him, around him, cradling him in her arms. "I'm here. I won't leave you."

Hours could have crept by, or perhaps only a handful of minutes. Olivia didn't know, and she didn't care. She was content to be where she was, whispering to him in the darkness, careful to keep her voice soft…soothing, gentling him until his breathing had grown calm. Eventually he lifted his head, the tiger's face close to hers as he stared deep into her eyes. He cocked his head a little to the side again, and she gave him a trembling, watery smile.

"You're so b-beautiful," she whispered, running her fingertips over his face, awed by the sheer, miraculous wonder of him. She had thought she would be terrified if she ever saw him in his animal form. That the beast would be foreign…unknown. But it was no stranger who stared back at her through those golden, hypnotic eyes. It was Aiden, and in that instant the horrifying realization burned through Olivia's mind that she was falling in love with him. The crazy, rushing, head-over-heels kind of falling that she couldn't defend against, couldn't fight. "I think…" She swallowed, working for her broken voice. "I think you're the most beautiful thing I've ever seen."

He gave a deep, rumbling purr, then licked the side of her face.

"Uck," she groaned, laughing as she wiped away the

tiger drool, and again she could have sworn the rough sound he made deep in his chest was laughter. In that moment, everything inside her churned into a desperate, needy ache that only he could ease, and she knew that she was tired of running from the inevitable. Tired of fighting what she wanted so badly to happen.

Olivia ran her hands down the sides of his face, his throat, her voice trembling with raw, devastating need as she said, "Change back, Aiden. Now. Change back for me."

He looked away, tensing, and she grabbed his thick fur, pulling until he was staring at her again. "Change back," she whispered, holding nothing back, letting everything she felt inside bleed into her expression. "I need you here with me. Right now."

He shuddered beneath her hands, then pulled away, slipping out of her hold. Panicking, she scrambled to her knees, ready to chase him down, until she realized he was already shifting back to his human shape, right before her eyes. It felt as if she'd fallen into some kind of magical universe as she watched thick fur melt into sleek, silken skin, his bones cracking as they reshaped themselves into the familiar, breathtaking body that never ceased to dazzle her, melting her down into a thick, molten burn of hunger and lust. As his muscles rippled beneath his skin, he fell away from her, sprawling across the floor on his back, the pale streams of moonlight illuminating his dark, dangerous beauty.

Before he'd even fully completed the change, Olivia crawled over him, straddling his ridged stomach, her hands reaching for his damp face. He shuddered beneath her, his golden eyes suddenly popping open, and he grasped her wrists, locking them in a manacle grip before she could touch him.

From one instant to the next, his expression turned savage, and he curled his lip. "I can't believe I let that happen today." The words emerged in a low, seething snarl, and he grasped her upper arms, giving her a little shake. "It was so stupid. I should have kept you locked in the truck. You both could have been killed. I could have lost you!"

"It wasn't your fault," she argued, fighting against his hold, mindless of the pain in her arm. "Damn it, Aiden. Let go of me and let me touch you."

His eyes squeezed closed as his head fell back against the floor, tendons straining in his throat from the arched position of his neck, his hands still gripping her arms, holding her away from him. "You shouldn't want me." Dull, emotionless words, as if *he* was the one shutting down now. "Not after what happened. Not after tonight. After seeing me like this."

Frustration welled up like a froth of lava getting ready to explode. "Why? Because you've shown you have emotions like the rest of us?" she burst out in a hot, angry rush, struggling against his hold even harder. "God, you alphas are so thickheaded sometimes! Now, let go of me before I scream!"

He released his hold on her arms and opened his eyes, his expression painfully grim as he dropped his hands to the floor. They curled into hard, tight fists, his body rigid beneath her, caught on a knife's edge between need and rage. "Get out of here, Liv. Now."

She lifted her chin, refusing to budge from her perch on his stomach. "No. I'm not going to go running just because you're in a foul mood. So you got upset? So what? What's the big freaking deal?"

"It's dangerous to let out what's inside me." His breath jerked in his lungs, lifting his chest, his golden eyes burning with frustration and fury and lust. "Trust me, Liv. It isn't all teary and tender. Most of it's ugly and raw and black. Most of it would scare the shit out of you."

"You don't scare me, Aiden. In fact, I'll show you just how *not* scared I am of you," she snapped, caught up in a complicated, powerful knot of desperation and love as she leaned down to press an openmouthed kiss against his left nipple. He reacted with a sharp jolt, as if he'd been struck by a crackling surge of electricity.

"What are you doing?" he snarled, staring with narrowed, suspicious eyes as she began to scoot back, kissing her way down his beautiful, muscular body. His massive erection jerked and pulsed between them as she kissed her way over his ribs, lingering on a smooth, curving scar. When her tongue dipped playfully into his belly button, the guttural sound that crawled up his throat was only part man. It should have terrified her, the sheer animal savagery of that sound, but it didn't. If anything, it only made her hotter…hungrier.

"Answer me, damn it." He was drenched with sweat, his eyes flashing between those of the man and the beast as she dared a quick glance up at his face, watching as his anger reshaped itself into something dark and erotic. "What the hell are you doing, Liv?"

With his hot male scent filling her head, she scooted lower, pressing a tender kiss to the healing welt on his thigh. The mind-boggling length of his erection bobbed at the edge of her vision, rising from its thick nest of caramel-colored curls, and she couldn't wait to touch it. Hold it. "You're a smart guy, Aiden. Figure it out," she said in a low voice just as she wrapped her cool hand around the heavy, vein-ridden shaft. His body went completely rigid, held in a straining vise of control, his eyes shocked wide, still red from his tears, but it only made him sexier, that ragged edge of emotion adding a fierceness to his features that spiked her need even higher. Or maybe that was just the excitement of holding him in her hand. The heady anticipation of knowing that she was going to take him into her mouth. Her body. Or maybe it was everything. God, all he had to do was look at her and she was ready, more turned on than she'd ever been before.

Salty drops of moisture leaked from the shaft's swollen, plum-sized head, and she used them to lube her hand, making her palm wet enough to glide along his length in a smooth, slick pumping action that had his lips pulling back over his sharp white teeth. His powerful body shuddered beneath her, his thick, ropy muscles defined in sharp relief beneath the burnished silk of his skin. And his eyes…his eyes burned with a hunger that was so savage and raw, she could only marvel at its existence.

"Last chance, Liv. You need to get up and walk out of here. Right now. Or it's going to be too late."

"It was too late for me the second I set eyes on you," she whispered, feeling as if she'd been caught up in a whirlpool that was sucking her down deeper…and deeper. But she wasn't fighting the current. She wanted to be pulled under. Wanted to be battered by the waves, crushed by the stunning force of the currents. She wanted to be swept away. Lost. Taken.

And she wanted it now.

"I'm not going anywhere," she told him, holding his burning gaze as she leaned down and licked the heavy, glistening head of his cock, the resulting tremor that shot through his body making her smile. "Not until we've finished what we've started, Ade."

CHAPTER SEVENTEEN

WONDERING WHERE the shy, stammering kindergarten teacher had gone, Aiden glared down at the stunning seductress, who was driving him out of his mind, her touch so damn good his eyes were nearly rolling back in his head. "You put your mouth on me again," he forced out through his gritted teeth, "and I won't be responsible for what happens. You understand me? And you're not ready for it, Liv."

"Like hell I'm not." A flash of temper sparked through her violet gaze, along with a heavy dose of frustration.

Reaching down, he fisted the fingers of his right hand in the silky strands of her hair, his voice a rough, guttural rasp as he tried once more to give her fair warning of what she was getting herself into. "I won't be able to control myself, which means it's not gonna be some sweet, easy ride. It's gonna be me covering you, holding you down, buried about a mile in your body, going at you as hard as I can."

"Good. Because that's how I want it."

Aiden eyed her warily, afraid to believe what she'd just said. The staggering implications behind her husky words. That this was actually going to happen, here and now.

He was too on edge to handle it, still reeling from the crazy, chaotic storm of emotion he'd been dealing with since the moment he'd realized that she and Jamie had been taken. The stark, chilling terror that had ripped him apart. Then finding that bastard with his hands on her. Hearing the vile things he'd said. It'd been like slipping into the most excruciating, heinous depths of hell, and now he'd been transported to heaven.

It made his head spin. Made him feel as if he was going to burst from his skin.

She tilted her head, pulling against his grip, and softly said, "Now let go of my hair, Aiden."

Struggling to keep himself as controlled as possible, he carefully exhaled the deep breath he hadn't even realized he was holding and relaxed his fingers. She pulled away a little, the silken strands of dark red slipping from his hold. Then she sent him a slow, hungry smile that made his muscles seize…and lowered her head again. Holding his narrow-eyed gaze, she opened her mouth and touched her tongue to the strained, damp head of his cock, the eager look in her eyes telling him that she was more than ready to handle the consequences of her actions. Lust erupted through his body with such savage, violent intensity that it arched his back, the sharp action nearly knocking her away. She gripped his hip with one hand to steady herself and opened her mouth wider.

"Deeper," he growled, her soft moan making him see red as she took him in. "Suck it hard. You won't hurt me. The harder you suck it, the better it fee—" He broke off, roaring, as his head fell back, a thick surge of hot fluid blasting into her mouth, though he hadn't come. Not completely. Not yet. When his beast was so close to the surface, his orgasms changed, becoming different, building up in sharp, wrenching bursts until he finally crashed over the edge in what would undoubtedly be an explosive, jaw-grinding release.

"I'm not done," he grunted, just in case she got the wrong idea and stopped, thinking he'd come—but she didn't question him about what had happened...or pull away. He spread his legs and she slipped between them, managing to work another inch into her hot little mouth. Reaching down, Aiden tangled both hands in the damp strands of her hair, pulling it away from her face so that he could watch her, the slick, wet suction breaking him down, destroying him.

"Wrap your hands around the base," he groaned, each word punctuated by a hard, gasping breath. "I need to push, but don't want to go too far."

She understood, sliding her hands down to the thick root, and his hips surged up, thrusting his cock past those lush, tender lips. Aiden had already known that it was too good for him to take much more, that he was pushing his control, and then she flicked her smoky gaze up to his face, her heavy-lidded eyes dark with pleasure, as if she was actually getting off on going down on him, and he almost lost it. "Stop," he growled, tugging on her hair, only seconds away from coming. "Liv. Stop!"

She pulled away, but not far, her shiny lips hovering over the dark, moist head of his shaft, her warm breath brushing against him as she said, "I don't want to stop. I want you to finish in my mouth."

"Next time," he snarled. "Next time I'll do whatever the hell you want. But right now I just need to be in you."

Instead of giving her time to argue, Aiden burst into action. Within seconds he had their positions reversed, her jeans unsnapped, unzipped and wrenched down her legs, along with a tiny pink pair of panties. Then he spread her legs, his chest working like a bellows as he knelt between her pale thighs, his burning gaze riveted on that sweet piece of flesh nestled beneath soft strawberry curls. He wanted to tell her how beautiful she was, how perfect, but the words were jammed up in his throat and he couldn't get them out. All he could do was make a rough purring sound that vibrated in his chest as he dug his hands into those soft white thighs, leaned down and licked the thick, juicy seam of her sex, working her open with his tongue. Hot, honeyed moisture wet his mouth, and he nearly cried with relief.

"You're ready," he grunted, mounting her, his hard thighs shoving her legs wider.

"Aiden...a condom?" she gasped, her damp palms clutching his biceps, her short nails digging deliciously into his skin as she arched beneath him.

"Shit. Right. Sorry," he muttered. Lust had obviously fried his friggin' brain, and as he reached for his bag at the foot of the bed, rooting in the side pocket for a rubber, he could only shake his head at himself. What had happened to the hard, detached bastard who never let anything get under his skin? Who never let anything or anyone rattle his composure? He didn't know. All he knew was that he was treading into treacherous territory with each hard, ragged breath jerking from his lungs, but he didn't care.

Refusing to whine like a pathetic loser, Aiden concentrated instead on the white-hot goddess sprawled before him, so perfect and sweet and gorgeous, he couldn't understand what she was doing there with a twisted, screwed-up jackass like him. But he wasn't going to question it. Later he could bitch and moan about things that could never be, but right now he was going to wallow in bliss and pretend, for a few stolen moments, that he could have everything he wanted.

With the condom firmly in place, he ran his hands up the smooth surface of her inner thighs, over the graceful curve of her hips, until his fingers were resting against the soft, velvety skin of her stomach. "You have no idea how bad it's been hurting, waiting to get you like this."

"It's been hurting me, too," she whispered, her lips curved in a provocative smile, her nipples thick and hard beneath her sweater. She wanted him, and the knowledge made Aiden want to roar with primal satisfaction. It also made him desperate as hell. Grasping handfuls of her sweater, he wrenched the soft wool up the sensual line of her torso, his only moment of caution when he slipped it over her head and carefully pulled the sweater down her injured forearm. Her bra quickly followed, and the sight of her naked breasts nearly killed him. Just about stopped his heart.

He was, by some miracle of biology, even harder than before. And his control was completely shot. He couldn't think, couldn't breathe. And he sure as hell couldn't stop.

One second he was rubbing his tongue against a sweet, berry-red nipple, stroking the head of his cock through her pink, slick folds, and in the next, he was driving in too hard, too deep, too quickly. She cried out, stiffening beneath him, and Aiden silently cursed himself for being so careless. He had to remember what she was. Human. Breakable. And he was an animal who liked to play rough.

"Damn it," he rasped, while the rawest, most intense wave of pleasure he'd ever experienced scraped down his nerve endings, just from being inside her. A part of her. It all but turned him inside out, and he struggled to hold himself still. "I didn't…I didn't mean to do that."

"You just caught me by surprise, but it's okay," she whispered, running her soft fingertips down the hot sides of his face, the tender touches so at odds with the sharp, visceral urges twisting him up inside, demanding satisfaction. "Trust me, Aiden. Okay doesn't even begin to cover it."

The way she moaned those husky words pushed him further over the edge, shoving him into that dark, feral place that was all hunger and craving and lust, and he found himself pulling back, then lunging back in with a hard, hammering thrust that nearly took him to the root. "S-sorry," he groaned against the side of her throat, bracing himself on his elbows. "Sorry. It just…it keeps getting away from me. You okay?"

"Better than okay," she gasped, her pale fingers digging into his shoulders as she arched against him in a sweet, sensual act of submission that drove him out of his mind. He pushed himself up on his arms and pulled his hips back again, until only the head of his cock remained snugged up inside her. Then he looked down between their bodies, staring at the way he stretched her open as he fed himself back into her, inch by inch, her glistening flesh straining around him. She was so beautiful it dazed him, as if he'd been slammed by some metaphysical hammer upside his head. He tried to drag in air. Couldn't. But hell, who needed air anyway? All he needed was this. Liv pinned beneath him, her pale body naked and held wide open to him. His cock buried hard and deep in that most precious, succulent part of her, clasped tight in the cushioned depths of her body, where she was liquid and melting and soft.

"It's too good," he panted, pulling back…thrusting, riding her hard…harder, pumping into her, the heavy rhythm shoving her across the carpeted floor. "I need more," he growled. "Need all of you."

And she gave it to him, a total surrender of self that made his brain melt down. His eyes burned, his throat, his muscles and skin and blood, his body sweat-slick and heavy as he moved over her, stirring her up inside, forcing her to take more of him with each grinding, slamming thrust. Rough, animalistic sounds jerked from his throat as she clutched him, pumping her hips up to meet him, making him crazed. He'd been so terrified that when this moment came, the beast would be doing everything it could to claw its way out of him. But for the moment, the creature was as dazed as he was. It purred with pleasure, drunk on lust, moving with him, beneath his skin, as desperate for her as the man. He growled as another thick burst of fluid pulsed from his body, into the condom, and he buried himself deep, shuddering against her, his breath jerking from his lungs in sharp, violent gasps.

She blinked up at him, curious, waiting to see what he would do.

"Not done with you," he muttered, barely managing to force out the rough, guttural words. He started moving again in hard, heavy lunges, loving the way he had to work against her body's natural resistance, fighting to get inside her. "This isn't over till you come for me, Liv."

A flare of panic chased away the pleasure blush burning in her cheeks, her small white teeth sinking into her lower lip. She was so easy to read like this, her emotions blazing up at him, bright as the stars in a winter sky. He could see her self-doubt, the shades of self-consciousness that had always made her too tense to enjoy sex. To just let herself go. On the one hand Aiden was outraged that she'd been denied something so many others took for granted, while on the other, there was a part of him that was savagely thrilled by the fact that no other man had ever been able to break through her walls and make her shatter for him.

"Why don't you see it?" He rode her with a slow, deliberate rhythm, seeking out all those inner sweet spots that made her tremble and gasp when he rubbed against them, whipping her into a frenzy. "You're so damn beautiful, Liv. Every part of you. Inside and out."

"I'm not, but it's…it's sweet that you think so."

His mouth twitched with a crooked smile. "I'm not sweet." The smile fell, his emotions roiling, surging from one extreme to the other with dizzying speed. "And I'm still furious with you for not listening to me today. I'll never forget what it felt like when I realized you were gone. It scared the hell out of me."

"It scared me, too." She lifted her hand again, touching the side of his face. "But I knew you'd come for us, Aiden. I knew you'd do everything that you could to save us."

It made him feel desperate, the way she gazed up at him. For a moment he almost thought there was a warm glow of trust shimmering there in the liquid depths of her eyes. A glimmer of faith. And something even sweeter, richer, that he couldn't put a name to. But he shook it off, figuring he must be mad. Hell, it wasn't as if there was enough blood left in his brain for rational thought, anyway.

"Watch it, Liv." His voice was a dark, grating slash of command as he gripped her behind her knees and said, "Watch it go in."

The color in her face burned even brighter, but she lifted herself onto her elbows, doing as he said. His name fell from her lips in a soft, stuttering whisper that slipped under his skin, burning through the center of his body.

"Look how deep you take it." He spread her wider, unable to get enough of how tight she was. How hot and wet and lush. "Sexiest thing I've ever seen, the way you're just swallowing me up. I want you to tell me how it feels."

Her heavy, luminous gaze flew up to his face. "Wh-what?"

"Don't think," he rasped, breathless. "Just talk. I've never…never asked a woman to talk to me before, but I love the sound of your voice. I want it filling my head while I'm filling your body."

She opened her mouth, but all that came out was a shy,

shaky gasp. Aiden slammed deep, then held there, rubbing against the sweet, swollen knot of her clit. Waiting. Teasing. Tormenting. Determined to get what he wanted. "I don't move till you talk."

"You can't do that!"

His chest shook with a deep, husky bark of laughter. "Wanna bet?"

"Don't you think that's being a little m-manipulative?" she stammered, licking her bottom lip.

"Probably," he conceded without an ounce of remorse. "But I need to hear it, Liv. And I know you can do it. Any woman who can come in here the way you did and demand I let her suck me off has enough courage to tell me what it feels like when I'm fucking her."

It was a physical pain to keep it slow, fighting against the intense, primal demands of his body so that he could keep himself from coming. Not yet, damn it. Not until she'd given him what he needed.

"It feels hot," she finally whispered, her face bright red. "F-full."

Shuddering, Aiden pulsed inside her, his beast beginning to prowl the confines of his body with restless, predatory aggression. "Keep going," he growled, fighting to hold the animal at bay.

"Thick. And d-deep."

He made a rough sound in his throat. "You want it deeper?"

Her eyes grew heavy and she nodded, pulling her lower lip through her teeth, the simple gesture inherently sensual. Impossibly erotic. And that was before the wild woman rose back up inside her and she said, "I want you to take me, Ade. As hard and as deep as you can."

He would have thrown back his head and roared with triumph if he hadn't been working so hard to keep it together. After all, it wasn't every day that a guy got the sweet, impossibly shy Olivia Harcourt to talk dirty to him. He didn't want to think about what his face must look like, the raw, savage intensity of his hunger for her no doubt cut into the grim lines of his expression, but she wasn't cringing. Wasn't shying away. She was glowing, as if some bright, incandescent light was burning beneath her skin.

"You're wet enough for me to get in the last few inches. But they're the…thickest part." The grittiness of his voice betrayed his need. "Your call. Don't wanna hurt you."

"You won't hurt me. I…I want them, Aiden. I want all of you. Everything that you have," she panted, falling back to the floor as he loomed over her, his fingers biting into the backs of her knees. He took her at her word, slowly working his broad shaft into her. Deeper…then deeper still.

"Keep talking," he demanded, forcing in those last thick, heavily veined inches. "Tell me how you want it, Liv."

"Harder," she moaned, writhing beneath him. Her face was cherry-red, her parted lips swollen and moist. "Faster!"

Her sex clamped down on him as he gave her exactly what she'd asked for. Aiden would have been terrified he was hurting her, if not for the way she grabbed his long hair and pulled him down to her. Her mouth attacked his with a feral hunger as dark and desperate as his own, a breathless cry spilling into his mouth as she crashed violently over the edge, her tender sheath convulsing around him in tight, greedy pulls. She would have broken the devastating kiss, gasping for air, but he took his hands from her knees, holding her head braced between his palms as he took control of her mouth, forcing her to keep kissing him while she kept on coming…and coming. It was, without any doubt, the most beautiful thing Aiden had ever seen. The most breathtaking experience of his life. Like being caught in the center of a lashing storm, the orgasm drenched him, going on and on in a lush, clenching caress that pulled him right along with her, straight over the edge.

Want to come inside her, the beast snarled. *Flesh on flesh. Fill her up.*

He groaned, undone by the idea, trying to wrap his lust-racked mind around how she would react. It was one thing to want him as a man, but to come inside her without latex would mean accepting the parts of him that were *more,* and he didn't trust her enough to take that chance. Hell, he didn't trust her at all. Which meant that he was just going to have to suck it up and accept the fact that this was all he could ever have from her.

And it wasn't as if he could complain. Not when the sex was already so good, it had all but blown the memories of every other woman from his mind, erasing them from existence.

"I'm going over," he growled against her mouth, coming so hard that it hurt, the violent sensations ripping through him like a mind-shattering blast of light and sound and bone-melting heat. As his body released in hard, thick surges that damn near blew the top of his head off, the beast launched its attack, fighting to break free, his fangs beginning to descend in a sharp, hissing glide. Aiden wanted to collapse against the lush cushion of her body, breathing in deep pulls of her warm, tantalizing scent as her heart beat against his, and stay there…forever, but he *had* to move. That instant. Before the beast pushed him to do those things that could never be undone.

With residual pulses of pleasure still firing through his system, he reached down to hold the condom in place as he pulled out of her as carefully as he could, while those tight inner muscles struggled to hold him inside her. Rolling to his back, he threw one arm over his eyes and gritted his teeth, using everything he had to force the animal back into submission. It wasn't easy. Was, in fact, one of the most difficult things he'd ever had to do.

Had he actually been stupid enough to think that he could screw this woman out of his system? What a dumb ass. The experience had been life-changing, head-twisting stuff, and it sure as hell hadn't eased a damn thing. He wanted nothing more than to go at her again, with nothing between them. His body shoved a mile inside her. His fangs buried in the smooth, tender curve of her throat, creating an unbreakable bond between them. One that would mark her sweet little ass as *his*—as well as make it impossible for him to ever leave her, no matter how deeply she grew to despise him.

I am completely losing it, he thought.

"Aiden, are you okay?"

The concern in those breathless words made him cringe, and he locked his jaw, forcing out a gravelly "I'm fine."

"You're not. I can...tell that you're lying. I wish you would just talk to me. Tell me what's wrong." Frustration bled through the quiet words, making them sharp. "God, I wish that you would tell me *anything*."

Shaking his head, Aiden rolled up into a sitting position, giving her his back as he moved to his feet and headed toward the bathroom. He got rid of the condom, then walked back into the room, grabbed a pair of jeans and a shirt and began pulling them on. He didn't look directly at Liv, but he was eating her up from the corner of his eye. She lay on the floor with her legs folded to the side, arms crossed over her naked breasts, her skin steamy and pink and damp, driving him out of his mind. Making him go as hard as a friggin' spike, as if he hadn't just unloaded so violently he was still reeling from the pleasure. He wanted to say something to make it right, but knew that anything that might come out of his mouth at that moment would just be a mistake.

Something had happened to him—broken him open—and now too much was crashing down on him. Lingering fear of what he could have lost earlier that day. Soul-shredding terror at what might happen if he failed to protect them in the future. Not to mention how she would react if she ever learned all the dark, ugly truths about him. And then there was the lust, stronger than anything he could ever have imagined. That biting, twisting need for possession. Somehow it was all wrapped up in a strange, fragile weave of tenderness and longing and things he had no bloody frame of reference for.

It was dizzying, disorienting, and with no idea how to handle it, Aiden sought the only option he could think of. Retreat. Hard and fast and necessary, if he was going to be smart and stop this thing before it snowballed any deeper into madness.

"Where are you going?" Her voice reached out to him across the moonlit room, her gaze burning against his back as he pulled on his boots.

"You take the bed," he told her. "It's time for me to head out on patrol."

It was a bullshit excuse, and he knew she thought the same. But she didn't argue or bitch or demand that he stay as she grabbed a folded blanket off the foot of the bed, wrapping it around her naked body. He didn't know whether to be relieved or absurdly irritated by her reaction, which didn't make any sense, considering he was the bastard running out on *her*. With each second that passed by, it was getting harder to hold himself together, but he stopped at the door, knowing he owed her the truth before he left. At least about Jamie. "Before I go, I need to tell you something. Something that bastard told me today. It's about your sister."

"Monica?"

"Yeah. You see, the way the Mallory magnify emotions," he explained in a low voice, still not looking at her, "it, uh, affected the Casus who took her life during the kill. That's why they're so desperate to get their hands on her daughter."

Shocked silence, and then a soft, shaky rush of words. "But…b-but Jamie's not even in her powers yet."

"Yeah, well, she will be soon."

"H-how do you know that?"

"For those of us who aren't human," he murmured, hating the fear he could hear in her voice, "it's easy to pick up."

"Are you telling me that they want to kill an innocent little girl because it will…" She could barely get the words out, not that he blamed her. "What? Give them some kind of sick power high?"

"No," he muttered, twisting the handle to open the door.

Aiden knew what his next words were going to do to her, but he couldn't be the one to stick around and comfort her. Not tonight. Not after what had happened between them. "The Casus don't want her power, Liv. They want to kill her because of how it would make them feel. Because to one of those sick sons of bitches, her death would be something that increased their pleasure. Something that made them feel...unbelievably good."

And with those gruff, ominous words, Aiden walked out of the room, shutting the door behind him.

CHAPTER EIGHTEEN

Prague, Czech Republic

KIERLAND HAD BEEN on the move, working to track down Gideon Granger, since the moment he'd walked out of his hotel lobby late that afternoon. The body count of his fellow Watchmen was stacking up, and he wanted to know what was going on. Despite hitting all the Deschanel haunts in town, as well as Granger's private apartment in the city, he'd been unable to find the vamp, and his frustration was mounting. Gideon hadn't been in contact, and Kierland wanted answers to his questions.

It would be dawn in a few hours, which meant that his time was running out if he wanted to find Granger before daybreak. There was one last nightclub that a young group of swan-shifters had suggested he check out, the club's clientele reportedly more clan than human, and he was making his way there now. Cutting through an alley in one of the seedier parts of town, along the east side of the river, he turned left and headed down a dark, foggy lane that dated back centuries. Stone-faced buildings crowded close on both sides of the cobbled road, the only light provided by the occasional flickering gas lamp, the orange flames casting maniacal-looking shadows against the pale stone walls. Up ahead he could hear the muted beat of some jarring, god-awful modern dance music, and he frowned, finding it hard to believe that Gideon would actually hang out in a club that played that kind of crap, even if he was a vamp.

Making his way down the center of the road, Kierland had covered no more than half the distance to his destination when a low, eerie thread of laughter whispered through the foggy night, raising the tiny hairs on the back of his neck. The childlike sound twittered like bells, but when he looked behind him, there was no one else standing on the cobbled lane with him. As he turned in a slow circle, a thick, rank stench reached his nose, confirming his suspicion that he was finally getting a visit from whatever kind of creature had attacked Aiden on Saturday morning.

"You gonna act like a coward?" he called out, his hard voice echoing off the ancient stone walls of the surrounding buildings. "Or show some balls and come out where I can see you?"

Turning in another slow circle, he struggled to see through the deep, impenetrable fog, but it was like staring through dark, murky water. He could find no trace of the creature…and then he heard a slight rasp of breath just behind his left shoulder. With a quick spin, Kierland found himself face-to-face with something that looked like death warmed over, but only for an instant. Acting as if he'd startled it, the creature immediately scurried back into the foggy darkness.

He'd have thought it had disappeared, except that he could still hear its harsh, erratic breathing. "If you went to the trouble of finding me," he said in a low voice, "why bother hiding?"

Coming forward once more, the creature slithered through the shadows as if it was nothing more than smoke, its form apparently as vaporous as the one that had attacked Aiden, which meant that he was going to have a hell of a time fighting it. "Granger was right," Kierland rasped, holding its yellow-eyed stare. "You're not Casus."

"Nice," it lisped, its white lips spreading in a slow smile that revealed jagged rows of sharp-tipped teeth. "One point goes to the vampire."

As it moved closer, he could see the bite marks that covered its pale, cadaverous skin, the wounds jagged, as if pieces of flesh had been torn away from its body. It was similar in appearance to the creature that Aiden had described, except for a few significant differences. For one, this thing didn't have any of the Regan characteristics that had been apparent in the other one. Instead, it had dark markings around its slanted eyes, reminding Kierland of the Vassayre, one of the more reclusive clans that seldom came out of the underground caves where they dwelled.

"Not to be rude," he muttered, thinking that if he could keep it talking, it might reveal something useful, "but you look like something that's been to hell and back."

It clapped its chalk-white hands together, its oval-shaped head tilting a little to the side as it scraped out another eerie spill of laughter. "Very good, wolf boy. And a point goes to you, as well."

"Yeah? You don't look like a demon."

"You're right, of course," it conceded with a low bow, the moonlight glinting off the small horns protruding from its forehead. "But then, not all demons dwell in hell, do they? And of course, not everyone in hell is a demon."

"If not a demon, then what are you?" he asked, shifting his body so that his back wasn't exposed to the open street, since he didn't know if this thing was on its own…or if it'd brought company.

"I'm something that has suffered more than any living creature should ever have to endure. Tell me, do you have any idea of the things they do to a body down there?" It glided closer, its feet not even touching the ground. "Some of it's so depraved, you can't even imagine."

"And how did you manage to escape? Far as I know, it's not exactly an easy place to break out of."

Another soft thread of laughter filled the air, its smile a

sadistic blend of horror and hatred. "There's so much that the Watchmen don't know. That you don't understand. You try to play God and everything gets all topsy-turvy."

"What the hell's that supposed to mean?" he grunted, quickly losing his patience.

"Oh, I can't make it too easy for you, Lycan." It seemed to be gaining substance, becoming less vaporous as it slithered through the air, slowly circling his body, careful to remain just out of his reach. "Some things you're just going to have to figure out for yourself."

"Then tell me how many of you there are," he growled, taking an aggressive step forward. He wasn't going to cower before this bastard, even if he didn't know how to kill it.

"Wouldn't you like to know." It laughed, clucking its tongue.

"You won't be able to take the Merrick, if that's what you're after. They're too—"

"Who said anything about wanting the Merrick?" it asked, cutting him off, its yellow eyes burning with purpose and passion. "It's the pets we want. You and the other Watchmen. That's who we're after. At least to kick things off."

"And just what do you have against the Watchmen?" he demanded, keeping his hands loose at his sides. He was ready to release his claws the second it attacked, which he expected to happen at any moment.

"What don't we have against you?" it murmured, slithering along one of the ancient walls, its claws clicking against the pale stone. "I mean, you ratted most of us out to the Consortium. Hunted us down. Killed us. Convicted us to hell. Nosy bastards, the lot of you. Always meddling in things that don't involve you. You can't imagine how long we've been waiting for payback."

Kierland jerked his chin toward the creature and snorted. "If you want sympathy, you're looking in the wrong place. In my experience, things end up in hell because they belong there."

"Do you want me to tell you how it's going to be?" it asked, the sharp bite to its words telling him that he'd gotten under its skin. "You see, while the Merrick and the Casus are busy ripping each other to pieces, it won't be the meek who inherit the earth. It's going to be *us*. The ones who feed on misery and pain, thanks to our time in the pit. Once we remove the Watchmen, there'll be no one to go tattling to the Consortium when we're naughty. We can kill amongst the various clans, picking them off one by one, making it look like the work of their enemies. And their pride, their conceit, will keep them from asking for help. But they'll seek revenge. They'll war, reviving the ancient feuds. And while the world bleeds, my brothers and I will feast on the spoils."

Ah, there it was. The thing that might finally help them piece this madness together. Kierland and the others had been racking their brains, trying to determine if there was any truth to the claims Ross Westmore had made to the Collective Generals about a time of anarchy coming to the clans. They hadn't seen how such a thing could be possible, but he could see it now. Could see the chaos that would overtake the clans if this crazy son of a bitch's words proved true.

It made him furious—the fact that Westmore had known this was coming, while the Watchmen had been left in the dark. But that was the problem with the Consortium. Everyone was so concerned about their political clout that half the knowledge got locked away as secrets, allowing important information to fall through the cracks. Westmore had obviously garnered his information through his involvement with the Deschanel, and it occurred to Kierland that Gideon could be an excellent source of intel, if he were willing to talk.

And are you actually thinking of buddying up with a Deschanel and making a deal?

Kierland curled his lip, but didn't bother denying it. Desperate times called for desperate measures, and he was man enough to own up to the fact that they needed help. There were still too many unanswered questions, the least of which being how this "creature" had escaped from hell, if his claims were to be believed.

"I can see the wheels turning in your brain, Lycan. You're trying to figure it out, but you won't."

"And why's that?" he muttered, wanting nothing more than to wipe the smile off its smug face.

"Because you're out of time," it whispered, and before Kierland could so much as blink, it attacked. It got in a lucky shot that busted his lip on its first charge, but he parried with a swift swipe of his lengthening claws that caught it perfectly across the throat, the same thick, black ooze that Aiden had described spraying out in a wide arc. With a sharp hiss, it came at him again, this time catching him on the shoulder as it sped by, its claws digging deep, though he managed to spin away before too much damage was done. Panting hard, Kierland spun in a circle, trying to pinpoint its location, his fangs descending as the wolf punched against his insides, eager to join the fight. A movement off to his left caught his attention, and he readied himself, striking first as the creature charged through the fog. This time he managed to rip his claws across its white chest before it punched him with a crushing blow to the side of his face, his nose cracking from the force of the impact. Ignoring the blood pouring down his face, Kierland gave a bloodthirsty growl and aimed for its throat again. But the creature was too quick, and he found himself swiping at air.

Readying himself for its next strike, Kierland accepted the frustrating fact that he was getting nowhere fast, but he was determined to find some way of weakening it. No way in hell was he going down without taking this bastard with him.

"Well, this looks like fun." The smooth, lazy drawl cut its way through the thickening fog, and though he couldn't see its owner, he recognized the distinctive voice of Gideon Granger.

"Where the hell have you been?" Kierland grunted, addressing the Deschanel while keeping one eye on the creature, which had scurried like an insect up one of the nearby buildings at the sound of Gideon's voice. Its breath hissed through its jagged teeth as it watched them from above, black ooze still pouring from its damaged throat.

With a dry dose of sarcasm, the vampire said, "I'd appreciate it if you didn't take that tone with me, considering I've been slumming my way through the Deschanel Court for the last two days. That place is so oily, I feel dirty just thinking about it."

"What'd you learn?"

"Not nearly enough. But I can tell you one thing. Your little friend up there is called a Death-Walker, and he broke out when a portal opened up for one of the Casus souls you and your friends sent to hell."

Shock reverberated through Kierland's system like a jolt of electricity. "Are you actually telling me that thing escaped when one of the Markers was used to kill a Casus?"

Gideon gave a slow nod. "You know what they say about how no good deed ever goes unpunished? I'm afraid the analogy is entirely true in this case. And it makes perfect sense, if you think about it," he murmured.

"Whenever a door opens, there's always a chance that something else might leak out. The portals that open for the fallen Casus lead into the part of hell that holds the tainted souls of the ancient clans. That's why the Watchmen deaths have each been slightly different. It's not one race that's making the kills. The Death-Walkers are made up of souls that come from each of the clans."

"He's right, you know," the creature lisped, shivering as the wind blew down the lane in a frigid blast. "Did I tell you that this place reminds me of home? It's so cold it hurts."

A bitter laugh jerked from Kierland's lips as he slid the creature, the *Death-Walker,* a wry look. "Seems to me you'd be used to something a little warmer."

"Ahh, see, that's where the living get it so wrong. Hell isn't a place of heat. Quite the opposite, actually. It's cold. The kind of cold that sinks down so deep into your bones, you feel the ice moving through your veins. And do you know why?" it asked with another eerie, childlike burst of laughter. "So that we can feel the fire better when we burn."

"Speaking of burning," Gideon drawled, pulling a small vial from his pocket and twisting the lid off, "I think this might do the trick." Lifting his hand, he flung the contents of the vial across the creature's face, making it shriek with pain. Steam rose from its scorched flesh as it curled its arms over its head, its body losing its definition, as if it were retreating back into a vaporous form. Peeking beneath its arm, it cut one dark, baleful look toward Gideon, then whirled away with a sudden burst of speed, disappearing into the moonlit sky.

"What the hell was that?" Kierland asked, sliding a curious, wide-eyed look toward the small vial still clasped in the vampire's hand.

"A little holy water," Gideon explained, balancing the vial on his open palm, "with some salt thrown in."

"Will it kill him?"

Gideon shook his head, one sable lock of hair falling over his brow as he returned the vial to his pocket. "Unfortunately, no. And don't ask me what will, because that's something I'm still trying to find out. What I do know is that the water will cause enough pain to scare them away."

Kierland lifted his right hand and rubbed at the knots of tension in the back of his neck. "Well, for what it's worth, I appreciate the help," he said in a low voice, managing to get the words out with only a trace of a grimace. "So, uh, thanks."

Gideon's mouth curled with a crooked smile. "Any time."

"Yeah?" A low, gritty bark of laughter vibrated in his chest. "Huh. I'd be lying if I said I wasn't surprised."

"You have bad blood with Ashe," the Deschanel murmured, rolling one broad, silk-covered shoulder, "but I'm not my brother." Looking up and down the narrow lane, he pushed his windblown hair back from his face, and asked, "What are you doing here anyway?"

Kierland jerked his chin toward the fog-shrouded end of the street, where the grating dance music could still be heard. "I was heading for that club down there to look for you."

The vampire threw back his head and laughed, revealing two perfect bite marks just above the thick line of his jugular. Kierland wondered who had fed from the Deschanel…and if Gideon had allowed his body to be used in exchange for the information they were after. As his laughter faded away, the vampire shook his head and snorted. "Does that sound like the sort of place I would hang out?"

"To be honest, I had my doubts," Kierland drawled, resting his back against the nearest building. He used his sleeve to wipe the blood from his face, and was about to ask how the vamp had found him, then realized that Gideon would have simply picked up his scent at his hotel, then followed the trail. Turning the conversation back to the creature, he said, "Westmore told the Collective Generals that a time of anarchy was coming to the clans. Before you got here, that…Death-Walker said that their goal was to take out the Watchmen so they could go to work turning the clans against one another. And once that's done, it sounds like they plan to just sit back and watch everything go to hell for the fun of it. This has to be what Westmore was talking about."

Gideon gave a slow nod as he pushed his hands into his front pockets, the corners of his mouth dipping in a frown.

"Westmore worked for one of the oldest Deschanel families in existence. It seems plausible that he could have learned about the Death-Walkers from them."

Wishing he had a cigarette, Kierland blew out a frustrated breath. "But why would the Deschanel know these things? I mean, this is stuff that the Watchmen have never even heard of."

The vampire arched one dark, arrogant brow. "You don't have a lot to do with hell, so how would you know its secrets?"

"And the Deschanel do?"

"What can I say? Sometimes it helps to be a little bit bad," Gideon murmured, slanting him a wry smile. "There are Deschanel legends about things like this happening in the past, long before the Casus even came into existence. They're told mostly as cautionary tales, full of dark magic and things no sane person would meddle in. But it looks as if the original Consortium was desperate enough to do just that. According to the Deschanel, portals like the ones being opened for the Casus can only be made from materials found in hell itself."

"So then you were right," he rasped, "about the leaders using dark magic to make the crosses."

The vampire nodded. "It looks that way. But if it makes you feel any better, I wish I'd been wrong."

Pushing away from the wall, Kierland forced himself to do the right thing and extended his hand. "You've got yourself a deal, if you still want it. Westmore will be yours, in exchange for anything else you can learn."

"I was hoping you'd feel that way," Gideon said with a low laugh, shaking his hand. They exchanged numbers, and then the Deschanel glanced at the silver watch on his wrist. "I need to get going," he said, "but I'll be in touch as soon as I have something more. In the meantime, be careful and watch your back. Until we understand more about what's going on, there's no telling what will happen. Believe it or not, the advice I was given is that you find a stone structure surrounded by water, and stay there, using it for protection. The Death-Walkers won't be able to get in. Not if the water's been salted and blessed by a man of God."

Kierland scrubbed his hands down his face, not liking the idea that instantly took root in his brain. Without a doubt, the others were going to fight him over it, thinking he was stark barking mad. But if it proved necessary, he'd find a way to make it happen—even if he had to drag them kicking and screaming across the bloody Atlantic.

"And Kierland."

"Yeah?"

"If I were you," Gideon told him, all traces of humor erased from his deep voice as the vampire settled his gray gaze on Kierland's blood-soaked shoulder, "I'd find it fast."

CHAPTER NINETEEN

Missouri
Monday night

IT WAS EVENING when they finally stopped for the night at a hotel on the outskirts of St. Louis. Though it'd been a long, confusing day, Olivia's body still thrummed with pleasure from the breathtaking things that Aiden had done to her the night before. She only wished the blissful sensation would bleed past the physical and into her emotions. But they were too edgy. Too raw.

And the day had been nothing short of bizarre.

At dawn she'd been pulled out of bed for an emergency meeting. The details had been confusing, but Olivia had finally succeeded in wrapping her sleep-fogged mind around the situation, understanding that Kierland Scott had gotten a lead in his search for information about the creatures attacking Watchmen all over the world. They were called Death-Walkers, and they were bad news—not that she hadn't been able to see that for herself. According to Kierland's source, the Death-Walkers were actually the condemned souls of clansmen and women who had been sent to hell for their crimes, and with each Casus death, at least one of these fiends was able to crawl its way up out of the pit.

The revelation sparked a spirited conversation, the topics including speculation as to how the Markers had been made and theories about why the Death-Walkers sought to create such chaos, though they all agreed that it sounded as if the creatures' minds had been warped by their time in hell. They also agreed that the Death-Walkers knew the Markers were responsible for their release, which would explain why the one that had attacked Aiden had been so fascinated by Jamie's cross. Then Kellan had told them that his brother believed there was a good chance they would need to move their base of operations, for safety purposes. Kierland hadn't given any specifics on the new location, claiming he needed to make some more enquiries first—but the idea had caused a whole new round of debate among the others.

All in all, it had been a chilling way to start the day.

Then, at around three in the afternoon, another call had come in, this one from Aiden's friends in Colorado. The security at Ravenswing had been breached and two Death-Walkers had infiltrated the compound. Thankfully, everyone had made it out okay due largely to their prac-

ticed evacuation drills, but the incident had only served to
set Aiden and the others further on edge. Now the group
from the compound was headed their way, and though
there'd been a lot of grumbling after they'd talked to
Kierland, it had been decided that everyone would head
to England. Kierland and Kellan had grown up there,
raised by their grandfather at a remote estate in the Lake
District that Kierland believed would be perfect for their
new headquarters, since it met the two requirements the
Lycan had been told they needed for protection—requirements that none of the Watchmen compounds in either
North or South America currently met.

It was surrounded by water.

And it was made of stone.

Though the inside of the house had been modernized,
its exterior walls belonged to the original stone structure
that had stood there for over eight hundred years…and it
was surrounded by a moat. While the estate was apparently in dire need of renovation after years of neglect since
their grandfather's death, it had been agreed that the
location just might offer the group the protection they
needed—an idea that Molly claimed had been backed by
Monica. Kierland had already made the necessary ar-
rangements not only to have the moat water blessed, but
for copious amounts of salt to be added. According to the
Lycan's source, the Death-Walkers wouldn't be able to
cross the salted holy water. Kierland had also told them

that the combination of salt and holy water could actually be used to drive the Death-Walkers away, scorching their flesh. But it wouldn't kill them…and they still didn't know what would.

And on a personal note, Olivia didn't know what she was going to do about one gorgeous, impossibly complicated shape-shifter.

Though she and Jamie had ridden with Aiden throughout the long day's drive, the conversation between them had been…strained. For a while she'd managed to keep him talking with questions about the things Kierland had learned and how the information would be passed on to the other Watchmen units around the world. She'd also touched on the admission Aiden had made during the dawn meeting, when she'd learned that he'd already started working to get his hands on the medication that Jamie would need in order to fly, since he'd wanted to be prepared for any eventuality.

She'd even talked to him about her father's marriage to Monica and Chloe's mother, which had been when she'd first learned about the secretive, mysterious world of the clans. Then they'd talked more about Jamie's father, who'd claimed not only that he couldn't handle the responsibility of a child, but also that he didn't like the way he always felt so "out of control" around Monica. He hadn't known about her dormant Merrick blood or the fact that she was half witch, but he'd obviously been affected by the Mallory curse.

That conversation had led to one about the ongoing search for her stepsister Chloe, but eventually Olivia's questions had dried up, since she hadn't been able to bring herself to broach the subject of Jamie's Mallory powers and how it related to the Casus's hunt for her niece, her terror and fear over that particular topic still too fresh. Aiden had fallen back into another heavy silence, leaving her to keep Jamie entertained. For a while they'd sung songs and played games, and then Jamie had asked for some paper and her crayons, keeping herself busy with her artwork for the rest of the drive.

Now, as Olivia stared at her reflection in the steamed surface of the hotel bathroom mirror, she could only marvel at the dazed, lovesick expression on her flushed face. She was too turned on, and not just in a sexual sense, though the guy had certainly blown her circuits. But there was an electric energy buzzing beneath her skin that made everything seem different. Sounds were clearer. Colors brighter. God only knew that she needed to shut down, pulling back into her calm, emotionless shell, but her old fail-safes had abandoned her, leaving her high and dry without any protection. Any armor.

As she finished pulling on some clean jeans and a T-shirt, she opened the bathroom door onto the small living room that joined their rooms together and found Aiden sitting on the floor talking to Jamie as she colored another picture from one of her coloring books. Kellan and Noah were out running patrol, all of them on edge, worried about what might happen next. Morgan had gone to bed to get some rest before her turn at running the perimeter with Aiden came up in a few hours, and though Aiden needed to get some sleep as well, he'd offered to watch Jamie so that Olivia could grab a quick shower.

Leaning against the doorjamb, she listened as he said, "You have weapons, Jamie. Ones you can use if you're ever scared or in danger."

"But I'm too tiny," her niece argued, her small face scrunched in concentration as she struggled to color within the lines.

"That's not a bad thing, sweetheart. You might be tiny, but you're still tough. Just remember that you're small and fast enough to get somewhere that an adult can't reach you. Use that against them. And whatever you do, don't ever give up. You're smart and you're strong, and don't ever let any jerk tell you otherwise, you understand?"

Jamie nodded, then set down her crayon, moved to her feet and threw her arms around Aiden's neck, giving him a fierce hug that made Olivia's eyes water. Forcing herself to move before she started blubbering like a baby, she walked into the room and grabbed Jamie's backpack, stowing her things away. "Come on, sweetie pie. It's time for bed."

"I don't want to go," Jamie protested, sticking out her bottom lip. "I wanna stay with Aiden."

Olivia reached down and affectionately ruffled her niece's silky curls. "You'll be able to spend all day tomorrow with Aiden while we're driving. But right now you need to get your beauty sleep."

Jamie gave in with a long, dramatic sigh, then took the backpack from Olivia and rooted around inside until she found what she was looking for. Taking out one of the pictures she'd drawn that afternoon, the little girl turned and handed the paper to Aiden. "I made this for you."

Olivia could see the shock of surprise in his hazel eyes, the warmth of his easy grin as he thanked Jamie for the "beautiful picture," making her feel as if something had reached inside her and taken hold of her heart, grasping it in a firm, unbreakable grip. Needing a moment to collect herself, she took a smiling Jamie into the room where Morgan was sleeping, and tucked her up in the second queen-size bed. Whispering one of the little girl's favorite bedtime stories to her, Olivia waited for Jamie to fall into a sound sleep, then tucked the covers up under her pointed little chin. When she walked back into the living room, she found Aiden still sitting on the floor, staring at Jamie's drawing. Color burned along the sharp crests of his cheekbones when he sensed her presence, as if he were embarrassed that she'd caught him still sitting there, and he moved to his feet, heading toward the other bedroom.

Hoping that he might open up and talk to her now that they were alone—and ready to *demand* that he do it, if he tried to avoid her—Olivia followed him. "You're good with her," she told him, standing just inside the open doorway.

"You think?" he asked, grabbing his duffel bag and setting it on the foot of the nearest bed.

She rubbed the slow ache in her wounded arm, reminding herself that if she could stand up to a psychopathic Casus, she could stand up to Aiden. "I do," she told him. "And in case you didn't notice, she adores you."

Aiden made a low sound in his throat that could have passed for a laugh, if it hadn't been quite so gruff with emotion. "She adores all men. Just look at her with Noah and Kell."

"She likes them, but you're different." He grunted in response, carefully sliding Jamie's drawing into his bag as she went on to say, "And speaking of Noah, we didn't get a chance to talk about it yet, but Kellan told me about…what's going on. About how Noah's trying to save his family. I feel like such a jerk for the way I reacted yesterday. I've apologized to Noah, but I still feel awful."

"He's a big boy," he drawled, knowing his jealousy was ridiculous. But he couldn't stop its slow burn through his body. "He can take it."

"Still, it was wrong of me to react that way."

He slid her a narrow, curious look. "Most humans wouldn't trust him, even knowing that he's trying to do the right thing."

"And I'm not like most," she said gently, holding him with that smoky, luminous gaze. "Or haven't you realized that yet?"

It wasn't easy, but Aiden forced himself to look away from her. "You're complicated," he muttered, rummaging in his bag for a fresh pair of boxers to put on after his shower. "I'll give you that. Hell, I'm still trying to figure you out."

She met the words with a blast of silence and he locked his jaw, his emotions so on edge, he felt like a high-tension wire. He hated the way things were coming down. The threat of the Death-Walkers thrown on top of their war against the Casus. The attack on Ravenswing. All of it. He wasn't crazy about going to England, but he wanted everyone in one place, where they could watch each others' backs. True, it was cold and wet there a lot of the time, but he'd suck it up and deal, if it meant it was best for everyone. But he hated the idea of getting on a plane, where they'd be pathetically vulnerable if those vaporous assholes decided to attack.

Christ, he hated the whole screwed-up situation.

From the corner of his eye he watched as Liv moved a little farther into the room...then shut the door behind her. "What's going on, Aiden?"

He took a deep breath. Slowly let it out. Then turned his head to look at her. "With what?"

"With us. Is this it?" she asked, the soft words vibrating with emotion. "We have sex and then you dump me? Was I that bad? Boring? What? If you're trying to spare my feelings, I wish you wouldn't. Just get it over with and spit it out already."

Hah! As if there was anything boring about Olivia Harcourt. The woman was like a force of nature crashing over him, ripping through him. She was electric. Hypnotic. And completely addictive.

Quietly she said, "I know you don't owe me anything. I mean, I knew exactly what I was getting into last night. But…I need to know where we are now. I need to know what's going on inside your head."

Oh, hell no, he thought, inwardly cringing. That was the last thing she needed to know.

Aiden figured the smartest thing he could do at the moment was turn his back and tell her to get the hell out of his room, but he couldn't even turn away from her. Couldn't take his eyes off her. Not when she was looking at him like that, her violet eyes smoldering with desire… burning with something deeper. Something powerful and strong and bright that rocked him to the core. Made him wish that he could be something he wasn't.

"I'm on a hair trigger tonight, Liv." He had to force the words out, fighting to make them sound human. "Don't push me."

Her lips trembled with emotion, but she didn't back down. Didn't run. "Why shouldn't I?" she said unsteadily, her hands knotting into small fists at her sides before she crossed them over her chest. "You're always pushing me. Maybe I've decided it's time I push back."

"If you're smart," he muttered, "you won't."

"Damn it, Aiden!" Her temper flared, blasting against him like a hot wind. "Just be a man and admit that you're sorry we slept together!"

"I'm not sorry," he growled, wishing that he was better with this kind of crap. Emotional confessions had never been a strong point of his, but then no one had ever twisted him up like Liv.

"If that's true, then prove it."

His head jerked back as if he'd been clipped on the chin. "What?"

"You heard me," Olivia whispered, taking a step toward him. "Prove it."

"It's not that simple, damn it." He started pacing from one side of the room to the other, feeling like an agitated animal prowling its cage. "You make me lose control. More than...anyone else. And that's dangerous," he muttered, scrubbing his hands down his face, then ripping them back through his hair. "When I was younger, I gave more of myself up to the animal than most shifters do at that age. I had to, if I wanted to stay alive."

He came to a stop in the middle of the room and just stood there, with his head angled forward, his hands braced on his lean hips. A husky rumble of laughter fell from his lips, sounding hollow and tired. "Hell, if it weren't for the animal," he rasped, "I wouldn't be here today. But there's a price to pay for it. I'm more aggressive than most. More feral."

"If you're trying to scare me off, it isn't working."

He let out a sharp, explosive sigh and turned his head, the thick waves of his hair falling against the side of his face. The corners of his eyes creased as he stared her down, the seconds stretching out like a body being tortured on a rack, until his mouth began to twitch with a boyish, lopsided smile. "I'm starting to think that nothing scares you, Liv. Not really. You'll fight till the bitter end, won't you?"

"If it's something worth fighting for," she whispered.

He looked down, staring at the dark blue carpet, while those soft words played havoc with his sanity. A full minute passed before he cleared his throat, his voice a rough rasp of sound as he said, "Yeah, well, that's the problem, Liv. That's what I'm trying to get through to you. I saw you and I wanted you, and was selfish enough to go after you. But the truth is that I'm not even fit to touch you."

"Is that what you think?"

His chest shook with bitter, breathless laughter. "It's what I *know*."

"That's such bullshit, Aiden."

"You think, Liv?" Frustration surged through him,

seething and sharp, pouring out in a rough, visceral growl. "Let me tell you about the guy you let cover you last night. About the animal you let inside you. You wanna know why I feel the way I do about humans? Because my mother was one. And you wanna know where I got these?" he snarled, holding out his scarred wrists as he stalked toward her. "When I was seven, my mother—my *human* mother—sold me to a man named Mueller."

Her mouth trembled and she shook her head. "I don't want to hear this."

"Well, you're going to," he grunted, dropping his arms to his sides, his hands shoved deep in the pockets of his faded jeans. The muscles across his shoulders were coiled with tension, his biceps rigid as he fought to keep himself under control. "You need to have it all spelled out for you, Liv, so that you've got a clear picture of the situation. See, Mueller made tons of money from running what he liked to call his little fun house. A place where loaded, sick-as-shit humans could come and get their kicks, working over kids in any way they chose. As long as you paid your money, you could have whatever you wanted."

"Oh, God." She pressed her fingertips to her trembling mouth, a violent shiver moving through her entire body. Her face was so white she looked like a sheet. Bleached and drained of color.

Aiden jerked his chin toward her, his expression twisted with a cocky smirk that he knew didn't hide the pain hidden beneath his surface. "Yeah, you're starting to get the picture now, aren't you? And Mueller's genius was in using kids who could take a licking and keep on ticking. With our ability to heal, shifters were like manna from heaven to a guy like him. The favorites in his little collection, he liked to say."

He went on, mercilessly telling her about the things they'd done to him. Confessing all the vile, twisted things they'd made him do. The drugs they'd given him to make his body hard. The way he'd given up more and more of himself to his beast as he'd grown older, just so he could retain some shred of his sanity.

Though he was shaking and covered in sweat, his insides twisting with shame, he forced himself to reveal just how thoroughly he'd been used, and in some perverse way Aiden knew it was because he expected her to turn away from him. One of them needed to end this thing before he screwed up both their lives by biting her… *marking* her—and he didn't trust himself to be the one to do it. So he'd force the issue into her hands.

"What about your father?" she whispered when he finally paused. Her voice was thick…broken, a wash of glistening tears overflowing those beautiful eyes. "Did he know where you were? Didn't he ever come looking for you?"

"Naw," he muttered, pulling his hand down his damp face. "I doubt he ever even knew he had a kid. He was just some guy my mom had a fling with while touring Europe. By the end of her trip she'd hooked up with another man. Turned out she'd moved on from a shape-shifter to a heroin dealer, and the rest was history. Once she finally clued in to the fact that I wasn't human, I became just a means to an end. A commodity that could be traded in to fund her habit."

Her voice quivered as she said, "Do you know what happened to her?"

He shook his head, another gritty laugh spilling from his lips. "She probably overdosed in some dark alley, stoned out of her skull, so far gone she couldn't even remember her own name. To be honest, I don't really give a damn what happened to her."

"I don't blame you," she whispered. "I'd feel the same way."

Rolling his shoulder, Aiden popped his jaw and got on with it. "Anyway, when I was fourteen, I hit my growth spurt. It should have been too soon for me to make a full change, but I did. At first I just wanted to get the other kids out of there…and I tried. But I was a young, stupid jackass who didn't know what he was doing. Not to mention scared out of my wits. Mueller's house was an hour outside Reno, buried in the foothills of the Sierra Nevada. There were too many of us to move quickly, and it didn't take long for his men to catch us. I'd managed to steal some weapons, and I told the others to fight back. It turned into a slaughter and they died. Every single one of them. The youngest was only five."

She covered her wet eyes, whispering something broken and hoarse under her breath, though he couldn't tell what it was. He coughed, forcing the last bit out, needing to get it over and done with before the knot in his throat choked him off completely. "I should have bled out, but somehow I managed to drag myself away. At least what was left of me. I spent three days hiding out in the woods before I recovered from my wounds. And while I was out there, freezing my ass off, I realized that I'd gone about it all wrong. If I left Mueller and his men alive, they were just going to keep on doing what they'd done to us to a whole new group of kids. So I went back and let the predator that lives inside me take its revenge. I hunted them down, one by one, and ripped them to pieces. But I saved Mueller for last."

For a long time the only sound in the room was that of their soft, ragged breathing, and then she finally said, "I hope you made it count when you killed him."

With a jerky nod, Aiden locked his jaw, trying to brace himself for the blow. The brush-off. He knew it had to be coming, any moment now. She was probably too polite to tell him what she thought to his face. But she'd bow out with some murmured excuse. Then find a way to keep a careful distance between them from that point on. Eventually act as if he didn't even exist.

He waited…and waited, his body sweat-slick and hot

beneath his clothes, as if he were burning with fever. But she didn't turn away. Didn't leave.

Instead, she came toward him, her energy hitting him like a blast of electricity, tingling and warm. He stiffened, his muscles coiled for flight. And yet his feet stayed rooted to the ground, even as she came closer…and closer. He shook. Trembled. But he couldn't move. Couldn't run.

"I don't know how you could think you're not fit to touch me," she said in a soft, tender spill of words. Heat crawled up his spine, curling around his shoulders…the backs of his ears, chasing away the painful chills. "You're the one who's strong. Who fought to survive something that would have crushed most people. You're the one with something to be proud of, Aiden. If anything, I'm the one who's not fit to touch you."

He felt himself swaying toward her, his brain fuzzy… thick. "Huh," he breathed out, shaking his head.

She stared deep into his eyes with that wild, hypnotic power that made him feel as if she was seeing right inside him. "What?" she whispered.

"It's just that…you never react the way that I think you will. The way you should. It's like you're…I dunno." He shook his head again, not knowing what to make of her. He'd been so sure of how she'd react…and now she'd gone and knocked him on his ass again. "I don't get it, Liv. It's not right."

She took a step closer, so beautiful and sweet it hurt just

to look at her. "Am I supposed to blame you for being strong and surviving, Aiden?"

He took a deep, shuddering breath, his face prickling with the blood rush that came just before you passed out. He didn't know what to make of the chaos swarming through his system—but there was something so much more powerful than lust fueling these strange new emotions awakening inside him. Something more potent… and infinitely more dangerous.

"You should be disgusted by my weakness. By my mistakes. Those kids died because of me." There was no heat in the words. It was just a quiet, desolate statement of fact.

"God, Aiden, that's not true! You were a child yourself. The only disgust I feel is for those monsters who hurt you. I feel nothing but absolute pride in you for being so strong. For growing up into the kind of man who could survive something like that without letting it blacken his soul."

One second she was wrapping her slender arms around his trembling body, and in the next, Aiden was attacking her. There really wasn't any other word to describe the fierce intensity of his actions. His hands were all over her, his mouth claiming hers in a wild, explicit kiss that was hot and wet and savagely hungry. The only thing that made it okay was the fact that she was kissing him back.

With his long fingers curled around her biceps, he turned, shoving her against the nearest wall. "Damn it," he gasped, nipping at her bottom lip, the salty taste of her tears only fueling his desperation. He grabbed her ass and lifted her off the ground, forcing her thighs to part as he lodged himself against her, grinding his denim-covered cock against her soft, tender core. "I'm being too rough again."

"Don't stop," she panted, wrapping her legs around his hips. "I love you like this."

His heart stuttered on the *L* word, even though he knew she meant it in a sexual sense. But the damage had been done. All that devastating angst that had been twisting him up inside turned into a raw, explosive sexual aggression that nearly floored him, ripping through him like a tidal wave. She knew his darkest, most shameful secret, and yet she still wanted him. He couldn't get his head around it. Couldn't get it to compute.

And the way she looked at him when he stopped kissing her long enough to check her expression, keeping his face close to hers, simply blew his mind. It was almost as if she…cared. Even after everything that he'd told her. She was so open, her emotions just blazing there on her beautiful face like a neon sign. All that heat and shimmering warmth just spilling out, melting him down.

In a distant part of his brain Aiden could hear someone shouting for him to wake up and take a reality check, but he was too far gone to care. Too desperate to heed its warnings.

Burrowing his face in the crook of her shoulder, he

pressed his open mouth against the side of her throat, flicking his tongue against the warm, salty sweetness of her flesh. He loved how she smelled. How she tasted. Loved how different her body was from his own. Soft where he was hard. Tender and pale where he was rugged and dark.

His heartbeat roared in his ears as he kissed his way back up to her mouth, and with his lips against hers, he said, "Get rid of your sweater."

She complied instantly, breathing in a sharp, excited rush as she reached for the hem of her sweater, yanking it over her head. He moved back a little so that she could have room to reach behind her back and unhook her bra, the satiny scrap of satin falling to the floor.

Lifting her higher, Aiden nuzzled his mouth against the inner curve of one soft, heavy breast, while staring up at her flushed face. The dark, crimson silk of her hair fell forward in wild curls as she gazed down at him, her lush, kiss-swollen lips parted for those gasping breaths. Aiden held her gaze as he opened his mouth over one thick, delicious, candy-pink nipple, trapping the tender bud against the roof of his mouth, rubbing it with his tongue. She cried out, trembling in his arms, her delicate hands clenched against his shoulders.

"I didn't pay nearly enough attention to these yesterday," he groaned, moving his eager mouth to the other breast. He swirled a slow, hungry lick around the puffy nipple, loving the way she squirmed in his arms. "They deserve hours of attention, Liv. Days. Months. Years. I've never seen anything so beautiful."

Her chest shook with a breathless flutter of laughter, her tender mouth curling in a shy, dazzling smile. "You're crazy."

"I mean it. That's not a line. You take my breath away," he panted. "Blow my mind."

Tears still glistened in her eyes as she leaned down and kissed him, holding his face in her trembling hands. With his head spinning, Aiden tightened his grip on her ass, holding her against him as he turned and quickly carried her to the closest bed. He laid her down, ripping off the rest of her clothes, then his own, and was beyond thankful that he'd put a condom in his back pocket so that he didn't have to go searching for one.

Racked with a violent, visceral need, he fumbled with the rubber like a green-eared virgin, nearly roaring with relief when he finally got the thing on. Then he crawled over her naked body, his muscles shaking so hard his damn teeth were chattering. "I need to fuck you," he somehow managed to scrape out.

"Then what are you waiting for?" Sweet, husky words that made him shake even harder as she ran her soft palms down the bunched muscles in his back.

Cursing a breathless stream of raw, erotic phrases under his breath, Aiden shoved her thighs wide and nudged himself against her opening, the slick, moist heat of her making him see red. With his muscles coiled hard and tight, he shoved deep, pulling a hoarse, shocked cry from her chest as he gave her every brutal, demanding inch… and began stirring the liquid depths of her body. He couldn't look away from her eyes, lost in the deep, smoky pools of violet, every intimate pulse of pleasure that thrummed through her body shining right there for him to see, so beautiful and sweet and bright.

Some kind of dark, primitive sound tore from his throat, and he heard himself saying, "Every time I get inside you, it just feels better. Like being caught in the middle of a hurricane, and everything's thrashing around me, while I'm snugged up tight in paradise, going out of my mind. It doesn't make any sense. I should be getting tired of you by now, and instead I just want you more. It's like you've put some kind of spell on me."

Her mouth curled with a slow, womanly smile, her eyes heavy lidded and dark as she ran her hands over the corded muscles in his arms, across his shoulders, fluttering them up the strained tendons in his throat. He rode her hard and roughly, caging her beneath his body as he thrust in deep, penetrating lunges that drove their sex-slick bodies across the bed. When she closed her eyes, he twisted his fingers in the thick hair at the back of her head, tilting her face up to his as he said, "Look at me, Liv. I need you to look at me."

Her lashes fluttered open, and his breath caught at the

glittering sparks of emotion burning in their luminous depths. He refused to let her hide, demanding she give him everything he wanted. He sucked on her breasts as if they belonged to him. Drove himself into her as if his life depended on it. And when she came, Aiden could have sworn her wild, sobbing burst of pleasure surged right into him, like some kind of crazy, breathtaking feedback loop.

She was liquid and soft and deliciously warm, hugging the thick, granite-hard length of his cock as if she wanted to keep him inside her forever. She stretched beneath him like a sated, well-fed cat and purred, "I thought things like that only happened in books."

"You like it?" he asked, riding her through the orgasm with slow, heavy thrusts, while she pulsed and throbbed around him. A stupid question to ask, but he couldn't stop himself.

She lifted her hand, stroking the tip of one finger across the slash of his brows, then along the hard edge of his jaw before sweeping it across his bottom lip. "Let's just say that I'm finding it hard to remember why I ever thought sex was overrated," she whispered, following the movement of her finger with her eyes as she traced the shape of his upper lip, a rush of shivering pleasure left in the wake of her touch. "I guess…I guess it's easy to understand why you've had so many lovers. Women probably follow you around, just throwing themselves at your feet, begging you to take them to bed."

Aiden frowned, suddenly feeling a little sick inside at the idea of Liv comparing what was happening between them to the sex he'd indulged in before meeting her. He wanted to explain the difference to her, but didn't know how. How could he make her understand that this heart-pounding, *throw the world off its axis* thing that they had eclipsed every moment of pleasure he'd ever felt in another woman's arms? God, it was like comparing water to the finest, rarest scotch whiskey.

Not knowing what to say, he let his body communicate for him. He tried to keep it slow, at first just rubbing against the damp, moist cushion of her sex, teasing her…loving the way she writhed and arched against him. But he could hold back for only so long before his hunger got the better of him, and the next thing he knew, he was riding her harder…deeper, increasing his rhythm until he was slamming his hips against hers, the slick, exquisite friction driving him out of his mind. As he lowered his head, pressing his open mouth to the fragile column of her throat, tasting the salty heat of her blush, he started to wonder if this blissful sense of perfection was what had the Buchanans so lit up, their normally rugged expressions always lovesick and sappy when their women were near. Was this what he'd been missing out on? This strange, mind-blowing connection that made him feel as if he'd finally, for the first time in his life, actually gotten something right?

And how in God's name was he going to live without it, now that he'd found it?

Not liking that particular question, his beast let out a bloodthirsty roar that echoed through his skull, punching against his insides as it tried to escape, more than ready to take matters into its own hands. It snarled with primal ferocity, demanding that he bite her. Sink his teeth into her. Mark her and claim her, while he still had the chance. Before it was too late and they'd lost her.

It took everything that Aiden had to fight it back, stopping the release of his claws and fangs—and although he managed, his control was weakening. Knowing each second he stayed inside her was madness, he shoved himself into the orgasm, and it was like throwing himself into the burning center of the sun. Like being tossed into a wild, storm-racked ocean, the waves crashing over his head, shoving him under again…and again…and again. His mind whited-out, as the teeth-grinding sensations went on and on, lasting longer than anything he'd ever experienced.

He had his weight balanced on his shaking arms, his head hanging forward, chest rising and falling in a hard rhythm as he fought for breath. She'd come with him, the narrow, cushiony walls of her sex still pulsing around him, a soft, shivery sigh of pleasure falling from her lips as she lifted her hands, running her fingers through the long, tangled mane of his sweat-damp hair. "You're shaking," she whispered, snagging his gaze as he opened his eyes, holding him with the sheer power of her will. "You're still fighting something, Aiden. I wish I knew what it was."

"It's nothing," he murmured, lowering his lips to hers, just needing to lose himself in the perfect taste of her mouth. Despite all that had happened, he still couldn't bring himself to make that next confession, admitting that everything about her made him want to sink his fangs into her, marking her body as something that was his. Or the fact that if he bit her, after falling in love with her, that mark would be permanent. Binding. Never to be undone.

Not yet, damn it, he thought, ravaging the tender depths of her mouth, so warm and moist and delicious. He wasn't ready to lose her. She'd been so sweet and accepting, but he knew better than to push his luck. It was hell fighting back the primal, predatory demands of the beast, but he'd keep doing it if it meant he could have her again. Just a few more times before he was forced to put an end to it.

Closing his eyes, he shoved away the stark vision of his future that lingered at the edge of his consciousness, taunting him with how things would be once he lost her, and did everything he could to cling to the moment. But the annoying voice in the back of his mind wouldn't shut up. Wouldn't leave him alone.

You're just living on borrowed time here. Eking it out.

When you know, in the end, you're still gonna crash and burn.

Panic settled in, destroying the hot, molten glow of bliss still filling his belly. The sweat on his skin cooled as he pulled his mouth from hers, the feeling in his gut twisting into a hard, tight burn as he stared down into her questioning eyes. God, he really hated that voice. But it was right. He'd never be able to put his trust in her. Not in the way she deserved. He was too wary and bitter. And no matter what she was feeling at the moment, he couldn't count on it to last. Not forever. Sooner or later she'd come to her senses. Realize her mistake. And by then, it would be too late.

MESMERIZED AND still a little light-headed from two bone-melting orgasms, Olivia watched the breathtaking play of muscle beneath Aiden's golden skin as he quietly pulled away from her and moved across the room, heading toward the bathroom. The low glow of light from the desk lamp illuminated the strong, rugged lines of muscle and bone and sinew, his body like a primal, enticing work of art. It dazzled her. Blinded her with its rough, masculine beauty.

But what truly captivated her was the wary, emotionally scarred man who lurked beneath that tough, beautiful surface. That was who had stolen her heart. Who she wanted to shower with tenderness. The man she'd fallen utterly and completely in love with. The feeling was so tender and fragile, like something soft and green just peeking up through the moist earth, seeking the warmth of the sun. She had to be so careful…so cautious, if it was going to have a chance to blossom and thrive.

"Are you going to run away again?" she asked, her stomach knotting as he came out of the bathroom and started to pull on the low-slung jeans he'd been wearing before.

"I'm not running, Liv." He reached for his thick watch, hooking it around his left wrist. "But it's going to be time for the guys to head back in soon, and they're going to need to get some sleep. I'd keep you in here with me all night if I could, but I don't want to put you in an uncomfortable situation."

She didn't argue, though she wanted to, for the simple reason that she wanted to stay with him. Be close to him. Instead, she moved to her feet, giving him her back as she collected her scattered pieces of clothing and began slipping them back on. When she went to pull on her jeans she had to steady herself against the wall, her body still shivering with lingering pulses of pleasure, like sensual aftershocks, the memory of what it felt like to have him buried inside her permanently imprinted on her brain. Between her trembling thighs she was swollen and sore, but ridiculously eager to have him again. She'd never known orgasms could be like that. So powerful and wild. A complete loss of self, without panic or fear, because she'd trusted Aiden to be waiting there for her on the other side of the dark, devastating pleasure.

She watched him from the corner of her eye as he pulled

on a black sweatshirt and raked his fingers back through the damp strands of his hair, wondering if he'd felt the same. If the experience had been anywhere near as mind-blowing for him as it had been for her.

Wondering, with an odd little pain in her chest, just what it was he was still hiding from her.

When they were both dressed, he walked with her to the door of the bedroom she was sharing with Morgan and Jamie. She started to tell him to be careful while he was out on patrol, but his big, calloused palms were suddenly clamped against the sides of her head, holding her in place as he put his mouth against hers, kissing her with a dark, savage aggression, as if he was starved for the taste of her mouth. When he finally let her breathe again, he pressed his forehead against hers, his thumbs brushing against her sensitive skin with soft, tender strokes as he said, "I don't have any regrets about what happened between us. I just…I wanted you to know that."

Then he gave her another hard, deep, bone-melting kiss, and before she could even take in enough air to speak, he'd turned away from her. As she watched him walk across the room, open the door and disappear into the dark, frigid night, Olivia reminded herself that only fools and dreamers wished for happily-ever-afters.

And though she'd never truly realized it until that moment, it had become blindingly clear that she was both.

CHAPTER TWENTY

Virginia
Wednesday

WHATEVER OLIVIA HAD BEEN expecting when Aiden's friends caught up to them, it was still a shock to her system when they came face-to-face on Tuesday afternoon. She'd never seen so many gorgeous, massive men in one place at one time, and the women were not only beautiful, but as easy to get along with as Morgan. In all, there were seven newcomers to their group. Ian Buchanan and his fiancée, Molly, along with Ian's brother, Riley, and his fiancée, Hope. Then there was their sister, Saige, and her fiancé, Michael Quinn, as well as a young British archaeologist named Jamison Haley. A quiet, twentysomething near her own age, with golden hair and an easy smile, Jamison seemed as human as Olivia. But he wasn't. According to Noah, Kierland had been forced to bite Jamison in order to save his life after he'd been tortured by the Casus, turning the Brit from a man to a Lycan. Amazingly, Jamison seemed to have taken to his new preternatural existence as if he'd been born to it, and Olivia had been fascinated by their conversations.

And Jamie, the little flirt, simply adored him, following Jamison wherever he went.

Wanting to spend as little time in the air as possible, they planned to fly out from Maine, and so they were now headed toward the East Coast. Though they could have split up, traveling in smaller groups, they'd opted for the old adage "safety in numbers," not knowing what to expect during their time on the road. After the attack on Ravenswing, everyone had worried that the Death-Walkers would find them again, but so far there'd been no sign of the creatures…or the Casus. Still, they moved as if they had something nipping at their heels, fully aware that danger was more than likely closing in, hard and fast.

It was Wednesday now, and they'd spent the morning traveling northeast through Virginia until they'd finally stopped at a wooded parkland to stretch their legs for a bit, while Kellan and Noah drove into the nearest town to buy everyone some lunch. Jamie was playing a game of catch with Jamison, and Aiden was on his cell phone, trying to sort out where they could pick up Jamie's medication, so Olivia settled herself against the weathered trunk of a maple tree and tried to read for a bit. But instead of focusing on the story, her mind kept wandering back to Aiden.

With the frantic pace they'd set, traveling through most of the night, only stopping at a hotel near dawn so that everyone could sleep for a few hours and grab showers, she and Aiden hadn't had a chance to snag any alone time together. They'd managed to steal a few hurried, desperate kisses—but it hadn't been nearly enough. She was starved for his touch. For the weight of his body covering her, holding her down. Her emotions might have been in chaos, but her body knew exactly what it wanted.

Problem was, her heart did, as well.

And it was definitely a problem. Despite his wicked smiles and the occasional teasing comment, she could see a tightness around Aiden's eyes that was more than just his worry for their safety, and she suspected he was having doubts about their relationship or affair or whatever you wanted to call it. He seemed to be keeping a careful kind of emotional distance between them…one that was knotting her insides, setting her on edge.

So much fear churned inside her, and so much hope, the combination making her head spin. Winning his heart wouldn't be easy, but as she'd lain in bed on Monday night, Olivia had realized that for the first time in her life, she was determined to try…to actually fight for what she wanted. She had let Chris go without a second thought. But she wasn't prepared to give up so easily on Aiden.

It awed her, the strength it had taken for him to survive what he'd gone through as a child and not let it warp his heart and his soul, turning him into something as vile as the monsters who'd abused him. Instead, he was one of the good guys. A knight in shining armor, bad boy though he might be. But she liked his rough edges. They were the perfect contrast to her nervous, stammering shyness, blasting through her defenses. She couldn't say no to him, and she didn't even want to try.

And so that tender shoot of hope inside her had bloomed, opening up, expanding until it filled every cell of her body. Anticipation thrummed through her veins, while her heart felt hot…sticky, soft in her chest, her pulse racing with nervous excitement as she thought about the topic she planned to bring up the next time she and Aiden were alone.

Last night, when Molly had noticed her stealing glances at the faint bite marks healing on the side of her throat, she'd offered to answer her questions. Olivia knew enough about the Merrick to understand that Ian needed to take blood in order to feed the primal aspects of his nature, but she'd been curious about how it felt…and Molly's answer had made her more curious than ever.

Looking up from the pages of her book, she searched for Aiden and found him leaning against the front of his truck, talking to Quinn, his powerful arms crossed over his chest, while the wind whipped at the long, caramel-colored strands of his hair. She studied the sensual shape of his mouth, and couldn't help but wonder what it would feel like if he were to ever bite her. Sink his fangs into her. Was that something he even wanted? Could it be one of the things he'd been fighting?

As if he could feel the force of her gaze on him, he looked her way, a hard, predatory wave of sexual aggression radiating from his body when he caught her staring. His mouth moved as he said something to Quinn, and then he was walking across the grass, heading straight for her. Whatever he'd seen on her face, it had awakened his own primal instincts, his amber eyes already smoldering with a warm, erotic glow, burning with heat.

By the time he reached her, she'd set her book on the ground and moved to her feet. Aiden grabbed her hand, and immediately started pulling her deeper into the trees. Riley and Morgan were running a perimeter on the area, so she knew they were safe, but she still worried that Jamie might need her, even as her body melted at the idea of being alone with him. Of stealing a few more of his dark, devastating kisses.

"We should stay close to the others," she burst out, breathless with excitement. "I'm sure Jamison's going to get tired of playing catch with Jamie and come looking for me."

"I doubt it," he murmured, suddenly stopping and crowding her against the wide trunk of a massive oak tree, "considering Jamie's already got him wrapped around her little finger, just like Noah and Kell. And Molly and Ian have headed over to join them." His deep-grooved grin was unbearably beautiful. "Ian said something about it being good practice, since he and Mols want to start having kids as soon as possible."

She was shivering when he leaned down to press a hot kiss against the edge of her jaw. Then stammering when he suddenly reached for the top button on her jeans and flicked it undone. "What are you d-doing?" she gasped, gripping his thick, powerful wrist. "Your friends could come walking over here looking for us!" She sounded so scandalized, Aiden couldn't help but smile, his chest shaking with a low bark of husky laughter.

"Do you know how much I love it when you go into teacher mode?" he rumbled, bracing his hands against the rough bark on either side of her shoulders, caging her in. "Is that kinky, Liv? You get all puckered up, like you want to lecture me about my spelling or my alphabet, and I go as hard as a rock." He leaned close, burying his nose against the side of her throat, and she tilted her head to give him better access as he kissed his way up to her ear. "I can hear it now, you using that prim little voice to tell me to ride you harder…to give you more. I'll refuse, saying you're too small…too tight, and then you'll dig your nails into my ass, pulling me deeper, fighting me until I lose it and end up giving you every hard, hungry inch."

She breathed out his name on a soft, trembling sigh. "We can't," she moaned, shaking her head, though he could see how badly she wanted to give in.

"Hmm. Then maybe I'll just drop to my knees, rip your clothes away and lick you until you're melting all over my face, screaming my name at the top of your lungs." He reached between her legs, rubbing his fingers against her tender, swollen flesh, her jeans a frustrating barrier that he wanted out of his way. "I think you need my tongue right here, Liv. Just licking you. Lapping at these sweet, juicy folds."

She gave a soft laugh, pressing her hands against his chest as she said, "You're obsessed with oral sex, aren't you?"

"Can't help it," he drawled, rubbing the base of his palm against the top of her mound. "I'm a cat, Liv. We like to lick things that taste good."

She moaned, her face flushing with color as she closed her eyes and tilted her head back against the tree.

"No one's going to come over here," he promised her. "I made sure of it."

He knew he had her when she opened her eyes, grabbed the sides of his face and pulled him down until she could nip at his bottom lip. "God, I love your mouth." No stutter. No hesitation. Just smooth, languid words, thick with desire. "You taste so good."

"Not nearly as good as you," he growled, tugging again

at the buttons on her jeans. "I want to make love to you, Liv. You okay with that?"

"Where?" she gasped, that single word shivering with excitement.

"Out here. Where I can see the sun shining on your skin. Where I can see every beautiful detail and know that it's mine to touch. To taste."

Aiden had never said anything like that to a woman before, but the strange, possessive words were true. The cracks in his composure were getting deeper, and infinitely more dangerous. Desperation filled him, pushed at him, because he knew their time together was coming to an end...that it was slipping away from him with each moment that went by.

Determined to make the most of it while he still could, he held her face in his hands, clutching at her like a lifeline. "Tell me something, Liv."

"What?"

"Anything," he whispered against her mouth, rubbing his lips against the petal-like softness of her own. "Everything. I want to know all your dark, dirty little secrets." *And I want you to tell me that this is about more than just getting laid.*

Wow. Another whoa moment, right there. One he hadn't even known was coming.

"That works both ways you know." She pushed against his chest until she could stare up into his eyes, daring him to look away. "I spill, then you have to spill, too."

He dropped his hands to his sides, a wry smile tipping the corner of his mouth. "I've spilled a lot, Liv. Enough to say I'm surprised as hell that you're still here."

Lowering her gaze, she walked a few feet away and braced her hands against a low-hanging branch. "You still have secrets," she murmured, staring straight ahead. "Things you haven't told me."

"Well, here's one of them," he said in a playful rumble, moving up behind her. "I absolutely love your ass."

Her head fell forward a little, and she gave a soft, feminine snort of laughter. "You're insane, Aiden."

"Well, yeah, that's probably a given," he drawled, running his big hands over her round, beautiful backside. "But I know what I'm talking about. And you, Liv, have one seriously gorgeous ass."

She laughed again, saying, "Chris thought it was fat."

"Yeah? Well, Chris was a blind jackass."

"I caught him having sex with one of the other teachers," she suddenly blurted, her hands tightening against the branch. "They were in her classroom. After school."

"Huh. Sounds like he was a dumb ass, as well. Wasting time on another woman when he had you." Reaching around her front, Aiden pushed his hand into her loosened jeans, under the elastic waistband of her panties, seeking out the slick, moist heat of her sex.

"You know what I think?" he said, loving the way her breath caught with a sexy little catch when he pushed two thick fingers up inside her. "I think your perfect ass scared him. Made him feel inferior. He knew he wasn't man enough to claim something so beautiful. And you *are* beautiful, Liv. We're talking white-hot, head-spinningly gorgeous."

She made a small, hungry sound and he kissed her shoulder, the smooth column of her throat. "I'll tell you something," he whispered in her ear. She tried to turn around, but Aiden stopped her, wrapping his free arm around her middle, holding her against him, his fingers still buried deep in her body, while he waited for her to soften around him. "You're the only woman I've ever gone down on since I got away from Mueller."

"That's…not possible." Quiet, shivery words, full of shocked surprise.

Nuzzling through the heavy silk of her hair, Aiden pressed a low, embarrassed laugh against the downy softness of her nape. "It's true."

"But you're a cat. You…you t-told me cats like to lick things."

"I told you that cats like to lick things that taste good. And that would be you, Liv. They made me do it at Mueller's when they wanted me aggressive, because it whips the animal into a frenzy. And since I escaped, I've never wanted to do that to a woman again. Until I found you."

With those hoarse, husky words hanging in the air

between them, he began thrusting his fingers, rubbing all those tender sweet spots buried deep inside her that made her shiver and moan. Aiden couldn't get enough of the way she clung to him, hot and moist and snug. He clamped his teeth onto the back of her neck, making her melt around his fingers, and felt himself losing it. Already, and he didn't even have his dick in her yet. But his beast was rising to the surface, like some primordial creature swimming up from the dark depths of an ancient lagoon. He tried to fight her pull, but the sight of her profile as she leaned forward and rested her face against one of her slender, delicate hands was too much. Dark lashes. Smooth, flawless skin. And that lush pink mouth, parted by her provocative moans. His ears roared. His eyes burned.

And his fangs broke free again, long and heavy in his mouth.

Gritting his teeth, Aiden pulled his hand from between her legs and grabbed hold of the branch on either side of her body. His fingers sank into the wood, creating deep impressions, and he pressed his forehead between her shoulder blades, fighting to get himself under control. His muscles twitched, his dick rock hard and ready, strangling inside his jeans, too stupid to know what it was getting itself into.

"Aiden?"

"Just…just give me a minute," he rasped, wondering

how he'd ever thought he could get his fill of this woman. God, he'd been mad. A blind, effing idiot. One who'd been shown paradise and was going to be left sucking wind when he lost it.

And damn it, he didn't want to lose it.

Not now, when he finally got what it was all about.

He couldn't say that sex with other women had ever felt bad. Just that…maybe he hadn't ever really felt it, like listening to music through thick, soundproof walls. He knew it was happening, but it'd never pierced its way through to him.

Then came Olivia, and she'd smashed his walls to pieces. Pieces he didn't know how to put back together. And now he was left standing there, with his face buried against her back, trembling like a leaf. Wishing. Wanting. Hungering. Craving with a visceral need that had bled into something so much deeper and devastating than physical desire—which was why he was going to be running, as hard and as fast as he could, the instant he had her safe and secure in England.

No, the animal snarled with a violent, primitive fury that echoed painfully through his skull.

Aiden hated the idea even more than the beast, but it couldn't be helped. Want had changed to need, and need was something he wasn't prepared to give in to. *Need* meant he was in this for the long haul—and that couldn't be. Hell, he didn't even recognize himself anymore.

Didn't understand what was going on in his head. He couldn't think, couldn't act. All he did was worry about her, feeling as if he needed to be near her to breathe, and it was scaring the shit out of him. He wanted to spend every goddamn waking moment in her presence. Hold her close to his body when they slept. Talk to her about the future, as if it was something they could actually share together. All bad, bad shit that was doomed to crash down on him, splattering him like road kill, if he didn't get the hell out of there. So he'd already talked it out with Kierland and made the plans.

Knowing the clock was ticking, Aiden pressed his mouth against the back of her neck, flicking his tongue against the salty, delicious taste of her skin. Pleasure rolled through him, as warm and sweet as the first rays of sunshine in spring. Not the hot, blinding flash of orgasm, but just as strong. Just as essential. "You always smell so damn good." His voice bled into a soft growl, his lips moving against the side of her throat as he nuzzled against her. "It drives me crazy, the way I can't get enough of you."

"Does that mean something?" she asked, suddenly looking at him over her shoulder.

Panic flared like a flame. "What do you mean?"

"Does it mean something about us? Am...am I special to you?" He didn't respond, simply staring back at her with a wary expression, but she wasn't deterred by his silence. "You wanted me to tell you something, so this is what I'm telling you. You're special to me, Aiden. And if you wanted to...to b-bite me, I wouldn't mind."

"What?" He could feel the color drain from his face. "Why in God's name would you say that?"

"Because I trust you."

Oh, Christ. He'd wanted so badly to hear those words from her, but they'd backfired on him. He hadn't realized the danger. How it would make him feel, all soft and hot in his chest, his face burning like a friggin' Broadway sign. "Well, don't, Liv. Not about this. I'm not even going to—"

He cut off the telling words, but it was already too late.

"You're not going to what?" she asked.

"Nothing," he muttered, looking away from her.

"I meant what I said, Aiden."

He closed his eyes, gnashing his teeth. "Get real, Liv. You don't have any idea what you're talking about."

"I do. I—"

"Goddamn it!" Within seconds he had her turned and shoved back against the trunk of the tree, his hands curled around her upper arms, holding her there as he leaned in close to her face. "Do you have any idea how dangerous it is, every time I touch you? How badly I want to bite you? I've been fighting it for days! And you know why?" he snarled, giving her a little shake. "Because if I bite you, it's going to stick!"

"Stick?" she repeated, her voice thick with confusion. "What does that even mean?"

"Your scent calls to me, Liv." He took a deep breath, struggling to get control of his anger, knowing he needed to make her understand. "It's called 'the Eve effect.'"

"Meaning?"

"Meaning you call to my beast. Meaning I should stay the hell away from you," he growled, "because of all the women in the world, you're one of the ones it would be a really, really bad idea for me to bite. Sink my fangs into you, and you could end up getting a lot more than you bargained for. Kinda like an instant marriage. Only, one you can't go and get canceled when you decide you don't like the husband anymore."

She blinked, a violent rush of color burning beneath her fair skin. "Are you s-saying that you would mark me as your mate if you bit me?"

He shook his head and let go of her as he took a step back. Then took another. Wishing that he hadn't smoked his last cigarette, Aiden raked his hair back from his face and said, "There would have to be an emotional connection between us for that to happen."

"Oh." She took a deep breath, and slowly let it out. "And…are your emotions involved?"

Instead of answering, he braced his hands on his hips, his gaze focused intently on the grass at his feet. "You should be considering yourself lucky that I haven't done it," he rasped. "I'm more animal than man, Liv. Nowhere near that perfect little world of normal that you want."

Even without looking at her, he could feel the way she flinched. "That's not fair, Aiden. I never said that was the life I wanted."

"Just the one you thought you were meant to have." His mouth twisted with something too tight and bitter to be a smile. "And you were right. Which is why I'm…"

"What?" she asked, refastening her jeans.

"Forget it," he muttered, not wanting to get into it with her, knowing it was going to be bad.

At least he knew, now, that he'd made the right choice in deciding to leave so soon. It had been hard enough not to bite her before, but now that she'd given him permission, there wasn't a chance in hell he'd be able to keep control. He could stand there and promise himself that he wouldn't slip up until he was blue in the face, but it wouldn't mean anything. Wouldn't change the truth.

"What were you going to say?" she whispered, unwilling to let it go. "You're not going to what?"

Pushing his hands deep into his pockets, he lifted his heavy gaze back to her face and said, "Saige is nearly done with the next map."

She stared back at him, puzzled, not yet connecting the dots.

Aiden cleared his throat. Forced it out. "She said it looks like the next Marker's buried somewhere in Finland."

Comprehension dawned like a slow spill of horror, widening her eyes. "And you're going to go after it? You're going to leave us?"

"Not yet," he rasped, hating the way she was looking at him. "Not until you're safe in England."

"But when we get there, you're going to leave?" she pressed, taking a step forward, her violet eyes swimming with tears. With dark, painful understanding. "And when you go, that's going to be the end, isn't it? I mean, for us. For you and me."

"I didn't say that."

"Tell me the truth." Her voice shook, trembling with emotion. "Tell me that when you leave it's going to be over between us."

He clenched his jaw, curling his hands into hard fists inside his pockets. "Don't act so surprised, Liv. You knew what you were getting into."

"Damn it, just tell me!" she shouted, taking another step forward. "I want to hear you say it!"

"Fine!" he growled, his voice so harsh it barely even sounded human. "When I'm gone, that's it. I won't come near you again."

"You bastard!" Olivia cried, slapping him as hard as she could. She hadn't planned to do it, but she hadn't been able to quell the primitive impulse, wanting to strike out and hurt him. Make him feel even a fraction of the pain she was feeling.

"This is for the best." He ground out the words, the left side of his face flushing bright red where she'd hit him.

"Why?" she demanded, feeling as if she was going to be sick. "Because I'm human, like Mueller and your mother? Because you're going to blame me for what they did to you? God," she cried, "all this time I've been telling myself that eventually, after you got to know me, it wouldn't matter. But it does. Because you won't let it *not* matter. I knew better, damn it. But I let my heart overrule my head and I'm paying for it now."

He made a low sound in the back of his throat. "I'm doing you a favor, Liv. Instead of being pissed, you should be thanking me. Better to cut our losses now, before things get any more complicated than they already are."

Squeezing her eyes closed against a hot rush of tears, she turned her head to the side for a moment, then forced herself to look back at him as she took a deep breath and said, "I feel sorry for you, Aiden. You probably don't care why, but I'm going to tell you anyway. I feel sorry for you because you're so buried in the past, you can't see the things that are right in front of you."

"No matter what you're feeling right now, the reality is that we don't have a future. We never did," he argued in a sharp, gritty voice, the lines in his face deepening, adding a grim edge of bitterness to his hard, masculine beauty. "You'll realize that sooner or later, because the truth is that I'm not a man, Liv. Not a human one. I might look like you, but I'm not."

"And you really think that matters to me?" Soft, tear-filled words that she wished could have been stronger.

"Maybe not now," he grunted, jerking his chin toward her. "But one day you'd wake up and realize what you'd gotten yourself into."

"That's such a crock," she snapped.

"Jesus, you just don't get it, do you?" he growled, his chest heaving, his golden gaze blazing with fury and frustration. "You think you know me, but you don't. And I don't like wanting something that I know I don't deserve. Sooner or later you'd come to your senses about the kind of man I am, about the differences between us, and then guess where that'd leave me? Getting fucked, that's where."

"So then you're going to screw me over instead?"

"No, damn it. It isn't like that," he argued, though he knew damn well that it was. "I think...I think you're a great person, Liv. One of the best I've ever known." His gaze slid away, his voice thick as he said, "Even after learning about my past, you didn't...you just...you surprised me. But we've got to face the facts."

"It's a fact that I care about you, Aiden."

He wanted to believe her. To believe that she wouldn't wake up one day and look at him with disgust. That she wouldn't ever hurt him or betray him. But he couldn't.

Maybe that part of him had been broken. Crushed out of him. Damaged and destroyed. Whatever the reason, he was incapable of trusting anyone now. Of ever truly putting his faith in another person. Even someone as amazing as Liv.

"You're just…confused right now," he grunted, barely managing to scrape out the hoarse words as he forced his gaze back onto her face, her shattered expression making him feel like the biggest bastard alive.

"So then that's it? You won't even give me a chance to prove myself?"

He wanted to say yes, that he would. Wanted to tell her so many things, but he couldn't do it. He was trapped behind a wall that he couldn't batter down. Couldn't break. "I can't. It…it doesn't matter what I want, Liv. The fact is that I don't have it in me. Why go through the trouble, when I already know how it's going to end?"

"That's not true. You don't know anything of the sort."

A muscle ticked in his temple as he held her stare. "No matter how you look at it, I know I'd never be able to give you a life that's anywhere close to a normal one."

Wrapping her arms around her middle, she said, "I wish you'd stop throwing that back in my face, because I made a mistake. I thought normal was where someone like me belonged. I thought that was all I could handle, but it's not. I was wrong, and I'm adult enough to admit it. Haven't you ever been wrong, Aiden? Haven't you ever changed? For the better?"

"People don't change, Liv."

"You're wrong," she argued, shaking her head. "We grow, Aiden. We live and we learn. And we find love, usually when we least expect it."

His reaction was instantaneous, his rage blasting against her like the hot, blistering force of an explosion. "This isn't love!" he snarled, cutting his right hand through the air as if he could swipe her soft words from existence. "Christ, you don't love me. You *can't* love me. You're just confusing pleasure with some ridiculous emotion because you don't know any better!"

His words were so sharp she felt bruised. Beaten. She reeled back, her face brittle, like a mask. One made of fragile porcelain that was about to crack, shattering into a million fractured pieces.

Not in front of him. Get away...and then you can break down. Then you can fall apart.

"I think...I think that you should just stay away from me," she whispered, the look on her face stopping him in his tracks. His hands shook. A muscle twitched in his hard jaw. And his eyes...no, she couldn't look at them, hating what she saw there. Distrust. Anger. Fear. "I won't run. I won't risk Jamie like that. But...just give me some space. I don't want to be around you, Aiden. Not anymore."

Choking on her tears, Olivia turned her back on him and started to walk away.

His rough voice reached out to her, painfully stark, as if it had been stripped down to the rawest, bleakest of emotions. "You don't trust me either, Liv. You might think you do, but it's not real."

Wiping the tears from her face, she kept walking as she said, "Open your eyes, Aiden. I've been putting my trust in you from the beginning."

Then she made her way toward the others…and not once did she look back.

CHAPTER TWENTY-ONE

The Lake District, England
Friday afternoon

IT HAD BEEN THE STRANGEST DAY. A beginning, since they would soon be arriving at their new home. And an end, because Olivia knew that Aiden would be leaving not long after they reached their destination.

She'd awakened that morning to find him giving a giggling Jamie tiger rides around the private garden of the cottage they'd stayed in overnight. Aiden had fully shifted into his tiger form, and Jamie had been riding on his back, clutching handfuls of his thick fur in her hands. She'd been worried that he might shun Jamie, after the things Olivia had said to him, but he was still as devoted as ever to the little girl. It was just Liv he gave a wide berth to, though she was doing her best to avoid him, as well.

After a harrowing drive up to the coast of Maine the day before, they'd chartered a private plane and flown across the Atlantic, to a rural airstrip in Scotland. Jamie's medicine had worked perfectly, and she'd slept through most of the flight, while Aiden had been a nervous, foul-mouthed wreck the entire time. Olivia knew he'd been worried about a Death-Walker attack while they were in the air, but she also suspected that the tiger in him didn't like soaring through the clouds, preferring to have its feet planted firmly on the ground. They'd spent the night near the airport, in the quaint country cottage that Kierland had leased for them, and after packing up that morning, they'd headed south, into England. The drive had gone more quickly than she'd expected, and they were already traveling up the winding road that led to the house she and Jamie would apparently be calling home. Olivia knew she should feel something about that, but there was nothing. Just a hollow void in her chest, emotionless and still.

Finally, after all that had happened, she'd gone into safety mode and shut down. Completely. It was either that or fall apart. And falling apart simply wasn't an option when you were on the run for your life...and the life of someone you loved.

At the thought of the *L* word, she inwardly cringed, remembering her heartfelt declaration on Wednesday. It had hurt, but she'd had to wake up and face reality, no matter how painful it was. Aiden didn't want her love, because he didn't love her in return. Or maybe he couldn't. Either way, he'd thrown the idea back in her face before she could even get it said, making his feelings clear.

Of course, she and Aiden weren't the only ones on edge. They'd met up with Kierland Scott when they'd landed, and the instant the Lycan had spotted Morgan in their group, tempers had flared. It was obvious, even to an outsider like Olivia, that the two had a turbulent past—one that caused the tall, auburn-haired Lycan to glower every time he was in the same room with the gray-eyed shifter. Morgan, however, had handled the situation with a cool, I-couldn't-care-less-what-you-think-of-me kind of attitude that Olivia secretly envied, wishing she could be that poised and in control. It was only when Kierland wasn't looking at the female Watchman that a powerful flash of emotion smoldered in Morgan's gray eyes, the flames vanishing the instant Kierland glanced her way again.

"We'll be there soon," Kellan murmured, pulling Olivia's attention back to the present. She and Jamie and Morgan were all riding with Kellan in a rented Land Rover, while the others followed in two similar vehicles. Morgan was watching a movie in the backseat with Jamie, while Olivia sat in the front with Kellan. "That's Harrow House up there," he told her, pointing toward the majestic rise of the sandstone building just visible through a mass of swaying treetops.

"My God." Squinting against the last rays of the late-afternoon sunset, she struggled to see the details more clearly, thinking it looked like a castle. "It must have been amazing to grow up in a place like that."

Kellan snorted. "It was actually kinda cold." His dry tone made it obvious he wasn't talking about the temperature. "My grandfather was about as soft as those stone walls."

"Oh. I'm sorry. That couldn't have been easy."

Rolling his shoulder, he said, "Aw, we did okay. I had Kierland, and he was the best brother any kid could have ever wanted."

She couldn't help but smile. "It's obvious the two of you are close."

"I drive him crazy," Kellan remarked with a husky bark of laughter, "but he loves me, faults and all."

Olivia laughed as well, but as they made the next turn in the road, the soft sound turned sharply to a gasp. "The bridge is out!" she exclaimed, staring through the windshield at what remained of the wooden structure that should have spanned the fast-moving stream on the road ahead of them.

"Yeah," Kellan murmured, bringing the car to a slow stop. "Smithson warned Kierland that it'd gone out a few years ago during a storm. We plan on getting the bridge rebuilt as soon as possible."

"Smithson?" she asked, trying to recall if she'd heard the name before.

"He was the estate's caretaker when my grandfather

was alive," Kellan explained, pulling the Land Rover onto the side of the private road, while the others parked behind him. "He's ancient now, living down in the local village. Kierland called him and got him to have the village priest come up and bless the moat."

Raising her brows, she said, "And no one thought that was an odd request?"

The Lycan snorted as he turned off the engine. "The locals have always thought everything that happens up here is odd. For centuries there have been rumors circulating that the estate is haunted. They say that if you listen at night, you can sometimes hear things howling at the moon."

Olivia slanted him a wry look. "Considering you come from a family of werewolves, it sounds like more than mere superstition."

"Not as far as they know," he drawled, giving her a wink.

Peering through the windshield, she asked, "So how are we going to cross the stream?"

"There's a stone pedestrian bridge that survived the storm, so we'll have to make our way there on foot. The bridge will take about ten minutes to get to, but there's a path through the trees that leads to it."

Well, hell. She didn't like the sound of that. Especially after the faint message that Molly had received from Monica during the night, warning that they needed to reach the house as quickly as possible. Jamie was still wearing the Dark Marker that Aiden had hung around her neck a week ago, and as a precaution, Olivia, Molly and Hope had been given Markers to wear as well, the ornate crosses now hanging around their necks from black velvet cords. Quinn had been carrying the Markers, which he'd brought, in a secured case, from Ravenswing when they'd escaped—but the Watchmen and Buchanans had agreed that they should be taken out today and used for protection.

Olivia only hoped they didn't need them.

It didn't take long to get everyone organized, no more than a handful of minutes passing before they found the path to the bridge. They traveled in a long line, with Aiden in the lead, while Kellan and Kierland brought up the rear. They'd opted to leave their luggage back in the cars for the time being, deciding it would be better to focus on getting everyone to safety first.

As they made their way along the winding trail, Olivia couldn't help but appreciate the beauty of the scenery, with its sloping, tree-covered hills and the occasional outcropping of rock. It was beautiful, in a strange, mystical kind of way, like slipping into a fairy tale, and Olivia whispered quietly in Jamie's little ear, pointing out each new discovery as she carried the child in her arms.

"I've got a bad feeling about this," Morgan suddenly murmured, walking at her side.

"You do?"

Morgan nodded, a frown tugging at the corner of her mouth. "The back of my neck is tingling, which is never a good sign. Just stay sharp and keep your eyes open for anything unusual."

Olivia rolled her eyes. "As if this whole situation isn't unusual," she muttered.

Morgan's mouth curled with a crooked smile. "You know what I mean."

She did, and the idea prompted her to go ahead and do something she'd been putting off for two days now. "Would you mind keeping an eye on Jamie for me?" she asked. "I need to have a quick word with Aiden about something."

"Sure thing," Morgan agreed, taking the little girl in her arms. "Jamie and I are best buds, aren't we, sweet thang?"

Olivia brushed a quick kiss against her niece's cheek, then took a deep breath and jogged ahead on the narrow path, around Ian and Molly, until she reached Aiden. He didn't turn to look at her as she moved to his side, but by the tightening of his jaw she knew he was aware of her presence.

She coughed, took another deep breath, then said, "I, um, I need to talk to you."

"Thought you were pissed off at me," he said in a low voice, sliding her a quick, wary look before focusing on the trail again.

"I am," she whispered, wetting her lips. "But…this isn't about me. I need to ask you a favor."

He gave a sharp nod, still not looking at her as he waited for her to go on. "If something happens to me—"

"Nothing's going to happen to you," he grunted, cutting her off.

"I know you'll do your best to protect us," she murmured, rubbing her wounded arm. It no longer hurt, but it was still a stark reminder of how close she'd come to death. "But things go wrong, Aiden. If something happens, I want your promise that you'll look after Jamie."

"You mean find her a good family?"

"No. I mean look after her yourself." She remembered his poignant reaction when Jamie had given him one of her drawings—how concerned he always was that Jamie was not only safe, but happy—and knew, without any doubt, that she was doing the right thing. "I want…I want you to raise her as your daughter. I realize that it's a lot to ask, but she…cares for you, and I know you would do everything in your power to protect her."

Olivia was so wrapped up in her thoughts, it actually took her a second before she noticed that he was no longer walking beside her. Turning around, she found him just standing there, in the middle of the path. "You want me to adopt her?" he croaked, looking as if he'd been smacked upside the head with a two-by-four, his expression completely dazed.

Nodding, she said, "Yes. If something happens, that's exactly what I want."

He muttered something foul under his breath, then shoved his hands into his pockets and started walking again. "Well, like I said before, nothing's going to happen to you, Liv."

"You don't know that," she told him, keeping her voice gentle, since he was certainly wound up enough for both of them. "Things happen, Aiden. Life's like that. I just…I need your promise."

It seemed like forever before he finally said, "I'd do it." His voice was gruff, edged with tension and strain and things she could tell he was trying hard to hide. "If it had to be done, I'd…yeah, I'd adopt her."

"Thank you, Aiden."

BY THE TIME AIDEN MANAGED to choke down the lump of emotion lodged in his throat, Olivia had already walked away, heading back to Jamie and Morgan. Scrubbing his hands down his face, he struggled to get himself under control. She couldn't have surprised him more if she'd asked him to get a sex change and start calling himself Lola.

Coming up beside him, Ian slapped him on the shoulder. "You okay, man?"

"Yeah," he muttered, reaching into his back pocket for his pack of cigarettes, then scraping out a coarse swear-word when he remembered he'd left them back in the car.

"You know," Ian murmured, "it'll be easier if you just give in."

Aiden scowled, but found he couldn't hold on to the anger. He was reeling, even harder than before. No matter how he looked at it, he couldn't wrap his brain around the idea that Olivia trusted him to be a good father to Jamie, and he was afraid of letting his thoughts run with it, not knowing where they might lead. What did it mean? He didn't know, and he was too damn tired to figure it out. His beast urged him to act from his heart…from instinct, but his fear still had him mired in doubt and denial.

"You should listen to Ian," said a soft, husky voice. "He knows what he's talking about, Ade."

Slanting a dark look toward the petite blonde now walking at Ian's side, he asked, "Why'd you do it, Molly?"

She didn't ask him to explain, knowing that he was talking about the way she'd insisted he be the one to go after Jamie and Olivia. "Because I thought she would be good for you," she admitted with a soft shrug of her shoulders. "She sounded like a strong woman, but one with a big heart."

He let out a sharp, explosive sigh. "And you didn't think it would matter that she's human?"

"It shouldn't," she murmured, her eyes gentle as she caught his dark gaze. "In fact, I was hoping that might help you get over your issues."

"I don't have issues," he growled.

Molly's sharp laugh earned her a heavy glare, but she simply smiled in return. "Honestly, Aiden. Olivia Harcourt is exactly what you need. A loving woman who won't let you walk all over her. At first it was just wishful thinking on my part that something might develop between the two of you, but after seeing how you are with her, I think I got it right."

"Well, don't go patting yourself on the back," he sneered. "Because in case you didn't notice, things haven't exactly worked out."

Molly rolled her eyes. "I've heard that animals can be ornery when they get cornered," she groaned, "but honestly, Aiden, you're taking this to the extreme. The only reason things aren't working out is because *you're* acting like a jackass. Think about it. A family would do you good."

A *family*. The word wormed its way through his mind, completely at ease there. He hadn't even realized what the word truly meant until Liv had shown him what it could be.

As the path wound around a massive outcropping of rock on their right that stood taller than Aiden's head, the narrow pedestrian bridge finally came into view up ahead of them. The house loomed in the distance on the other side of the stream, and Aiden suddenly had the strangest urge to run back, grab Olivia and Jamie and race for the safety of its walls. Pulling in a deep breath, he searched the air for any signs of danger, but a strong headwind was blowing down the valley. He knew nothing was ahead of them, but that didn't mean something couldn't be sneaking up on them from behind.

"You got the same feeling I've got?" Ian suddenly muttered, scanning their surroundings with a narrow gaze. The outcropping of rock completely blocked them on the right, while a small area of moss-covered ground spread out on their left, bordered by a thick wall of trees. "Like we're not alone out here anymore?"

Before Aiden could answer, Olivia came running up to him with Jamie clutched in her arms. Hope followed just behind with a gun clutched in her hands. "Morgan and the others sent us ahead," Olivia panted. "She wanted me to tell you that they've picked up a scent, but it's faint. They're checking it out now."

"We need to get the women up to the house," Aiden said in a low voice, reaching behind him for his Glock. "And we need to do it quickly."

"It's too late." The whispered words came from Jamie, and everyone stopped, staring at Jamie's pale face, her brown eyes shocked wide with fear. "They're already here."

"Who's here?" Olivia asked, sliding a worried look toward Aiden.

"All of them," Jamie whispered, lifting her face toward the sky. Following her line of sight, Aiden felt his gut clench as he caught sight of three Death-Walkers flying in over the swaying treetops. As they came closer, their rank stench reached his nose, their yellow eyes burning through the thickening, lavender shades of twilight. The creatures were each different, and yet similar. The same cadaverous white skin. Same small horns and eyes, as well as jagged fangs.

The ground began to vibrate with the hard, heavy pounding of fast-moving bodies, but Aiden could tell from the scent that it was Kierland and the others. They came rushing around the curve in the path, their weapons drawn and at the ready. "Casus are coming," Kierland growled, his rugged face etched with grim lines of worry. "From the scents we picked up, there's a lot of them."

"We've got Death-Walkers, too," Ian told them, jerking his chin toward the sky.

Holding a Beretta in one hand and one of his knives in the other, Noah muttered, "Shit, this just keeps getting better and better."

"I say we make a run for it, hard and fast," Quinn grunted, keeping close to Saige's side.

Sniffing at the air, Aiden shook his head. "There isn't time. If they catch up with us on the bridge, we'll be trapped out in the open. We've got to make a stand here." Looking around at the other Watchmen, he said, "Get the women against the rocks and fan out around them. We're not going to waste time tonight trying to use the Markers to fry these assholes. Just fight to kill. Does everyone have their flasks?"

Nods went around the group as everyone pulled out the flasks of salted holy water they'd picked up on their way through Tennessee, and then they quickly got into position.

CHECKING TO MAKE SURE that Jamie still had her Marker hanging around her neck, Olivia clutched the little girl tighter against her chest and pressed her back against the craggy wall of rock, while Aiden positioned his tall, muscular body in front of them for protection, his friends fanning out at his sides. She wanted to reach out and touch his shoulder, asking him to promise her that he'd be careful, but right then a howl sounded in the distance, echoing through the thickening twilight. It was a stark, sadistic sound, conjuring images of torture and pain. The kind that made chills break out across the surface of her body, and she felt the bonds of her emotional lockdown begin to strain and snap.

One second everyone was locked in that tensed, charged moment of terrifying expectation…and in the next, more than twenty tall gray forms burst through the trees, and the battle with the Casus began. All around them, muscular bodies exploded into action, the darkening evening filled with the sickening sound of flesh being ripped by claws and teeth and bullets. Riley used his telekinetic powers to pull the weapons away from those Casus who were armed, but the monsters were still a formidable enemy. They attacked with a fast, brutal savagery, and while Kierland and the others fought to hold them back, Aiden's deadly aim with a gun was being put to good use. He'd already managed to shoot three Casus through the head when a Death-Walker swooped down on him. The heinous creature slammed him to the ground, his gun knocked away as it slashed at him with its deadly claws. Panicked, Olivia was still fumbling with her flask, trying to get the lid off while holding Jamie, when Hope came to the rescue, flinging a stream of the salted holy water across the Death-Walker's pale back. An unearthly scream ripped from the creature's chest, and then it was gone, disappearing as quickly as it had come.

As Olivia breathed a sigh of relief and Aiden moved swiftly back to his feet, a man stepped casually from between two nearby trees. He was still in the form of his human host, rangy and tall, with chiseled features and shaggy mahogany-colored hair that whipped against the sides of his face, but she could tell without any doubt that he was Casus. A cruel smile curved his thin mouth as he looked out over the violent scene, his pale eyes smoldering with anticipation, as though he couldn't wait to see what happened next.

Tilting his head back, he drew in a deep breath, then smacked his lips, his ice-blue gaze sliding toward Olivia with a hungry, sexual look that made her skin crawl.

"Josef," she whispered, knowing she was right. "Aiden!" she called out, raising her voice to be heard over the rough sounds of fighting. "It's Josef! The one I told you about. The one who's hunting Jamie!"

Quickly finishing off the Casus he'd been grappling with, Aiden turned and followed the direction of her terrified gaze.

Looking for all the world as if he was out for a Sunday stroll, the Casus came closer, his smile widening as Aiden moved nearer to Olivia and spread his arms out from his sides in a protective stance. "Well, well, well. Look who we have here," Josef drawled, sliding his gaze toward Jamie. "Do you know who I am, sweetheart?"

Jamie tightened her arms around Olivia's neck as he bared his teeth in a grin and said, "I'm the monster who ate your mama."

Gasping, Olivia pressed Jamie's head against her shoulder, then covered her other ear so she couldn't hear. It terrified her how silent and still Jamie had become since the fighting had begun, and she silently prayed that the little girl was okay.

"Mmm, she is sweet-looking, isn't she?" Josef said with a low, husky rumble of laughter. "She's meant to be saved for Calder, but I'd be lying if I said I wasn't tempted to do both the runt and the aunt."

"Shut your damn mouth," Aiden snarled, flexing his claws at his sides.

"Or what?" Josef asked, lifting one brow in an arrogant arch as he slid his icy gaze toward Aiden. "You're going to kill me, shifter?"

Aiden's amber eyes narrowed to menacing slits. "You'll die no matter what you say. The only question is how much I make it hurt before you go."

"Ooh, you are a cocky one, aren't you?" Josef said thoughtfully, rubbing his chin. "I wonder how cocky you'll be when I'm covered in Olivia's blood, shoved deep in her broken little body."

The dark, visceral sound that tore out of Aiden's throat was that of a deadly predator protecting its territory. He launched himself at the Casus with his claws and fangs fully extended, and Olivia could only watch in horror as they tore at each other, Josef's fingers transformed into gnarled, claw-tipped weapons. Aiden was magnificent in his fury, his skill far superior to that of his rival, but Josef wasn't looking for a fair fight. Almost immediately he screamed for backup, singling out two of his fully shifted brethren for the job. The massive creatures raced across the clearing and joined the fight just as Aiden and Josef disappeared into the trees—and Olivia knew she had to do something. It didn't matter how good a fighter Aiden was, he was desperately outnumbered, and his friends were all too busy with their own battles to come to his aid.

Which meant that it was up to her. She might have lost her hope for a future with the stubborn, bitter shapeshifter, but that hadn't changed the fact that she was madly in love with him.

Looking around, she spotted Molly standing close by, the blonde's terrified gaze focused on Ian as he fought off two Casus at the same time, his body shifted into its lethally powerful Merrick form. Grabbing Molly's arm, she quickly said, "I need you to take care of Jamie for me."

"Why?" Molly asked, dragging her attention away from Ian to send a worried look toward Olivia. "What are you going to do?"

"Please," Olivia begged. "I don't have time to explain, but Aiden's in trouble with the Casus. I need your help."

Molly hesitated, her troubled gaze going from Olivia's face to the battle that raged a few feet away.

"Molly, please," Olivia pleaded. "If it was Ian, you wouldn't just stand by and watch."

"Okay," Molly answered swiftly, slipping the Marker she was wearing over her head and handing it to Olivia. "On one condition. You take this with you."

"But I already have one," she argued.

Molly's brows drew together, her brown eyes steely as she reached for Jamie and pulled her against her chest. "Which means they won't think that you have another one, will they? You can use that against them."

"Right," Olivia whispered, slipping the second Marker into her pocket. "Wish me luck."

As Molly squeezed her hand and told her to be careful, Olivia pressed a hard, quick kiss to Jamie's cold cheek, whispering that she loved her and would be right back. Then she turned and made her way through the swirling battle as quickly as she could, heading toward the trees where she'd last seen Aiden. Following the sounds of their grunts and snarls, Olivia reached them just as the two fully shifted Casus got hold of Aiden's arms and trapped them behind his back.

"Kill him," Josef spat out, wiping his bleeding mouth with the back of his hand.

"No!" Olivia shouted, and all four heads whipped toward her, their faces revealing various levels of surprise.

"How sweet," Josef murmured, his mouth twisting with a snide smile. "The little human's come to watch you die."

"She has a Marker," Aiden snarled, his muscles bulging as he strained to break free from the two monsters holding him. "You won't be able to hurt her."

Josef shrugged. "I can still take her prisoner. Sooner or later I'll find a way to get the Marker off her. And then she'll be mine."

She could see that Aiden was seething with fury, the tendons in his neck sticking out in stark relief as he growled, "You stay the fuck away from her!"

Returning his attention to the Casus, Josef said, "What are you waiting for? Gut the bastard."

"No! Wait! Don't hurt him!" Olivia screamed, rushing forward and falling to her knees. "Please! I'll go with you. Do whatever you want. Just…just don't hurt him!"

"Get the hell out of here, Olivia!" It was clear from the savage sound of Aiden's voice that he was beyond furious with her.

Taking the Marker from around her neck, Olivia held

it out to the Casus on her open palm, offering it up to him. "Here, you can take this," she whispered, shaking so hard that her teeth were chattering. "You can have it. Just…let him go. Please!"

"What are you doing?" Aiden roared, and though she wasn't looking at him, her watery gaze focused purposefully on Josef, Olivia could hear him struggling to free himself. "Put that bloody Marker back on!"

Watching her carefully, Josef walked toward her. "You're playing a dangerous game," he murmured.

"No game," she told him, her voice breaking from the tears that were pouring down her face. "I swear. Here, take it. Just…just let him go."

Josef came closer, and a low snarl rumbled deep in Aiden's throat. "I'm warning you," he growled. "Touch her and you're going to pay for it."

Ignoring the guttural threat, Josef took the Marker from Olivia's hand, his eyes glowing as he reached down and stroked his gnarled, claw-tipped fingers against the side of her face. "You're not very clever, are you, sweetheart? Still, I didn't travel all this way because I'm interested in your intellect, now, did I?"

With tears pouring from her eyes, Olivia forced herself to hold his stare, the terrified look on her face one she didn't have to fake. Turning his back on her, he began walking toward Aiden, and she could hear the smile in his voice as he said, "I can't decide whether I should kill you now, shifter, or keep you alive long to enough to watch the fun your little human and I are going to have together. Do you have a preference?"

"Go fuck yourself," Aiden grunted, and Olivia could hear Josef chuckling softly under his breath as she moved slowly to her feet. She was careful to keep her head down, lest the monsters holding Aiden looked up and saw her intentions written all over her face. Josef was still talking, his voice low and taunting as he began to describe in vile detail all the things he was planning to do to her. Reaching into her front pocket, she curled her hand around the cross that Molly had given her, pressing it against her palm in the way that Kellan explained it had to be done in order to release the Marker's power. The pain was instantaneous, the blistering sensation radiating from her hand into her entire arm so excruciating, it was as if she'd reached into the heart of a fire. She ground her teeth together to keep from screaming, and knew she had to act quickly, before the others noticed what she was doing.

Only a handful of steps separated her from Josef, and as she pulled her hand from her pocket, Olivia sprinted toward him, aiming for the base of his neck, just as Kellan had described. A sizzling, crackling noise filled the air, accompanied by Aiden's roar of shock…as well as Josef's outraged cry of pain. He tried to twist away from her, but a scorching ball of flame engulfed her arm, and in the next instant her hand sank deep into the son of a bitch's body, locking her into him. His skin instantly began to blister, a hot, molten glow of crimson and orange burning beneath its surface, and Olivia turned her head away from the gruesome sight, her agonized screams blending with the horrific sounds tearing from Josef's throat as the pain in her arm intensified. His tall body jolted and shook with violent spasms, wrenching her shoulder as she fought to keep her balance, and she was thankful that he was in his human form, since she never would have been able to reach her target if he had fully shifted.

Praying that it was going to be over soon, Olivia struggled to breathe as the flames grew hotter, the stark sound of the Casus's cries echoing painfully through her skull. Just when she was sure she was going to lose consciousness, his body finally exploded in a powerful, bone-cracking blast, the force of it knocking her clear off her feet.

She could feel the air rushing past her body as she soared over the ground.

Could hear Aiden's choked cry of horror.

And then there was nothing but a blessed, silent darkness.

CHAPTER TWENTY-TWO

AS OLIVIA SLOWLY CAME TO, she realized the blast had knocked her a long way from where she'd been standing. She also realized that the roaring in her ears was actually Aiden shouting at her as he crouched over her body, checking for injuries.

"What were you thinking?" he demanded in a rough voice the instant she lifted her swimming gaze to his grim, blood-spattered face.

She shook her head, wincing as she tried to sit up. "I don't know. It was the only thing I could think of."

"Here," he grunted, offering her his hand, so that he could pull her to her feet. He gripped her shoulders, waiting for her dizziness to pass, then let go of her, shoving his fingers back through his hair so hard that she winced for his poor scalp. "Is your arm okay?"

Olivia nodded, surprised to find that there wasn't any lingering pain, considering how badly it had hurt when the

Marker had gone into weapon mode, creating its Arm of Fire. Somehow she'd retained her hold on the cross, and she slipped it over her head.

"How did you even know how to use the Marker like that?" he asked, forcing the words out through gritted teeth.

Looking around at the smoldering piles of ashes that littered the ground, she coughed, then managed to say, "Kellan explained it all to me during the drive today. At first, I was worried Jamie might accidentally hold her cross against her palm, but Kell said her hands are too small to make it work."

He let out a sharp, explosive sigh. "Olivia, look at me."

"Yeah?" she said, lifting her gaze back to his beautiful, angry face.

"I can't believe you took that kind of risk." The words were hoarse, thick, his eyes burning with a look of pure, savage fury.

"I had to do something, Aiden. They were going to kill you."

He stiffened, his narrowed gaze boring deep into her eyes, as if he was trying to read her mind. "And why the hell would that matter?" he rasped.

"You'll have to figure that out for yourself." She sighed, looking around again. "What happened to the other Casus? The ones who were holding you?"

Scrubbing his hands down his face, he said, "The blast

knocked us all to the ground, and they weren't so lucky against me when it was just the two of them."

"Where are their bodies?" she asked, noticing that fresh claw marks were torn across his arms and chest, his shirt completely shredded.

"I hid them," he muttered, jerking his chin toward a thick cluster of trees.

Olivia shivered, glad the monsters' bloodied corpses were hidden from her view. God only knew she'd already seen enough blood that evening to last her a lifetime.

"We need to get back to Jamie," she whispered, filled with a sudden sense of urgency as her thoughts finally began to clear. "I had to leave her with Molly when I came after you."

Walking over to the spot where Josef had been standing, Aiden quickly reached down, snatched up the Marker that the Casus had taken from her and slipped it into his pocket. Then they rushed through the trees, back toward the path, and found Aiden's friends fighting what looked to be a losing battle. Though there were Casus bodies littering the ground, all of them slowly transforming back into the shape of their human hosts, too many of the creatures still stood, more bloodthirsty than ever.

"Stay close to me," Aiden commanded, taking her hand as they began working their way through the surging press of bodies. Olivia nearly wept with relief when she spotted Jamie crouched against the craggy outcropping of rock, flanked by Molly and Hope, who were both holding guns and firing bullets at any Casus who tried to come near them. Jamie's beautiful little face was completely blank, like a doll's, until she spotted Olivia and Aiden coming toward her. The little girl blinked, and then her lower lip began to tremble, just as her small body was suddenly racked by violent tremors, and even with her human senses, Olivia could tell that something was wrong.

"What's happening to her?" she gasped.

"I have no idea," Aiden grunted. "But she's throwing off power like crazy."

They wove their way through the battle as quickly as they could, trying to reach her, but when they were no more than ten yards away from Jamie, one of the two Casus who'd been fighting Kierland caught sight of them. With his bloodied jaws gaping, the monster turned suddenly and began to charge. Aiden shouted for Olivia to run as he released his claws and turned to face the quickly approaching Casus, its open mouth revealing rows of sharp, jagged fangs. Knowing Aiden could handle the monster on his own, Olivia was trying to make her way around Kellan and the two Casus he was fighting when one of the bastards slammed into her as he reared away from a lethal slash of the Watchman's claws. Losing her balance, Olivia hit the ground. Hard. Her head spun from the impact, until a high-pitched cry suddenly filled the air, jarring her back to awareness, the sound so sharp she wanted to cover her ears. For an instant everyone stopped fighting, while the strange cry filled the air, becoming louder, sharper. And then it stopped.

Everything was silent. Still. And then the most bizarre thing began to happen.

"What the hell is going on?" she asked Aiden, unable to believe what she was seeing as he quickly pulled her to her feet. The Casus had turned on one another, their heavy gray bodies rolling over the ground as they tore at their brothers with their muzzled mouths, ripping their gnarled claws through tough, leathery flesh. And it wasn't just the Casus. Even the Death-Walkers were fighting amongst themselves up in the sky, slashing and biting at one another, the sounds they made reminding Olivia of screeching alley cats. "Why are they doing that?"

"I don't know," Aiden muttered, looking around, his gut cramping with a fresh surge of worry when he realized what was happening. "Oh, shit," he rasped. "I think it's Jamie. She's doing it. Somehow she's making it happen."

"What?" Olivia gasped. "That's not poss..." Her denial died as quickly as it had started when she turned and saw the same thing that had snagged Aiden's attention. Jamie was standing on her feet, her small face deathly white, while her dark eyes shone like twin beams of blinding light. And some kind of strange, fiery blue glow seemed to be burning from inside her body, radiating out through her skin. Hope and Molly were both trying to reach for her, but it was as if they were going up against an opposing force that was pushing them back, keeping them away.

"Everyone get across the bridge and up to the house! Now!" Aiden shouted, knowing they needed to get out of there while they still could. Grabbing Olivia's hand, he ran toward Jamie, the power emanating from the child nearly knocking him to the ground. Gritting his teeth, he refused to go down. He snatched Jamie's glowing body up into his arms and crushed her against his chest. She trembled against him, then threw her arms around his neck, hugging him tight as he started running, pulling Olivia along behind him as they all raced across the pedestrian bridge.

Jamie's body was no longer glowing, the power pulling back inside her, which meant that any surviving Casus or Death-Walkers might very well start coming after them again. Pounding up the path toward the house, the group finally made it to the sprawling lawn that wrapped around the building's wide, circular moat. Ian was up ahead, shouting for everyone to hurry, and their whoops of triumph blended with groans of pain as everyone made their way across the ancient drawbridge that spanned the moat.

A swift head count confirmed that everyone had made it, and Riley began working the levers to raise the drawbridge, just in case any Casus decided to follow. Though from the looks of things, it seemed that any remaining

Casus had decided to turn tail and run. The Death-Walkers, however, were a different matter. As the tired, blood-covered band stood on the deep stone porch waiting for the drawbridge to close, they spotted the Death-Walkers speeding through the sky, their bodies silhouetted against the moon as the creatures headed straight for them.

"Anyone who has anything left in their flasks, get them ready," Aiden grunted, putting himself in front of Olivia after he'd placed Jamie in her arms. The Death-Walkers picked up speed, moving faster, soaring high above the ground. Then they suddenly came to a crashing stop, slamming into some kind of invisible wall when they reached the moat. Hissing, they hovered in the air, glaring down at everyone gathered on the wide porch, their yellow eyes burning with hatred, before finally turning and dis-appearing into the night.

"Holy shit," Noah grunted, his deep voice thick with surprise. "It actually worked."

"Remind me to thank Gideon when I see him," Kier-land panted, leaning his back against the massive, double wooden doors that led into the house.

"Thank him? Hell, I'm gonna kiss him," Kellan drawled, bracing his hands on his knees as he bent for-ward, still struggling to catch his breath.

"I think we owe Jamie some appreciation, as well," Ian murmured, sliding Jamie a gentle smile. "You were amaz-ing, sweetheart."

THOUGH SHE WAS still shivering in Olivia's arms, Jamie managed a shy grin before burying her face against Olivia's throat. Olivia could see the questions burning in everyone's eyes as they all looked at her niece, wondering how Jamie had managed to turn the Casus and Death-Walkers against each other. It had been nothing short of amazing, and Olivia could only thank God that Jamie seemed to be fine now, if a little shaken.

Rubbing her hand against Jamie's small back, Olivia stood off to the side, listening as the others talked, until Riley finally managed to get the drawbridge completely raised and Aiden suggested they get inside.

And that was when the real work began.

Because of the local legends surrounding Harrow House, Smithson had apparently been unable to round up a full staff willing to come in and tackle the cleaning. Still, he'd managed to get the process started, but they still had a long, tiresome evening ahead of them. Keeping Jamie close to her side, Olivia had worked with Saige and Morgan, rummaging through the endless number of rooms until they'd managed to get beds made up for everyone to sleep in. She hadn't seen Aiden since they'd come inside, and figured he was either busy with the others or doing his best to avoid her. Not that she'd expected anything different. Despite what had happened that afternoon, he'd given no indication that his feelings toward her had changed, and she knew better than to wish for a miracle.

After all, they'd already had their fair share of miracles that day. To ask for another seemed greedy, and she didn't want to press their luck, no matter how sweet it would have been on a personal level just to have the stubborn shape-shifter seek her out for some simple conversation.

It was late, and they were finally done for the night. There'd been an anxious hour when most of the men had gone back out, heavily armed with weapons that Kierland's grandfather had stocked in the cellar, and taken care of the bodies that had been left at the site of the battle, but they were back now. They'd also managed to retrieve the luggage from the cars, which meant that everyone would be able to sleep in clean clothes. While Morgan took Jamie downstairs to show her the game room they'd found, Olivia went upstairs to grab a quick shower in the suite of rooms she and Jamie would be sharing.

She also needed just a bit of time to herself, to try to sort out what she was going to do about Aiden.

"You need to just get a grip and forget about him," she muttered to herself as she entered the shadowed room, the only light provided by the milky glow of moonlight that spilled through the leaded windows.

Pulling off her dust-streaked sweater, she headed into the bathroom, shutting the door behind her. It was a good twenty minutes later when she came back out, dressed in a loose T-shirt and a ratty pair of sweats. She'd taken no more than one or two steps into the bedroom, her head lowered as she rubbed a towel through her hair, when Aiden's deep voice rumbled through the shadows. "If it's all right with you, I'd rather you didn't. Forget about me, that is."

Gasping with surprise, she looked up, and the low wash of light spilling through the bathroom door reached just far enough into the room to illuminate Aiden's long, beautiful body perched in a chair beside the bed. He sat leaning forward, with his elbows braced on his knees, his bruised hands hanging loosely between his parted legs.

"You scared me to d-death," she stammered, noticing that his hair was damp and his clothes were clean, which meant that he'd already showered, as well. She also couldn't help but notice that he was staring at her as if he wanted to eat her alive, his eyes burning with hunger, glowing a bright, mesmerizing shade of amber. "What are you d-doing here?"

Scraping his fingers back through his hair, he spoke in a halting, gritty rumble. "Yeah, well. See, I realized something tonight."

Too afraid to think of where this might be leading, Olivia clutched the towel against her fluttering belly with both hands. "And what's that?"

"I, uh, realized that I'm a total jackass."

Snuffling a soft laugh under her breath, she said, "I find it hard to believe that this revelation never came to you sooner."

His mouth twitched with a wry, crooked smile, and he shook his head. "I might be pretty, but I never claimed to be brainy. Sometimes it takes me awhile to figure this emotional stuff out, and it doesn't help that I'm stubborn as hell."

"Sounds like you know yourself pretty well," she murmured, tossing the towel on the foot of the bed so that she could cross her arms.

He gave a rough laugh, the husky sound melting down her spine, turning her insides to honey. But she wasn't ready to give in. Not yet. Not when there was so much at stake. "What do you want, Aiden?"

Instead of answering the question, he asked, "How's Jamie doing?"

"She's good," Olivia told him. "Smiling. Laughing. Molly and Saige think that what happened was some kind of psychic release of all the emotion Jamie's been bottling up since Chloe first disappeared and Monica was killed. When she saw us surrounded by all the fighting, and thought she might lose us, it finally all came pouring out. Saige thinks it might even be a sign that the Mallory curse could be nearing its end."

"Christ. Is she going to be okay?"

"With all the love and attention she's getting, I think she's going to be just fine," she murmured. "But you didn't answer my question. What do you want?"

He blew out a rough breath, looking for a second as if he was going to bolt, but then he scrubbed his hands down his face and said, "I'm no good at this, but I can't deny you anything." Surging to his feet, he braced his hands on his lean hips in a purely masculine pose and just stood there, his chest rising and falling with his hard, ragged breathing. He was glaring at her, but she had to bite back a smile, because she could see the emotion he was trying so hard to deal with shimmering in his golden eyes. "I guess what I'm saying is that I'm an even bigger jackass than I realized, not to have been able to see what's right in front of me."

Olivia had never imagined she would see Aiden looking so nervous and unsure. So…hopeful, the un-guarded look on his beautiful face melting what was left of her anger, transforming that cold, brittle ache into something soft and shivery that filled her chest, warming her from the inside out.

"You asked me once if I'd ever changed, and I have," he rasped, his head turned a little to the side. "At least, I have now. I wouldn't have believed it was possible, but it happened. I don't know how, except to say that it's because of you. Because of how I feel about you. And to think that I could have lost you today…Christ, it almost killed me." He raked his hair back from his face again, and she noticed that his hands were trembling. Shaking. When he realized what she was looking at, he shoved his hands into his pockets and went on, saying, "I don't want to have any more secrets from you, Liv. So I guess I came here so that I can go ahead and just get it all in the open."

She nodded, her heart beating like the frenzied wings of a hummingbird as she waited for him to go on.

He took a deep breath, and then in a low voice he said, "I got my tats when I was fourteen. Just after I escaped from Mueller's. One of the other kids there, Adam, was from one of the other clans called the Feardacha. He told me that in their culture it's bad to leave the evil souls of the dead unchecked, so the warriors tattoo themselves with symbols that are meant to draw the souls back to them, if they ever escape." He paused and glanced down at his tattooed forearms. "These markings are sort of a memorial to Adam, I guess."

Moving a little closer, she kept her voice soft as she asked, "Why didn't you want me to know?"

His chest shook with a low, gritty bark of laughter and he tilted his head back, staring at the high ceiling. "Because I guess there's always been a part of me that wonders if they might actually work. Not exactly a big selling point for a relationship. Can you just imagine me saying, 'Hey, check out my tats. Oh, and by the way, if any of the psychopathic assholes that I ripped to shreds ever crawl out of hell, these are supposed to pull them to me, so that I can try to figure out a way to kill them all over again'?" Lowering his head, he looked right at her, another wry smile lifting the corner of his mouth. "Call me crazy, but I kinda figured you had enough baddies coming after you already, without throwing something like that in the mix."

"Aiden," she whispered, taking another step, drawn toward him as if there was some kind of powerful magnetic pull between their bodies, but he held up his big hand, silently telling her to stop. She wrapped her arms around her chest, vibrating with emotion, and waited, though it was killing her to stay away from him.

"I don't make much of a slice of normal," he said huskily, rubbing his fingers against his scratchy jaw as he stared so deep into her eyes, she felt as if he was sinking into her. "But hell, who wants normal anyway? You've had normal all your life, Liv, and look what it's gotten you. A pathetic ex who wasn't worth the time it took you to drop him." Like a swell rising up over the wide expanse of the ocean, she could see his confidence building, rushing against her like a warm wind. "You need me, Liv. You need someone like me to show you what you've been missing. You need someone like me, because I might be a pain in the ass, but I'd lay down my soul before I'd let anything happen to you. It's a hell of a thing we're mixed up in right now. I know that. But you're going to be in danger wherever you go, and I'm the best man for dealing with that. I'm not going to let anyone hurt you or Jamie, because I refuse to lose you."

He paused, glancing back down at his tattooed arms. "And if these markings ever do bring those bastards back to me, well, I figure you're strong enough to help me take them on." Lifting his gaze, he said, "You're an amazing woman, Liv. One who can handle whatever life throws at her, even if it is a screwed up smart-ass like me."

Realizing that this was the most important moment of her life, she forced herself to take a deep breath and see it through, afraid that if she let herself go she might throw herself at him and tackle him to the ground. "What exactly are you saying, Aiden?"

He rolled one muscled shoulder, and this time he was the one who took a step forward, his voice a dark, delicious rumble as he said, "I realized that you matter, Liv."

She shook her head and smiled. "Is that the best you can do?"

"Aw, hell," he groaned, taking another step closer. "You're gonna make me say it, aren't you?"

"You're tough," she whispered, trying to sound sultry, though she suspected the happy, goofy grin on her face was probably ruining the effect. "You can take it."

He took another deep breath, then let it out. "Fine. Enough of acting like a pussy. I can do this." He walked right up to her, standing so close that she had to tilt her head back to see his face, and then she was drowning in the golden depths of his eyes as he said, "I'd just tell you that I love you, because I do, Liv. But I don't see how that one little word can do justice to what I feel for you."

Suddenly all the pieces that had been so broken inside her were mended into something that was perfect and pure. Her heart felt hot, melted down into a molten glow that burned in her chest. She was afraid to blink. To breathe. Because she didn't want to break the spell.

She recalled the feeling she'd had when she'd first met him, that strange, exhilarating rush of awareness that had told her she was going to need this man in her life. Need the physical presence of him to live and breathe and exist.

And in so many ways that was true. Yeah, she could have walked away, and she would have survived. She would have woken up each day, gone to bed each night. But she wouldn't have been whole. She would, in fact, have been only half alive.

"Does this mean I get that chance to prove myself?" she asked unsteadily.

"You don't need a chance. What you get is *me*. That is, if you still want me."

She blinked, trying not to cry as she said, "You trust me not to hurt you?"

"How could I not trust you, Liv? Right from the start you took everything I always thought I knew about humans and turned it on its head." He lifted his hand, hooking her hair behind her ear. "So yeah, you have my complete and total trust. But what about you? Do you trust me not to break your heart?"

"I trust you," she whispered. "And I love you, too."

"God, woman. You don't know how good it feels to

hear you say that." And then his mouth was on hers and he was lifting her into his arms...carrying her to the bed. Excitement shivered along her nerve endings as he laid her down on the cold sheets and started stripping off her clothes, then his own, the wicked glint in his eyes warning her that she was going to be in for one hell of a night.

"Are you still leaving?" she asked, the words turning into a shivery moan as he pressed a hot kiss against one sensitive nipple, and then the other.

"I'm not going anywhere," he rasped, bracing himself over her so that he could look into her eyes. "I talked about it with Kellan before I came up here. He's going to take Noah with him to Finland, and I'm going to stay here with you and Jamie."

"Thank God," she whispered, curling her hands over his hard, muscular shoulders. "I mean, I know you still have a job to do, but I couldn't stand it if you had to leave us. Not this soon."

He leaned down and claimed her mouth with a long, ravenous kiss that made her head spin, a rush of sweet, shivering chills spreading over her body as he pressed himself between her legs. His breathing was ragged as he worked his way back down to her breasts with slow, open-mouthed kisses, his tongue lapping with savoring, deliberate strokes, as if he found pleasure in the simple taste of her skin. He took his time, sucking and nipping and licking until she was writhing from the pleasure…from the biting anticipation, her nails digging into his muscled backside as he rubbed the heavy length of his erection against her slick, sensitive folds.

"I need to get a condom," he said in a raw voice when he finally pulled himself away from her breasts, his heavy-lidded eyes smoldering with a sharp, feral glow. "I didn't want to jinx myself by coming in here prepared. I need…I gotta go grab a rubber from my bag. I left it out in the hall, by the door."

"Leave it," she whispered, stroking her palms up the length of his back, loving the feel of all those bunched muscles beneath his sleek, fever-warm skin. "You don't need a condom, Aiden. We're in love and I'm on the pill. So just take me already."

"Are you sure? I mean…" He swallowed, his breath rushing in hard, ragged bursts as he shifted his gaze to the side. "There are things…that will happen if I come inside you. And once I start, I won't be able to stop. Are you sure that's what you want, Liv?"

Her answer was to reach down and eagerly take him in her hand, fitting the swollen, heavy head of his cock against the damp opening of her body. "Don't make me get rough with you," she teased him, arching her hips, a smile on her lips as the first few inches slipped inside her.

"Wait!" he growled, his body shaking as he straightened his arms, his biceps bulging beneath his dark golden skin. "I haven't…haven't even told you exactly what will—"

"I don't care," she whispered, cutting him off. "Whatever it is, I'll love it, Aiden. If it's a part of you, I'll love it."

He squeezed his eyes closed, his nostrils flaring as he obviously tried to keep himself under control.

"Look at me, Ade." She waited until he'd opened his eyes, then reached up and held his beautiful face in her hands as she said, "I love you. Every part of you. They're mine, and I want them—"

Her words broke off with a thick gasp as he suddenly drove her against the mattress, shoving hard and deep, a rough, guttural growl tearing from his throat as he pumped his hips, working against the tightness of her body until he'd buried every inch inside her. "Oh, God. I didn't think it could feel any better, being inside you," he groaned, lowering his face close to hers. "But it does."

"I know," she whispered, loving the wild, animal intensity of him as he moved inside her. She couldn't get enough of the way he stared down at her as if she was the most gorgeous woman in the world. She knew she wasn't. That she was just plain, average Olivia. But in Aiden's eyes she was beautiful, and that was all that mattered.

"It's gonna happen," he growled, his lips pulling back

over his teeth as his back arched, and she felt his cock give a hard pulse, almost as if he'd had some preliminary kind of orgasm. She'd felt the sensation the other times they'd made love—only this time there wasn't anything separating them, and the hard, thick pulse was immediately followed by a hot, molten heat that felt indescribably good as it spread through her body, and Olivia could feel herself tightening around him even more. With a low growl vibrating in his chest, Aiden rode her with hard, heavy lunges, thrusting against some deep, impossibly wonderful spot that damn near stopped her heart. Her head shot back, her mouth open for the silent screams pouring up from her throat as a voluptuous wave of pleasure rolled through her, her body convulsing around him as he began to make raw, thick noises in the back of his throat. It took a moment for her to focus through the blinding, piercing ecstasy, but she finally realized he was asking her the same question, over and over again.

"Are you sure? Are you sure? Are you sure?"

Knowing exactly what he was talking about, Olivia reached up and wrapped her arms around his strong neck, pulling him down to her as she turned her head to the side, revealing the vulnerable curve of her throat. "Do it, Aiden. Please. I love you so much. Just do it."

He shuddered, his hips slamming against her, powering his body into hers, and then she felt his warm lips brushing against the tender skin just beneath her ear. "You don't know how close I came to biting you before," he said in a dark, velvety voice that was roughened by need. "Every time we made love, it was so hard not to mark you, Liv. To hold myself back."

"You don't have to fight it anymore."

Groaning, he buried his face in the curve of her shoulder, and she dug her nails into his biceps. She felt the scrape of his lengthening incisors against her flesh, and then a thick cry of shock was ripped up out of her as he drove his fangs deep. She could feel his cock growing harder…thicker, her body stretched around him to the point that it was a crazy blend of both pleasure and pain as he growled against her shoulder. Then he pulled back his fangs, licking the wound with slow, provocative strokes of his tongue. For a moment Olivia was almost frightened, as he became even thicker, his body driving into her with a visceral, savage intensity—but then the pleasure won out over the fear and she gave herself up to it, falling into a crushing wave of ecstasy with him that was so violent, so extreme, she knew she'd never be the same.

She lay there, panting and wrecked, for a long time after, loving the heavy weight of his body draped over hers. Loving his warm breath in her ear. The lingering pulses that twitched from that powerful part of him that was still packed deep inside her.

She thought she'd known what pleasure was, but she'd been wrong.

She thought she'd been prepared for how this moment would feel, but she hadn't had a clue.

With his hot face pressed close to hers, he finally managed to say, "Damn, woman, I think you killed me."

She smiled and stretched beneath him. "You stole the words right out of my mouth."

Bracing himself on one elbow, he stared down at her flushed face as he lifted his hand and pushed back the damp strands of her hair from her cheek. "I thought I knew how it would be, but I wasn't even close."

"Better?" she asked, thinking that she'd never known a more sinfully, impossibly sexy man.

He lowered his head and kissed her deeply...hungrily, his lips moving against hers as he said, "There's nothing in the world that could compare."

With the tips of her fingers she touched the bite mark Aiden had made, a strange warmth still pulsing beneath her skin that felt unbelievably wonderful. "Does this mean that I'm your mate now?" she whispered, filled with a powerful, stunning surge of pride.

His eyes tightened as he threaded his fingers through the hair at her temple. "You're more than my damn mate, Liv. You're my everything."

"So what now?" she asked, knowing without any doubt that she was the luckiest woman in the world.

His mouth curled with a boyish, lopsided smile as he said, "Now we go downstairs and get Jamie. We bring her up here and tuck her into the little bed that's set up in the connecting room. Then I carry you back in here and lay you down. Make love to you again…and again, until our bodies are too exhausted to move. And after that, I want to sleep with you, Liv. Hold you in my arms through the night, just watching over you…listening to you breathe." He shook his head a little, saying, "God, there are so many things that I want from you."

"You can have them all, Aiden. Just name them, and they're yours."

"Good," he rasped. "Because I know just what to start with."

"And what would that be?"

"A baby, so that Jamie can have a little brother or sister. For you to marry me, so that I can call you my wife. But most of all," he whispered, brushing his lips against hers, "I want forever with you, Liv. One lifetime just isn't going to be enough."

The tender words melted into her heart, stunning her with their beauty, her happiness so powerful and vast and intense, she didn't know how she kept it all inside. Somehow, in the midst of the nightmare surrounding them, Olivia had managed to find her version of heaven, and now this gorgeous, loving, incredible man was hers.

She didn't know what she'd done to deserve it. To deserve him.

But she had a tiger by his tail, and she was never letting him go.

* * * * *

 NOCTURNE™

Coming next month

THE HIGHWAYMAN
by Michele Hauf

Feared in the paranormal realm, Max kills demons
as well as their conduits – familiars. But it is the demon
he harbours within his own soul that plagues him the most.
Familiar Aby would normally be on his hit list, but could
she be his only salvation?

WILD WOLF
by Karen Whiddon

There's a new wolf in town and it's up to Simon to assess
the threat. To his shock, the female, Raven, is young
and undeniably attractive. When he is ordered to
exterminate her, Simon knows he must protect her.
Can a werewolf be tamed by love?

On sale 16th July 2010

SHADOW OF THE VAMPIRE
by Meagan Hatfield

Alexia has been undead for over a century, so it's been
a while since a man's made her pulse race. Until Declan Black.
Alexia is ordered to torture and kill him. Yet with each
reckless encounter, she finds herself further consumed
by his fiery passion…

On sale 6th August 2010

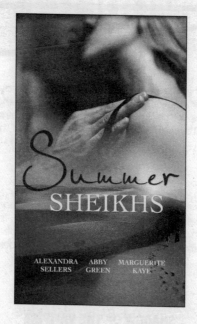

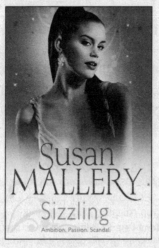

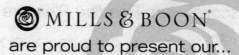

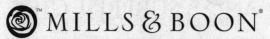

2 FREE BOOKS
AND A SURPRISE GIFT

We would like to take this opportunity to thank you for reading this Mills & Boon® book by offering you the chance to take TWO more specially selected books from the Intrigue series absolutely FREE! We're also making this offer to introduce you to the benefits of the Mills & Boon® Book Club™—

- **FREE home delivery**
- **FREE gifts and competitions**
- **FREE monthly Newsletter**
- **Exclusive Mills & Boon Book Club offers**
- **Books available before they're in the shops**

Accepting these FREE books and gift places you under no obligation to buy, you may cancel at any time, even after receiving your free books. Simply complete your details below and return the entire page to the address below. You don't even need a stamp!

YES Please send me 2 free Intrigue books and a surprise gift. I understand that unless you hear from me, I will receive 5 superb new stories every month, including two 2-in-1 books priced at £4.99 each and a single book priced at £3.19, postage and packing free. I am under no obligation to purchase any books and may cancel my subscription at any time. The free books and gift will be mine to keep in any case.

Ms/Mrs/Miss/Mr _____ Initials _____

Surname _____

Address _____

_____

_____ Postcode _____

E-mail _____

Send this whole page to: Mills & Boon Book Club, Free Book Offer, FREEPOST NAT 10298, Richmond, TW9 1BR